TESTIMO

"This book will resonate in the heart and soul of every person who reads it. The author has a way with words that draws the reader in. A riveting emotional experience that I greatly enjoyed. Job well done."

Barney Barnes

Corporal, USMC, Vietnam 1967-1968

Commentator: Ultimate Warfare, Hue: Vietnam's Bloodiest Battle

"I laughed and I cried. I didn't want the story to end."

Julie Cordray

Guidance Counselor & Educator

"Knowledge of the topic was outstanding. Terminology was time appropriate. One-liners, music, and places; they all took me back in time. I would, on occasion, find myself kinda daydreaming if you will, I don't know how else to describe it."

Raymond Barry

Sergeant, USMC, Vietnam 1967-1968

"Intense and heartbreaking yet told with great sensitivity. The younger generation will find familiarity here. I lost friends as I finished the last page, then found myself tearing up."

Ellen Stocum

M.A. Clinical Psychology & "Girl of the Sixties!"

i

"I loved this story. So much of me resonates in these pages. The author got it damn close. My time in Vietnam came to life again."

Howard Boyte

Corporal, USMC, Vietnam 1968-1969

"A fascinating insight into the Vietnam War and the turbulent times of the Sixties; hauntingly parallel to present-day America. A tribute to the strength of character of Marines and the women they loved. I love learning. This book does not disappoint!"

Debbie Doblar

Business Owner

"Impressive. Well written with an interesting combination of characters. Good job describing what life was like in the military, the language and behavior, the fighting and not fighting. Very good book. Good story!"

Leo Harris

Corporal, USMC, Vietnam 1968-1969

COME NOW THE ANGELS

FIVE MARINES IN VIETNAM

A WOMAN'S STORY OF WAR, DEATH, LOVE & HOPE

SUSAN KUMMERNES

A Seat at the Table Publishing, LLC
Jacksonville, Florida

DISCLAIMER

This novel is inspired by true events but is not a biography of any character depicted in the novel. The story should not be construed to represent a true or accurate recreation of actual events that transpired. The story, the characters, and the relationships between the characters and the names, businesses, places, events, and incidents depicted in this story have been fictionalized. Any insinuation or resemblance of any character to any person, living or dead, or the resemblance of the story to any real occurrence is purely coincidental.

The true soldier fights not because he hates what is in front of him, but because he loves what is behind him."

G.K. Chesterton

"The most ferocious fighting machine in the world is a pissed-off 19-year-old Marine"

John Ligato

"Basic Rifleman"

USMC

DEDICATIONS

FOR J.

So, my green-eyed boy … are you smilin' down on me?

May we meet again.

FOR GEOFF

You are my angel here on earth.

Thank you. Thank you. Thank you.

Come Now the Angels

Five Marines in Vietnam

A Woman's Story of War, Death, Love & Hope

All proceeds from the sale of this book are donated to:

The Vietnam Veterans of America, Organization

PROLOGUE

A nine-year-old boy once told me that a broken heart was not necessarily a bad thing. He drew two heart halves with a large gap zigzagging down the center.

"See? If we pour glue down the middle of the zigzag, the heart will mend, and it will be bigger." What a wise child he was.

A Motown singer asked, what becomes of the broken-hearted?

Did he sing an answer? Did I miss it?

I want my heartache to live.

Nineteen sixty-seven was called the "long, hot summer," in the States, referring to the 159 race riots that swept through our country. Yes, it was hot and violent here in the U.S., but it was nothing compared to the heat and violence you knew the day you were killed in Vietnam. On that day, it hit 105 degrees, and the battle you were in was horrific.

For you, my love, it was the summer of death.

The month before you died, America took part in an outdoor music event, the Monterey Pop Festival. Fifty thousand traveled to Monterey, California, to attend. It was America's first festival of this magnitude and preceded Woodstock by two years. It provided the template for all music festivals to follow. And it was called the *Summer of Love*.

Music was a moving force in the sixties and well into the seventies. Lyrics embodied the frustrations and yearnings of a generation, "War," "Give Peace a Chance." "Get Together." "What's Going On," "Teach Your Children Well," "A Change Is Gonna Come," and "Blowing in the Wind."

Music impacted societal consciousness and values, and often ripped families apart. It was brutally honest, and frequently controversial. Not only did it reflect the times, it shaped thinking and attitudes for generations to come.

On Sunday, June 18th, at the close of the Monterey Pop Festival, Scott McKenzie, a relatively unknown musician, stepped up to the microphone wearing a white robe. Brown curls framed his face. He looked almost angelic. He sang a song that captured a generation, "San Francisco (Be Sure to Wear Some Flowers in Your Hair)".... His gentle words and melodic voice moved the hearts of those listening, especially the flower children whose mantra embodied the heart of the matter... "Make Love Not War."

For you, they played Taps .... "Day is done, gone the sun, from the lake, from the hills, from the sky. All is well, safely rest. God is nigh."

There are places in this world that move the spirit - sacred ground.

Places that connect with your soul in a way you cannot explain. Places that tell stories of loss, heartache, and sacrifice. You may or may not feel an intimate connection with the place, but you feel its sacredness in your bones. An unseen presence reminds you to remain reverent and humble when standing upon this ground. It is the collective energy of the place, the feeling of timeless solitude. The more you quiet yourself, the more you are in touch with the moment and understand the word *hallowed*.

Arlington National Cemetery is hallowed ground.

You rest on a quiet hill under a large oak tree in this sacred place. When I visit, I hear birds sing nearby and feel good for that. They leave droppings on your headstone, and I guess I like that too. It means you have friendly company. It means you aren't alone.

Yours is but one story of one grave in Arlington Cemetery. There are over 400,000 graves and doubtless that many stories waiting to be told.

I cried, "I love you," into the night. I wonder what happened to my words? Did they find you? Or were they lost to the universe?

~~~

A curious thing occurred after my last visit to Arlington. Almost daily, something related to Vietnam came my way. I confided to a friend about these occurrences, I needed to tell someone but was afraid. I thought they'd think I was crazy. I expected my friend to minimize the situation or perhaps laugh at me, but in a serious tone, he told me the universe was speaking, and it was my job to listen.

I got in my car to drive home and thought about his advice. His reaction surprised me because he was someone who operated in a rational world, whereas I usually operated a little left of center. So why was it hard to accept that the universe was reaching out to me about Vietnam? I had had similar thoughts but dismissed them. Who was I, after all? And even if that was the case, that the universe was talking to me, why and what was I supposed to do about it?

I smiled at the absurdity of the situation as I stopped at the first traffic light. My eyes wandered to the car next to me, an inconspicuous baby blue vehicle from another era. The driver, an Asian man about my age, sat alone, his left hand on the steering wheel, his right arm resting casually along the top of the passenger seat. Hanging from his rear-view mirror, I saw a gold-fringed white flag about the size of a three-by-five-inch index card. "South Vietnam" was embroidered diagonally across it. He glanced over. Our eyes met. He looked into me as though he knew me ... then nodded "yes" twice, slowly. Sure, that could have been a hello ... but it wasn't. I knew it wasn't. Driving into my community, still a little unnerved, a car with a Vietnam Veteran sticker on its bumper pulled out in front of me. At home, I sat down to watch the news with a bowl of Rocky Road. I turned on the TV, "Platoon" was playing.

How does the universe, or God, speak to someone? I believe in God, but unlike Noah, or Moses, or for that matter Joan of Arc, God never spoke to me, no message whispered in my ear, no voice from above. Then a revelation. The universe or God, take your pick, speaks in distinct ways to each of us … the universe or God showed me what I needed to see by delivering a message through people or things around me. Okay. I got it. My job was to see and listen.

I listened. I thought. I came to realize this was about you, Jesse. And then I understood what you wanted, what this was all about. You wanted me to give remembrance to you and your brothers-in-arms. To tell your story. You wanted to be remembered.

My eyes welled up with tears when that understanding swept through me.

I began a two-year search and read. As Americans, we knew many of our Vietnam Vets fell on hard times after the war and came home to medical and psychological systems ill-prepared for their complex needs. Interestingly, current research shows a large majority of you became more successful than those who hadn't fought. I learned our infantry in Vietnam averaged 240 days in combat during their 13-month tour of duty compared to the infantry in WWII, who averaged 40-days during their four-year tour. That statistic was an eye-opener. Given the horrific nature of guerilla warfare in 'Nam coupled with constant combat days, the above success rate was so very inspiring and significant!

I discovered your Division in the Marines received the Presidential Unit Citation during the time you served. Quite an honor!

I found your name in a book and learned about your year in Vietnam. I learned how you died in battle. I stumbled upon an e-mail sent by a Marine, remembering a particularly horrific battle fought in May. Your name was in that e-mail as one hell of a machine gunner. I learned you fought relentlessly for days to save those trapped in an ambush, showing up everywhere to take the enemy down. You were a hero.

And in the end, I knew this. It was not the soldier who lost the war in Vietnam. Our soldiers won the battles, Tet, Khe Sanh, Hue. Battle after battle won. We lost the war because we in the States grew weary. We grew weary from the dissension and unrest that grew from this "undeclared war," weary of fighting against the spread of a doctrine manifesting on the other side of the world ... communism. And we grew weary of our sons and husbands battling an enemy who skillfully fought in the moonlight. We watched our soldiers win ... against all odds. And we watched you die.

I lived through the Vietnam era and lost someone I loved. I lost someone. You.

My heart said, write this story for others to know. I can't do this, I argued. I know nothing about writing a novel, or fighting, or the war in Vietnam. A writer is supposed to write about what he or she knows. Right? How can I write about something of which I know nothing?

"Then learn," came the answer.

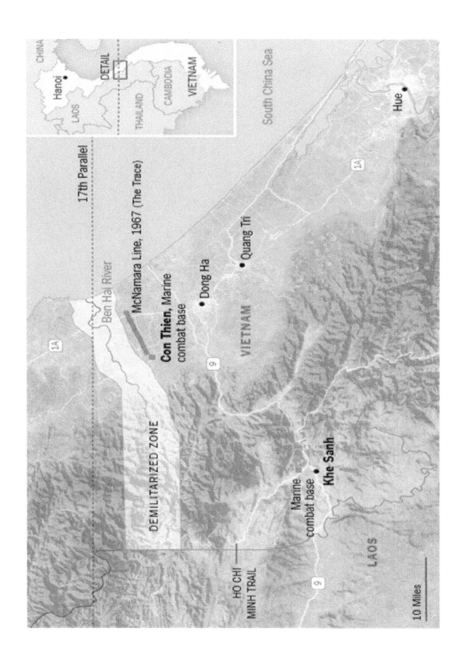

xix

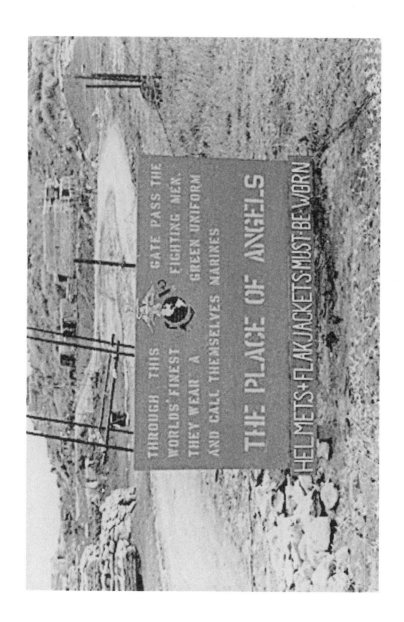

ONE

FAR APART BUT NEVER PARTED

ANNIE & JESSE

August 1967

I sit on a grey metal chair in Arlington National Cemetery. You have returned to us from Vietnam. Your casket is before me. Sunlight penetrates through tree branches and casts dappled shadows on the American flag draped precisely over your new home. A bird sings in the distance. A soft breeze cools my face ... *is that you telling me you're close? Are you comforting me the only way you can?* While we sit in silence, I hear a young woman sobbing somewhere behind me. The sound is muffled, perhaps she's crying into a handkerchief. The breeze billows your sister's skirt. Her hand travels to it. It becomes still. I'm aware of the scent of a man's cologne ... English Leather?

Imprint the moment, I tell myself.

I will return to this memory often; these details will support my acceptance of your death.

Today, I discover the exact location of my heart. The ache is intense, sharp. *I know you can handle pain, my love. I know Marines can handle anything. I hope you didn't suffer. I pray death came quickly when you could fight no more.*

You lie inside the casket. *It's only the casket that keeps us apart.* Inside, your eyes are closed, at rest. I know you're wearing your uniform proudly, in death as in life.

I wish I could see you ... more than that, I wish I could touch you one last time ... place my hand against your face. Would that bring you comfort?

1

The rifle volley shatters my thoughts, our thoughts, our reverie. In one trigger pull, I am part of the war you left behind ... *The sound is terrifying. I wonder what hell you knew.*

Noise from the rifles reverberates through this quiet place of honor. Its unnerving contradiction recognized by each person present, and I wonder why the instrument of a soldier's death is the instrument of his salutation. The answer comes before the question fully forms.

I realize this volley is not only for you lying in death but also for the living, we who reap the benefits of your sacrifice. By hearing what you heard at your final moment, if only for an instant, and in a small way, I'm given the privilege to participate in the gruesome reality of the war you fought. In the sound's violence, I understand the sacrifice you made. I recognize it is my obligation to listen if I am to accept the gift of your sacrifice. I listen gratefully. *Jess, do you hear these rifles fired in your honor? They bring it home. Thank you.*

Thank you.

War. What irony. We fight for peace, a never-ending example of the duality of our world. We fight for peace!

Too soon, you left too soon .... My life is before me, and yours is over. Did you know I loved you? You were my Marine, and you've been gone too long. No tears have brought you back as sometimes storybook tears can. You were my Marine. You will always be my Marine.

TWO

Colliding worlds.

As a boy, Beau stood in the street with arms outstretched, face to the sky, meeting the storm. A wall of water stung his face and body, hard rain, needles pushing into his skin … but only on his left side. His right leg, arm, face, and nose felt the warm sunshine. He stretched farther into the enigma and surrendered to it.

~~~

The memory of that moment reverberated. Rain and sunshine, war and love. He'd chosen war but also love and was trying to reconcile the two.

Marine Lance Corporal John Beau Parker had been granted leave to return to "The World" to marry Helen, his high school sweetheart. He'd flown from Vietnam to Florida to attend her graduation from nursing school. The following day, Beau married the most beautiful woman he'd ever known and now hoped she carried his child.

On his last day home in Fort Myers, he stood in the shower, hot water streaming over him. It was a luxury Beau took advantage of many times during his leave. He'd promised himself to never again miss an opportunity to shower, but this morning he regretted that promise and the need. Beau and Helen loved hard all night. The future might not be theirs, but last night was … they consumed, tasted, possessed, raged at the unfairness of life, understood its fragility, and loved. Their souls, like their bodies, were given to the other and nourished. Needs were satisfied. In ecstasy, in joy, they melted into the other and became one.

3

He wanted the scent of their lust with him on the other side of the world, to keep Helen close, but knew it was impossible.

He stepped from the shower as Helen came to him, naked, towel in hand. She dried him off, hung the towel on the rack, then turned … for Beau's eyes to see her … all of her …. She stood unashamed before her husband. Her eyes never wavered from his as she walked toward him, put her arms around his neck, and pressed her flesh against his. She kissed him softly, then with more demand. She bit his lip, tugged with her teeth as the sinewed arms of her Marine lifted her and carried her to their marriage bed. Filling need more than want; they loved one last time. Beau did not shower afterward.

~~~

Every step away from Helen took him farther from the safe and tender world they'd created and closer to the possibility of death. He trudged slowly to the waiting plane and even slower when his boots touched Vietnam soil. The light fragrance of their love was all he had, just as he wanted it to be. He was grateful.

One boot in front of the other, just keep moving.

~~~

"Couldn't stay away from us, huh, Parker?" "Welcome back, old man!" "Hey, Beau, how's that new wife?" Men he'd fought with welcomed him back. His heart lightened. These were his brothers and hearing them now lessened his ache. He admitted he'd missed them.

Craters from incoming artillery pockmarked the earth, acrid fumes of spent explosives hung like fog as he struggled to breathe. These Marines had been hit hard and often. He remembered someone saying, "Bombs don't choose. They hit everything." They sure as hell had hit everything! Beau thought the shelling from the North Vietnamese Army (NVA) would have lessened or stopped, but no.

Fucking NVA. I'm a sitting duck on this hill … again!

Since boarding the plane, the memory of standing in the street with rain and sunshine had stubbornly remained. War and marriage … a

4

contradiction no different, and for the first time in his life, Beau sensed a deeply rooted fear. It gripped his gut the moment he boarded the plane, and it made the 9,000-mile trip with him to Da Nang.

Now that he was married, would he fight as hard as always or play it safe … perhaps give in to a split-second delay that lessened his risk, maybe find a position that could shield him … keep him better protected in some small way … increase his safety … for their future, for Helen? But at what cost? Place another Marine in harm's way? A brother injured, possibly killed? His squad or platoon placed in jeopardy? His stomach ached from the dread and the thoughts that dogged him. *Oh God, let me be a better man than this! Help me, Father, please.* But before the prayer was complete, the selfish thoughts took hold again. *What about Helen … doesn't she count … don't we?*

Beau realized the quandary, but also the potential madness of second-guessing his actions. Helen or his brothers in 'Nam … he had to get it straight, now.

He looked toward heaven for an answer and, not receiving one, looked down on those ragged Marines grinning at him. His heart filled with tenderness and pride. These men were his brothers in every way. They'd lay their lives down for him. He would do no less for them. Ashamed of what he'd been thinking, he resolved to do what he was trained to do. He'd fight as hard as always. Let the cards fall where they may. To do less would ruin his integrity and his marriage, not to mention prove him unworthy, the greatest unspoken fear of every fighting Marine. Beau Parker would not be found unworthy. He'd give his best to these men who counted on him, then give his best to Helen when he returned to "The World." *Please, God, help me keep this resolution.* His pace quickened as he looked for his squad.

"Hey, any of you deadbeats seen McGowan anywhere?" yelled Beau to a group of weary-looking Marines sharing C-Rations. "Yeah, check over toward the CP!" one replied. He walked toward the Command Post through the remnants of the early morning artillery barrage and caught sight of Jesse McGowan, gun team leader. Jess was walking toward him through the smoke. His M-60 machine gun rested squarely across broad shoulders as though it was part of him, arms up, wrists draped over the barrel and stock. The light changed for a second, maybe a cloud sailed past the sun, but in that moment, Jesse's silhouette looked like Christ on the cross to Beau and caused him to shiver. Beau blinked to see better, but the moment was gone. Jess ambled closer with his easy gait and grin. Beau's tension eased. He'd be alright; Jess would make sure of that. Jesse was his closest friend in 'Nam, his "brother from another mother." Jess set down the M-60 to give his friend a mighty hug, and Beau realized Jess was his closest friend in the world. "Hey, Bro! Good to have you back!" A few feet behind Jesse trailed the rest of the gun team.

Beau had not forgotten these men, brothers-in-arms, who'd sworn never to leave a man behind. Semper Fi. Always Faithful. He returned to 'Nam with five cigars in his seabag, one for each on the team and one for himself. Yes, it was hard to return, but now he was back. What the hell, this was a home of sorts too. *Man, I have it all! A beautiful wife. Good friends. A chance to serve the country I love and do my duty.* He was in awe of it. Life was good, even in this hellhole. *I've made it so far, and God willing, I'll make it back to Helen soon enough. Nothing's changed.* He pushed away his fears. He'd not be less of a Marine because of Helen, he'd be more of one. Beau Parker greeted his friends, and with ease, resumed the familiar persona of noise, laughter, and confidence, a big Marine not afraid, the fun-loving warrior he was before marriage. He promised himself to never return to those fears as he passed out cigars.

"Hey, Lieutenant," he yelled, "Can you take a picture of us?" The five Marines struck a pose, Beau, Mike Redd, and Jesse stood; Angel and Chingas kneeled in front. They were a good-looking group.

Marines in Vietnam didn't have much more than each other. The men based at Leatherneck Square were as good as Marines got. They were men who looked out for each other, cared for one another, and treated each other with kindness and regard. Steadfast in their courage, no sacrifice was too great, and to save the life of a brother, some sacrificed all. They did as ordered and did their best. These young sons of America exhibited valor in and out of battle. Some came from upper and middle-class families, more from the working class and poor, but each saw a chance for honor and accepted the challenge. They represented the best of America.

Each Marine sported a celebratory cigar as the Lieutenant pressed the shutter release, none aware that this picture would be the thread that wove their lives together.

THREE

SMILE WITH YOUR BROTHERS

1967

Jesse turned to Beau and said, "Parker, honest to God, I want a copy of this picture, all of us alive and smilin' in sunny Vietnam, with you lookin' like a grinning fool!"

"Hey, hey," Beau drawled, "watch yourself, Chief, that's no way to talk to someone when you're askin' a favor. Where are your manners? You want something, ask nice, use 'please,' and you could always add 'kind sir.'"

"The hell you say," Jesse chuckled. "A copy of this picture, or I might have to send your pretty wife a picture of our last R and R ... conduct a little blackmail operation!"

"Yeah, I want a copy too, Parker," Redd chimed in. Mike Redd, a young, black Marine hailing from Macon, Georgia, who at five-foot-eleven, was dwarfed standing between Jess and Beau for the photo. A grin spread on Redd's face, and with velvet poise and a voice of innocence, he delivered a customary "Reddism" to Beau Parker, a verbal "coup de grâce" that cut to the quick. "I dig what you recall, Jess. I do believe you're referring to Hotel Company's very own Lance Corporal pink fringed coolie hat Parker, wearing only a smile with Mai Mai on his lap."

The unlit cigar Redd clenched between pearly whites wagged Groucho Marx style. Beau felt his face getting hot. Redd saw he'd hit a nerve, and more, they were back to the banter he'd sorely missed. He knew the big guy's tongue was faster than most and that he was good for a loquacious, prolific rebuke. Vietnam was entertaining once more! Beau Parker had returned!

8

A journalism major, Redd attended the University of Georgia until his funds ran flat. "Flatter than a pancake pounded by an eighteen-wheeler," he was known to say. He worked odd jobs to pay for school, and the scholarship money made ends meet. But the jobs and scholarships were not enough to cover his last semester. Mike thought his dream to be an investigative journalist was all tied up ... but there was too much knot with too little string. Redd had to drop out, the prized diploma just out of reach.

One stinking semester! So close and yet so far ....

~~~

Quitting went against his grain. Ever the focused fighter, Redd promised himself to be different from most coming out of his neighborhood. He wanted to count for something, to be of value, to make a difference. One way or another, he would persevere. When he graduated, he'd hang that diploma in a gilded gold frame and pay folks to come inside to admire it. In his mind, he already saw it hanging in the entrance of the two-story brick home, which would one day be his. He could and would make this happen.

Redd took on two full-time jobs and worked on the side doing any job that paid a buck or two. He did without. "Without" meant without much food, damn near without sleep, and definitely without a life to speak of when compared to other males his age. His sole focus was to save every red cent that came his way. He had enough time to generate the funds necessary for the fall semester. He could do this.

By the third month, life stepped in and snatched his dream. No longer protected by his student exemption status, the draft found him. It found him scrounging through a week deep stack of mail strewn on his grocery crate table, stuffing Ramen noodles in his mouth to avoid being late for his second job. When he saw the nondescript white envelope, with the return address, **United States Government**, his hand began to shake. With a sinking feeling, he realized that being late for work was the least of his worries. He put his feet on the grocery crate and settled back into the only piece of furniture in the room ... a very faded, somewhat frayed, blue and white flowered, older than old, overstuffed chair. With

9

trembling fingers, he tore open the envelope and pulled out the twice-folded piece of Government Issue paper. He unfolded it. It read, **ORDER TO REPORT FOR INDUCTION.** He stared at the words while they sank in.

The Ramen noodles churned in his stomach. Redd did a cursory review of the contents. The closing statement told him everything he needed to know – **"Willful failure to report at the above place and hour of the day named in this order subjects the violator to fine and imprisonment."**

Redd leaned back and rested his head on the chair, feeling its thick, cushioned comfort for the first time. He stared into space and chewed his noodles slowly to relish their taste. He no longer needed to rush. No thoughts of, "I should have moved to Canada as soon as the money ran out," or, "I should have become a conscientious objector." Instead, he told himself this was just a glitch regarding his future … a hiccup. He'd stay positive. He absorbed the inevitable. *Well, well, so this is one hell of a way to say goodbye to two boring and dead-end jobs. Goodbye, Piggly Wiggly, my stock boy days are over. So long, Valet King, guess some other joker can replace me as a King parking attendant. It will be their turn to hear swank Georgians say, "Boy, keep your hands on the wheel of this ve-hic-le, ten o'clock – two o'clock, easy on the brakes, and shake a tail when I come for it …." Or, "Boy, don't be parking this here vehicle near any puddles or mud now; I just had this here vehicle cleaned, and if you want a tip, shake a tail when I come for it …." Shake a tail, shake a tail …. Ah, the wealthy, always in a hurry, always expecting the best but usually giving the least. "Hands full of gimmies and mouths full of much obliged," he'd once heard a folk singer sing, and it stuck with him because it was true. Sonofabitch! I'm getting drafted!*

His mind drifted to the Marine Recruiting billboard he had seen many times, capitalized letters maybe three feet tall, emblazoned against the sky … summoning: JOIN THE MARINES AND BECOME A MAN. Mike Redd wanted to see the world, why not start as a Marine?

Within five months, he found himself no longer eating Ramen noodles; instead, he was eating the red dirt of Vietnam as he dove face down into the mud, dodging incoming artillery, trying to stay alive.

~~~

"Well boys," Beau proclaimed in his bigger than life way, "I might have only been wearing a birthday suit at that most bodacious soirée, but let the record note that this young Marine walked away from all the boom-boom offered by Mai Mai and her friends! Before God and The Corps, I was true to my Helen, and you're each a testament to that fact!" His eyes softened as he glanced at the gleaming gold band new to his finger. The mask of banter faded away.

Jesse caught the glance, and not wanting Beau to wax nostalgic, worked to keep the joking going. "Ooo-weee, Parker, that's some band you've got there. Man, you're just too damned happy with all that shine on your finger! I'll bet you haven't had time to say hello to the 'honey-do list' that comes just after the 'I do.'" A frown crossed Beau's tanned face as Jess continued, "Or maybe you've made friends with it already? What's on the 'honey-do' list for you, amigo?" Imitating Redd, Jess too wagged his cigar and made his eyebrows twitch as though they were living things, caterpillars that moved across his broad forehead. They framed hazel eyes and thick lashes any female would covet, intelligent eyes, warm eyes, eyes that now twinkled with fun and humor at the look on Beau's face.

"Beau, you'd make a piss poor poker player!" Jess finished, laughing out loud.

"This band of gold won't ever know a 'honey-do' list, my friend," replied Beau. "It's the symbol of pure unadulterated sweet love, never to partake in advantage seeking or list-making, but more than that, boys, it's a symbol of a man in his prime, ready to be a love machine to the woman of his dreams, rearing to please, you might say!"

He calmed the snickers and laughter with a wave of his hand and tried hard to quell his urge to laugh and laugh hard, as he realized just how wrong those words sounded. Shit! He made every attempt to appear serious after the realization hit. "Enough," he ordered. "Any more talk Jess, that includes you, Redd, and you both might have to forget about copies of this undoubtedly very fine photo, representing at least three of the best fighting Marines on Vietnam soil!"

"And who would those three be, my friend?" asked Jess.

"Why me, of course, and those two smart, refined gentlemen who kneeled below us, keeping their mouths shut and dutifully respecting the gift-giver in this group!"

Jesse laughed. His old friend was himself once more. With a wink, Jess reached around Redd for Parker's ear. He gave it a tug, like an uncle catching a favorite nephew doing something wrong. Redd moved fast to create distance. He understood all too well horseplay was starting, and two very large Marines were about to do damage. Anything or anyone in the way was small potatoes in the rucksack of life! Let the games begin! As Beau yelled, "Your ass is grass, McGowan!" Jesse McGowan locked up Beau's arms in a move they learned in boot camp, and they ended in a collective heap on the ground.

Redd found a pile of sandbags to sit on. Not a cigar man himself, he took a long pull on his last Chesterfield, feeling content. Before him, two grown men scuffled in play, like kids on the playground. The bantering, the joking around, the horseplay, was like a cold beer. It took the edge off the fear. He glanced at the other two Marines who were part of his life. Angel pulled out his Zippo, and with an animated flourish and a deep bow, he lit the cigar for Chingas. Redd smiled because he remembered there was a peace sign engraved on the Zippo along with the words, "Why me?" scratched near the bottom. That lighter epitomized Angel. He'd signed up without a clue what he was signing up for but loved the adventure, anyway. Not to be outdone and looking much like a Shakespearean bard, Chingas returned the favor with a stiff bow and gruff, "Thanks, man."

Redd knew the NVA could strike at any time. It's what they'd been doing for weeks, but for this precious moment, he allowed himself to ease out of hypervigilance and to groove on the sensation of peace and goodwill. Not much older than schoolboys, these Marines played hard when they could. It cut the stress and moved them forward to take on their next crises.

He looked to see where the Lieutenant was. Redd had expected to see him by now, saying, "Pack it up, boys, we're movin' out." It surprised him the Lieutenant had made the time to take their picture. He was busy, but Beau was the one who'd asked, and the Lieutenant had a good heart.

It was almost 0900 hours, and Redd figured it would take most of the day to cover a mile or so, moving a battalion of 400 men to their first position. He wondered how long it had taken Hannibal to move several thousand soldiers and thirty elephants over the Italian Alps. Something to see, but not something a sane man wanted to do, he concluded.

Perhaps time was on their side this morning, and they'd bombard Beau with questions of "The World." He'd made it back and was now obliged to share news of "The World" with them. "Spread the wealth," so to speak, and give them a chance to put Vietnam on the back burner. Redd could imagine the questions they would ask. "Any hot new musical groups? What about the Monterey Pop Festival - they had heard about it before Beau left ... who performed? Any new hit songs they hadn't heard on Armed Forces Radio before he left? What cars were 'in'? What movies were out?"

Redd wanted Beau to bask in the memories, he deserved it, and his happiness would spill over to the others, they deserved that too. Redd understood that in giving them information about "The World," Beau was reminding them that home still existed ... that's what each man was seeking, a renewed connection with the world they'd left. He hoped there'd be time for that. It'd make today's trek easier to bear.

In the distance, Redd caught sight of the Lieutenant stopping by a group of men. His heart sank. *Damn. Maybe tonight the boys and Beau could talk ... no time for it now ....*

Redd hated being the spoiler of parties, but someone had to be the bearer of bad news. Better it came from a member of the gun team. He walked over to where the scuffling was still on and told Beau and the others to get ready.

13

"It's called 'Operation Kingfisher,' Beau, and 400 of us are entering the Demilitarized Zone to find the fuckers that keep shelling us." Beau's face told him he understood that Operation Kingfisher was a big deal. They had to move carefully to find the artillery sites. What a shitty return for Beau, Redd thought. It was a perfect example of "expect the unexpected," a state of being every Marine in Vietnam understood only too well.

It was an "anything goes" war, and the infantry was "on" pretty much twenty-four hours a day, seven days a week. There were no safe-zones as in WWII, let alone safe-moments. The day you expected a firefight was the day you got a taste of peaceful serenity. The day you expected safety, hoping to let your mind wander to your girl or family, well sure as shit, that was the day you got ambushed, or a shell exploded close to you, or a buddy stepped on a booby trap. Life in this overgrown jungle of soul drenching heat was endless anxiety and dread of the unknown because the unknown came swiftly and carried a big stick. It came in the form of war-hardened communists, either the Viet Cong (VC) or the NVA, armed with accurate and reliable Russian-made AK-47's and light artillery. The "certain uncertainty" is what made Vietnam macabre and surreal, and this was not lost on this team of eighteen to twenty-two-year-old grunts humping in the bush. They lived and died by Hotel Company's motto, "Hell in a Helmet," and these Marines were America's collateral for freedom from communism.

To a man, they paid the price. Some with their lives, others on the installment plan with loss of limbs or body function, or Post-Traumatic Stress exhibited with guilt, nightmares, substance abuse, and suicide. And then there was Agent Orange. Exposure to Agent Orange, and if you served or lived in 'Nam, you were almost surely exposed to it, produced cancer, diabetes, peripheral neuropathy, blood pressure, and heart issues. For the 5,000 women who served in Vietnam, usually as nurses, exposure could cause reproductive problems and stillbirths. The children of Vietnam Vets exposed to AO could experience deformity, spina bifida, and again, a higher rate of stillbirth.

Each Vietnam Veteran wore the price tag of freedom; it was just not visible to the naked eye.

14

These five Marines served their time "in-country" in a barren, bombed-out place known as Con Thien. The name translated to mean the "Hill of Angels."

FOUR

HOTEL COMPANY

1967

With the horseplay over and more than a little stunned by Redd's news, Beau absent-mindedly ran his hands over his now exposed six-pack, having pulled his shirt off when the wrestling began. "Yes sir," he said to no one in particular, "still have what it takes to fight those sons of bitches." He looked at the sky, keenly feeling the Vietnam heat. He'd forgotten its intensity while in Fort Myers. It was a sledgehammer, pounding him down, and August would be worse. *Get yourself hydrated, Beau, and keep yourself hydrated–this body is already out of sync with Vietnam.* He got some water and found a sandbag to sit on. *Well, well, so here I am ... two hours back and facing who knows what for the next few days. Good thing I got my head straight and figured out what's important! Guess I have a date with the DMZ!*

No negative thoughts, he reminded himself.

His parents were first-generation Norwegian immigrants. The middle child of three brothers, Beau looked every bit the Viking with his massive frame and white-blonde hair. If his parents had named him Thor, it would have suited him. He was born happy and could be counted on.

While lying under the stars one night, neither able to sleep, Beau and Jess talked about home and their families. Beau chuckled at a remembrance. "My Mom told me God placed me in the middle of her three boys so I could teach my older brother, Kristian, how to have fun and at the same time keep an eye on my younger brother, Ronny, who has too much of it. The problem was I got Kristian into trouble, and both of us got into trouble when we hung out with Ronny. Guess I wasn't much help to Mom, but we Parker boys sure knew how to have a good time!" Beau smiled at the memory. "Yeah …. Kristian wanted to join the Marines but was turned away when the results of his physical showed a heart condition. He took it hard. Not because he had a heart problem, but because he couldn't enlist. The first thing I did after I signed up was find a phone and called him. I told him I joined up … for both of us." That was Beau.

Beau had taken Jess under his wing and showed him the ropes from the first day Jess stepped on `Nam soil, and he was grateful for Beau's help and friendship.

So much differed from what they were taught at Parris Island. Not to say the Drill Instructors had done a bad job. No. But when reality hit in this war zone, there was much Jesse wasn't prepared for. Beau taught him the things that made the difference between comfort and discomfort; how to pack sixty-plus pounds of supplies into a rucksack, to keep socks dry to avoid immersion foot which led to bleeding cracks or chunks of flesh falling off, how to remove leeches that crawled on you at night and sucked your blood, and whose head could remain embedded in the flesh and cause infections if removed incorrectly.

Beau also taught Jesse the things that could make the difference between life and death; Halazone tablets used to purify drinking water, salt tablet management to reduce the possibility of heat exhaustion and death … and the importance of a clean rifle since the M-16 was a weapon known to fail if mud, grit, or moisture was not thoroughly removed. A faithful cleaning of your M-16 meant you at least had a chance.

The most important lesson to combat survival Jesse learned on his own. He learned it the hard way his first night in `Nam; the importance of maintaining communication with others. He and his platoon were in the bush. Jess stepped away from his squad to relieve himself … not letting anyone know. Upon his return, he was mistaken for the enemy and was confronted with several M-16's, aimed directly at him and ready to be fired! A small shiver invariably came with that memory. He felt it now as he talked survival skills in the moonlight with Chingas, new to Vietnam and the gun team.

"I was whistling past my grave and didn't even know it! Looking into the barrel of weapons ready to blow me apart ... would've scared the shit out of me if I hadn't just gone!" Jess shook his head and chuckled as he went on. "That little incident might have 'soiled' my reputation as a Marine... for life! I would have been the fucking green Marine who shit himself his first day here!" He looked at Chingas and added, "I don't tell this story to just anyone, Chingas. Only Beau knows about it, and now you. I'm telling you, so you don't make the same mistakes I made. Communication, it's vital." Chingas understood and appreciated this story because it was told in confidence. He was trusted. From that day on, he hung onto every word uttered by Jesse as though his life depended on it because it did ... just as Jesse had hung onto Beau's words.

~~~

That night, Jesse thought about what he had not brought up with Chingas ... a topic taboo to some Marines, but that came up in private conversation, usually before or after a firefight. It was "the kill." The action of taking a life that sometimes froze a Marine with deadly consequence or put him in a tailspin afterward.

The Corps taught you to kill the enemy with deadly efficiency. They did not address it as taking a life—a huge difference in attitude and approach. The Corps took it for granted when you signed your name on the line that you accepted killing as part of the job. In fact, you accepted it as the most essential part of the job. Yet after you killed, you were left with the realization that you took a life. That detail wasn't broached.

Jesse remembered his first kill and the subsequent emotions he experienced. *How do you get emotionally prepared for that? Yeah, you think you've got a handle on it 'til it happens. You know this is the enemy and know what it means to be a Marine. In battle, survival instincts kick in; training and muscle memory take over. But when searching dead bodies and you find a picture of a loved one tucked away in a pocket, the enemy becomes a human being. It's then you know you took a life... a heavy burden for some to justify ... it was the elephant in the room ....*

18

In the still of the night, in quiet conversation, fears were sometimes revealed. Jesse overheard someone say, "Yes sir, said he'd rather have his own life taken than to take someone else's." Jesse never heard that, but it came from a Marine he trusted, so Jess considered the information authentic.

"'Rather be killed than do the killin' ... I heard that said in my battalion when I first got to 'Nam," added Redd, who was awake and in on the conversation. "But I tell you what," Redd stopped to laugh under his breath, "When that Marine went into his first firefight, he wrapped his head around what had to be done quick enough when the bullets came at him! He was dancin' and jumpin,' dodgin' bullets and all the while firing like there was no tomorrow! Man, it's hard not to laugh out loud, all of us witnessing firsthand the birth of a killing machine!"

Redd knew men froze sometimes, and not always the quiet, intrinsic type. He saw a rowdy newcomer freeze ... really freeze ... and get killed ... three days in-country and dead. *Killing someone is the hurdle you overcome if you want to live.* Redd took that thought further, in a different direction .... "And then there's the killing that can enslave you if it comes from hatred," he mused. He mentioned a song by Billy Holiday called "Strange Fruit," a song about black men hanging from trees after a lynching. The black Marine he was talking with got it. "Yeah bro, there's that kind of killing too," he muttered.

Jesse didn't know much about Billy Holiday songs, but the conversation got him thinking about Chingas. Jesse promised himself to keep an eye out for the team's newest member, make himself more available to this quiet guy, especially if he got wind of Chingas having any reservations about killing.

~~~

As the gun team got their gear together to begin the spoiler mission, Jess glanced over to Beau. His bulk was comfortably familiar. Jess didn't have a brother, only his older sister Janine, but no one could have asked for a better friend or Assistant Gunner than John Beau Parker.

For all his fooling around, talk of women, and preoccupations with his "manly physique," Beau Parker's face lit up like a schoolboy's when he received a letter from Helen. He had been the six-foot-three-inch lineman for the Fort Myers High School football team. Helen was a cheerleader and voted school Homecoming Queen. The quintessential American couple.

Beau was a big man in every way at twenty-one years old. Jess understood early on that he and Beau complemented each other. Jess was an observer, more subdued than Beau, and his ability to listen garnered loyalty. Beau was the consummate entertainer who loved people, loved the limelight and the audience. He was happiest when he could talk and joke around. "I could sell a rat's asshole to a blind man as a wedding ring if it came down to it," he'd bragged once. And he probably could. Jesse didn't know why, but that saying brought a chuckle every time he heard it, no matter how bone-tired or emotionally exhausted he was from the carnage of the day.

Parker's exuberance was catching, but when too much ego spiraled out, as it sometimes did, Jess would remind him he himself was almost twenty, only a little over a year younger than Beau, one inch shorter, and had played some high school football himself, as the Maryland Football State Champion quarterback. Alpha males both, Beau just used less filter between brain and mouth than Jesse.

Jess was a natural leader. He'd known for a long time, maybe since 5th or 6th grade, that looking out for others, especially the little guy, made a difference to everyone. It pulled people up and seemed to Jesse that when egos were in check, everyone on the team slept better and seemed to have fewer problems. Marine training had reinforced the concept. The whole is greater than the sum of its parts when teamwork was in place. All for one and one for all ... brothers ... each man having value. These were ideals that resonated with Jess and made sense. This, and the Corps solid edict that no Marine, alive or dead, would be left behind, were the reasons Jesse chose to be a Marine. It meant something to him to know that no matter what, he'd make it home.

Jesse had learned from a friend's father to give thought before action. "Come from a position of strength. Think of your alternatives, then calculate the outcome for each ... only then do you come from a place of strength, not before." That advice stuck with Jess, and it was advice he knew he'd use for the rest of his life.

Beau's bravado and impulsiveness were an innate part of who he was, but they occasionally backfired and created conflict. In these ways, he and Jesse were different, but these two Marines adhered to the same core values. From the start, their connection was strong. They knew each other's worth, and over time, their respect grew, and their loyalty became absolute. They were not brothers by birth, but in these killing fields, they were brothers by choice.

Jess remembered an especially brutal firefight a couple of months earlier. It lasted for days. Each Marine wondered if he'd live to tell about it. Never let it be said the VC or NVA were ill-prepared or in any way inferior. They were not. They were fighting machines, especially the VC, who had been fighting for much longer. Their advantage over the Americans was twofold; they were playing a home game on their own turf, the terrain, climate, and customs were all part of who they were, and they were relatives to many in South Vietnam and expected, often demanded, help from "family" in the South, regardless of which side their relatives' political views fell.

During that firefight, Hotel Company was on reconnaissance patrol, crouching in the shadows. Low on ammo, Jess concentrated on the next ammo belt being fed into his M-60 by Redd. Beau was normally Jesse's Assistant Gunner, but he was providing gunfire support for Marines trapped in a crossfire, and Redd was filling in. From the corner of his eye, Jess saw Beau return and heard Beau emit a low guttural "Fuck." Jesse glanced up and saw Beau aiming his M-16. Jess's eyes skipped toward Beau's aim point and saw an NVA pointing his machine gun, an AK-47, at Jesse. At that moment, nothing existed for Jess but silence and the face of the NVA soldier. Jess was about to be shot.

The sound of a shot filled the air, followed by silence. A vaporized burst of pink replaced the soldier's face. Nothing existed but the pink spray, a soft, beautiful firework exploding. The soldier collapsed, falling almost gracefully to the ground, a puppet released from its strings. Silence and timelessness continued. Jesse was captured inside a snow globe, watching ... waiting ... in frozen silence ... seeing only pink snow while the world around him no longer existed ... and a part of which he was not. The ear-shattering gunfire, the sight of human massacre, and the smell of fear snapped him back to reality. Jesse knew it was Beau's shot that killed the soldier. Jesse's adrenaline pumped hard. He was alive, and he fought with every fiber in his body to stay that way.

Return fire eventually stopped as night closed in. It was over and time to tally the cost in equipment and men. It would take a while to determine who was missing. All hoped the missing were well concealed or beyond caring any longer. Screams in the jungle would tell the whole story until daylight returned and they could resume searching.

~~~

"Fucker didn't know who he was dealing with," Beau said to the gun team that evening, slapping Jesse's back with his left hand while gulping down his second round of spaghetti C-Rations with his right. "We might be like a blind man in these hills ... not always sure where we are ... but we can smell a stinkin' bill of goods when it points a gun at us."

Listening to Beau, Chingas grunted. He looked over at Angel. They shared a nod.

The world was simple for Beau. The enemy was the enemy, not a person. Jesse was envious of his friend's ability to compartmentalize his world. When it came to killing, Jesse wished he could think more like Beau. That night, Jess stayed awake wondering about the world of that NVA soldier, what he left behind and who would mourn his death. It certainly wasn't Jesse's first kill, but it was his closest face-to-face dance with death. But for a fraction of a second, it would have been him.

22

FIVE

YOU COULD BAKE COOKIES

1967

Chingas, also 19, didn't say much but saw everything. Some teachers thought he was slow when he first entered their classroom but soon realized that "quiet" had nothing to do with "slow" in his case. He'd taken his fourth-grade teacher aside, and with all the courage he could muster, told her even if she thought he was slow, it didn't mean he wasn't going somewhere.

He felt safe being in the company of Jesse, Beau, Redd, and Angel. They were Marines who hadn't lost their minds like some had. They cared about fighting the good fight and expected to win, not like other Marines, recent arrivals, touting an attitude of, "It don't mean nothin'," or who were giving in to the "fuck its," or were frequently complaining of "FUBAR's" … "Fucked up beyond all reason."

Before coming to 'Nam, Chingas wondered how he'd fare as a Mexican-American in this war, living in proximity with white boys. He discovered Angel wondered the same about being Cuban. It was not an issue with these men. He never heard the word "gook, fish head, slant eye," or other derogatory terms come from Jesse's mouth when referring to the Vietnamese, and it comforted him. As the gun team leader, Jesse set a fair tone and treated each man as someone of value. That meant something to a kid who grew up tough on the streets of New York. He thought it meant something to Angel and Redd as well.

Chingas recalled riding in a convoy with Jesse in the back of an open Deuce-and-a-Half truck. Left behind for maintenance by an Army Materiel group, the convoy returned from Cam Lo, the southwest corner of Leatherneck Square, to retrieve the truck then head for Da Nang on a supply run. Leaning against the metal rod of the open truck, a new grunt pretended to shoot villagers as the truck passed by. Jesse watched but didn't say much. The grunt's game intensified. It became a reality when he took serious aim at an old man herding an even older water buffalo. Without warning, Jesse lunged forward, pushed the rifle up, and caused the private to miss his shot, ruining his sport. The grunt tried to swing at Jesse, but Jess already had him in a chokehold.

"They're not worth less because they're different from us," Jesse growled before he shoved him away.

Those who took the time to know Chingas Ramirez discovered a nice guy. One of his few non-Mexican friends wrote in his High School yearbook, "You have a heart as big as Texas. You need to let people see it!" Chingas opted to disregard that advice. It would mean he'd need to reveal himself, let people in, and trust, something he didn't do easily or quickly. He was a private person, and that was okay in his book. Few Mexicans lived in New York City. Those who did, stuck together, bonded through La Familia. They trusted their own. Chingas only trusted his own. In the city, he had family, trust, and security. He needed nothing more. He did not need to stretch his comfort zone or extend himself into unknown arenas. Then came Vietnam, and as different as New York City was to 'Nam, one constant remained; a Mexican boy alone was vulnerable and might encounter trouble, perhaps death.

He tried to reconcile who he was with what he needed, a loner in need of La Familia. When Chingas heard Jesse say, "They're not worth less because they're different from us," his heart opened. Here was the solution to his dilemma; God was good and looking out for him.

"Thank you, Jesús," he'd whispered to himself. The unspoken prayer had been answered! In a New York minute, Chingas knew he could trust Jesse, and without knowing it, Jesse's ticket to La Familia had been punched. From that time forward, Chingas traveled close to Jess and made a personal vow to be a friend to this Marine and protect him if he could. Chingas would do all he could to keep this part of La Familia alive because Jesse was a good man and being close to him could ensure his own safety.

24

~~~

Angel Santiago, born in Havana, Cuba, was another city boy. In 1961, Angel, along with 14,000 other Cuban children, took part in a little-known airlift called "Operation Peter Pan." The children were sent by their Cuban parents to relatives or Catholic orphanages in the United States to escape communism. This was the most extensive exodus of unaccompanied minors in the Western Hemisphere, and the U.S. government waived visa requirements.

Aunt Rosalina and her husband Maximo welcomed 13-year-old Angel into their lives and their small apartment above the bakery they owned near Lincoln Park, Chicago.

Aunt Rosalina. Good Aunt Rosalina. Always admonishing the easy virtue of those mini-skirted, sexy smelling, "devil with the blue dress on" type girls which Angel had recently discovered. Who in their right mind wanted the chaste good girls Rosalina wanted for him? She'd selected Corinna as the girl best suited to be his betrothed, but Angel didn't wish to be betrothed to Corinna or anyone else ... not now ... not yet ... he had oats to sow! The Marines looked more promising to Angel than settling down to what he referred to as early retirement, so he enlisted. And he knew exactly why he enlisted. Angel was not ready for the mundane, the ordinary, the routine that sucked life away. He wanted excitement and the big life. Mostly, he wanted to avoid a marriage to Corinna del Salvadore.

Extolling the virtues of "good girls" had fallen on deaf ears, and in fact, it was what pushed Angel to enlist in the Marine Corps, the most machismo branch of the military with the best-looking dress uniform. If nothing else, the uniform might be a magnet for the women Angel Montoya Santiago desired.

Angel enlisted for many wrong reasons, but as he signed his name, he thought of the mother and father he hadn't seen in years, the friends he lost when leaving Cuba, and the beauty of the green island he said goodbye to from the plane window. He realized that Castro and communism had stolen everything he loved. He'd lived in a world with his head in the clouds and never connected the dots. Now, as a Marine, he realized he would have the power to fight communism and those who'd ripped his world from him. It would feel damn good to kick them in the ass and help the United States, the country that took him in and kept him safe. He spat on the sidewalk as he walked away from the Recruiting Center, pretending it was Khrushchev's face, and smiled. *Watch out, Khrushchev, Angel Santiago is coming! And looking good in dress blues, thank you very much!!*

"Oh my God in Heaven, what am I to do?" Rosalina cried to Father Roberto during confession. "How could he enlist now? And in the Marines! I tried to do for him what I believed my sister would have wanted," she sobbed, afraid of the repercussions should anything happen to her girl-crazed nephew. Would her sister ever forgive her? "What can I do?" she lamented.

"You could bake him cookies," Father Roberto said. "Boys love cookies." It was a simple solution to a complex problem. Rosalina began a baking frenzy to keep her soul out of hell. She would bake magnifico cookies worthy of kings. She would bake to keep Angel alive!

Rosalina sent weekly care packages to Hotel Company, delicacies the likes of which most of these boys had never tasted, and for this, they christened Angel, "Sweetness." For Angel, the name "Sweetness" catapulted him into a world he desired and wished to conquer ... the delicious world of women, red-hot mamas, and sizzling Chiquita's. With this nickname, his imagination took flight. He hoped the name Sweetness would get him to first base during R&Rs and any other opportunity that involved womankind. It would distinguish him as a sweet man, a kind man, a man who would look out for the best interest of "woman," and perhaps, if he got lucky, "woman" would look out for the best interest of Sweetness. Oh yes, this name was just the beginning of something right, and it had happened thanks to Aunt Rosalina!

The universe opened its doors to Angel the day he enlisted. He would make peace with God, his Aunt, and his mother still living in Cuba later. Good fortune had come his way. He could feel it. He would capitalize on it. Now it was time to receive Nirvana from the Gods. In a quick motion, he crossed himself, just in case, and hastily added under his breath, "Forgive me, Father."

~~~

Angel spotted Beau Parker's massive body as he approached the group upon his return from "The World." "Beau's back!" Angel shouted in the team's direction as he gave Beau a warm handshake, hands wrapping around thumbs, palms sliding together, fingers hooking.

"My man, welcome back to Hell! How is it you can walk, bro?" he asked Parker. "Trashcan banter," Beau called it, but as usual, he threw Angel a comeback.

"Sure, I can walk Sweetness because I know better than to use my feet … is that what you use? No wonder your ladies never come back for more!"

Laughing hard, Angel replied, "No man, I do not use my feet!" A mischievous grin spread over Angel's face, and not accepting failure, he tried once more. "So, tell me, big man, how did Johnson like his nights of marital bliss?"

With a look of disbelief at the audacity of this young Marine, Beau replied. "Johnson loved his nights of marital bliss. Don't you ever give up, kid?" Beau shook his head, not wanting to engage in further lowlife conversation involving time with his new wife, but bravado reared its ugly head. Before he could stop the words from leaving his mouth, Beau added, "Johnson knew what to do, hold out until the troops were ready and when the signal came … start shootin' for the moon!" And the howls from the squad began. "Hey man," Beau continued smoothly, "I thought you knew 'Get the job done before it gets us done,' is our gun team's personal motto? Did you think I would fall down on the job?

Seeing the Lieutenant in their vicinity, Beau shouted, "Hey Lieutenant, can you take a picture of us?" And with everyone still laughing, they moved into a pose.

SIX

Except for Chingas, the team had served for many months at "Leatherneck Square," a remote U.S. Marine firebase made up of four outposts: Con Thien at the northwest corner, Gio Linh at the northeast corner, Cam Lo the southwest, and Dong Ha the southeast outpost. It made up an area of 54 square miles of barren, cratered, and scorched earth.

In 1967, Con Thien captured worldwide attention because it was the gateway into South Vietnam, and the NVA were hell-bent on taking this area. Their shelling had been relentless during Beau's leave as it was the closest U.S. base to the line separating North and South Vietnam. Robert McNamara, the Secretary of Defense, designated the outpost to keep North Vietnam from invading South Vietnam. Only two miles south of the Demilitarized Zone (DMZ), also known as the "Dead Marine Zone," this area would become known as "The Meat Grinder," and serving there was "Doing Time in the Barrel."

Con Thien. Hard to imagine that a place whose name meant "Hill of Angels" could be the site of such gruesome acts of violence. "Hill of Angels, my ass," Angel said with disgust when a particularly horrific shelling ended. "We're losing two Marines a week! The only angels here are dead Marines!"

There were many other reasons the Hill of Angels was perhaps the worst spot in Vietnam to serve. The earth of Con Thien consisted of gritty red dust. Explosions from enemy artillery hurled huge clouds of it into the air, which then attached itself to everyone like a second skin. The red dust smothered pores and intensified the heat they felt. It

28

wormed its way into every moving piece of machinery and weaponry. Every can of C-Rations had a gritty texture. Pages of letters going home were smudged with its pink blush. The Marines breathed it in and, on a good day, washed it from their bodies.

July's heat was intense. It burned the nose to breathe it in. From October to March, monsoons poured cold rain measured in feet and gorged the rivers the infantry waded through. It made Con Thien's mud so deep that Marines sank to their knees in it, knowing part of its deep redness was Marine blood.

Then there were rats. The ongoing war between who was in charge, rats, or Marines. It was exhausting. Clearly, the rats were in charge as they scurried wherever they damn well pleased. More the size of fat cats, no Marine wanted a bite from the fangs of these scurrilous creatures. Vietnam's equivalent to the cockroach, and like the cockroach, the rats ran when noise or light came their way. They were repulsive.

Many a Marine opted for a recon mission to get away from this seething death trap, and the incessant shouts of "Incoming!" They were young Marines staring down death daily. Angel was right. It was a place of angels because it was a place of death. Who would die next, Angel wondered? He crossed himself.

~~~

During a recent barrage, Jesse and Chingas caught in the open, laid next to each other, waiting for a chance to sprint to a bunker. Between blasts, Chingas yelled out, "These guys have a serious hard-on for us!" Out of character, he stood in full view and shot a middle finger from each hand in the direction of the enemy. Strangely, the firing stopped! Jesse looked at Chingas with renewed respect and laughed.

"You know Jess, I don't even know why we're over here or how we got into this war," confessed Chingas as they bedded down for the night.

"Simple Chingas," replied Jess. "Ya gotta know the history.

"It's always been a country occupied by someone else. China was here for two thousand years, then the French showed up in the 1800s, colonized the place, and built large rubber tree plantations. During World War II, the Japanese occupied the country but let the French continue to run it. In 1954, the Vietnamese kicked the French out, and we're here now. The Vietnamese are tired of everyone running their country except themselves. What do you know about Ho Chi Minh, Chingas?"

"Not much, man."

"You wanna know?"

"Yeah, man."

"Okay! For starters, he's a revolutionary who wants an independent Vietnam. Ho tried to get help as far back as Presidents Wilson, Roosevelt, and Truman but struck out. He went to Russia's Stalin, but Stalin wouldn't meet him. He turned to the Chinese Communist revolutionary, Mao Tse Tung, where he found help. Mao would help with weapons and artillery, but most importantly, he would train Ho's Vietnamese soldiers in guerrilla warfare. This would be done in exchange for rice and the agreement that Vietnam would accept communism. They struck a deal.

"In `54, after eight years of fighting, the French surrendered, and Ho's guerilla army declared victory. The French agreed to peace talks in Geneva, where it was decided Vietnam would be divided into two countries at the 17th parallel, right here where we're sitting!" Jess spread his arms wide to emphasize this fact, then continued.

"South Vietnam would be democratic, and North Vietnam would be communist with Ho as President. But Ho always stood for a united Vietnam. 'It was patriotism, not communism that inspired me,' he said. The peace talks promised an election of a new ruler for a unified Vietnam within two years, and that new ruler would likely be Ho Chi Minh.

"In 1955, everything fell apart. A politician by the name of Diem proclaimed the formation of a new country called the Republic of South Vietnam, assumed the Presidency. Then he refused to acknowledge the promise to reunite North and South made at the Geneva Accords.

"The U.S. supported Diem. Hell, we made his victory happen. He was a dictator, but on paper, Vietnam was a democracy. In the early 60s, the North, led by Ho and General Giap, attacked South Vietnam and its government. Ho had waited patiently for the promise of Vietnam's reunification and the election of its president. The promise was never kept.

"President Johnson believed in the Domino Theory, if one country fell to communism, then neighboring countries would topple … falling dominoes. Johnson considered Vietnam the gateway to Cambodia, Laos, and Thailand. He feared Ho would spread communism if he became its President. He feared communism would spread throughout Indochina, and South Vietnam was where President Lyndon Johnson drew his line. South Vietnam would remain a democracy. If it meant a fight, so be it. In 1965 he deployed 3,500 Marines to Da Nang to fight the Communist North Vietnamese and contain the Red threat.

"So, that's why we're here, Chingas." Jesse noticed Chingas' eyes had glazed over. "That's also why we're fighting the Viet Cong. Some of them have been fighting for a unified Vietnam while you and I were still in diapers. They wear black pajamas by night and often fight alongside the North Vietnamese Army Regulars. By day, they wear coolie hats, act like peasants, and travel at will between North and South Vietnam.

"Hey, are you listening or sleeping with your eyes open?" Jesse kidded with Chingas.

"Yeah, man, I'm listening! We're here to stop a global communist threat, fighting the people who only want to reunify their small country, right?"

"Wow, man, that's it in a nutshell! You were listening! Two very different motivations are fighting for the same turf. They're fighting as hard to reunite their country as we are to keep communism out of ours. High stakes for both sides. Aim well, Chingas, they will be!"

Chingas yawned and said, "Thanks Jess, that was a lot of info to cover!"

"Yeah, I guess it was … just trying to help," Jess muttered and yawned himself.

"What do you know about the history of Mexico and its war with the United States?" asked Chingas with a grin. Jesse slapped Chingas in the back of the head for that smart-ass comment. Chingas was the surprise card. More to him than meets the eye, Jess thought more than once.

"That lesson is for another day, my friend, and it will cost you," Jesse joked, rolling over on his poncho to get comfortable. He needed sleep.

What did he know about the Mexican American War? The Alamo? Sam Houston? Did he remember his history teacher calling it a "land-grab" by the United States? *Didn't we take almost half of what was Mexico? Do I remember right?* Tomorrow he would see what Chingas knew about it …. He yawned again and was asleep as he finished his last thought.

SEVEN

ANNIE

April 2006

It was seven-thirty in the morning, and golden sunlight streamed through her bedroom window. A ringing phone pulled Annie Miller from a deep sleep. She hit the snooze button, but the noise persisted. Damn! Her plan had been to sleep late. She squinted, not ready for the brightness. She groped for the receiver of her pink-beige retro phone, a parting gift from her first boss who'd said she wouldn't be complete without it attached to her ear. To her chagrin, he was right. Any reporter who worked in the seventies would vouch that the phone and typewriter were essential to producing the story of the day, second only to coffee and cigarettes. In Annie's world, there was always a story worth addressing, a cause worth exposing, and a justice worth securing. Annie was nothing if not a fighter for the underdog and justice.

She put the phone to her ear and pulled the quilt over her head, a habit from childhood when she and Grammy would hide, tell stories, whisper secrets, and pretend to be invisible from the world. She gazed through the quilt's red and white pattern. It looked more like a piece of stained glass than a quilt, the cotton translucent, worn thin by decades of use and washings. It was a treasure, a friend that shared much of her life's journey. It had been her solace when tears needed a place to fall, heartaches needed consolation, and decisions needed timelessness to be processed. These pieces of fabric, sewn together by her Grammy, mother, and aunt, were a testament of a family who loved one another. Many treasures had found a home with Annie, but she cherished this one.

A reluctant tenant of the new day, she begrudgingly accepted the morning's interruption. "Hello," she grumbled into the receiver,

33

resenting the anonymous caller who'd taken away any hope of awakening to the sound of birds ….

"Morning, Mom," replied Thomas, her only child, "I understand you're hot to trot to get in trouble, true or not?" Multiple possibilities raced through her foggy but never quiet mind. She waited and hoped he would give her what she needed to answer coherently. It was too early to go on a fishing expedition. *What did he mean hot to trot to get herself into trouble? What trouble?* He apparently expected her to know what he was talking about. All male, his world was the center of the universe, and all who entered should be mind-readers, but she was not … especially this early … also, as a man, he expected all the inhabitants of his world to be linear thinkers, just like him … again, she was not …. Men and women, so differently wired, she thought for the hundredth time. *We multi-task, and their brain is task-focused. For the female, a simple question doesn't necessarily lead to a simple answer. A question to a female produces a party of possibilities igniting the brain … a virtual network of synaptic explosions flirting with options.* Annie liked the sound of that phrase. *I should use that in a story.*

"Not fair to be ambiguous when you call your Mom this early, Thomas." *Do most males truly lumber along, unaware of the effect of an open-ended question on a woman?* She would not try for an answer. It was a trap. The probability of a correct response negligible.

Annie let him question too much as a child. But then, she'd read Dr. Spock. She explained too often when she should have answered, "Because I said so." Maybe if she had put her foot down more, she would have a polite, ever respectful, perfect son. *So much trial and error in raising a child, the grand experiment … who knew? And who would want a perfect child, anyway? Perfect child meant perfect mother … no, no, that would never work …. And he better not throw another senior citizen remark my way!* Annie Miller would have a word with him if their conversation took that turn.

"What are you getting at, Thomas? What was the question?" She needed coffee.

"Mom, stay with me here, you can do this," came the reply, followed by a solid chuckle. He knew her so well. They'd almost grown up together; she barely twenty-one when she had him. *Thomas, how good it is to have you close again.* Annie savored the moment, telling herself to imprint this as a good memory. Yes, he was all male, but he was her male, and she loved him dearly. And truth be told, maybe her world was as important to her as his was to him. Oh well, Thomas was back, and she felt complete!

Her classic features let the tensions go, and her face softened. She pushed back a strand of blonde hair and let the quilt billow down onto her lap as she sat up to engage more clearly. Recrimination made way for laughter on her end as well.

"Mom, a few of us met at the Hawk and Dove last night after work, where I ran into your boss, Sam Wallace. I should have figured it was his watering hole. It's a sardine can filled with wall-to-wall politicians. He mentioned your trip to New Orleans. That totally blind-sighted me! Are you going to New Orleans? It doesn't sound safe yet, for a single, slightly older woman," he teased. *Damn if he didn't do it again!*

She shook her head. *Two can play this game.* "You are merciless, not to mention irreverent and intolerable. Haven't you heard, Thomas? The late fifties are the new thirties! Hell, I'm your age!" she quipped. "Stop worrying, old man. Do you see me with a cane yet? Aging is a state of mind, and my state does fine! But to answer your question, I'm going to New Orleans to see what's happening. It's been eight months since Hurricane Katrina, and I want to see how it's coming along for myself and the paper. I'm hoping to help with whatever's needed, progress seems slow. Anyway, I have the time, and Sam says go, so I'm going."

"I knew talking you out of this would be unlikely, but I had to give it a shot," Thomas responded, hoping she would understand his call came from a place of caring, not controlling. He would never try to inhibit her. He had only admiration for his mother and knew full well the many and varied accomplishments of this self-sufficient woman.

Professionally, she'd had a long career as a writer for the Washington Post. "I stay in my truth when covering a story," she was once quoted.

She'd proven herself not afraid of taking on corrupt systems or challenging those in power whose views or actions she believed to be immoral or to the country's detriment. Above all, Annie was an advocate for justice and the disenfranchised. She credited her professional strength to the Post, a newspaper that always supported her.

~~~

As a young teenager, Thomas, trying to be "cool" with a new friend, said sarcastically, "My Mom believed in truth, justice, and the American way long before Superman became a hero." Annie overheard the remark. The next day she took him to the local animal shelter, where they walked past cages of animals, many suffering from signs of abuse.

As they drove away, she asked, "What did you see, Thomas?"

"I saw puppies and cute dogs that will probably get adopted and some that won't."

"What's different about those that won't?"

"The mistreated ones won't get adopted; they're kinda broken."

"Do you think all sentient life deserves proper and equal treatment?"

"Sure," he replied.

"That would be just, Thomas. Justice is served if laws and moral consciousness work for the good of all. Justice sees that everyone, every being, is valued and entitled to the same treatment as everyone else. Some of those animals were beaten and neglected and might well be euthanized through no fault of their own. Laws are made to prevent that mistreatment. That's justice, too. Always walk on the side of 'right,' Thomas. The sting, no, the hurt of injustice, exists all around us and pulls us down to a base place. We must fight it. Martin Luther King. Jr. said, 'Injustice for one means injustice for all,' and he was right. Just so you clearly understand, I feel privileged that I can fight for justice. And when I fight for justice, I'm also fighting for truth; you see, truth is the chrysalis tucked inside justice." He looked at his Mom differently from that day forward, through new eyes. Yes, she was a force to be reckoned with. She dared to think for herself and act on her convictions. He'd remember this conversation many times throughout his life.

Annie proved to be a Mamma lion when he needed an advocate, but simultaneously she encouraged self-reliance and independence … especially independent thinking. She supported Thomas' goals in every way she could. No boy had a stronger ally, and he was grateful for it.

~~~

The University of Maryland had recruited him as a history professor, and he'd recently purchased a fixer-upper on the Chesapeake Bay. The forty-minute drive to the University was more than worth it to live on this beautiful stretch of water. And he was closer to his aging mother, should she need help, although that wasn't likely for a good while yet, after all, she was the "new thirties!" Still, you never knew.

"Call me when you get there, Mom, and check in now and then, or I might miss all those hard times you give me!"

"I give you?? Rethink that statement, my friend!" Annie laughed. They both knew the truth. "Wait, before you hang up, how's the remodeling coming?"

"Just laid down the tile."

"How does it look?"

"Great Mom, it came out great. I read the directions." In her mind, Annie could see the smile take shape on her son's face as he teased once again.

"Yeah, yeah, Thomas, I read them too, when it's necessary." She laughed again. She hated directions and too often just "began." That spontaneity had gotten her into trouble more than a few times, and she knew Thomas knew.

"Gotta go, kiddo," said Annie, dodging any more potential bullets. "You stay safe with all those new power tools!" She was as comfortable in a hardware store as she was rummaging in her favorite boutique, but this was his first go-round with renovating. *Good, he's using his hands and getting them dirty.* There was satisfaction in that work, a beginning and an end, with sweat equity endearing the result.

"You stay safe too, Mom," Thomas responded. "Call once in a while."

Thomas smiled to himself and looked around for an empty spot to put down his cell phone, then turned to evaluate the full-scale mess around him, material, tools, machinery, and dust. Mostly dust. Everywhere. *Where to begin?*

~~~

Annie hung the phone up, enjoying the warmth and coziness of her king-size bed a moment longer, still hoping for a bird's song. It was not meant to be. *They must all be sound asleep with no baby bird named Thomas to wake them.*

Canadian geese honked their "hellos" to her. They often flew over her townhouse near the Potomac River. She admired them. They were monogamous, and if one was hurt, it was never left alone. They shared the driver's seat while flying chevron, each taking a turn at leadership. They understood and incorporated three essential life concepts. First, keep your partner; life is better with a mate. Second, always, always, help someone in need and stay with them until the need passes. And finally, share the lead. Strength comes from the weight of leadership, and lightness results when others take the lead. *So much smarter than the human species!*

She swung her legs out, and her feet touched a white fur rug. Annie smiled as she wiggled her toes in its softness, a happy way to start each day. She walked down marble stairs to the kitchen. She had the luxury of time now with no need to rush for her flight. Perhaps it was good that Thomas called early.

EIGHT

THE PICTURE

April 2006

With coffee brewing, Annie set an oversized mug on a black granite counter embedded with shards of silver, gold, and bronze. She ran her hand over the polished stone, enjoying its cool smoothness. Precious hours had been dedicated to securing the perfect piece of granite. She completed her own kitchen renovation, and as her eyes took in the stainless appliances, the black granite counter, and white cabinets looking fresh and ultramodern, she felt a deep sense of satisfaction. Annie's home was a two-story brick townhouse in historic Old Town Alexandria, with a view of the Potomac River and Washington, D.C. She particularly liked that the Potomac was a working river, and from her bedroom window, she could watch ships come and go. Cargo from the world over was unloaded at the docks nearby. People visited from all parts of the world, all walks of life, to explore the streets of her neighborhood. Annie frequently observed people of different cultures or backgrounds navigate through their differences to find common ground. When that happened, she felt a special satisfaction; it restored her faith.

Yawning, last night flashed through her mind. She'd made a quick stop at the Fish Market after work, a local eatery around the corner from her townhouse. Inside, the Norwegian Captain of the *Labrador,* docked for unloading, introduced himself and asked if he could buy her a drink. A few of his crew were sitting with him, and like Annie, were seeking warm food on this chilly April night. They'd sailed from Newfoundland, delivering paper goods, and the glow of amber candlelight outlined rugged faces. They told her stories of trolls, mermaids, and fjords in the land of the midnight sun and downed multiple rounds of Heineken, all the while making sure her glass of Glenfiddich remained full and bowls of steaming clam chowder were served to everyone. After many "No thanks" to tour their ship, Annie made a getaway, glad she was walking and not driving, definitely feeling light-headed. *What a crew!* It had been a long time since she'd enjoyed herself that much! They were storytellers alright, and bad boys, each flirting and joking with her, the handsome Captain the worst.

Walking home, Annie reflected on her life and decided she was in a good place, even after two failed marriages. She had many good friends, her health, and could still turn an eye if she said so herself. She was not only an established writer but one who enjoyed renown that reflected her integrity. Sam, her editor, and boss valued her. Best of all, Thomas was near.

This morning, leaning on her kitchen counter, hands cupping a coffee mug, her eyes traveled to the den beyond and rested on a black-and-white photo standing alone on an end table. The picture was of five Marines in Vietnam; three standing and two kneeling before them, each with a cigar in hand or held fast, unlit, between clenched teeth. A picture of perfect symmetry. "Morning, Jess. Morning boys," she said, as she did most mornings. This morning she permitted herself to look into their faces a little longer than usual, especially Jesse's. They were so young, and it was such a terrible war. It claimed so many. To this day, she felt ambivalent about Vietnam and what it meant to America. Jesse, how she missed him.

She carried her coffee upstairs and thought about what to pack.

NINE

MOONLIGHT ON THE MISSISSIPPI

April 2006

New Orleans, no other place in the world like it! Annie's room at the Hilton was within walking distance of the French Quarter, Jackson Square, restaurants, jazz clubs, and historic buildings. Jackson Square, considered the heart and soul of New Orleans, sheltered the best of the city's creatives, a sanctuary where artists flourished in every medium, especially the chefs who induced culinary orgasms. Musicians played soulful saxophones or lonely trumpets into the night, their inky shadows blending them invisible against the backdrop of the mighty Mississippi. Musicians played not for the dollar, but their soul; not as a want but a need, a catharsis, each note resonating a story, echoing a memory, or touching a feeling already felt or waiting to be discovered. Their music was an outpouring of all they were and all they hoped to be. Their melody was for the wind, the river, and the evening dew forming on all things verdant. It was for any passerby whose heart was open to receive it, who understood the ache, who allowed the song to bring them closer to the Almighty.

This area escaped the wrath of Hurricane Katrina, and for this, Annie was grateful. It may have been shallow, but in truth, part of her excitement in returning here was to eat the city's unique food once again. French pastries, crepes, breads, gravies, seafood, red beans & rice, papaya, the earthy flavors of field and chickpeas ... she remembered them all while flying down, the cuisine in this city reflected the intricate ethnic blend of its French, Caribbean, and African residents.

Her mouth watered at the thought of the charbroiled oysters she planned to eat at Drago's, the on-site restaurant at the Hilton. Annie realized how hungry she was. "Would you care for a package of peanuts," the flight attendant had asked? She stubbornly refused on principle. Could the airlines get any cheaper?

~~~

In the hotel lobby, a loud growl came from her stomach. She gave Thomas a quick call, as promised.

This trip had been one of those great ideas, made in casual conversation with Sam. He made a quick decision for her to head down and to follow-up on Katrina's impact and recovery. She hadn't much time for research, but that was okay. She remembered Katrina's murderous blow and the horrific statistics that followed. Knowing Annie's penchant for "letting the world come to her," Sam stressed, "I want you to go there on the condition you relax and let it happen, let this trip be … what's your name for it … an 'experiential assignment'?" He smiled the smile of a friend. "You've earned this, Annie. Now get out of here." She had complete freedom to engage with New Orleans and write about whatever came her way. That suited her fine. She also enjoyed going there without preconceived goals. Let the universe show her what it wanted her to see. This was her kind of assignment! Coming four years after 9/11, Katrina's size and ferocity was an acute reminder to America that feeling safe was fleeting and security elusive. She sighed. She would see what she would see.

~~~

Annie had grown up on "Gruesome Fairy Tales" as she liked to call them, where ordinary people or animals needed to find the courage to overcome great odds like wicked witches and evil stepmothers. Fairy tales paved the way for her to understand the concept of courage and to compare a character's actions to her own. In so doing, she practiced at being brave. She learned that being brave didn't mean not being afraid. Instead, she learned that being brave meant being afraid … and acting anyway.

By age ten, with flashlight in hand and under bed covers, she consumed first Nancy Drew, then Sherlock Holmes mysteries. She read far into the night with appreciation for these fearless crime solvers, especially admiring Nancy who sleuthed in a man's world.

It was little wonder she found the world of investigative journalism riveting. Annie Dillard, a favorite author of Annie's, wrote that we can either seek the world or let the world come to us. That made sense to Annie Miller. Her style of investigative journalism was a little of both, but the excitement came from the latter. As a writer of controversial issues, Annie liked nothing more than the cat and mouse of making her presence known, asking hard questions, then sitting back to see who and what would come her way. Like detective work, her job required she sift through information and motives, find the truth of the thing, report it, and hope for public remediation to right the wrong. It was this she loved and needed from her job, to be an operative for justice and a vehicle for change.

This trip was not that. It was more a "weather report," offering Annie's readers an update on an American crisis. She hoped a few human-interest stories might result from her week's stay. That would be a plus. Mostly, Annie hoped she would find herself in a position to help. She had old jeans and sweats packed for physical labor. She was ready and excited to see what the world would bring.

~~~

Annie stepped from the Hilton into the street. The air was that unique southern crisp, balmy with a splash of cool breeze. Azure blue sky with no cloud in sight, palm trees, and eye-catching crepe myrtles cascading with blooms of lavender, pink, white, and burgundy. She smelled sweet jasmine in the air. What a place!

Her stomach growled louder as three teenage girls with purple boas wrapped around their necks walked by and giggled. She needed food!

Annie knew the French Quarter and Garden District were saved from the nightmare of Katrina, but she looked for hurricane damage regardless, trusting her eyes. Along Decatur Street, Annie recognized the roasted chicory's heavy scent and knew she was close to her favorite coffee shop, probably the world's favorite, Café du Monde. She entered and glanced at the walls for a water line, then at the roof for telltale stains or cracks. *No visible damage.* "Welcome to NOLA," someone shouted from the back. "NOLA," the acronym for New Orleans, Louisiana, was used by those most familiar with the city. This iconic building appeared to have been spared! Over eighty percent of the city had not been so lucky and experienced catastrophic damage. Relieved that this treasure was safe and feeling more relaxed, Annie let herself enjoy the surroundings.

"Yes ma'am, what's your pleasure?" asked the waiter.

"Coffee and two beignets, please," Annie replied to the elderly man behind the counter. She noticed that he, like many others in the city, was wearing purple, the color of New Orleans, as though proudly saying, "This city is mine, in ruins or not."

Terrance, his nametag read, was her server. Annie believed everyone liked hearing their name, and its use formed a connection.

"Terrance, how did the area around here fare with Katrina?" His happiness disappeared for a moment, but Terrance was not willing to let go of good energy on such a beautiful day, so he smiled even larger. In that split second, however, she'd seen the sadness in his eyes. They told the real story, and Annie was nothing if not a good reader of faces. He'd most likely been questioned by every tourist coming here for the past eight months. She felt more than a little uncomfortable for having asked but accepted questioning as necessary to her profession. Asking probing questions was always intrusive and proved to be a constant quandary for even the most seasoned journalists. She knew her question now brought it all back to Terrance.

Suddenly, in the middle of the sights, smells, and sounds of New Orleans, Annie imagined the fear and horror these people had faced ... 140-mile per hour winds that slammed into people, homes, vehicles, machinery, trees ... anything big or small, sharp or dull, accompanied by a 20-foot water surge that churned and smashed things together like a colossal concrete mixer. Anguish and pain, known by too many. She couldn't stop a small shudder, and Terrance noted that.

He understood her unintentional shake and said kindly, as though speaking to a child, "We here in the French Quarter, we was lucky ... but about two-thousand people in this city wasn't. Lots of souls lost. We's like a big family here in NOLA, ma'am, and when two-thousand of your own don't make it ... well, there ain't nobody this side of heaven who come out of this hurricane not being hurt, 'n hurt bad. All of us lost family or friends. We was just lucky here in the Quarter," he mumbled to himself, shaking his head slowly as he moved away. "Just lucky."

While Terrance served with his left hand, Annie noticed his right had only a thumb and the first two fingers. His ring finger and baby finger were stubs covered with skin that had the texture of rough orange peel. He saw her glance at the mangled hand and held it up for her to see. Almost proud.

"Yes'm, Katrina," he offered. "I mustered enough strength to pound my hand through the roof of my sister's house. The lower 9th Ward got it the worst. That's where she was. I pounded and tore a hole in the roof big enough for her and the kids to get through. We wasn't sure we'd get outta there with the wind trying to split us up and whip us to death, everything wet and cold, things flying past our heads. I don't know to this day how we made it. Will of God, I s'pose. House still standing and the hole's still there – you can see it if you's so inclined. Florida Avenue, hardly a house left standing. Woulda gave my whole hand, both hands, if that's what it took to get them outta there safe."

Then, in typical New Orleans fashion, he lifted his hand, formed a fist, and shook it at the sky. He brought it to his lips and kissed the stubs that were once his fingers. He flashed a wicked smile toward Annie as if to say, "No matter, we're alive in NOLA, and today is another day!"

Between customers, Annie spoke with Terrance, and when she told him she was a journalist, he listed places for her to see. There were the damaged areas like Plaquemines and St. Bernard's Parish, where all but a half-dozen houses remained habitable out of almost 27,000. He suggested she see the areas of renewal, where the community was working together, neighbor helping neighbor to renovate and reconstruct. And he agreed to a photo, and as Annie was focusing her camera,

Terrance was raising his fist and smiling. She had her first story. The universe was good.

Annie thanked him for the information. "By the way, Terrance, do you know what's going on at Jackson Square? I noticed TV crews and reporters during my walk here."

"I ain't sure ma'am, but a customer told me the Vietnamese community of St. Bernard Parish was boiling mad over the Mayor's office wanting to dump trash from Katrina into their neighborhood, could be that."

~~~

Intrigued, she brushed white confectionary sugar from the front of her blouse, crossed St. Ann Street, and headed for Jackson Square. She approached horse-drawn carriages stationed in front of a palm-lined walkway, leading to St. Louis Cathedral, the oldest cathedral in North America. Each carriage was decorated, the horses outfitted with colored feathers, ribbons, and rhinestone flowers that sparkled in the sun. Idle drivers carried on casual conversations with each other while waiting for passengers, their horses swatted flies. Interested tourists climbed aboard, hoping for an informative ride or a chance to rest sore feet. Often couples wished for romance and an unhurried moment together in this charming city of culture, rich history, sin, and depravity.

Drivers became historians, offering a deluge of information, some of it even factual. Ranging from hauntings to black magic, they also included information on Andrew Jackson's pipe-smoking wife, Rachel, purportedly still married to another man as she said "I do" to Andrew. So much information, so little remembered after the drinking and drugging.

As Annie approached the square, she noted the television stations represented. Near them, a group of Asians gathered and were listening intently to a female speaker. Annie moved in unobtrusively, stopping next to a tall, well-built man around Thomas' age. She was sorry to have missed the beginning of this speech.

"She's eloquent," Annie mentioned to the man next to her after listening for a few minutes.

46

"Yes, she is," he responded, his eyes never leaving the speaker. Almost as if talking to himself, he continued, "She lost both parents to Vietnam, I lost one."

"I'm sorry," responded Annie, surprised at such a personal disclosure from a stranger. "It was a terrible war," she replied in a conciliatory way.

As though transformed to another place, he added, "He was a Marine."

Annie was touched at the tenderness in his voice as he said those simple four words. She looked into his face. There was something familiar about him, but she couldn't place what it was. "Annie Miller, good to meet you," she said, as she reached out her hand.

"John Parker, Jr. Pleased to meet you."

A large, strong hand met hers. Memories of Jesse washed over her for the second time that day ... the way he kidded her, his warm eyes.

TEN

A HARD ROAD HOME

April 2006

Long straight black hair whipped wildly across her face and flew up as though reaching for the sky. Like a raging tiger not to be tamed, Lucky pulled it into place, impatient with its power over her.

Lucky Dai stood defiantly before the news cameras wearing a traditional Vietnamese garment, the ao dai. She wanted all to know who she was, a Vietnamese American. Born of a Vietnamese mother and a black American father, she was stunning and compelling. Her wild black hair was like her mothers, and in the style of her mother, she wore a crimson tunic over black silk pants. Her mocha skin, full red lips, and rounder eyes defined the other half of her heritage, that of her father. Today, she was the culmination for which each parent had sacrificed their lives.

Lucky was prepared for this speech, having chosen each word carefully for the precise meaning she wished to impart. She'd read it aloud frequently, in front of her bedroom mirror, and had grown comfortable with its rhythm.

She understood her speech had the potential of life and death for her Vietnamese family and beloved community.

Lucky calmed her fluttering heart with a deep breath. She was ready to present.

ELEVEN

THE HEARTACHE THAT IS VIETNAM

April 2006

The night before her speech, Lucky sat alone on her balcony, staring up at a full moon. She sent her mother a prayer, asking for help in making tomorrow's speech moving. Moving enough to save lives.

She remembered a night long ago in Vietnam when she was a young child. Lucky's mother, Tweet, held Lucky in her lap as they gazed at the moon. It was a memory of contentment and feeling safe.

~~~

Appreciating the moon's beauty, her mother asked, "Shall I tell you a story about the moon?" pointing toward the champagne circle against a midnight sky.

"Yes, Mamma."

"Very well, but the price is a kiss."

Lucky chuckled, took her mother's face in her small hands, and planted a warm kiss on her lips. Her mother smiled and, in return, tenderly kissed Lucky's cheek. The story began.

"Many describe Vietnam as a land of exquisite beauty. Native folklore says that in the beginning, one of Vietnam's first mortals forgot to 'see' the beauty of the country and thus walked around in a 'blindness' of sorts, stumbling into bushes, tromping on flowers, scattering and sometimes injuring small creatures as he walked. He created discord and imbalance everywhere he went.

"The moon watched him from above and felt sad for the country and the mortal. She decided to help. She breathed in the night sky and

49

became so full and round that her children, the moonbeams, spilled out from her, onto the countryside, and like warm, translucent milk, they rolled over majestic hills, skipped on vast wetlands, and danced upon ambling rivers. Silver-blue moonlight glazed every blade of grass, every leaf, every ripple of water, every cloud in the sky, creating a most beautiful place of quiet splendor for the mortal to see and behold.

"Overtaken by the majesty, his eyes filled with tears of gratitude. He bowed to the moon in humble thanks and promised her he would never again fail to see the splendor of Vietnam and would always be grateful.

"Pleased with this mortal, but knowing a mortal was only a mortal and could not always be counted on to keep his word, she promised him she would become round and full once each month to remind him of the wonder, lest he forget .... She knew when the mortal's world felt balanced, he would know peace. A kind moon indeed, caring for us and aspiring to keep our heart's content and peaceful."

Lucky remembered her mother's arms had tightened around her at the end of her story. She could almost feel them now.

"This story teaches us that when we open our eyes to the beauty around us, our hearts will feel contentment. It is then that peace and hope can thrive.

"Look for beauty, Lucky, and you will find it. Embrace what joy comes your way, and like the mortal, live a life of gratitude, contentment, peace, and hope, my daughter," she'd whispered.

~~~

Thank you, Mother. You have reminded me of the importance of hope and assurance in the only way you can, by sending me a memory. I am listening. I am grateful for all things. I miss you terribly and your strength of spirit. Please stay near me.

Stepping up to the podium the following day, she reminded herself that this speech was not about her but about the good that could come from her words. A New Orleans breeze blew past her. *Mamma?*

Today, she would be heard.

~~~

Marine Lt. Col. John Parker, Jr., had arrived the evening before from a visit with his grandparents in Fort Myers. Walking from his hotel, the Place D'Armes, he came upon a gathering of news reporters and a small contingent of Asian speakers, Vietnamese, he guessed. They were getting ready to address a crowd. His eyes fell on a Vietnamese beauty, next in line to speak. Regarded as a "man's man" by his military friends, he also had it in him to be a "ladies' man," attracting women with his blonde good looks and sense of humor. He waited for this woman to get the crowd's attention, looking composed and ready. It had been a long time since a woman's looks had taken his breath away. This one was afire. His eyes stayed riveted on her, and he wondered what she would say….

"Hello, my name is Lucky Dai, and I come to speak to you about an injustice, a grave injustice that our mayor, and his council, believe we, the Vietnamese community of New Orleans, should accept with a humble spirit, and with the smile of 'Cong Khi,' the monkey.

"But we come here, not with a humble spirit. We are ready to be jailed for what we believe. We cannot smile like the monkey when we feel anger; the anger a tiger feels defending her cubs.

"We, the people of the Versailles community, St. Bernard Parish, gather today in the destructive wake of Hurricane Katrina. We come as citizens of the United States. We come to be heard. We come still believing in the phrase that many of us studied in our citizenship classes, 'Justice for all.' We are here to remind our political leaders that justice was a concept most highly valued by America's founding fathers. We pray it is still a value held dear in every American heart.

"We believe each of us faces poison and death at the hands of our Mayor. He plans to bury one-third of the debris from Katrina in our community's backyard. There has been no investigation or safety evaluation conducted on this plan. There is no consideration for a protective containment to prevent the seepage of contaminants into the

51

soil. There is not even an understanding of what contaminants may be present. Asbestos, Ethylene, and its by-products, oil, and other petroleum products, all known carcinogens, are present, and the Mayor is hoping to get rid of this quickly and inexpensively.

"We gather today because we are afraid. Afraid that once again, we will lose all we are, all we own, from ill-conceived government action. As a community, we have kept ourselves apart. Perhaps because of fear or pride, or maybe because as refugees from war-torn Vietnam, we have experienced so much death and destruction that the peace which comes from anonymity is something we cherish. For better or worse, we have stayed to ourselves. But now is the time for us to be known. To be heard. Now is the time for our neighbors in New Orleans to understand why we hold so dear our small space in this community.

"We, like many of you here today, have survived the devastation of Hurricane Katrina last August. Five hundred of us huddled together with our priests in our beloved church. We listened as trees were ripped from the earth. We heard screams in the wind and feared we'd be blown to oblivion. But thankfully, that didn't happen. We survived. We survived this catastrophe as we survived our terrible days in Vietnam many decades ago. The families that came to Versailles Arms came here as refugees through a re-settlement housing program established by the U. S. government. We already lost all we had in the war. To survive in Vietnam, and then in the United States, many of us were forced to relocate … often.

"Some here today left their homes in North Vietnam when the communist regime took hold. About ten million of us became refugees and sought safety in South Vietnam, but sanctuary did not come when we moved to the south. Two million men, women, and children living in South Vietnam during the war were killed. We had bombs hailing down upon our villages and our land. We lived in fear of death.

"Perhaps you think because many of us had no kitchen sinks or faucets with running water, our lives were of less value, but I promise you, I dearly miss my mother, as would any little girl in this world. My father, an American Marine, lost his life because he loved a Vietnamese

52

woman. We were left behind, not knowing what to do, and became boat people two days before the North Vietnamese Communists took Saigon.

"Half the nation of South Vietnam fled communism and left any way possible, even our President Thieu fled. My family's fate was to sell what little we owned to become part of the hundreds of thousands of boat people exiting South Vietnam. Thai pirates overtook our boat and preyed upon our weak bodies and broken spirits. They took the little money left in our pockets and raped the women. They raped my mother, then killed her because she tried to protect me from their violence.

"My great-grandfather, cousin, and I traveled to the Philippines as refugees, and because we had the necessary documents, came to the United States. We were fortunate. Others were not. Eleven million Vietnamese became refugees of the world, and country after country turned them away. Government records say 400,000 boat people died while trying to flee Vietnam.

"Because my father was a U.S. citizen, our little family resettled in the United States, first in Arkansas, then in Versailles Arms in 1976. My mother sacrificed her life, so I might enjoy the freedoms she would never know.

"I tell this story to remind all who listen that my people have been born to suffering. We know its face, inside and out, but we don't lie down and accept it. We survived bombs, brutality, torture, and death, and still, we live to see another day!

"Our Mayor believes he can place us in yet another life-threatening situation. Place a landfill in our backyard, again I repeat, a landfill comprising one-third of all refuse left by Katrina! He would create for us a Love Canal, where our children and friends might well die of toxic chemicals leaching into our water.

"Mayor, if you're listening, I'm here to tell you we survived Vietnam! We survived Katrina! Like you, we are residents of New Orleans, and our lives are of no less value than the lives of those living on Charles Street! We will fight you to keep out the refuse! We will fight you to keep from poisoning us! We will fight for our right to preserve the lives

53

of our children and community! We will fight you, Mayor, and we will win!"

~~~

As the applause continued, Annie remarked to John, still standing beside her, "Wow, that was quite a speech!" John had heard many political and military speeches, hell, he'd given a few himself, but this woman and her stirring words captivated him. As Lucky finished with a few closing words of thanks and recognition to those who helped in the movement, John realized this resolute woman had mesmerized him.

Lucky's mention of being an orphan hit home. Had she lived with his demons?

TWELVE

I MISS YOU, MOM

1971

The nightly news, featuring Walter Cronkite, highlighted footage of the war in Vietnam for family's back home. Each evening John would hear Grandma June say, "Come on, Ben, let's see what's happening in our daughter's world." She would scoop John off the tiled floor and place him on a rug littered with blocks, books, and toy cars. Grandpa Ben would appear and sit next to June. "Are you okay, darlin'?" he would ask. Taking a deep breath, June would nod yes, a routine that lasted years.

Only later in life did John understand that Ben was cryptically asking June if she was prepared to see the worst. Prepared to learn that something had happened to Helen while serving at Da Nang Station Hospital. They knew the Station Hospital received all wounded Marines fighting in Tet, Hue, and Khe Sanh, Vietnam's longest and deadliest battle of the war. Ben and June were watching when the news reported an errant rocket had found its way to "Helen's hospital," with minimal damage, but damage, regardless.

John Parker Jr. lost his father to the Vietnam War and was left by a mother to be a Vietnam nurse when he was only a toddler. He was raised by his grandparents, never knowing his father, and barely knowing his mom.

Surprising everyone, he followed in his father's footsteps and joined the Marines after college. It was a choice fraught with conflict. John joined the Corps to serve a country he loved and honor the father he never met.

55

He lost his father legitimately fighting in a war, and his death remained a constant loss for John. His mother's absence, well, that was another story. For her to leave him and then place herself in harm's way … that was hard to understand, hard to forgive, and it angered him. He loved his grandparents dearly, was forever grateful for their care, but these circumstances left scars.

As he grew older, John tried to understand what his mother felt when her husband was killed in Vietnam, three days after leaving her; the two of them just married. He'd been told by his Uncles Kristian and Ronny that his dad's groomsmen were ready to be pallbearers if burial in Fort Myers would take place. All so young. Everything moving so fast. Then his mother discovering she was pregnant only weeks later. John wondered if he was ever a consolation or simply a tragic reminder of her loss.

Once, when he was older, she'd confided in him. "Those were my darkest days, John. I prayed continuously. I think if I hadn't been pregnant with you, I might have tried to kill myself … the pain was so bad. I felt scorched inside, blistered. Your father was so much a part of me."

Everyone in the family, Beau's parents, brothers, Ben, and June knew Helen's reason for going to Vietnam. Purportedly, God had spoken to her. "Go to Vietnam," he said clearly into her ear. And though each shook their head in disbelief, Helen left when John turned one.

She used her nursing skills to minister to those who would benefit from her care, as her beloved had not. Her letters home, frequent at the beginning, became less frequent as time passed. They told of a woman who now had a reason to live, to get out of bed each morning. Her profession was her salvation.

~~~

Helen had come home maybe once a year until John was five, then less so. She left Vietnam for another job, another mission, and eventually became a stranger of sorts. He heard from Grandma June that Helen now worked at the Veterans Hospital in Washington, D.C., near where he

56

would soon be stationed. Well, good for her, he thought with ambivalence.

John believed she never accepted Beau's death … never worked through it.

THIRTEEN

COINCIDENCE OR KISMET

2006

O thers spoke after Lucky, but none with her passion or eloquence. The crowd disbanded, and Annie approached Lucky to introduce herself.

"Hello, my name is Annie Miller. I'm an investigative journalist for the Washington Post. Your speech was powerful and moving. I'm interested in your experience as a refugee. I believe your story could be important to refugees from the Middle East. Concerning your landfill issue, I'd like to offer you my help, as well as coverage by the Washington Post."

Lucky looked at the smiling face of Annie Miller, then looked down. She spoke softly, as though her answer troubled her.

"I am a pharmacist, and as you might imagine, still busy with concerns from Katrina. I must focus my effort and energy on that first. I live with my great-grandfather, and after work, I care for him and help with the reconstruction of my community. Any extra time I have is for fighting the landfill project. I have no idea how long it will take, but my first responsibility must be to my people.

"We Vietnamese are hardworking, Ms. Miller. This hurricane has brought with it the chance for all in our community to work together to rebuild. For many years we have been a community in conflict, the old wishing to live in the old ways and the young wishing to be 'Americanized.' We've been a house divided, as the Bible says.

"Now we are a house united, young, and old, working together with a common purpose, to rebuild and fight the Mayor on his plans for the landfill. We've been reminded that the young and the old can contribute in valuable ways. It's been a wonderful experience for us and a reawakening. One day, when these hard times are over, I'll gladly speak with you so we might help others, but now I must keep my focus here. I hope you understand.

"That said, if my community sees the need to seek outside help to resolve our landfill concern, rest assured, I will contact you. And I thank you sincerely for your offer, as I'm sure you would be a strong ally."

Annie smiled. She liked this woman! She liked that Lucky said, "we, so we might help others." That sounded like Lucky was on board.

Lucky extended her hand, and Annie took it. They understood they were focused on helping others. The handshake was one of camaraderie and promise. Annie gave Lucky her card. "Please, call me Annie. I feel like I'm on the clearance rack of life when you call me Ms. Miller!"

Both women laughed. "Then, thank you, Annie."

"I hope to hear from you, Lucky ... but only when you're ready," were Annie's closing words.

Annie walked away, chuckling, and felt sorry for the Mayor. He didn't have a snowball's chance in hell of winning this issue. *Better find another spot or way to eliminate the refuse; you're not beating that fireball. I'll make sure of it if that's what it takes!*

~~~

John wanted to speak to Lucky but saw she was preoccupied with the woman who'd stood next to him. He walked away, not wanting to leave. Lucky's impassioned speech had moved him.

Hungry and wanting a drink, John looked at his watch. *Is it too early for a drink? Hell, no, it's noon somewhere, and this is NOLA, where it's ALWAYS the right time!*

He recalled seeing an outdoor café nearby and headed in that direction.

~~~

59

John took a long pull on his vodka tonic. It toned down the edge he felt from the speech and thoughts of his parents.

How many times had he stood at his father's grave in Arlington, seeing the name with no personal connection to it? There was a time he was angry with a government that churned out young men to die in wars, and downright mad that his father volunteered to fight. Didn't he consider the price too high when a woman like Helen loved him? The prom queen loved by everyone. Things could have been so different, had he stayed home.

Most of his anger, however, was reserved for his mother. John could understand, perhaps, admire Helen wanting to serve in the war that took her husband. But the sledgehammer to his heart was when she left Vietnam and worked everywhere in the world except home.

She didn't come back for him. She did reach out to him long ago, but the hurt was too deep, the chasm too wide to traverse. He no longer called her Mom. She was Helen to him. His therapist had an explanation for that.

Did you ever consider what leaving would do to me, or did you not care? Was there no place for me in your heart? Were your needs so much more important than mine? When do we put others before ourselves? I thought mothers did that.

In theology class, John learned about a sect of monks who were not permitted to ask for more when their bowls were empty. They waited in silence until someone saw their need and attended to it.

Will there ever come a time when we put the needs of others before our own? Is that what peace looks like?

Before he accepted a commission as an officer in the Marine Corps, John read many books about Vietnam. He concluded his father made the right decision. Some things were worth the fight. Freedom was one.

John accepted the cards dealt him, and those dealt to a father raised in an era of innocence, chivalry, and ideals. "Camelot," some called America during that time. Khrushchev, leader of the Soviet Union, threatened Camelot. "We will bury you," he promised. No one bullied the United States! He understood his dad's choice and elected to be close to the man he never knew, but respected, nonetheless.

His mother's choice was a different story. Chaps helped John understand his feelings, accept them, and regain control of his drinking. But forgiveness, well, that might have to wait for another day.

John took another long drink to get the bitter taste out of his mouth.

As a Marine Lieutenant during Desert Storm, John realized his men faced challenges, some bigger than others, but with rare exception, most had solutions. He taught his men to be their best, understanding that "their best" was not perfection, nor was "their best" determined by others, but rather measured by their own true heart. Sometimes he heard the voice of Chaplain Daniel, his "therapist," in the words John spoke and the ways he cared for his men. As Chaps predicted, John still had occasional feelings of doubt, hurt, and anger, but with less frequency or intensity. He let go of perfection and moved toward the acceptance of imperfection, the ultimate freedom.

Desert Storm was the flame that tempered the metal of his heart. It was what he needed to become "real." He came out of Desert Storm a man. Changed. Stronger. He'd turned a page.

~~~

Assigned to Intelligence, John traveled throughout the world and gained knowledge of customs and cultures during embassy duty in Seoul, South Korea, and Kabul, Afghanistan. Quick-witted and able to speak multiple languages, John was promoted in The Corps and transferred to George Washington University for his post-graduate program in International Affairs. His present assignment would return him to Washington, D.C.

Too many wars, too many politicians cashing in, too many lives lost. Why do we fight? All life is precious and worth saving. We live in paradise on a beautiful blue planet, yet we're never satisfied just to live and appreciate its grandeur. Why must we destroy each other?

John recalled Eisenhower's warning to America during his Presidential farewell speech, "Beware of the military-industrial complex."

Yeah, incestuous bedfellows those two. Lots of money to be made from war. Unfortunately, from the blood, sweat, and tears of the men and women on the line. The longer the war, the more money to be made. How many millions had one Vice President made from the war in Iraq with his company Halliburton? And how was that not a conflict of interest?

~~~

Good drink. Good po'boy sandwich. Good to be saying goodbye to the Middle East. Nice to have surprised Grandpa Ben and Grandma June with a visit!

~~~

John smiled as he recalled Grandma June saying, "Johnny, Johnny! Can I get a hug from my broad-shouldered grandson? Let me look at you! Oh, you look fine and more like your father every time I see you! What can I make you for supper?" And Grandpa Ben's voice right behind, friendly and warm. "How long can you stay, boy? I got a fishin' pole for you and some Crown Black at the bar with your name on it! Good to see you, son!"

They fished. A fishing trip with Ben was always a good time, peppered with jokes and entertaining conversation. This visit had an objective, however. It was to give back to them for all they'd provided through the decades. To say thank you for letting me be king of the rock pile once again! Thank you for seeing the good in me. Thank you for appreciating me because it allowed me to become a good and capable man. Thank you for loving me. Let me honor you by sharing laughter, kind words, happy memories, and appreciating YOU! These were the ways John would give back to them before they were no longer here.

~~~

Yes, it had been a great trip. Lots of happy times. Entering his room was like walking into a memory. The smell of Banana Boat and rubber from his wet suit, trophies, and banners on display. On his dresser sat the wedding picture of Helen and Dad, next to it, one of Uncle Kristian and Ronny, taken of the three of them celebrating his commission as an officer. John's sides hurt for days from laughter after their get-together. Always a great time with those two. There were more pictures of his dad's Norwegian parents, Bestemor and Bestefar, and of course, a picture of June and Ben.

On the other end of the dresser, standing alone, a black-and-white photo of his dad in Vietnam with four other Marines.

~~~

John's eyes focused on movement across the street. A red tunic. The woman who captivated him in Jackson Square. *What was her name? Lucky? Lucky Dai? Great name! How did she get that?*

Lucky unlatched and lifted the hood of her Toyota and stared inside. John watched her for a few moments; his eyes lingered on her form and fluid movement. Something was wrong.

John stood up from his table and walked to her as she rummaged through her handbag.

"Can I help?"

Their eyes met. For the second time that day, John Parker caught his breath. Her eyes were warm amber, no, more like smoky honey, edged in bluish chocolate. Red stained lips the color of poppy fields he'd seen in Iraq.

Lucky recognized the face of the man she'd noticed in the audience. She had been keenly aware of him, his head high above the others. He was tan, in shape, and handsome.

"Yes, thank you. I can't start my car!"

My God, she's lovely. To his surprise, her hair blew again as though captured by a breeze that wasn't there.

Seeing his look of surprise, she stated, "Static energy."

With a look that seemed to doubt her explanation, she added, "I can't seem to control it."

Then, returning to reality, she asked, "Can you help?"

~~~

That evening at the Hilton, Annie was replying to her waiter, "Yes, I know those charbroiled oysters are your specialty, and I would like to order a dozen!"

In her room, head on the pillow, Annie thought of Lucky's speech and the young man standing next to her. Both had lost so much to Vietnam. Strange, thoughts of Jesse and Vietnam had been with her since saying hello to him and his gun team this morning in her townhouse.

For a long time after Jesse was killed, Annie felt he was nearby. She felt it today. Remembrances of Forest Heights and Jesse flooded over her as she closed her eyes ....

FOURTEEN

A METRONOME LIFE

1957-2006

She remembered the summer of '67 when Jesse was killed, "The Summer of Love." In April of that year, Cassius Clay, later known as Mohammed Ali, refused induction into the Army. He was tried and jailed. Detroit suffered violent race riots in July. Eight-thousand National Guardsmen and almost 5,000 soldiers were deployed to restore law and order.

When peace was established, the cost was 43 dead, 7,000 arrested, 2,000 stores looted or burned, and over 400 buildings burned to the ground, with many families finding themselves homeless overnight. The peace movement against the war, along with racial inequality, was fanning the flames of societal change in America.

Gut-wrenching times. Breakfast began with the morning paper inundating Americans with reports and pictures of our country torn apart by riots. Work now involved discussions about the state of the nation with co-workers, trying to make sense of it. After dinner, the nightly news showed footage of the fighting occurring that day in Vietnam, and there we were, staring into the faces of the 500,000 troops stationed in Vietnam, fighting for numbered hills, with precious ground taken, lost, and retaken. As Americans, we saw the futility reflected in the young faces of our soldiers serving there. Later in July, America would hear of a little-known place called Con Thien, located just south of the DMZ. It was being bombed daily and mercilessly.

The United States was in conflict, inside and out.

~~~

Annie was taking a summer class and studying in her dorm room when someone knocked on her door. "You have a phone call, Annie." She walked to the only phone on the floor of her women's dorm.

"Hello?" There was a brief silence before she heard a reply.

"Hello Annie, this is Elizabeth McGowan, Jesse's Mom."

Annie felt her stomach churn. She could tell Mrs. McGowan had been crying. Annie knew what was coming. The unspoken words slammed into her. "No!" she silently screamed and squeezed her eyes tight. She leaned against the wall to keep her balance. The spent and broken voice went on, "Annie, Jesse's gone. He'll be buried in Arlington Cemetery. It's a short drive to your dorm. Do you want to come? We can pick you up and take you with us if you'd like."

~~~

Now in her hotel room in New Orleans, she remembered it as though it was yesterday. Her thoughts drifted back to that divisive period in America. The topic of Vietnam seldom surfaced anymore, and when it did, it was usually met with a shake of the head, a guarded look, a downcast eye, shame. She herself continued to struggle when it was brought up.

It takes courage to speak of that war, the anguish, the opinions, the many ghosts of every sort. What happens to a wrong never righted? Does it fester like most wounds? Do we sweep it under the rug and hope it doesn't stain … send it away like an unwanted stepchild? To speak of it might give it life again. Better to leave it alone, let it wither on the vine, die a slow death and be forgotten …. This was America's way of handling the Vietnam War … AND those who fought in it. Self-induced amnesia.

Her thoughts went to her life in Forest Heights.

~~~

When her family moved there in 1957, it was a sleepy, white-picket-fence community. One house looked just like the next, except for the color of the painted wood above the red brick base. Not like today,

66

where builders ensure each house is different, and individuality is the norm.

The adults and kids knew each other by name. Adults could chastise or redirect any child who looked like they were misbehaving ... or even thinking about it. It was a village, and the kids stayed in line. Neighbors knew each other. Doors were left unlocked, and windows left open to enjoy the breeze. Dinners were made from scratch and eaten in dining rooms with conversation between family members. Mothers borrowed sugar from neighbors glad to share, and borrowers returned it promptly. "Borrow" meant you owed, which meant you paid back—no moochers in the 1950s. Well, not many, Annie chuckled, remembering Mrs. Stone, who was the exception. "We as much as paid for that woman's baking this Christmas," her mother had grumbled. "I don't mind her borrowing, but couldn't she return something just once?"

It was a time that smacked of clockwork contentment—a metronome life.

School always began the day after Labor Day, with students wearing a new outfit. Those lucky enough to get to the ocean over the long weekend, like Annie and her family, returned with sunburns and peeling noses. The last great kickback before another year dedicated to learning.

Annie was starting sixth grade, and it was her last year in elementary school. As with every previous year, the first day back included a school-wide slide show of Mrs. Anderson's summer vacation. As principal, "her" students saw people, places, and things that many might never have the good fortune to see ... totem poles in Alaska, giant redwoods in California, or donkeys weighed down with tourist "stuff," heading towards Old Faithful ... this year's trip. There was Mrs. Anderson, wearing a white Stetson hat, red curls peeking around a chubby sunburned face while she pulled on the reins of her donkey, stubbornly refusing to keep up with the others. That brought laughter from all the kids.

During the assembly, Billy Jackson, a fifth-grader, whispered to the boy next to him he wished Mrs. Anderson would go to Tahiti next year and bring back slides of the topless Tahitian girls he'd seen in National

Geographic; the primary source of sexual knowledge for boys in the '50s. Dominic Giovanni didn't need a National Geographic; he knew where his father's Playboy magazines were hidden and occasionally shared them with the neighborhood boys.

Annie hoped Dominic had charged money for a viewing. It might have made the whipping he got from his father worthwhile following an irate call from Tommy Sanders' mom, the busybody of the neighborhood, who made no bones about her disgust to Mr. Giovanni - that he'd purchased "trash" in the first place and then, in the second place, that he hadn't hidden it well enough from his son to see.

Billy's comment about Tahitian girls brought on a flurry of seat shifting by those girls who'd overheard what he'd said, and muffled laughter from the pre-pubescent boys as the delicious image wormed into each of their male minds.

Overhearing his remark, Billy J. was whisked to the rear of the auditorium by his teacher, and upon completion of the slide show, invited to join Mrs. Anderson in her office. The following year he sat quietly, front row, next to his new teacher during a Hopi Indian presentation, and seating was boy-girl, boy-girl.

The leaves of fall framed the elementary school. Halloween costumes were judged inside a warm cafeteria. Annie's Martha Washington costume won 1st place. Her prize, a Silly Putty Egg, felt secure in Annie's hand as she and her mom walked home under a canopy of twinkling stars. "Thanks, Mom," Annie said, looking up at her, "You did a great job on my costume." Her mother smiled. "Measure twice, cut once."

Winter was all about sledding. Good sledding required at least two on a sled. Sitting was okay, but real speed was gained when bodies were piled on top of each other; two went fast, three went faster. Kids stayed outside until they could stand the cold no longer. They knew the rules about going out in the snow. Dryers weren't plentiful, and kids only had one pair of snow pants, gloves, or jacket to wear. If you came in, you stayed in. So you stayed outside until your feet burned into numbness, and your nose dripped snot that should have been removed for shame's sake, but with freezing numbness, nobody knew they had snot on their nose, and nobody much cared.

The kids believed what Bobby Dougherty, the Down syndrome boy a few houses up, told them. He warned that if they weren't careful, their frozen noses might break off like icicles.

Bobby had outlived the normal sixteen-year life expectancy for Down syndrome children back then. Because he'd beaten the odds, and because he was "different," the kids believed he had something special going on, so when he said something important like this, they listened, and more often than not, believed his warnings. He was like a smiling Buddha and their personal mystic of sorts. They gave Bobby his due and looked out for him when they played, which was pretty much any time they weren't eating, sleeping, or doing homework.

April meant door-to-door sales of Girl Scout cookies, Thin Mints, hands down the best cookie on the planet. Annie knew if she sold the most boxes in her troop, she would receive a red and white record player along with an Everly Brothers record. She planned on winning and hoped the record would be, "Wake Up Little Susie." She identified with the star-crossed lovers in the song who, on a date, fell asleep to wake up in the middle of the night, and to a world of trouble. Her female intuition already recognized this could easily happen to her one day.

"Come on, Mary, come to Jesse's house with me," Annie begged. Mary refused to join her in the "selling of her wares," as she called it. Mary knew cookies would open the door to Jesse McGowan, and she knew Annie had a crush on him. With a raised eyebrow and a slight edge in her voice, she rebuked Annie for using the Scouts for personal advantage.

"It's less than honorable," Mary chided. "You're better than that."

"No, I'm not!" Annie told her. They broke out in laughter, happy to be alive and young.

Mary was a good Catholic girl and still preferred horses to boys. She was Annie's best friend, an eccentric of sorts, and could be counted on to think outside the box. That was their connection. At that early age, they were both already outliers. Annie's father, seeing Nancy Drew books on her Christmas list, said to her, "Why read common books when you can read the classics which have withstood the test of time?" Annie knew he was right, and her life was changed with that observation. She continued reading Nancy Drew because she loved Nancy's independence. Still, because of her father, she read Sherlock Holmes, followed by the Iliad and Odyssey by age eleven, then Crime and Punishment by twelve. Annie and Mary were voracious readers, consumed books like food, and, by reading at an early age, expanded their world exponentially.

The McGowan house was across the street. Jesse was one year ahead of her in school, which made him an "older" boy.

"He's going nowhere, Annie," her mom said. "Not the boy I want you to spend time with." Annie wasn't sure what she based that on, but Annie and Jess had fun, and they laughed … a lot.

Jesse had a "bad boy" reputation of sorts with the elementary school teachers perhaps because he wasn't a "yes" person, and made sense of the world in his own way, but they kidded around with him and asked him to run errands and help with things. They spoke to him as though he belonged to their club. He didn't seem to care about "fitting in," yet he fit in with everyone, everywhere. Jesse hadn't been a designated leader in the school, but was one.

After a short consideration, Annie decided she didn't much care what her mom or the teachers thought of Jess. She knew she liked him, "bad boy" or not. He looked out for her, and that mattered. In fact, she knew he looked out for all the kids in the neighborhood. And then there was his hundred-watt smile … When he smiled, it came from a place deep down inside.

~~~

He was thirteen and in the 7th grade, and Annie twelve when she walked up the McGowan front porch steps. The sweet fragrance of honeysuckle floated from long vines wrapped around rusting wrought iron. Until recently, Jesse had only been a friend, and she would have felt

70

comfortable knocking on his door. But things had changed. Her feelings had changed, and that made all the difference.

She stood alone, holding her breath, and knocked.

"I'll get it," a voice yelled. The door swung open, and there stood Jess. Soft brown hair a little longer than a crew cut, masculine, squared shoulders, strong jaw, warm green eyes, big hands. Solid. And there was that smile.

"Hey, Jess," Annie said, shifting the weight on her feet, trying to look natural.

"Hey," he returned, looking at her with questioning eyes. She felt her heart beating faster and wasn't sure what to say. Should she make small talk, like, "How was school today?" Should she blurt out, "You know you were in my dreams last night?" Such opportunity hanging in the air! "Want to buy some Girl Scout cookies?" were the words she settled on.

"Mom," he shouted over something sizzling in the kitchen and smelling good! Annie heard Gunsmoke on the TV. Chester was talking to Miss Kitty, resplendent with big hair and a much-coveted beauty mark, high on her cheekbone. Later, as color TV came their way, they would discover the real brilliance of Miss Kitty's flaming red hair, and it would take their breath away! Matt Dillon entered the scene, talking to Doc. "I went to bed mean last night, Doc, and I woke up meaner." Classic straight-shootin' Matt talk.

"Annie's selling Girl Scout cookies. Wanna buy some?"

"Two boxes of Thin Mints," she yelled back. Jesse looked at Annie for a second.

"How about some for Aunt Flo? Doesn't she like them?"

Was he looking out for her? Annie's heart pounded even harder. Maybe he liked her ... just a little. Her mind flashed back to a few days before, when she was getting dressed in her favorite pink sweater set with the white pearl buttons.

"You're developing," announced Mary. Annie had placed a necklace over her head, trying out a look. She stood before her mirror, studying herself. So she was—the necklace hung between two small mounds, which were definitely noticeable. With resignation, she realized if Mary noticed, Mom would notice too. It meant Mom would try to harness her into some stupid training bra, and eventually a garter belt with stockings.

Until a year ago, Annie was an uncomplicated tomboy who enjoyed playing in the treehouse with boys. She'd kept her Superman cape in a secret hiding place, just in case …. She sighed, not wanting to face the inevitable changes she knew were coming. She wasn't ready to grow up.

"We'll take four boxes," Jesse repeated a second time, a little impatiently.

Annie's cheeks burned. She'd recalled the necklace scene while standing there before Jesse McGowan and hadn't heard him. Annie was glad he wasn't a mind reader.

He looked at her red cheeks, and a flash of curiosity crossed his face.

"You okay?" He asked.

"Yeah, thanks, Jess," she said.

As she walked down the porch steps, she mumbled, "Sleep good tonight, Matt."

The tune, "Riverboat ring your bell, Annabelle fair thee well, Maverick is the legend of the West," was now playing. *It must be 5:30.* Maverick was the next western in the television lineup. James Garner, a glib, silk-vested gambler, was replacing straight-talking Matt. The living room light turned on at her house across the street. Dad was home.

She crossed Jesse's yard. *Jeez, could I have been any more awkward?*

Every season had its time and events—clockwork regularity. Everyone knew the rhythm and what to expect. It was a safe world, predictable, and shaken only by the occasional A-bomb duck and cover drill, where kids kneeled under their school desks, hands and arms over their heads, all the while wondering if it would really do any good.

72

America was strong, and Annie felt secure.

Those passages in time coincided with nature's passages as they themselves were growing up. All appeared in synch, balanced. But for those listening, the metronome was ticking a warning. The winds of change were coming, and destruction was about to fall upon the Garden of Eden. Norman Rockwell's comfortable Americana was to endure severe cracking on many fronts, and America would be tested to its core.

~~~

Sleep was descending upon Annie in her New Orleans hotel room. She had read, "Love is a decision of how we treat people," and Jesse had always treated her with kindness. At twelve, she'd given him her heart. It was the right decision.

FIFTEEN

It was Easter Sunday, and Annie sat on the front porch glider next to her little sister Debbie, waiting for Mary. The glider converted to a futon and became a bed for sleepovers. Many nights were spent looking at the stars through the screened porch and talking "life" before falling asleep. Mr. Thomashefski, the mailman, often found the girls there in the morning when delivering mail.

Mary arrived shortly after Annie and Debbie's Easter egg hunt. Annie could read Mary like a book and knew Mary had something important to say.

~~~

They walked upstairs to her room, heavy with the scent of lilac coming from a tree her father planted under the window years ago. Fat black and yellow bumblebees moved from blossom to blossom, occasionally bumping into the screen but not seeming to care. Glancing at the bee's, Annie wondered for the hundredth time how those tiny wings supported so large a body?

As soon as Deb left, Mary turned to Annie, and said dramatically, "Remember last week when you told me Tommy Sanders looked up from his kitchen window to see you up here in your training bra?"

"Sure," Annie replied, not knowing where this was going.

"Remember you said you wouldn't have cared if it was Jesse McGowan looking up at you, and I told you that was disgusting?"

"Yeah, so what?"

74

"Well, I was wrong, Annie, and I take it back. If any boy in the neighborhood should see you in your bra, it should be Jesse McGowan," she stated, cheeks turning red. It was blasphemy coming from her Catholic mouth.

She now had Annie's full attention.

"Why do you say that?" Annie asked, anticipating something delicious.

Mary's voice lowered. "I came home from church and was in my backyard checking on the pups, waiting for you guys to finish your egg hunt. I had on those stupid lace knee-highs Mom made me wear, totally ruining the look of my patent leather stacked heels."

"Go on, Mary, get to the point," Annie demanded impatiently. *She should be a book writer!*

"Well, by the time I got home from church, my left knee-high was down around my ankle. I didn't care, but something got in it and stung me, twice! I screamed! I stomped and shook my leg and screamed more. Jesse was playing football with some guys in his backyard and must've heard me and came to see what was going on. I was crying and tried to tell him I'd gotten stung, but just blubbered and pointed to the knee-high. He stooped down, unfolded it, and found a wasp. He held it in his fingers, and Annie, he placed it gently on the ground … like he cared about it. Then he told me I'd be okay and asked if I needed some ice. He helped me in front of those boys, me, the nerd girl of the neighborhood. I think I'm in love! Have you ever noticed how big his hands are?"

"Yes!" Annie replied as lustily as a thirteen-year-old coming from a picket fence community could. "And you can't like him, you like Shane Williams, remember?"

Once again, Annie's reason for loving Jesse McGowan had been validated. Her love confirmed …. *Oh, thank you, Mary!*

That evening, Annie pulled Lady Chatterley's Lover, by D. H. Lawrence, from under her bed, where she hid it from her parents. "Too

Racy!" her mother had exclaimed with disdain. Annie liked Lady Chatterley because she lived life on her terms, defying expectations of proper behavior of a "Lady" in 18ᵗʰ century England. While her husband chased the "bitch-goddess success," Lady Chatterley surrendered herself to the gentle gamekeeper who appreciated and loved her. At thirteen, Annie was becoming aware that gentleness and caring bonded a relationship. "He helped me in front of those boys, me, the nerd girl of the neighborhood," Mary had said, and Annie understood.

As she finished getting ready for bed, Annie studied her reflection in the vanity mirror; the last vestige of a girl-child stared back. Through her nightgown, Annie's breasts and small waist were illuminated by the lamp on her nightstand. She was transforming into a woman, a woman yet to be, but the foundation of a beautiful woman was in place. She stared at herself, almost as though in a trance, and realized the power she might one day wield over the male species.

She knew she would live within her own truth as a woman, and like Lady Chatterley, had choices. Annie fell into a contented sleep.

~~~

Time passed. Still insulated, still safe. Small treasures came Annie's way in what would be her last year in Forest Heights. She loved dancing every morning at the Robbley Junior High School Sock Hop. It was required that every student enter the school through the gym, take off their shoes, and dance for fifteen minutes before classes began. There was never a fight at Robbley, perhaps because its teens were forced to dance away excess energy each morning.

In the spring, Jesse saved Annie from a water moccasin as she walked through the woods, coming home from school. He killed it with a stone while standing on a boulder overlooking her path. His aim was amazing. He was amazing. He continued to watch over her.

And then they danced together. Jesse's older sister Janine promised her parents she wouldn't be alone with her boyfriend while they were away. She kept her word by having Jesse and his friends, Annie, Mary, and Jeff Carson, come over. Janine's boyfriend played DJ, and they danced in the basement of the McGowan house.

The kids were watching Janine and her DJ dance when Jess turned to Annie. "Want to dance?" he asked. It was a slow dance. Annie saw Mary and Jeff snickering. She didn't care and said, "Yes!"

"Would you like to dance?" Mary asked Jeff. "Heck no!" he shot back.

Annie looked at Jesse and smiled, knowing she would return often to this sweet moment. Duchess, the McGowan's French poodle, barked and wagged her tail. One two, one two, Annie and Jess danced like proper robots, but they danced ... and he asked her ... they were close to each other, and it was exciting!

Then it was over.

SIXTEEN

ONE SUMMER NIGHT

1964

At the end of ninth grade, Annie's dad landed a job in Louisville, Kentucky, and they were gone ... but not completely. They returned while making a trip through Maryland the following summer, and Julie Stone gave a surprise "Welcome Back" party for Annie.

Sixteen-year-old Annie cautiously walked down the steps of the Stone's basement, wondering about all the noise. She'd just finished reading Gone with the Wind, and there ... looking like Rhett Butler watching Scarlett descend that antebellum staircase ... stood Jess. His arm rested on a well-crafted banister, his loafer on the bottom step .... *He's changed over the past year .... He's become a man.* His hair was longer and looked like Jack Kennedy's, a Princeton cut. He wore a madras short-sleeved shirt and jeans. His shoulders were broader than she remembered. Ah yes, there were those hazel eyes and thick long lashes she'd envied, and then came his smile, the smile she knew all too well. Jess.

In a blur, Mary, Julie, Jeff, and the rest of the kids, said hello, and shared hugs, but the moment was given to Jesse, whose large, warm hand met hers with his own. Annie didn't remember them speaking. The perfect song began to play. With rock hard arms, he pulled her close, surrounded her, and tenderly held her against him. She remembered their last dance in his basement. This was nothing like that. Annie was lost in the song, Jesse's warmth, the faint scent of soap, and his aftershave, British Sterling. They danced like lovers while the Danleers sang.

The haunting melody filled the room and echoed beyond the open doors ... for the night sky to embrace then pass on to the galaxy ....

"One Summer Night" … a favorite of hers. And she knew, as the song said, no one could ever take Jesse's place or take this moment from her. *It must be playing for us.* She was in Jesse's arms once again, her head against his chest, feeling safe.

"Welcome home, Annie," he said in a husky voice. "I missed you."

~~~

Somehow, they were in the Stone's backyard, she and Jess lying on the grassy hill, loving all the stars that looked down on them … They talked, then kissed, making up for time lost. They had come of age, and this was their time to show what they had always felt for each other … felt when they were too young to express it. All was magical. The moon was round, and though it was summer, it had the pink glow of a Harvest Moon. Stars twinkled like fireflies, thicker than honey, and sparkled as she'd never seen before. A soft breeze cooled their skin.

Annie had boyfriends in Louisville, and she'd "made out," but that only involved kissing. This was different. These kisses were deep and long. His touch was skillful and oh so tender. He kissed each closed eye, her cheeks, her chin, her mouth. It felt as though he would devour her, and the only word that came to her mind was, "yes."

When he could hold her no closer, he lowered his body on hers, and through their clothes, they knew each other. They moved to a rhythm that belonged to them and them alone. Annie was fully aware of the hardness pushing against her and felt her own body push back. She was a virgin, but every cell in her body wanted more of Jesse, and she knew he wanted the same.

"Annie … Jesse … you guys out there?" Julie was calling to them. The spell was broken, and like intoxicated bumblebees with too much nectar, they moved ever so slowly away from each other. They became two people once again. Life had stolen the moment. *Aw Jess, do you feel how much I want you?*

Then it was over. Really over. Annie returned to her family and left. It was the last time she would be with Jesse … alive.

SEVENTEEN

DRUMBEATS

1965

"Hold on, Paul, I want to see this on the news," Jesse spoke into the wall-mounted phone, pulling its spiraling cord into the living room. He glanced out the window to see if snow was still falling. It was March 8th.

"Hey man, are you hearing what I'm hearing? Walter Cronkite just said that President Johnson dispatched 3,500 Marines to South Vietnam for combat. They're in a place called Da Nang, and the South Vietnamese girls are lined up with red and yellow-flowered necklaces for each Marine.

"The troops are in trucks driving under a sign that says, 'THANKS TO THE U.S. GOVERNMENT AND PEOPLE FOR THEIR DETERMINATION IN PROTECTING FREEDOM IN V.N.' The roads are lined with people waving, smiling, and cheering. I don't believe it! Man, this country is going to war! I gotta go. I gotta call Russ. He's gonna go crazy when he hears this. He'll be full of 'I told you so!' Wow, I bet he'll sign up tomorrow!

"Catch you later, Paul. Oh, hey, I mentioned to Cheryl that you and Linda wanted to double date for Spring Fling. She's been bugging me about it all week and is looking at magazines for dresses. Women! Yeah, anyway, she's good with us going together. You driving, or you want me to ask my dad if I can borrow the Bonneville?"

As Jess dialed Russ' number, he glanced out the window again. Big marshmallow-sized snowflakes were coming down, and Jess decided a trip down the street to the Stone's house would be better than a call. He loved snowfall at night when all was silent.

It swirled around him as he stepped outside. He pulled his coat collar up and put his hands in his pockets as he walked toward Russ' house. Maybe he'd get invited to dinner. Mrs. Stone was an exceptional cook, even if she borrowed half the food from the neighborhood. Good-hearted yes, organized no. He smiled.

~~~

After a perfunctory knock, but without waiting, Jess opened their door and entered. This was his second home.

The Stone's house was full of noise and activity and smelled like a wonderful meal was on its way. Spaghetti and maybe garlic bread?

"Hey Julie, where's Russ?" Two years younger than Russ and a junior in High School, Julie sat at the dining room table with a black and green geometry book Jesse recognized. She looked overwhelmed.

"Hi Jess," Mrs. Stone said, passing by. "You staying for supper?"

"Would love to, thanks!"

"I'll add more noodles and sauce," she replied, not slowing her pace.

"Jess, you any good at Algebra?" Julie asked, hopefully.

"You wanna play Chinese checkers?" came two voices from somewhere else.

"Yeah, I'll give ya a hand in a sec Jules; tell me where Russ is first."

"Raincheck on Chinese checkers!" he yelled as he walked down the basement steps.

Russ and Mr. Stone were working the lathe in a partitioned off part of the basement. Mrs. Stone had set down the law when they bought the house that part of the basement could be her husband's work area, a small part, but the larger part would be for their growing family. The law held. "How do you argue with a woman," Russel Sr. muttered when a large piece of wood needed a larger space.

Tonight, Mr. Stone was making a new cocktail table to replace the one the twins broke. They'd used the old table as a chair to tack up

Beach Boys posters in a room already chock full of Pipeline and Surfin'
Safari "stuff." Their double weight collapsed the table, an event Mrs.
Stone quickly recognized as a genuine opportunity.

She'd saved the 1964 Sears and Roebuck Spring Catalog for almost a
year now, coveting an inlaid coffee table on page 24. Lucky for Beverly
Stone, she had a husband who was a carpenter by trade. She was in the
living room with page 24 in hand before the twins even ditched the
broken pieces. She smiled. She envisioned. *God worked in mysterious
ways!*

Russell Stone, Sr. could craft something beautiful out of nothing. As a
regular at St. Andrew's Church, he was always busy helping with
repairs. Jesse looked into his broad smiling face and remembered when
he drove "Russ Jr.," and Jesse to Dr. Dave's a few years back to learn
"the facts of life."

It was a meeting arranged between the two men, both being
parishioners of St. Andrew's, and Jesse's dad okay'd the meeting. What
a fiasco! Dr. Dave told Mr. Stone it was a good thing he'd brought them
because they were green, green, green! They knew nothing about
anything. Russ and Jesse feigned "green" because to share what they
knew would put them in the hot seat, knowing more than they should.
Dr. Dave and Mr. Stone laughed with relief that the boys were "good
boys" and knew so little, and Jesse and Russ laughed with relief that the
two men bought their act.

Russ was a year older than Jesse and out of school. He worked in his
dad's business and had been dating Sally for three years. Two years into
the relationship, Russ Jr. stopped by the McGowan house, and as he
closed the door to Jess's room, confided with a big grin of satisfaction,
"We went all the way last night." Recently, he confided that the
"withdrawal" thing Dr. Dave had recommended for birth control was
getting harder and harder to do. And they laughed again, remembering
that meeting.

Jesse hadn't scored yet. He was content in getting it right with
someone special and figured that piece of information might surprise
many people, but he was okay with that. Jess knew who he was and

realized he frequently wasn't who people thought he was. That was okay with him too. He and Cheryl seemed to be doing fine. He liked her well enough, and maybe things would happen for them ... who knew ... maybe at Spring Fling ... or Senior Prom ....

"Have you listened to the news?" Jess asked. Mr. Stone and Russ slowed down to hear what he had to say. Without pause, Jesse continued, "We're at war, well not exactly war, Johnson calls it a 'conflict,' but troops are ready to fight." Both men stopped their work and looked at him, each with a different expression.

Mr. Stone looked first at Russ with concern on his face, then at Jess, and sighed in resignation.

Russ looked excited and blurted, "No kidding? This is gonna be short and sweet. Guess we'll show the commies who we are fast enough and about time too!

"That son of a bitch Khrushchev needs to get a bona fide U.S. government issue boot up his fat ass! We'll knock that grin off his wart-ridden face! He says he can bury us, our children, our grandchildren, and our great-grandchildren. That he'll defeat us without firing a shot. We'll show him who he can and can't 'bury.'"

Not on the college track, Russ nonetheless watched the news nightly and stayed current on world affairs.

Mr. Stone had served in World War II and with a perceptible, resigned sadness in his voice, said, "You never know what you'll get when it comes to war, boys." Then added, "Watch your mouth, Russ, your mother might hear you."

EIGHTEEN

EVERYONE MATTERS

1966

M r. Stone passed a folded piece of paper over to Jess.

"Found this note for you tucked in Russ' letter to us."

It was a cold day outside as Jess entered Stone's Carpentry, Inc. He blew into his cupped hands before reaching to take the note, aware of the warmth he'd stepped into and appreciative. Mr. Stone had known severe cold while serving in Europe during WWII. He'd promised himself never to be cold again. His house was always warm in winter, and so was his new shop.

Three men were working on a project for the new community college, scheduled to open in June. The college had awarded his company a large project, and Mr. Stone had been hustling since he'd signed the contract. He was a mother hen, supervising everything. Each cabinet, table, desk, and chair had to be perfect. He was proud to have landed this, the largest project since opening his business. The word "quality" was said by him fifty times a day if it was said once.

Russ had been in 'Nam for four months. This was Jesse's fourth note from him. He unfolded the letter. No salutation or greeting ....

> Don't even think about coming over here, Jess. It's bad, really bad. I have the craps-they call it Ho Chi Minh's revenge. I'm shitting nonstop. Men are shitting while they're firing and they're not sure if it's fear or Ho's revenge, I figure it's both, but it's bad either way. Some got it so bad they ended up in the hospital on IV's. I guess I'm

lucky, not that bad for me yet, plus my feet are still good. Most important thing we got from the government was socks. Lotta guys are dealing with a thing called immersion foot. It comes from having wet feet for so long that chunks of flesh fall off. Pretty raunchy when parts of your foot come off in your fingers. Then there's the leeches. They crawl on us every fucking night and suck our blood. Only way to get them off without the mouth staying in and infecting us is to use salt or a cigarette on them. We'll be sorry motherfucker's if the salt runs out! Jesus, what a place! And in case you're not getting the straight news over there in "The World," let me tell you the North Vietnamese know how to fight. Don't believe it if the government is saying this war will be short! That's bullshit, man! These bastards know how to kill and don't mind doing it. Don't think about enlisting Jess. Listen to me, stay there; stay safe. Stop in for a meal at the old homestead and let Mom and Dad see your face, maybe give Julie a hand with her math. That would be great and would make a difference. You being there is a little like me being there. Tell Jules to keep the sweets coming. It's the only thing sweet over here, and she's getting better at baking with each package.

I'm thinking of re-upping Jess. I know it sounds crazy, man, but some of us need to stick around to 'edumacate' the poor green bastards coming here straight from the farm ... man, these kids get picked off so fast. Never even know what hit 'em. Keep a lid on this re-upping thing, Jess ... nobody knows. I sure might change my mind by the time my tour is up. I don't want you thinking I'm doing this because I enjoy fighting or think it's some kind of glorious war. I don't, and it's not. It's as close to being in hell and still being alive as anything can be. Just feelin' sorry for the new kids on the block.

Don't be a knucklehead. Stay put. Take care, my friend.
Russ.

~~~

Russ was the first in Forest Heights to enlist. Mrs. Stone cried for days at his decision and begged him to reconsider. He would have signed up the day after he heard the Marines had landed if not for his mom's begging.

She remembered when Russ Sr. served, and she wanted no more of the agonizing fear she'd already experienced with her husband. Once was enough. War was not an abstract to her but a reality, and she'd already "served" thank you very much.

The twins were in awe of Russ' decision but were still too young to understand the potential consequences. Julie was now a senior in High School and cognizant. When she heard, she sat quietly for a few minutes, deep in thought, wondering what she could do to keep her brother safe in a place so far away. Then resolutely, Julie went to the kitchen and pulled out her mother's cookbooks, turning to the baked goods section. Brownies; Brownies with nuts, Brownies with toffee. Cake; Pound Cake. Lemon Cake. Cookies; Chocolate Chip, Coconut Macaroons, Lemon Bars, Oatmeal Raisin. They were all there, Russ' favorites. Sweets he loved that probably every guy loved. "You will be the most popular guy in your platoon, Russ," she'd promised. "I'm baking you something wonderful every week while you're over there, and I'll bake enough so you can share with the fellas. You must share Russ. Promise you'll share. As long as you get sweets and pass them along to the others, they'll work just a little harder to keep you around." She'd come up with a strategy to keep her brother alive. Then the tears began.

Mr. Stone walked over to Russ, extended his hand for a long shake, and put his other arm around his son in a hug. "I'm proud of you, son." Then repeated, "I'm proud of you."

Sally was the surprise card. Russ expected her to make the same scene his mom made. In a tone more serious than he'd ever heard before, Sally said, "Russ, I love you, and I've listened to your feelings for months now about how America needs to take a stand in Vietnam. I know you're afraid that if we don't fight now, the communists will keep taking over other countries, maybe they'll even try to take on the U.S. I'm planning on having kids with you, Russell Stone Jr., and I figure you and I both want our kids to grow up in a free country. I'm glad you're going. You're going for our family's future, and I'm 100% behind you. But you better make it back, sweetie, and do what you have to do to get our babies started."

She smiled, and Russ, at that moment, knew true, deep love. He fell head over heels in love with Sally Pallao then and there. He knew now he could count on her to be his "true north" ….

Within two weeks, they shipped Russ to Parris Island for thirteen-weeks of Basic Training, followed by six weeks of Infantry Training. He began his thirteen-month tour of duty in Vietnam in October 1965.

~~~

The Selective Service issued draft calls each month, depending on the need. Robert McNamara, President Johnson's Secretary of Defense, always seemed to need more fighting men. That summer, draft calls were up to 35,000 within a month. By the winter of 1965, Vietnam was "home" to over 184,000 combat troops.

Like most 18-year-old males in Forest Heights, Jesse had now become friends with Mr. Thomashefski, the mailman. Since registering with the Selective Service and meeting with the Local Draft Board, Jesse was scrutinizing the mail daily. Induction notices were delivered to males between the ages of 18 and 26 in an envelope that looked like any other … but wasn't. It was a death knell of sorts and directed the recipient where and when to report for induction into the Armed Forces.

Every guy looking at that notice knew any plans had just been deep-sixed, maybe permanently. That he would report to the Induction Center and probably make a left turn for Vietnam. It was one hellacious "anything goes" war from what everyone saw on TV, and only a fool would not be thinking of his own mortality as he approached the Center.

~~~

After watching the news together one night, Jeff Carson tried consoling Jesse. "This war can't go on much longer, plenty of guys are going every month, and you'll probably never get called up."

Jeff was safe, not yet 18, and would get a 2-S classification, "Deferment for College Studies." Both of Jeff's parents were teachers and intent on Jeff furthering his education for many reasons, avoiding the war in Vietnam certainly not the least. Jesse figured their reasoning was solid enough.

For the working-class community in Forest Heights, most boys received a 1-A, "Available for Duty."

On a cool, quiet night, Jess sat on the front porch steps, Russ' letter in hand. He'd thought hard about the words written in that letter, and a heaviness came over him. He'd considered following in Russ' footsteps to take control of his life, instead of waiting for a notice to arrive. Now he was having second thoughts.

"Hey, Jesse, whatcha doing?" He looked into the almost Asian eyes of Bobby Dougherty, the Down syndrome kid who lived up the street.

"Hey, Bobby."

"Who's the letter from?"

"A friend," Jesse replied, not wanting to talk.

"You look pensive."

"Pensive, huh?" A smile crept over Jesse's face. "Where'd you learn a big word like 'pensive'?"

"Oh, I know a lot of big words, Jess; I learn a new word every day from Mr. Webster. He wrote a book called the Webster's Dictionary, have you heard of it?"

"Yeah, I have." Jesse's smile grew larger.

Bobby looked hard at Jess, then moved closer as though to confide in him.

"You know I'm different, Jesse, I know it too. I know I'm not smart like you or Jeff. Dad sometimes tells me I'm not the brightest bulb in the package. Yes, Dad really says that to me sometimes!" Bobby smiled, and Jesse smiled wider, both recognizing the liberation which comes from truth.

"But he always says afterward that it doesn't matter how bright we are; all that really matters is that we shine."

"Yeah, Bobby, I guess that's right."

Bobby fervently nodded his head, seeing that Jesse understood and agreed with his dad.

"My dad also says the way for me to shine is to stay happy and be true to myself. He says when I'm happy, then everyone around me will be happy too. Do you think he's right, Jesse?"

"Yeah, Bobby, I think your dad's a wise old bird."

Bobby beamed. "Yes! I think so too! I'll tell him you said so! Well, Jesse, I have something to ask you then."

Jesse sighed, there was an agenda in place, and he might as well put his thoughts about his future on the back burner.

"Okay, Bobby, what do you want to know?"

Bobby paused as if making sure he had permission to speak again.

"You don't look happy right now, Jesse, and you're my friend. I want to know what will make you happy, and how I can help make that happen for you?"

Those simple words surprised Jesse. No one had ever asked him what would make him happy before.

"Wow, Bobby, that's a good question."

And there, on the steps of his home, Jesse poured out his thoughts about enlisting or not enlisting to this Down syndrome man-child. And in so doing, he decided on a course that would change his life.

That night, lying in bed, Jesse thought how strange life worked. It was all there. All you had to do was listen and receive the answer. He secretly thanked Bobby for coming to his rescue and "shining."

Year's back, Jess had accepted John F. Kennedy's charge, "Ask what you can do for your country." He heard these words with his heart, and they rang true. His heart responded. The problem was that Kennedy was dead, and he didn't much care for or trust the politicians or military leaders running this war. Nothing had been the same since the assassination of JFK, and America's spirit was depleted.

Vultures swooped in where eagles once soared, and communism was on the rise. Johnson intended to stop the spread of communism in Indochina, starting with its spread to South Vietnam. The problem was China. China was a protector to Communist North Vietnam and, if necessary, would purportedly send troops to defend the North. A U.S. invasion of the North might well unleash the wrath of China … evoke a retaliation and possibly provoke a third World War.

Congress refused to declare this a war. It would remain "a conflict." It was decided ground fighting would occur south of the 17th parallel in South Vietnam. The fighting would be against any invading Viet Cong and NVA who crossed the 17th parallel and entered South Vietnam.

Military success was historically based on territory taken, but this was no longer a viable approach. Believing his hands were tied, Johnson agreed with McNamara to use dead bodies in determining whether battles were won or lost.

Winning would be determined by which side had the least dead bodies after each battle ….

There were logistical questions Jesse wondered about when considering this "body count" war.

How would we win a body count war when there was a never-ending stream of fighters coming from the North? The Viet Cong were already sending second-generation soldiers into the fight. If the North never ran out of motivation or fighters, would this become an endless war?

90

Would the higher-ups escalate battles to produce increased body counts, especially when the war lasted too long in the eyes of America? Questions worth considering.

Then there were the moral considerations that weighed heavily on him. A body count concept seemed un-American, unclean, and twisted to Jesse. Dead bodies defining winners or losers. Unbelievable. In measuring success by counting the number of soldiers killed, McNamara, and by default Johnson, had reduced each soldier to a number. Fodder for the fire.

A stinking number. Not a person. A number. McNamara had anesthetized death, making it a clean numerical operation, and in so doing, had cut the heart out of the thing. He lessened the humanness of serving, not to mention the dignity of the soldier offering to lay down his life for his country.

Given that war was the ultimate act of barbarism for humanity, the concept of a body count war took barbarism down to an even lower level and offended Jess to his core. Each time he heard the phrase, he cringed inside and knew he could never respect men thinking in these terms. It devalued life.

Jesse researched McNamara, where McNamara worked before going political and taking the position as Secretary of Defense. He found McNamara was one of the "smart new politicos," a technocrat, one of the nation's "best and brightest" who had served as President of the Ford Motor Company and had admitted that his knowledge of military matters was scant. Scant! *Jesus, his background is all about numbers. So why was he Secretary of Defense?* Jesse had no answer. Jeez, hadn't some politician warned America not to let business and government get too friendly? It had a name, but Jess couldn't remember it .... There was truth to that warning. How much of that was already happening?

Then there was Army General Westmoreland, who sure didn't seem to care about the troops the way Eisenhower or Major General Walt of the Marine Corps did. All of this was a big crapshoot, he ruefully accepted. These pivot points could go on forever when considering whether to enlist.

On the front porch steps in the cool of night, he decided that the country would elect Bobby Kennedy as President, perhaps in the next election, and Johnson would be out. Jesse believed Robert Kennedy was someone to trust and could turn things around. He had the strength of character and conviction to "correct things." Hell, he'd taken on the entire mafia almost single-handedly. Jesse decided it was his job to help America until this could happen. Jesse put his money on Robert Kennedy and drove to the Recruiting Center the next morning.

Because he could be honest with Bobby Dougherty, Jesse confided that he wanted to be the best man he could, and in the company of other men who felt the same way ... the Marines. He knew basic training would be tough, but he'd make it; he was fit, self-disciplined, and had the courage to handle what would come his way. Sure, Jesse wanted to be a hero, and yes, in his eyes, the Marines, by definition, were heroes. The Corps would provide him with the skills necessary to protect himself and the country he loved. It would give him the brotherhood he needed. But when it came right down to it, his loyalty to the United States propelled him forward. Democracy would have one more patriot in its ranks to fend off the threat of communism.

He drove past the billboard he'd seen and admired a hundred times, "THE MARINE CORPS BUILDS MEN!" and signed his name on the line. He felt good. Very, very, good. Gung-ho!

~~~

Russ wrote that he arrived in the South China Sea in what he called the "snail ship," a U.S. Navy transport jam-packed with men. "Sardine ship" might have been more appropriate. The crossing took several weeks, and onboard, war stories were rampant. The journey was fraught with seasickness and frayed nerves, which infected the spirit and morale of crowded men. They expected to storm the beaches as troops did in WWII, only to find them empty. It was unnerving. This was the first of many uncertain and strange situations Russ would encounter. Nothing in this conflict was quite what it should be, he wrote. Jess wondered what his first encounter with Vietnam would be ....

~~~

92

Months later, at boot camp in Beaufort, South Carolina, Jesse stumbled upon a gift shop. Inside, hung on a wall, was a saying called "Desiderata." One section read, "Speak your truth quietly and clearly; and listen to others, even the dull and ignorant; they too have their story."

Jesse thought of Bobby Dougherty and walked to the postcard display. There, he found a card with large oak trees indigenous to the South, looking all the while like misshapen swamp creatures with hairy moss hanging from limbs akimbo. They lined a path leading to a beautiful place called Magnolia Plantation. Jesse liked the card … it felt … what was the word … his mother would know the word … she would call it … enchanting. He hoped it would make Bobby feel good to get this. On the card, Jesse wrote:

> Hey Bobby,
>
> Thanks for being a friend when I needed one. Keep shining, Bobby.
>
> You made a difference! Give my best to your dad!
>
> Your Friend, Jesse.

NINETEEN

Jess, like Russ, was sent to Parris Island, South Carolina, for Basic Training, where he learned quickly enough what being a Marine was about. When the DI (Drill Instructor) shouted, "What is your job, Marine?" The words, "I am a Marine trained to kill, Sir!" had damn well better be the first words spewing out of each recruit's mouth or there'd be hell to pay, not only for the Marine who failed to perform but for every recruit in the company.

When one screwed up, they all felt the consequence. These recruits were not a company of sixty-some individuals, sixty-some marbles in a jar; they were the jar, a cohesive body working together and used coordinated firepower in a deadly efficient manner.

Early on, each recruit learned that in combat, his actions affected lives and outcomes. The Marine on either side of you held your life in his hands. The Corps taught that victory or failure was determined by how well they worked together. Synchronized effort maximized success, and the whole was greater than the sum of the parts.

Jesse learned scalable tactics, such as how to move forward under fire while being protected ... leapfrog ... one Marine passing another, the Marine being passed providing the fire cover, all the while the group running toward a destination. A unified whole. He became part of something greater than himself. He accepted the responsibility of being his brother's keeper, gaining admission to the brotherhood—a*ll for one and one for all.*

94

Jess was the first to help any Marine in need. At his most bone-tired, he would hear his mother's voice, "God gave us two hands for a reason, Jesse, one to pull ourselves up and the other to pull up those in need."

One night, the DI stopped at his bunk. "Saw what you did today. Whittaker wouldn't have made it without you. Keep it up."

Just that. Supreme praise.

It felt good, maybe better than when Mom praised him with a cookie for each hand and a kiss on his forehead. Maybe not. He laid back and smiled.

He missed Dad and his sister, Janine, but especially Mom. Jess thought of them often during his thirteen-weeks of Basic, followed by his Infantry Training. He'd never been away from them, and it was harder than he imagined.

He thought of his girlfriend, Cheryl. She was livid when he told her he enlisted. Jesse supposed he should have talked with her first, but once his conversation with Bobby Dougherty was over, he was determined and at peace.

Like her parents, Cheryl believed the U.S. had no business in Vietnam, fighting the Vietnamese "on the other side of the world," and they were sure President Johnson had done something underhanded in the Gulf of Tonkin to instigate this mess. They might have been right, but Jesse believed stopping the spread of communism said it all, regardless of how it started. Cheryl didn't agree with Jess's volunteering to fight, but mainly she was furious that he'd made such a major decision without talking it over with her. "How can I ever trust your judgment again when it comes to us?" she'd yelled at him. "It involved me! We should have talked!" They were never the same after that and became increasingly distant from each other. Amplified by their polarized opinions of Vietnam, their view of the world soon arrived at the point of vanishing returns, and they knew it in their hearts.

~~~

Jesse was washing his car the day before he left for boot camp when Cheryl stopped by. She looked different, her hair, usually in a ponytail, was hanging long and free, and a choker of small red beads hung around her neck. Blue jeans had replaced her normal pleated skirt, and she looked like she needed a flower in her hair. Her cheeks were bright spots of red. He knew they got this way when she was angry or nervous.

"I heard you were leaving tomorrow, and I wanted to say goodbye and wish you good luck." He stood there, not sure what to say or do. She kissed him on the cheek. Not a girlfriend type kiss, but a "goodbye friend" type kiss. She turned, and he watched her walk away. *I never had a chance to say a word, not even goodbye ....*

He went back to washing his car. He'd be going to boot camp without a girl. *Maybe I don't need a complicated relationship. I need to stay focused on the job at hand.*

~~~

Jesse missed her. Perhaps more than Cheryl, he missed what other guys had, a girl to write to and receive letters from. A girlfriend who cared. He told himself that would come in time after he'd served, and the fighting was over. He thought about Annie, where she was and what she was up to. Probably better not to think about her either. Stay focused, he told himself.

"Perform whatever good you can," was part of the code. That was the higher-order thinking that appealed to Jesse. It included leaving no brother behind. That was the grabber. Sure he would sacrifice, sacrifice his life if need be ... but not to be left behind, or rot in a country not his own ... that was the other draw to the Corps, not just for Jesse, but for most men going through Basic. The code removed the fear of being left behind or dying alone.

While the concept of "unit" was paramount to the Corps, the value of each man, each Marine, was absolute .... Every Marine mattered. Every Marine had the same value. The Marines honored their own so much that rather than leave a dead or wounded brother behind, they would risk, even sacrifice themselves, to retrieve the fallen. Loyalty to each other meant everything. They were a family. The code was the foundation of "Semper Fidelis." Semper Fi. Always Faithful. Oorah!

TWENTY

FLIGHT

1966

Jesse flew to 'Nam via a TWA commercial jet. A dozen or so Marines traveled with him. He was glad for their company, but they were not Marines he knew well. Going to war on a commercial plane was not what he'd expected. It was certainly not like a John Wayne movie where men arrived en masse, full of camaraderie.

To rapidly increase manpower, Boot Camp was reduced from eighty to sixty days in September 1965, for all Marines save infantrymen. As an infantryman, Jess spent eighty days at infantry boot camp, Parris Island, then an additional four weeks of Individual Combat Training, and two weeks of Basic Specialist Training. He was sent home for one month before being flown to Camp Pendleton Staging Battalion, California, for a three-week training of Southeast Asia Orientation given to Lance Corporal's or below headed for Vietnam.

Jess spent nearly five months with hundreds of other Marines eating, sleeping, and shitting, rituals, and routines they had in common, becoming brothers. Daily they were reminded they were THE CORPS. Jess could hear his DI yell, "Whether you live or die, you live or die as part of The Corps! If you live, you live as a Marine forever, and when you die, you'll meet up with Marines in Marine heaven."

Here on the plane, he didn't much feel part of anything. Looking out the window at the clouds, he felt alone and scared for the first time since he'd enlisted. The Corps and Forest Heights felt far away. Jesse's home was now with the Marines. His first exposure to President Johnson's war wasn't reassuring. It left him wondering.

Russ and his buddies might have been seasick and worried on the Navy ship that carried them to the South China Sea, but at least they were seasick and worried together. They had camaraderie. They complained to each other. They shared fears. They shared stories and told terrible jokes. They bonded and felt stronger for it. It made for good morale. They were warriors going to battle … together, an ancient brotherhood that spanned time, nations, and causes.

"Together" was the cornerstone of the Corps, but now he was part of Westmoreland's campaign. Russ had written Vietnamese women greeted them holding flowered garlands for each Marine's neck. More weird shit. Had honor and respect for the warrior been devalued.? They weren't arriving in 'Nam as tourists. *Please, let this not be an omen of things to come.* Talking to himself, he took charge of his negative thinking and realigned his perspective.

Jesse thought about the great send-off Mom had orchestrated. A perfect meal, her best Maryland fried chicken, and somehow, because she knew how much he loved them, she'd wrangled up some Chesapeake Bay blue crabs, pretty expensive for the McGowan budget. Janine gave Jesse a small silver compass with the latitude and longitude for the State of Maryland engraved on it to remind him always of where "home" was. And Dad, well, Dad sat in the distance and watched the neighborhood kids and their parents wish his son well.

Mrs. Stone brought a big dish of macaroni and cheese after she'd borrowed two boxes of elbow macaroni from Mom. Jesse smiled to himself as he heard his mom talking to Janine in the kitchen while they were making preparations.

"Can you believe it?" she asked incredulously. "Borrowing from this house so she can bring a dish for us! If Russ wasn't in Vietnam, and she didn't have such a good heart, I'd give her a what for."

Janine giggled, knowing well her mother's frustration with Mrs. Stone. Soon both were laughing at the ridiculousness of it. Jesse ducked around the corner to avoid being pulled into the conversation, having a hard time not laughing out loud.

Paul and Linda, Jesse's friends from high school, stopped by to show everyone Linda's engagement ring. He thought of Cheryl again and wondered if there wasn't something he could do to make peace between them.

The Carsons dropped in to wish Jess well, as did the Dougherty family. As Bobby Dougherty was leaving, he pressed a rabbit's foot into Jesse's hand without a word spoken, just a smile of recognition between two friends sharing a secret.

Jess went to where his dad was sitting, "Come join the party?"

"No, no, son, this is your day. You enjoy it. I enjoy watching."

As Jesse left for Camp Lejeune the following day, it was his dad, with teary red eyes, who hugged him longest and strongest. He would never forget that hug.

All his life, Jess had done things to get his dad to be proud of him, but he sat in the shadow on the front porch step, or in the backyard absorbed in his own thoughts and memories. Jesse didn't know which. His dad drank too much and had his demons. Jess would try to get close and win his praise, but it felt as though he couldn't provide whatever it was his father needed.

Deep inside, Jess never felt smart enough, fast enough, or good enough to improve the relationship with his father. He wanted to give his dad the comfort he needed, and in so doing, provide what he needed himself. He longed to hear words from his father that would ease his doubts, smooth over his fears of self-worth. Words like, "Son, I'm proud of you, and I love you." But those words were never spoken. Jess exuded confidence and leadership to the outside world, but the doubts were there, hanging around the edges of who he was to himself. He joined the Marines not with misgivings about who he was, but with an awareness that some corrections needed to take place if his life was to go in the right direction. Without putting his finger on it, he was seeking affirmation of who he was as a man. Boot camp and the Corps gave him the strength and confidence he sought; he knew he could be counted on to do the right thing.

~~~

The stewardesses sent them off in Okinawa with words of, "Your connecting flight is Braniff Airlines. Your destination will be Da Nang, South Vietnam. Have a safe stay." *Weird .... This whole thing is weird .... It feels like I'm heading for a vacation instead of a war.* He boarded the connecting flight to Da Nang.

~~~

The notion of "vacation" was immediately dispelled as explosions from rocket attacks vibrated the aircraft during descent. He took deep breaths until the plane touched down on Vietnamese soil.

Nothing about this war was quite what it should be.

Stepping off the plane in Da Nang, he smelled the fresh air of the South China Sea, best known for China Beach and R&R, the Rest & Recreation retreat where dreams came true for many a GI. As he walked across the tarmac, Jesse's senses were assaulted by the smells of humanity; even in this heat, there was the smell of smoke from wood-burning fires cooking food.

He watched a helicopter land by a hospital. It was a Huey, a massive piece of machinery with a cockpit that was perhaps eight feet wide and six feet high. It had a commanding presence. The whop, whop, whop, of the blades never stopped as it landed, ready and prepared to lift off at a moment's notice. This airfield would likely be the place from which he would leave when his tour was complete. He guessed this would be the hospital they'd take him to if he ran into trouble. That was a sobering thought. Don't go any further, his mind warned.

He entered a tent smelling "American GI," a familiar mix of canvas and grease. It was controlled chaos with "boots" like himself, lined up. They were handed manila folders that contained orders, then told where to go next by Marines with clipboards.

They ordered Jess to 2nd Battalion, 9th Marines, or "2/9". He was to report to Phu Bai Marine Base, located a few miles from Hue. Scuttlebutt from the Marine giving him his orders was that 2/9 would head to an outpost called Con Thien sometime soon. He waited. Then he waited some more.

With no one directing him, Jesse pushed aside the flaps of the tent and stepped out to a bustling world. He saw wooden barracks, bars, more bars, tattoo parlors, supermarkets, bowling alleys, cinemas, shops, pagodas, shanties, and more bars. The kaleidoscope of color and movement and cacophony of sound overwhelmed the senses. The streets bustled with villagers, soldiers, monks, bicyclists, cars, trucks, pimps, prostitutes, peasants, and refugees pushing carts or carrying packs filled with belongings … a different world from Maryland.

So, this must be what Marines call "Dogpatch."

A Marine on the plane mentioned the population of Da Nang had exploded from 20,000 in the 1940s to 85,000, primarily due to the exodus of North Vietnamese refugees fleeing communism. Since Da Nang was the first major city in South Vietnam protected by the Americans, the refugees settled here. The population grew even larger as South Vietnamese were forced to leave their homes located in "free-fire zones," areas where everyone was considered the enemy, and anyone was a target.

Hello Vietnam. God, please keep me safe.

Hurry up and wait was the order of the day, and Jesse wondered about the Corporal who said, "I'll be back in a flash."

Jesse felt good about his assignment to the Ninth. Without a girl, Jesse used his free time during Basic to read about the military, the history of the Marines, and Vietnam. He remembered the 9th Marines distinguished themselves in World War II for valor against the Japanese in the Solomons, Guam, and Iwo Jima. He knew the 9th was stationed 1,500 miles away in Okinawa since the '50s and were the first conventional ground combat unit to arrive in Da Nang on March 8th, 1965, tasked to defend the Da Nang Station Hospital and airbase.

~~~

"Marine! You goin' to 2/9? Follow me!"

Jesse looked around and saw a Marine pointing at him and waving for him to follow to the waiting Huey, blades still spinning, dust blowing in all directions. Jesse grabbed his gear and ran after the Marine, ducking down as he stepped near its blades. His guide jumped into the hold of the Huey and turned toward Jesse, holding his hand out while still waving for him to hurry. He grabbed Jess's gear and tossed it into the chopper. Jess climbed in, and with one foot inside and the other still on the skid, the helicopter lifted off.

The Marine grabbed Jesse's arms and pulled him into the belly of the beast, where Jess was unceremoniously dropped into a jump seat. "Grab the straps and hold on!" he barely heard over the noise of the engines as the blades beat the air into submission.

In the blink of an eye, they were airborne, the swirling dust left behind, the ground rapidly disappearing. He was taken aback at the swiftness and smooth maneuverability of the "bird." He also had a death grip on the strap above him while the helicopter sped along, skimming the treetops.

Jess looked at the Marine who took him from the airfield. Grizzled was the only word to describe him. The Marine returned the look, smiled a tired smile, then shook his head slowly, almost imperceptibly. If Jesse could've read his mind, he would have heard, *Another FNG, wonder how long he'll last? Lambs to the slaughter.* Jess broke the stare to look at the other two Marines nearby. Door gunners, each secured with a safety harness to keep them inside, each held the handle of a mounted M-60 machine gun. A belt of ammunition was loaded, and the gunners watched the terrain underneath speed by, ready to return fire, or fire at targets as directed by the pilot.

Jess was still looking at the ground when the helicopter suddenly slowed. The nose pitched up, and he was pushed back into his jump seat. They landed. The ride to Phu Bai was over; his guide pulled him out of the jump seat by his arm. Jesse grabbed his gear and was led quickly out of the helicopter toward an area where other Marines were standing in a small group, other "boots," also trying to figure out what the hell was happening. "Stay here!" was all Jesse heard before his guide turned and ran back to the waiting chopper.

~~~

A Marine Corporal collected Jesse and the others and led them to a wooden building. As they entered, another Corporal yelled, "FNG's line up here!"

"What's an FNG, Corporal?"

"Fucking New Guy! Over here!"

They were given multiple forms to complete and stood in line for supplies. Jesse was told someone would take him to the 2/9. He was handed a rucksack filled with supplies he'd need, his "782 gear," and that was that.

As Jesse walked out of the tent, he searched for the Corporal assigned to transport him. Since he was in a wait situation with no meet and greet in sight, Jess decided to get acquainted with his supplies. He sat on his helmet and opened the green canvas flap of his rucksack.

He pulled out a blanket, poncho, one drab olive green towel, several pairs of socks, shaving kit, an entrenching tool, tent pegs, ridge pole, flashlight, compass, knife, canteens, mess kit, sandbag liners, Halazone pills to make water drinkable, salt, probably for the leeches Russ had written about, three packs of Marlboro, and one Zippo lighter.

Jesse was also issued a machete, a bayonet, and an M-16 rifle with several ammo magazines. He was told to expect mission-related weaponry, to include trip flares and wire, claymore mines, firing wire and blasting caps, as well as frag and smoke grenades when he got to his platoon. Additional pairs of boots and uniforms would come on an 'as needed' basis. A conglomerate of goods weighing somewhere between 60-80 pounds, including C-Rations, and a flak jacket. *So, this is the reason we're called grunts.* He began to repack.

"Hey man, let me give you a hand with that. I've got this down to a science, son. Name's Parker, John Parker, but my friends call me Beau."

"Thanks, man. I'm Jesse, Jesse McGowan."

And so it began.

TWENTY-ONE

GUNNER TAKE HEED

1966

Y ou're the new gunner, McGowan," the Lieutenant told him when Nudge, the previous gunner, was killed. Nudge was the nickname given for his shooting strategy. "A little nudge here, a little nudge there gets the bulls-eye," he said, explaining his incredible accuracy.

Everyone knew the M-60 machine gun's raw power was an accident waiting to happen if placed in inexperienced hands. It could accurately fire six hundred rounds a minute that traveled the length of twelve football fields in 1.3 seconds. Six-pound belts of ammunition, each containing 100 rounds, fed the machine gun. It was a good weapon but drew attention during a firefight. Nudge was almost sliced in half by an NVA gunner who was just a second faster on the draw. The M-60 reminded Jesse of a beautiful woman who required care and attention. She'd love you and make your life wonderful if you took care of her. Ignore her at your own peril.

Jesse had mixed feelings about being Gunner. He'd been in 'Nam for several months and felt honored for the responsibility and that his gun team played a vital role in warfare, but he was also legitimately concerned. The gunner, radio operator, and officers were often the first to be killed, and usually in that order. Taking out the gunner produced an instant reduction in firepower, which in turn, provided an immediate advantage for the enemy.

Besides the risk factor, there was a physical aspect. No part of him looked forward to carrying close to forty pounds of machine gun and ammo belts, adding to his already heavy rucksack. There was no refusal of duties. It wasn't like you could bow out with a polite "Thanks, but no thanks ...." Come hell or high water, it was part of the job, and he was selected because he was good at it.

~~~

"Hey Pard, at least you won't be using this lame-ass M-16. I'd give a lot to ditch this piece of shit and get the control you've got with that bad boy," Beau said, as he nodded at the M-60.

Both Beau and Jesse had served as part of Nudge's gun team, and Jesse was surprised Beau wasn't the assigned gunner and gun team leader.

"Thanks, man, I guess there's a silver lining to everything." Neither discussed the risk shadowing Jesse's new position. That wasn't what Marine's did. Beau was pointing out what Jesse needed to hear to allay his misgivings and accept his new responsibilities. Jesse's M-16 had jammed on him twice, and it was the most unnerving thing that could happen during a firefight. It was like driving on the beltway at rush hour, and your steering wheel comes off in your hands, you're at the mercy of God and fate, and once it happened ... you never felt safe again.

Jess had seen Marines cut down while trying to clean their M-16's, the cleaning rod pushed down the barrel to clear the jam and keep them in the fight. They looked like Revolutionary War soldiers reloading black powder rifles.

Almost 200 years later, the U.S. government issued inferior weapons for an undeclared war. A travesty Washington was slow to correct, and it was a source of bitterness. Grunts fumed at the situation and demanded to know, "Why the fuck can't we get weapons that work?"

The M-60 was one less fear to deal with. Jesse might not have much control in this foreign land, but the upgrade in weaponry sure leveled the playing field. He felt reassured, and Beau validated his feelings, and that made everything okay. Jesse would be a good gunner and like it.

"Don't slip on a banana peel after you start shootin' friend!" Beau jabbed, getting in the last word.

~~~

107

Jesse and his gun team distinguished themselves during a battle in May when they took action upon hearing mortars and AK-47's in the vicinity of a nearby Marine platoon.

Upon arriving, Jess saw Marines trapped by NVA fire. Almost single-handedly, he exacted severe damage by flanking the NVA and firing his machine-gun into two of the bunkers where they commanded the field of fire. The firefight raged for hours, and when the battle was done, members of his platoon commented that Jess had been everywhere. Jess felt good that the team was safe; no one was killed or wounded.

That evening, the squad sat together as they usually did, C-Rat's or cigarettes in hand. Angel pulled on his cigarette, and his eyes followed the curl of the blue-gray smoke. He took a few more drags, then snuffed it out with his fingers, thinking better of it with night fast approaching ... a cigarette could reveal their location.

Redd spoke first, "Man, Jess, today was something ... I mean REALLY something," all the while shaking his head back and forth.

"It was your day, bro, beginning to end. You were like a fucking superhero, here, there, and everywhere!"

Chingas laughed, "Dig it, man, you weren't the little engine that could, you were the engine that DID!!"

Soon they were recounting the events of the day, recalling a memory, adding a moment of importance, or recollecting a feeling at a specific time. In so doing, they blew a second life into the battle and processed with each other, recounting their coordinated strategies and maneuvers.

In this informal way, they learned how to support each other in future fights, but in this battle, they recognized it was what they'd trained for. All the blood, sweat, and tears spent in training paid off. They had successfully applied the knowledge and skills garnered to defeat a worthy opponent. Each had given their all for themselves and their brothers. They were not found wanting. It had culminated in a stunning, flawless operation. They knew they were a finely honed team.

Each man's mettle had been tested, and all proved worthy.

A Marine from the platoon walked by, "Shit Jess, you're the man today. Everyone's talking about you!" Another Marine from the group that was trapped sauntered over, a slight limp to his gait. He was older, and Chingas noticed a wedding band on his finger. While holding his dog tags to his chest, he squatted down and spoke with Jess, who was sitting on his helmet. "Jess, the boys, and I want to thank you and the team for the rescue today. We won't forget it." He patted Jesse's shoulder as he stood up.

Each Marine on the gun team assisted in the rescue, and everyone recognized who and what Jesse was to the day's outcome.

The gun team knew they had been part of a valiant effort all around and that Jesse had been a savior of sorts. To a man, they were proud of him.

"Here man, you deserve this," Chingas said, half in jest, half-serious, as he passed over his can of peaches to Jesse. Peaches held a five-star rating in C-Rations' hierarchy and were regarded as a culinary delight of "fine feasting."

"Thanks, man! I'll take it!" Jess said with a grin, holding the full can up, sending a toast to Chingas. Yes, it had been the day they'd trained for.

Before falling asleep that night, Jesse prayed, *What's done is done, but Father, please don't let the ghosts of all those I killed today crash into my dreams tonight.*

TWENTY-TWO

A DAY IN THE LIFE

1967

Action came fast for Jess and the gun team. The NVA had positioned artillery in the DMZ, just north of the Ben Hai River. The Hill of Angels was shelled daily, ripping to shreds all things animate and inanimate ... flesh, bone, earth, and rock. Artillery didn't choose, it hit everything. Con Thien had a bullseye painted on it.

Aim here, you sons of bitches. Yeah, right here, we're here, waiting to be killed!

The joke among these Marines was what to write when Mom or Dad asked, "How are you doing?" or "What's going on?"

How are we doing? Well, we're stuck in a meat grinder and scared shitless.

What's going on? Well, we're spending time in a barrel waiting for incoming rounds, so we can once again be scared shitless!

This might have been the honest reply written by every Marine at Con Thien, but family and friends wouldn't understand their horrific plight until they heard it on the evening news.

There is an adage that every nightmare ends with daylight. For Jesse and his squad, there was no daylight at Con Thien.

The Marines woke up shell-shocked from the previous night's rocket attacks. "Nowhere to run to, nowhere to hide," sang Martha and the Vandellas in America, but at Con Thien, it took on a whole new meaning.

They lived in the randomness of death. Life could be extinguished in less than a second, but how they lived and died, well, that was the story that would be remembered.

General Westmoreland mandated longer, more frequent patrols. Headquarters created strategic plans that increased the number of companies on patrol for extended periods, from days to weeks, to accommodate this missive. Each Marine understood what this meant, humping, always humping. More time in the bush equaled longer exposure to death or injury.

Resentment was fast becoming the order of the day.

~~~

The Spring of `67 found 2/9 on patrol outside Vietnam's ancient capital of Hue, searching for enemy troops, then doing time in the bush near Phu Bai, an area southeast of Leatherneck Square.

"Dammit, Gunny," Lieutenant Tom grumbled to the Staff Sergeant. "Pull out that map again." Gunny pulled the area map in its protective clear plastic case from his fatigue jacket. He'd marked their previous location on the plastic with a grease pencil.

Through sweat-filled eyes and the heat of a mind-numbing sun, he looked hard at where they'd been, compared to where they were. He sighed. The Lieutenant was correct. They'd traveled in a circle.

Anger mounted at the unrelenting wasted time Marines were forced to spend in the bush, dedicated targets wandering around in the enemy's backyard. Sitting ducks once again.

The men Jesse fought with showed courage, bravery, and valor at every turn. Jesse had come to the Corps alone but now belonged to this band of brothers. War was a proving ground where men learned to depend on one another, for without each other, they would die. In all their glorious imperfections, they held his life in their hands. Understanding that power, they came through time and again, not falling prey to fear but rising to the magnanimity of the human spirit.

~~~

Headquarters carried out General Westmoreland's orders with swift compliance. Too swift, it seemed to the grunts. Westmoreland was just a name, but HQ was real and easy to blame. Marines had hard feelings toward those who were "in the rear with the gear." Easy for them to send grunts on patrol, it wasn't them doing the dying.

Rear echelon Marines lived a relatively harm-free existence. The war was less real to HQ as they conducted business with a good cup of coffee and chowed down a hot breakfast. They shared beers at night while they watched television and read mail.

To the grunts, it seemed like it was easy for HQ to minimize the blood and guts of this war as staffers settled into a state of "comfortably numb." Staffer's rationale was that they were assigned to HQ through no fault of their own, but their conscience understood the truth. Some scuffed their boots to erase the look of the good life. Others failed "to see" the aging faces, vacant eyes, and broken bodies of their brothers in arms, who lived without the benefit of well-being.

Grunts were acutely aware of HQ's power over them when the basic comfort items like toilet paper, cigarettes, or toothpaste ran out, but when they were thirsty from lack of water or stomachs growled from inadequate food supplies, it was unconscionable.

"Bad enough we're forced to fuckin' hump the bush and wander through this infested countryside day after fucking day, but to send us out without enough fucking supplies, not even a decent can of food now and then, well that just ain't 'red, white and blue," Angel exploded, his last despicable can of Ham and Lima Beans held high.

Sure, HQ staffers and grunts served in the same war, but it was an entirely different experience for each.

~~~

The mosquitos, like the Cong, arrived in hordes, attacked at night, and craved blood. Night noises echoed of men snoring and smacking themselves. These drained Marines highly prized sleep, but sleep was a seductress who made promises she seldom kept.

"Nobody better ask me for blood when I'm back home," Beau grumbled, swatting hard at his haggard face, looking worn, dirty, and much older than his years. "This boy has already given." No one responded, each felt as miserable and cranky as Beau. They'd been on patrol just shy of two weeks and were lucky not to have met the enemy.

Neither the VC nor NVA were ever far off, but on this patrol, they were never close enough to generate a conflict. Fine by these grunts.

~~~

Because of the continuous shelling and ground attacks on Con Thien, and Gio Linh, a large offensive movement into DMZ was planned. The platoon leaders were briefed, and the Marines prepared to move out.

All had gone well for the grunts as they humped to the mobilization point. No disturbance or noise that would indicate an enemy presence. No smoke or smells of food, just the incessant hum of mosquitos.

Jolted into action by a massive rocket attack on Dong Ha, Marines knew they would be engaged in a battle of major proportions.

In mid-May, entire Marine Divisions were called to the area, along with soldiers from the Army of the Republic of Vietnam (ARVN), to launch Operation Hickory.

Jesse's gun-team, part of the 60-Marines that made up Hotel Company, moved toward a small hamlet identified on their map as Marketplace.

TWENTY-THREE

MARKETPLACE

Late May 1967

Marketplace was a mix of jungle, elephant grass, rice paddies, and hedgerows, some 10-feet tall that bordered Vietnamese homes.

Hotel approached a gutted Catholic church that provided shade, a sanctuary in every way. The coolness of its walls soothed the Marines' backs as they established bearings on reported enemy locations and developed a plan of attack. Open fields were visible beyond the church.

The calm was shattered by machine guns and rifle fire as an avalanche of NVA poured from bunkers, nooks, and spider holes. The area was infested with them, and they had the upper hand. The Marines had walked into a trap.

Redd sought cover near a row of trees. He saw a flash of movement at the edge of the clearing. The area was perfect for another ambush. He motioned to Jesse that he'd seen something and crouched lower as he moved in that direction. Alarmed, he saw a young Vietnamese boy walking toward him, crying.

The boy had stumbled into the ambush at the same time as the Marines. He was terrified, not knowing what to do or where to go. Cautiously, Redd crept closer, waved his arm, pointed to a bush, and hoped the boy would hide there.

"Tran," a woman called out.

The boy turned as the young woman appeared from the trees, motioning for him to return. She wore a blue short-sleeved cotton dress and a pink and yellow headscarf to keep her long billowing hair from her face. To Redd, she looked like a porcelain doll, with pink cheeks, and

114

red lips. He thought she was beautiful. Surprised that he'd captured so much detail as bullets whizzed past, Mike Redd regained his focus.

Bullets struck the ground around the boy, dirt thrown onto his body. He stood frozen, his eyes wide with fear, and Redd knew the child would be dead in seconds. He broke from cover and yelled to the woman, "Go back!"

As he sprinted, Redd focused on the boy, and without breaking stride, scooped him up and headed toward a ditch. He felt a white-hot heat explode in his shoulder and side and heard himself shout again, "Go back!" The words were prolonged, as though in slow-motion. His legs buckled as he dropped his M-16 to hold the boy in both arms. They fell into the ditch, and Redd covered the boy with his body. Blackness swept over him.

TWENTY-FOUR

THE MYSTIC MONK

1967

R egaining consciousness, Mike Redd became aware of a presence.

"What are you doing here?" the presence asked.

The head was clean-shaven, and he wore the orange garb of a Buddhist monk. In his hand, a strand of wooden beads, seeds from the Bodhi tree. Like a rosary, each bead touched meant a prayer for someone or something.

"Who are you?" Redd asked.

"I am a traveler in life, like you," was the reply.

Again, the monk asked, "What are you doing here?"

Redd studied his surroundings. In the distance shimmered a blue mountain capped with white. Green grass made a path that led to its base. He saw a river and bamboo trees, their delicate leaves bedazzled by the sun, and the sparkle from the water. It appeared as if the river ran through and beyond the monk. Redd saw buildings on the far side of the river and thought he recognized them. *Have I been here on a mission? Hue? Am I near the banks of the Perfume River? Why are my thoughts so unclear?* The smell of incense drifted past.

Redd was confused. He searched the gentle eyes of the monk, looking out from an expressionless face. He seemed harmless enough … no need for fear. This was a lovely spot, and Redd realized it had been too long since he'd relaxed.

"What are you doing here?" the query posed a third time.

116

Apparently, this was an important question, and Redd contemplated an answer. *What AM I doing here?*

"I don't know."

"Then, is it not time you seek to understand?"

Not wanting his peace interrupted further, he asked the monk pointedly, "What are YOU doing here?"

"I am seeking balance," said the monk, now looking very much like the Buddha to Redd. "What do YOU seek?" questioned the monk.

Redd stared into space, thinking about this second question ... *What DO I seek?*

He had never asked himself that question. He had always been too busy living life.

Redd watched cherry blossom petals fall slowly around them ... as if alive and seeking the perfect spot to rest for eternity. One petal landed softly on the monk's outstretched hand. He placed it carefully in the palm of Redd's hand as if there were no other place but that perfect spot, for that perfect petal.

Benevolently, he said, "You are like the petal, drifting in the wind. You are not long for this earth, soldier. Find yourself and the perfect spot to land. Plant your seed. Create a garden of happiness."

Redd looked deep into the monk's eyes, and they became the river. He heard a chuckle and noticed colorful squares of silk above him ... Buddhist prayer flags ... each disintegrated slowly into the fragrant air.

"A prayer is being made and delivered to the universe," thought Redd, somehow knowing the significance of those flags, wondering if perhaps the monk had said a prayer for him. He reached out to touch one before it disappeared, but instead of cloth, he felt a hand take his own in a gentle clasp .... Warm, soft. Redd opened his eyes and looked into the face of the Vietnamese woman he'd seen before being shot ... blue eyes ... deep blue ... the color of the Perfume River. *Such an unusual color for a*

Vietnamese. She was looking down at him, smiling, and had clasped his groping hand with her own.

"You have been dreaming. You've been shot through your shoulder and have a surface wound on your side. I have cleaned and dressed your wounds, and they are healing.

"You are in our home and safe. You have been here for two days.

"When the fighting stopped, and all the soldiers were gone, my grandfather and I pulled you from the ditch and brought you here in our cart.

"The National Police Force had ordered us to evacuate the area because a large battle was to begin. I returned to help my grandfather. We were late leaving because he had come from a nearby hamlet with our buffalo and cart. The fighting started when we were nearing Marketplace, so we hid in the woods.

"Tran saw a rabbit, ran after it, and found himself in the battle, and there you were, at the same moment to save him. Tran is my nephew and my sister's only child.

"You were wounded and lay in the ditch unconscious. We got Tran out from under you, but you were too heavy to pull into the cart with the NVA close by, so we covered you with branches and leaves, hoping the NVA wouldn't discover you, take you prisoner, or worse. A blessing must have found you. You stayed safe, and when they left, we hid you in our cart and brought you here to care for you. Thank you, soldier, for saving us.

"Because today is Buddha's birthday, there is no fighting. We're all safe. We're burning incense to celebrate the Buddha. I hope it does not bother you."

"Tran," she called, and the young boy who had been walking toward him during the battle appeared.

"Bring the willow bark tea and a cup of fish soup for our guest."

Tran shyly approached Redd, smiled a thank you, and then touched Redd's hand lightly to make sure he was real.

Redd opened his hand to the boy, and a cherry blossom petal fell to the floor. The young woman picked it up gently and examined it. She wondered where it came from since she'd washed Redd when he was brought to the hut and had washed his hands. There had been nothing in them. Besides, cherry blossoms were no longer in bloom. Strange.

Tran returned with soup and tea and she began to feed Redd.

"Sleep soldier," he heard her say. He closed his eyes, once again drifting in and out of consciousness.

He remembered his grandmother once made fish soup from the bluegill he and Jaybird caught while fishing on Macon's Ocmulgee River. They'd relaxed by the water, felt the warmth of the sun, and waited for a tug on the line. That trip was the closest thing to a vacation Mike Redd ever had.

~~~

A rooster crowed, waking him up. Redd's hand slowly traveled to his aching shoulder, then to his side, where he felt bandages. *Did I dream about the monk, or was he real? What did he say before he disappeared?*

Redd knew it was important to remember the monk's words, real or not. He sensed they were significant. In his mind, he heard the monk say something like, "Find yourself, soldier, and your own perfect balance. Your time is short. Find a place to land and plant your seed. Find happiness." A deep sleep washed over him again.

~~~

His dream was like no other he'd ever experienced, vivid, filled with memories, good and bad, of his life, all of it, recounted. He relived incidents he'd buried inside and forgotten until now; the night his mother had left them, the day teammates had berated him in the locker room because he'd selfishly taken the glory and failed to recognize their part in the win.

From his grandmother "Moms" beatings, coach's guidance, and the mentoring from Jaybird and Mrs. Hamilton, he'd learned. Not quickly at first, but steadily, he'd learned. He grew comfortable with the concepts

119

of discipline, practice, and attitude, and how each of these affected his chance of success.

He'd discovered the resolve to win was the primary force that resulted in winning. He learned a win could measure success, but also that winning was yours to claim when you gave all you had, regardless of the outcome. Redd learned he didn't walk this earth alone, and along the way, people were ready to help, especially if asked. He had come a long way since Macon, Georgia.

Slipping into his dream, his life played out and brought back his Mother, Father, Moms, brothers, Mrs. Hamilton, Jaybird, and Coach.

TWENTY-FIVE

A PLAN

1958

In his dream, he was again a young boy in the kitchen of MaeBelle and Jaybird Hamilton.

"Why you're skinny as a rail," Mrs. Hamilton said, looking him up and down, "When was the last time you ate a proper meal?"

"Well, Ma'am," Mike began, not knowing how to say a good meal in his house was a rare commodity. "Well, Ma'am," he stammered some more. "You see, my Moms doesn't have so much time to be cookin' for us. She's always busy takin' care of the folks on the street and doin' charitable type work for them. 'Sides, she knows me and my brothers can take care of ourselves."

He lied, knowing full well Moms' idea of a good meal was a slice of bread smeared with bacon fat, or on a better day, peanut butter sandwiches the boys made themselves. On very, very, good days, like Sundays, Moms would make grits. Not the golden cheesy kind he saw resting in a bowl a few feet away on the red Formica table, but plain grits, boiled in water, salted and peppered. As for helping people on the street, well, later, when he played this conversation over in his head, he'd laughed to himself. That had been a bold-faced lie! He didn't recall Moms ever helping anyone, quite the contrary. It was them that had gone to neighbors begging and asking for help.

Mrs. Hamilton studied Mike's face, and a soft smile formed. In her thick southern drawl, she said, "Young man, this is your lucky day! Jaybird says good things about you. Since Jaybird knows better than to lie to me and him bein' a good judge of character, I do believe you are a hard workin' young fella, pumpin' gas at his station, and lookin' out for our interests. Guess the only neighborly thing to do would be to look out for you in return. C'mon and have a seat."

"Yes, Ma'am!" he'd said with gusto, and with that, MaeBelle went to the kitchen cabinet and pulled out a plate. She heaped it with all the food Mike had taken in with his eyes, fried chicken, biscuits, mashed potatoes and gravy, grits, greens with bacon grease floating on top, and black-eyed peas swimming in butter. He sat where he was told, at the end of the table, on the chrome steel and vinyl-covered chair.

He knew he'd died and gone to heaven. He hadn't thought angels were plump white women with gray frizzy hair and smile wrinkles around their eyes, but he realized he'd been thinking wrong. He ate as if he was at God's table in the Kingdom of Heaven.

Then it happened.

MaeBelle turned on their television, and to Mike's unbelieving eyes, a colored man appeared, reporting on something that Mike couldn't make out, but it didn't matter. He could've been reporting about Martians landing on the backs of flying pigs. He was a colored man on television, reporting the news, speaking clearly and with authority.

Once, when they were in downtown Macon, he'd seen a TV through the doorway of a restaurant. On his street, folks didn't pay attention to much more than where the next meal was coming from. Now, in MaeBelle Hamilton's home, Mike stared transfixed at the colored man reporting news, and at that moment, he knew beyond a shadow of a doubt what his goal in life was. He wanted to be that man who spoke clearly and with authority. He took a chance and asked, "Mrs. Hamilton, Ma'am, if someone was wanting to be a reporter like him, how would they go about it?"

"You interested in becoming a reporter, Mr. Redd?" she asked, understanding the meaning behind his question.

"Yes, Ma'am," Mike confessed, allowing her to see the hunger in his soul through unashamed eyes.

"That man there is Mr. Bradley Rudolph, and he surely went to college to get where he is today. I already know you're a hard workin' boy, but are you smart and filled with ambition too?"

Mike thought for a moment and asked, "What's 'ambition' mean 'xactly, Mrs. Hamilton?"

"Well, Mr. Redd, for me, it means you want to be somebody successful, make a difference in the world, change lives, have some nice things for yourself, like maybe what you see in this house.

"It means to leave something behind for your kinfolk or for the world if your ambition is big enough. Jaybird had nothing when I met him, but he sure had ambition. That's why I chose him, so we put our heads together and made a plan, then we put our backs together and got that plan to work.

"Between his jobs and my cookin' at The Rooster, we got 'nuf money put together to buy that gas station. THAT'S ambition, Mike Redd. Do you have a fire in your belly like that too?"

"Yes, Ma'am, I sure do."

MaeBelle squinted hard at Mike and scrutinized him. He looked back at her unapologetic and eyes unwavering. Was she trying to see into the future like one of those gypsy women he'd heard of ... or maybe she had the power to see the man he would become ...? Either way, he continued to return her stare, resolute. Finally, she nodded, mind made up, also resolute.

"Your Principal, Mrs. Elvira Johnson, goes to the River of Life Baptist Church." Mike knew where it was, right next to the Sleepy Hollow Motel. "She sits two pews behind us. Want me to ask her to send help your way?" Mike was dumbstruck. Nobody in his whole life had ever offered to help him with anything, important or not.

"Yes, Ma'am, I sure would be grateful for that, Mrs. Hamilton." On that day, they struck a deal. Mike Redd's life would never be the same.

~~~

As he walked away from the Hamilton's white picket fenced home, he glanced at a reflection on the living room window of a house he was passing. He saw kids dancing on TV. He had heard there was a TV show somewhere up north that allowed kids, white and colored, to dance on the same dance floor while rock-and-roll singers performed.

Afraid to look too long to see if this was the show, him being a colored boy in a white neighborhood, he averted his eyes, put his head down, and walked home. His brain was reeling! What a day this was for a thirteen-year-old boy living in the slums of Georgia!

~~~

While lying in bed that evening, thinking over the events of the day, and still full of the best food he'd ever eaten, Mike put his hands behind his head and sank into thought. The material of his hand-me-down pillow was stained with grease from too many unwashed heads. The seams had come apart and had been re-stitched more than once by a novice hand, but one that was able to unite two pieces of ticking into a pillow once more. Oblivious to its greasy smell and deaf to the bickering of his twin brothers Hector and Achilles, or Moms yelling at his youngest brother, Messiah, he began to consider how to improve and what he knew needed work on.

Mike needed to figure a way to release the ever-present anger he carried in his heart, first against his father and now his mother, who had left a few months back. He had to harness these emotions and get them to submit. He needed to clear his heart and head and stay focused on the promise of a future.

What was important was that a colored reporter existed, and that Mrs. MaeBelle Hamilton had promised she would help him and get help from his Principal. The way he saw it, he was halfway there. The rest was up to him. Mr. and Mrs. Hamilton made their plan. Now it was time for him to make his.

He had a chance at being someone in the white man's world, and he would not allow anyone or anything to stop him. If one colored man had made it, made it outside the sports or entertainment arena, he could too.

Feeling more adult than child, he vowed several things that night. He would do anything necessary to get out of this shanty neighborhood. He would change the poverty thinking that rotted life in the colored world. It was the acceptance of that thinking that perpetuated misery and slavery of the soul. He would not be kept "in his place," and he would stay out of the welfare lines.

I will develop my inner strength. I will use this strength to become someone of value. I will not give in to the way of dependent life or be a slave to any master, and that includes doing drugs or alcohol, cheating, stealing, or being lazy. I will become a good man, and I will earn respect.

He wrote his plan on a scrap of paper, then carefully folded it, and pushed it under his mattress for safekeeping, to read over and over again. He walked into the bathroom, scrubbed the filthy toilet, then scrubbed himself. It all started now.

Mike went to church with Moms, occasionally. With her New Orleans roots, she believed in Catholicism and dabbled in Voodoo. Mike believed in only one God. That evening he prayed to God to help him on his journey and help him in his resolve. This day was the first day of Mike Redd's journey toward enlightenment.

Resolve, while growing up in Moms four-room shanty shared with Mike's three brothers, was no easy thing to sustain. Crowded, so crowded, especially later as the boys grew larger ....

Moms' tongue was always clicking, a habit of hers, and she muttered, devout muttering, usually directed at a population of Saints. It was her way of coping when life failed to go as she wanted. Sometimes the muttering was directed at the devil himself.

She cursed the devil about the "unholy foursome" as she called the boys, disparaging one or all four simultaneously with the foulest language. She asked the devil to curse them for acts they'd committed, real or not. The angrier she became, the louder the clicking.

From toddler to teenager, they accepted the accusations spewing from her mouth because it was her house. She held all the cards, and they were

125

kids with no money, no resources, and in time, no parents. They were powerless, except for their attitude.

And so, they lived together in a continuous cacophony ... arguing, yelling, sometimes laughing—the bumping and thumping of four boys.

From the house next door, mangy dogs barked endlessly. Their leash, clipped to a clothesline, determined the extent of their world, a path devoid of grass. They served as watchdogs, not pets. Overhead, crows cawed in continuous flight, as if they flew without feet, cursed never to land. Seldom did the boys hear a bird's sweet song.

The single tree in their yard was a gnarled thing, branches reaching for the sky as if pleading for something better. Few leaves bloomed, and no children graced it by climbing or swinging from tires on ropes. It was not a happy tree; it was not a happy place. People didn't live in this neighborhood; they were sentenced to it, some for life.

The boy's lives were a blur of motion ... shooting paper or small rubber balls into a box hung from a nail that once held a picture of flowers in a blue vase. Bought at the five and dime, it was Moms only touch of beauty. Paint on the walls had faded to a nondescript greige, but fortunately for the boys, the area behind, where the picture had been, remained a true pewter gray and now served as the backboard for their inside basketball games.

They wrestled, jumped, roughhoused, goosed, made farts with hands in their armpits, gave "wet willies," and were boys doing boy things ... feeling free.

Something green and black was always growing inside the toilet bowl, and now and then, little mushrooms sprouted around the base. The bathroom door remained shut. To leave it open would permit the stench to permeate every inch of their living space. Worse, it would force someone to clean it, an event that happened only around the holidays when one of the boys was desperate for money, and Moms was forced to dole out coins from her Mason jar for the deplorable job.

The bathroom stink mixed with the odor of four boys going through puberty on hot Georgia days was a ripe force not to be ignored. Each boy's first and only instruction on personal hygiene was invariably from a teacher who pulled him into the hall with an Old Spice deodorant stick discreetly in hand. "Go to the boy's room, wash your pits, rinse out the sink, then use this. Take it home with you, it's yours!" they would say.

After "the talk," there was more concern with hygiene for the boys, but when girls entered their lives, each brother became an expert in the art of cleanliness, fastidiously scrubbing not only their pits but private parts as well, using a communal rag, holier than Pope John, that was dubiously referred to as a washcloth. A liberal dousing of some cheap cologne completed this wash-down and promised the possibility of a trip to first base and maybe, just maybe, a home run.

True to her word, MaeBelle made sure that Principal Elvira Johnson helped Mike, and later both she and Mrs. Johnson kept their eyes out for opportunities, knowing him to be competent and likable.

Mike worked even more hours at the gas station, and his money went into a college fund set up for him by Mrs. Hamilton at the bank. Mike recognized she knew a lot about organizing finances and that she was a go-getter for a woman who came from little to nothing. She made things happen for herself and those she cared about. Never in his life did he imagine he would have a college fund, let alone go to college. It was becoming a reality.

He studied hard, often late into the night, because he knew the extra effort now would produce exponential gains in the future. At an early age, Mike Redd understood the concept of cause and effect.

As awareness grew, he saw how tempting the insidious shackles of enslavement were and the challenges he faced. He noticed that most colored folk fought each other for the scraps left to them from the white man's world.

The white man was privy to the finest cuts of meat; the colored man made chitlin's from its entrails and was happy for it. Most colored folk seemed to accept that it was good enough to live with less, perhaps never knowing better. They were grateful for the food stamps and government handouts. Grateful for the welfare lines ... the path of least resistance.

127

Mike came to understand the white man's world didn't concern itself with his or anyone's beginnings, but rather the ability to produce. The system would measure him against its white definition of success and then increase the ante because he was black. His performance would need to be better than the white man on either side of him, but now it was at least possible to compete.

Mike became discerning, realizing that thoughts, emotions, and behavior were the moving parts of the human triangle, to change one element led to a change in the other two. He chose thoughts that made him emotionally stronger, not "I can't," but instead, "It's possible if." He chose words carefully to precisely honor his thoughts and feelings. He refused to own Moms scorching words toward her grandsons because to do so would reduce him. He chose friends who were uplifting and involved in efforts that were positive for themselves and the community. He began to see that more was not necessarily better, only more, and realized the beauty of simplicity. To be strong within yourself, to stay in your truth, to be a humble servant, those were the things that gave him peace and reassurance.

In High School, Mike refined the goals he'd written at thirteen, realizing he had more work to do regarding the anger he still felt over his parents' choices. *I must not stay angry about things I have no control over. Anger is another form of enslavement. I must develop a genuine sense of gratitude for all that has come my way and not give power to ill will. Gratitude will strengthen my resolve and help me in my responsibility to my race and my country. I will look out for my family and remain a positive role model for my brothers and my children yet to be born.*

Again, he prayed for help from God.

~~~

Mike graduated with honors from high school with both an academic and athletic scholarship to the University of Georgia, sorry only that Mr. and Mrs. Hamilton were not present. His "Angel of Mercy" as he thought of Mrs. Hamilton, had suddenly passed just months before. Jaybird sold their business and moved back to his hometown of

Cleveland, where family remained. Elvira Johnson and Coach had hearty handshakes and hugs for him.

~~~

Two years later, while sitting in a college philosophy class, Mike learned no matter who he was in life, there would always be those greater and lesser than himself and that finding happiness within was the game changer and much more important than comparing himself to others. He came to understand that he could make plans and work toward goals, but in the end, all he could control was his attitude and how he reacted to the circumstances of life. Daily, Mike Redd made a conscious choice to be a man of integrity, knowing that worth and respect would follow.

He was on his way to making his dream a reality.

TWENTY-SIX

THE DREAM

1967

Mike continued to drift in and out of consciousness, aware of his aching shoulder and that he was burning up. His earlier life resurrected itself, and his dreams remained vivid. Perhaps the dreaming was part of the healing process he needed ... or would need .... He woke up long enough to wonder ... *Am I about to die?* He'd heard a person's life flashed before them just before death ... then he fell back into a sleep state.

~~~

The dreams suddenly morphed from memories into something bizarre and ominous. He felt immobilized by the sweat that encapsulated his body. He was being pulled into a dark underworld, real memories blending with the surreal fragments of truth that supported untruths and brought fear. Mike "told" himself to wake up, but like a sleepwalker unable to obey, he became the unwilling voyeur to his own twisted reality.

As the dream progressed, Mike stood within a grove of magnolia trees. Fireflies flickered here and there, and he stood alone in the jet-black night. Stars moved, swirled, and coalesced into a figure who tentatively descended toward him. Mike felt a primal fear but recognized something familiar about this apparition. He remained guarded. "It" came closer, cautiously ... no ... as if it sought permission ....

~~~

Big Redd, Mike's father, showed himself, but with downcast eyes as though ashamed, with little right to be in Mike's presence.

130

Seeing his father materialize brought memories fresh as rain ... explicit, detailed, intense. And against his will, Mike remembered. He remembered the smell of Big Redd; cologne doused over unwashed yesterdays ... his sniffling, scratching, and nodding out ... veins pulsing with heroin. Mike hated him for many reasons, but mostly because he'd gotten his mother addicted.

Big Redd's hand now rested on Mike's shoulder, a gesture long forgotten as hatred for this man had intensified with time and with his disappearance.

But then there were his eyes, smiling and emitting love even when glazed over, as they so often were.

Almost against his will, Mike was forced to remember Big Redd's kindness, taking Mike and his brothers for ice cream, even though the other boys weren't his, or letting Mike sit on his lap steering the car as they drove down country roads, and later, when Mike ran track, bringing him a stopwatch to measure time.

Tears welled up in Mike's eyes. It was seldom he'd received kind words in that world, and during those occasional kindnesses, Mike loved his father more than he'd hated him. His father ....

When he was around, Big Redd was restless and on the take. Veronica, Mike's mama, had followed in Big Redd's footsteps, each wanting something from the other, neither able to give, having so little in reserve. The kindness and caring they had, they held onto tightly, afraid they would be bereft and soulless, lost in darkness forever, if they gave that final bit of humanity away. Mike had instinctively known what those precious offerings of kindness had meant to his father while he lived in a life of defensiveness and hypervigilance. Mike realized now that Veronica and Big Redd never understood the law of reciprocity. They were too young to know that if they gave freely, they would recoup good things many times over, like compounding interest. Early on, their worlds were too hard, and their hearts too hardened to trust or surrender. Neither could trust themselves to the vulnerability that is love.

By seven, Mike learned what heroin was and that his mama and Big Redd used it. He watched as Big Redd took out a spoon and syringe from the faded black case he carried, pull his belt off and tie it around his mother's arm above the elbow. As Mike stood inside the bathroom, looking through the crack of its door, Mike smelled its foulness while he watched his father put the white powder in the spoon, cook it over a flame from his lighter, and draw the liquid into the syringe through a cotton swab. Big Redd injected the needle into Mike's mother's arm, then into his own. Their eyes rolled back as they lost contact with reality. Mike leaned over the dirty toilet and retched.

~~~

The vision that was Big Redd was translucent. He raised his eyes and looked squarely at his son.

"Boy," Big Redd began, "It wasn't that I didn't love you, I did. I couldn't love you the way you needed to be loved because I didn't love myself the way I should've. I was twisted by doubts that left me crippled inside. The drugs took me away from the pain of feeling lost.

"Your mama was a flower I didn't deserve. I know she loved me as good as she could, but I also know she thought I could get her out of Macon, away from Moms yelling and jealousy, claiming your mama was a beautiful package on the outside but plain, brown, and empty on the inside. Why would a mother say things like that to her daughter? Your mother was beautiful inside and out. I was unworthy of her and didn't believe in myself. Thought nothing good in life would come my way, and I figured anyone who loved me would end up just like me. A wasted piece of nothing' ... a shadow going nowhere.

"That's why I stayed away from you so much. The only good thing I did in my life was to marry your mama and give you a name. I figured I'd pull you down like I did with everyone I loved. I got locked up for shooting a man during a drug deal. He didn't die, but I might as well have killed him. It crippled him for life that shot did, and Moms wouldn't let anyone tell you they locked me up because she wanted to protect you. Yeah, I bet you're as surprised at hearing that as I was. Didn't expect Moms cared that much about anybody.

"When I got out of prison, the first thing I did was look you up. I watched you walking with your friends at the University, but I didn't have the guts to talk to you because I felt ashamed. I figured I had no draw on your time, that I had only been a bad father to you. So, I walked away, then did exactly what I promised myself I wouldn't do. I got back with my same drug-shootin' friends. I was comfortable with them. It's what I knew, Mike. I overdosed one night and passed, and as I was letting go, I realized there would never be another time to meet up with you. That was my greatest sorrow.

"I sure would've liked to have known you and seen you grow up, and I'm sorry I let you and your mama down. You both deserved better. Son, I hope you can forgive me somehow because I promise that forgiving me will make a difference to you. It will still make a difference for me too; we keep learning on the other side."

Before Mike could say a word, Big Redd vanished.

~~~

In true dream fashion, Mike's mama replaced the space occupied by Big Redd. There she was. Beautiful. Smiling.

Nature had both blessed and cursed Veronica Redd. Moms was a Creole who had loved a man Veronica knew nothing about. Try as she would, Veronica could not pry a word from her mother about who her father was, except that he was white. Once, she heard her mother mutter under her breath, "Just like all sons of bitchin' white men," when a car driven by a white man came close to the curb where Moms stood, splashing water on her skirt. She had no love for white men and had likely been treated less than well by Veronica's father.

Veronica's skin was the color of coffee, with plenty of creamer. She had soft amber eyes inherited by Mike. Her hair was wavy, and she was often told that she looked like a white actress named Natalie Wood. By age thirteen, males, not only from Macon but also from surrounding towns like Gray, Centreville, even Jeffersonville twenty miles away, knew of Veronica Redd's sultry beauty and were drawn to Live Oak Street like bears to honey. There was never a shortage of black Georgia boys around the run-down turquoise shack. She was pregnant by fourteen and had birthed Mike by fifteen. To Big Redd's credit, he married Veronica to give Mike a name and legitimacy, although Mike knew his father only as Big Redd, not Dad. Mike's brothers came into this world in quick succession, each from a different father.

~~~

One night, Veronica came to Mike, where he slept. She woke him with a kiss. "Wake up, Mikey. You gotta listen careful to me," she whispered hurriedly, afraid Moms, who was snoring in her bedroom, would catch her. "Mama's gettin' out of Macon tonight to make a fresh start with a new man, a man who loves me and will take care of us once we're settled. I'm losing myself here, honey. If mama don't go now, she'll die hungry in this little town. I's goin' to Atlanta to sing. I'll come back for y'all, I promise." She held him close. Then quietly slipped out the door.

~~~

Now in his dream, his mama reappeared in a sequined, coral gown smelling of vanilla. She sparkled like the Christmas gifts Mike had seen in expensive store windows. She put her face close to his and wrapped her arms around him. She smelled so good, and her skin was soft as velvet, "I'm here to get you, Mikey," she almost purred. "I'm a jazz singer in Paris, France, and I'm loved and respected there. I have a beautiful apartment for you and your brothers, and we can all live together … a happy family. Wait 'til you see the Eiffel Tower, honey, and eat whipped cream on your pancakes." She began to float off. Looking back, and with her hand outreached, she grasped Mike's hand and continued her conversation. "In case we get separated darlin', I sing on St. Germaine Street. They call me 'Chantilly,' it means 'whipped cream' in French. Come on with me now, darlin'," and she continued to float off, becoming a thin mist of coral, leaving behind the scent of vanilla, but continuing to hold his hand in hers, warm and soft, not letting go. He'd tried to hold on too, oh how he tried. He tried to fly off with her like Wendy flew after Peter Pan, but like Big Redd, she was gone …. "Mama, mama," he woke up to the sound of his voice crying out for her, still smelling her scent in the back of his throat.

Redd laid back, tired, clear on the details of his life. They were the poorest family on Live Oak Street, and Live Oak was the ghetto of Macon. His family members seemed crippled by circumstance or opportunity, ill-equipped to pull themselves out from their poverty. Mike remembered his family having to beg for food. He remembered Moms yelling at his mother, "Veronica, you'd better stay away from that 'her-o-ine,'" as she pronounced it … Heroin with a long "i" sound. "That heroin be the death of you, girl! Stay away from Big Redd, he gonna do you in with that shit. You hear me, girl? And I ain't raising no mo' chillun, I done raised mines and musta done a piss poor job, what with you using that shit. Ain't raisin' yours too!"

Coming up, how often had Mike heard that conversation. But, like so many grandmothers of that time, Moms did raise Mike and his brothers.

With mama and her male friends gone, life for Mike and his brothers settled in, after a fashion. The neighbors seemed friendlier, and they'd sometimes bring over barbequed ribs or sticky buns or leave greens covered with waxed paper on the porch "for the growing boys." Mike guessed they were glad the yelling and fighting between his mama and Moms had stopped, maybe they were happy to be helping the four brothers living in the shanty. In any event, Live Oak Street got a little calmer.

His uncle Robert got Mike the job at Jaybirds. Mike walked a couple of miles to the station and worked late to make money. In his spare time, he worked a deal with the nearby grocery store manager to carry customer's bags to their cars. Any tips they might give were his to keep. He'd get a quarter, and sometimes fifty cents if the load was large. Once a fat cat from Atlanta, breezing through, handed Mike a dollar. Mike asked him if he'd heard of a singer named Veronica Redd in Atlanta, but the man shook his head. "No."

His side jobs helped Moms put food on the table, and the rest went into the bank account MaeBelle had established for him. Messiah held his own academically, and Achilles and Hector were scoring big points on the football field. His teachers liked Mike because he produced and showed responsibility. Mrs. Fitzsimmons, his 9th grade English teacher, diligently helped him with his writing skills, sometimes even staying after school to tutor him. MaeBelle, true to her word, had kept all her promises and was always there to help.

~~~

He remembered them all. He wondered if the monk had anything to do with this second dream.

Clearheaded and awake now, Redd created a list once again ... a mental one this time, as in this little Vietnamese shanty, there surely would be no paper or pencil. *How do I always end up in shanties?* He smiled, feeling right at home.

In his mind, he wrote a plan to find the balance the monk spoke of.

Item 1. Write mama a letter and give her the words she so desperately needs to hear, words that will give her strength. Let her know she is a good woman and that I forgive her for leaving us. Tell her I understand what made her seek a better life, that I understand her need to fulfill her soul. If she's still using drugs, convince her she doesn't need them to deal with the world, she's strong enough to deal with life on her own terms. Promise her I will always be there to help her, that she's not in this world alone.

Plan: Ask Uncle Robert to find her wherever she is, and if possible, deliver my letter personally.

Item 2. Get back to school and finish my degree. Become the journalist I want to become. Make a difference.

Plan: Go to the local VA stateside and find out how to apply for the G.I. Bill within one week of returning to "The World."

Item 3. Forgive Big Redd.

Plan: Forgive, pray for guidance on forgiveness, and seek the wisdom of forgiveness.

Item 4. If she will have me, ask this beautiful Vietnamese woman to marry me. She has risked her life to get me to safety and then cared for me. She is the one. In my bones and my heart, I know she is the one.

Plan: …?

For this, Redd had no answer, but he was sure it would come. He just needed time. Somehow, he knew they found each other, the circumstances around their meeting seemed almost prearranged … the monk? Sow my seed. Find happiness. Yes, maybe the monk! He instinctively knew they were part of something bigger; she was part of his destiny. Mike knew he would love her; he already did. He knew she would love him because he would be a good man to her. He would tell her of his desire to be a good man, a good father, and a role model for the children they would have. Those were the things he'd promised himself on his day of enlightenment in Macon. This was the goal he had written on that scrap of paper, probably still tucked under the mattress in Georgia.

And then a plan came to him ….

Plan: Be kind, be gentle, and listen, really listen to her story. Take care of her needs.

He would find a place for the two of them, as the monk had instructed. He would sow his seed with gratitude and love.

TWENTY-SEVEN

THE WILL TO WIN

1967

Jesse and Chingas watched Redd run toward the child and grab him, stumble forward and dive into a ditch at the edge of the clearing. Too late, they realized they'd walked into an ambush, maybe what Redd was trying to signal to them.

The grounds around the Catholic Church were swollen with NVA troops, the air thick with bullets from their AK-47's.

"Put grenades into the back of those bunkers hidden at two o'clock! Fire's coming from them!" shouted the Lieutenant to two Marines with grenade launchers who quickly went to work on the bunkers, leaving only silence afterward.

Jesse saw several NVA troops moving between trees and bush to the church's left beyond the clearing, where Redd went down. *Where was Redd, and where the hell was Beau?* Beau usually fed the ammunition for Jesse's M-60, but he'd disappeared like Redd. Chingas had taken over for Beau, and they fell into the routine they'd developed and relied on.

Jesse set the barrel of the M-60 onto its bipod, and Chingas began feeding the ammo. Angel appeared out of the smoke with two new belts of 7.62mm full metal jacket rounds. The weapon of war reverberated in Jesse's hands and the machine gun opened its symphony of death, a staccato familiar to any who fought.

Jesse took in every color, movement, and sound, his hearing sensitized, his sense of smell heightened, his pupils dilated. Adrenaline pumped through his body, easy to pay attention when any second could be your last. He scanned the area for the enemy and Beau with a single sweep.

He spotted Beau trapped in the crossfire between the church and woods. *Shit.* Beau was a sitting duck and likely to become a dead duck if fortune didn't smile on him, and fast!

"I'm going for Beau!" he yelled at Chingas and Angel.

Jesse stood up with the M-60 and ran toward Beau. Firing in bursts, Jesse picked his targets carefully while the ammo belt draped over his arm became shorter and shorter. Beau spotted Jesse and ran toward him. He wore ammo belts for the M-60 across his chest and felt their weight while zigzagging from the bullet with his name on it. Beau's size-13 boots were kicking up dirt when he heard American voices yelling, "Here, over here!"

Beau recalled his DI saying, "Death smiles at everyone, and Marines smile back," followed by a loud "Gung Ho!"

Beau smiled, "Gung Ho," he shouted as he turned toward the Marines that yelled for him.

Beau's battle-cry was answered as Jesse ran past yelling, "Gung Ho, let's get them outta here!"

They ran toward a berm where the Marines had clustered to return fire.

The taste of pennies in Jesse's mouth told him he'd been scared as he and Beau found cover. *Where was the Lieutenant or the radio operator?*

Crouched near a tree with the radio beside him, the Lieutenant shouted into the radio mouthpiece, "I'm telling you this place is crawling with NVA. They must be twenty deep. We need reinforcements before we're all dead. Hotel to HQ, do you read? Do you read?"

"Estimate of enemy numbers?"

"Too many!" was the Lieutenant's curt reply.

A pause at the other end, then hearing the desperation in the Lieutenant's voice, the Marine on the other end said what the Lieutenant needed to hear.

"Sending Echo Company. Hold On."

~~~

"Corpsman!" Chingas yelled, trying to get help for Redd, whose body had fallen into the ditch while rescuing a small boy. Redd's location was becoming more obscured with smoke from the battle and smoke grenades used to conceal movement.

Chingas saw the corpsman in a thicket tying off the bloody stump that used to be an arm of a Marine. There went the morphine shot to ease the pain.

"Get to Redd," Chingas shouted to the corpsman, but there were too many nearby needing help and the bullets too thick to move. Frustrated, Chingas realized Redd was on his own when suddenly, an NVA soldier was upon him, a bayonet poised like a deadly spike against a blue sky.

The bayonet plunged downward as Chingas swung the barrel of his M-16 toward the attacker's head and pulled the trigger. Bullets jerked the soldier's head to the side as they all but severed it from his shoulders. Like a grotesque and bleeding rag doll, the soldier collapsed on top of Chingas, blood spurting from the neck and chest, soaking Chingas' flak jacket and shirt. The blood ran down his face and neck and stank of iron.

Chingas rolled the body off, grabbed his canteen, and poured water over his head, wiping off blood, flesh, and brain. He laid back, stared at the blue sky and white clouds, then began to shake. *Move! Move now! Get back into the fight before you die lying here.* He was trained to kill, and while his skills were sharp at long-range, this was different. It was personal. Close. This wasn't an "enemy soldier," but a man whose life he'd taken. Chingas put an end to this moral discourse to preserve his sanity. He looked at the soldier lying next to him in a pool of blood and yelled, "Fuck You!"

~~~

As suddenly as it started, it stopped. Night approached, and the NVA were strangely quiet. Second Battalion/Ninth Marines sent out scouts to patrol and gather intelligence. They reported that the NVA had retreated, and it was decided not to pursue the enemy. There was no sense in risking men to booby-traps or ambush. Command ordered a security perimeter while the dead and wounded were evacuated.

Jesse and the gun team hustled back to the clearing to look for Redd.

They found the ditch, but nothing more. No Redd. They asked if any corpsman had treated him, placed him on an evacuation chopper, or, worse, tagged him KIA, "Killed in action."

No one knew. There was a strong possibility that the NVA had captured Mike Redd, and the gun team was sick about it.

~~~

A soft rain fell as Chingas and Angel shielded their Marlboro's with cupped hands to light up. The four had searched beyond the field and into the trees, beyond what was safe, with no sign of Redd. No one spoke. Each reflected on their unspoken oath of "No Man Left Behind."

Feeling numb, Jesse sat and stared at two C-Rats cans of Ham and Lima Beans, lids open, catching raindrops. Some grunt evidently couldn't stomach the first can and must've hoped the second would taste better, a "green grunt," for sure. Jesse smiled. Didn't know yet that shit is still shit. The cans reminded him of two children standing on a sidewalk, mouths open to the rain. Did children throughout the world catch raindrops in their mouths? He guessed so. Were we so different? Was not the sound of a child's laughter the same everywhere? And even with the differences, were we not more alike than different? Would we never get along? Learn to play together?

He watched the raindrops splash on a stone. Each produced a perfect crown, adorned with sparkling round beads that soared upwards, glistening and refracting colors of light. They were tiny creations of perfect beauty offered by nature for eyes that took the time to see and appreciate.

He'd heard that the water on our planet was the same water since the beginning of time, only recycled. Was the rain on his face the same that ran down the nose of a Tyrannosaurus Rex? A caveman? A king? A mutant? Was water the unifying experience between man and nature? Was it the ultimate unifier of all life? He'd allowed his mind to drift with random thoughts. It eased him.

It had been a horrific battle. He felt drained. How many lives had he taken today? Hungry, he began digging in his rucksack for his own C-Rats. He found two. Ham and Lima Beans and Ham and Lima Beans. Dog food must be better than this, he thought, now searching for the piece of ham that was in every can. No one wanted the Ham and Lima Beans, and for good reason. One of "the brothers" said it was the closest thing to chitlins a white boy could eat, and everyone knew what chitlins were. Shit in a skin.

Where's Redd? We'll look again in the morning. No brother left behind.

Well, there's that piece of ham after all. Eat it before all the flavor gets washed away. Jess knew this can of food would cause gas, foul even by 'Nam standards. But he needed nutrition. He heard a blowout nearby and smiled. *Everyone must be in the same bad spot, saving the worst for last.*

Again, the face of the battle showed itself, as memories encroached upon him. He had been reloading the M-60 when he saw the soldier charging at Chingas with a bayonet. Just as quickly, Chingas had raised his M-16 to fire into the head of the attacker. The bullets entered the soldier's neck and had blown out the back of his skull.

He'd fallen, collapsing on Chingas, head jerking sideways, as though surprised.

When the fighting stopped, and bodies were collected, Jesse had walked past where he lay, a young kid, mused Jess, maybe sixteen or seventeen. Small, delicately framed, about half the size of a big Marine but a killing machine, nonetheless. Fearless, Jess thought begrudgingly, always so fearless. They commanded respect. The eyes remained open and looked upward, maybe to heaven. Brown eyes. Soft. His face looked like he might be awake and able to return home to his mom and dad, more grateful for them than any day in his life.

This warrior had been reduced to a crumpled sack when Chingas had pushed him off. The uniform which camouflaged him in life had continued to serve its purpose in death. He'd blended with the earth of Vietnam and was already becoming an indistinguishable part of nature.

Jesse gripped his M-60 tighter and walked on, not looking back. He'd heard a battle-tested Gunny Sergeant once say he could kill the enemy as easily as he could eat a steak.

~~~

The day ended with Death, the winner, retrieving extensive spoils from both sides. Its smell hung heavy in the air and would creep into nightmares years later.

Jesse looked for Chingas to check on him ....

TWENTY-EIGHT

CONTENTMENT

1967

Full lips pursed together. "Tweet, my name is Tweet," she replied to Mike Redd's question.

She knelt beside him, having removed the dressing from his shoulder; her hands skillfully touched the flesh around the wound, examining for infection. Upon completion, she tapped his other shoulder.

"Why did you do that?" Mike asked.

She lowered her eyes, embarrassed, and replied, "It is a superstition in my culture. We believe a genie resides on each of our shoulders, and if I touch one shoulder, then the other shoulder must be touched as well, to keep us balanced. Much like you Americans sometimes believe you have a devil and an angel on yours, a good spirit, and a bad spirit vying for your conscience. I suppose for both our cultures, it represents the duality of life."

"Yes, I see," he said, moving to get comfortable. Mike propped his pillow against the wall of the hutch. He rested on a thin mattress, chest bare. Although outwardly nothing but methodical, Tweet was not oblivious to his muscled torso or warm amber eyes. She looked away.

"Tweet? That's an unusual name. Is it Vietnamese?"

Her high spirits transcended her modesty, and she grinned.

"Oh yes, my name is Vietnamese. It's spelled T H U Y and pronounced 'Tuwee,' but you Americans have changed it to satisfy your discomfort with an unfamiliar name. So, you call me Tweet. You have Americanized me in a way."

144

She saw a look of confusion in Mike's eyes, followed by a glimmer of defensiveness. Not wanting to offend the man who saved her nephew Tran, she bowed her head slightly and added, "Don't get me wrong, soldier, I don't mind, really. I think it's what you Americans do well. You homogenize the world to meet your need for the familiar, take what's different, shape it to be like you, then own it. You are like the wind that shapes all it touches but never sees a need to change itself, even after all things are worn to sand. The world yields to power; it's been that way since the beginning of time. The strong survive, and the weak learn to change or die," she said philosophically.

As though he was a confidant, she continued, "You are the power at this moment, so I forgive America and will let you call me Tweet." Then with a twinkle in her eye, she said, "At least you don't practice 'Jus Primae Noctis,' the 'right of the first night,' allowing a nobleman to take the virginity of the brides of the enemy." She patted his arm in a motherly way. "The willow bark has worked well to soothe you, and your body heals."

Many thoughts flooded Mike's brain as he listened to her, looked at her. *Who was she?* She was unlike any Vietnamese woman he had known regarding looks. Today she wore a flowing light blue top with a yellow bandanna tied around her neck, Girl Scout style, and black pants. Sporting a pert ponytail, she blew bangs from her face while casually mentioning "Jus Primae Noctis," as though it was an everyday conversation in sunny Vietnam.

Wow, she's something. Why pigeonhole her by saying she's unlike any Vietnamese woman I've known? She's unlike ANY woman I've ever known, especially her knowledge. She's confident, skilled, and competent. She's special alright.

Mike wondered how she'd learned to speak English so well and how she'd learned about these things.

Tweet moved to get up.

145

"Wait, where did you learn English, and how do you know about 'Jus Primae Noctis?'" Redd's hand rested lightly on her arm, detaining her. She looked at the hand on her arm, then at him. Her features softened.

"The teacher in our village was a Jesuit priest. He taught us numbers, biology, and physical sciences like geology, but we also learned of logic, and abstract thinking, history, and cultures of the world. We learned to speak Latin because it is the root of many languages, and we learned to speak French and English. French because it's the second language spoken in Vietnam and English because it's the language of those who rule the world."

With a playful smile, Mike said, "Sit with me a moment, please, and tell me about yourself, after all, you saved my life. I've read that in some parts of the world, I am beholden to you and am required to stay with you until that debt is repaid." His smile broadened.

Fascinated with her, Mike drew on every bit of charm he could muster. With an exaggerated lowering of his voice, he slipped into his best southern drawl and began to sweet talk Tweet.

"That said, I think I have a right to know more about my savior so I can get out of debt sooner rather than later, or does my savior want me to stay and be beholden?"

Tweet laughed at his bravado and felt herself blush. It felt like something was happening between them.

"You have no rights here Marine, and no obligations. And stop calling me your savior," she chided, laughing more. "Papasan and Tran are working in the rice paddies today, and they'll be hungry when they return this evening. I have cooking to do, but I will tell you some things about myself because I choose to."

The nineteen-year-old paused, then shyly asked, "What is your name?"

"My name is Mike, but many of the men in my company call me Redd. It's my last name. Sometimes they call me other things too, but that's for another day, and I don't know you well enough yet to say those names out loud!" Tweet knew precisely what he meant as they laughed together.

"Well, let's see," she began. "I was raised in a village a few miles south of Da Nang. I work at the Da Nang Station Hospital and rent a small room in what you Americans call Dog Patch. My sister lives here but is also trying to get employment in Da Nang at the Military Exchange, where the pay is good. She was there for an interview when she heard bombing was expected here at Papasan's home and that an evacuation of the area had been ordered.

"To ensure my sister, Thanh, could have her interview, I came home to help Papasan and her son Tran to evacuate. Papasan is my grandfather, and we were leaving when caught in the crossfire at Marketplace.

"We knew returning to this hamlet with an American Marine was risky for us, and to you, Mike, but it was a risk we had to take. You saved Tran's life, and for that, we would have done anything to keep you safe. It is we who owe you, Mike Redd! We've kept your presence from those few villagers who haven't left the hamlet and prayed the Cong would not come here while you were healing."

Tweet spoke about her younger brother Bao, who'd joined the ARVN when the fighting between the North and South began. From their Jesuit teacher, Father Joseph, Bao, Tweet, and her older sister, Thanh, learned that democracy was the only road to their country's ultimate freedom and that communism would crush them all. So Bao had enlisted. He was a scout working with the American Army when he was killed during a mission near Pleiku.

"Fighting broke out near here a few months ago, and American planes dropped napalm. The planes accidentally dropped napalm on my parents and other Vietnamese civilians seeking sanctuary in the foliage nearby. They were killed."

Two more names to the already incomprehensible number of civilian casualties, each with a family to mourn their loss, Mike thought.

"Seeing money was needed, I traveled to Da Nang and secured a job at the hospital. I sent money to Papasan. That little bit, coupled with the meager food they could still harvest, was enough for them to survive.

"Thanh hasn't heard from her husband in two years. He followed his beliefs and joined the NVA, who, as you know, patrol and fight you Americans mostly by day. Very different from the Cong, who are amiable peasants by day, smiling and pretending to be your friend. But who, at night, attack you or go to our villages singing songs of heroism and proclaiming praise for the doctrines of Ho Chi Minh; Uncle Ho, as they lovingly call him. Hidden by darkness, they enter our villages and hamlets. Many have family members here. They seek help from us with food or military information. They ceaselessly attempt to gain our allegiance to either serve or fight for their cause.

"Yes Mike, for us it's a Civil War much like yours was, with families, even husbands and wives, divided in their allegiance, fighting against each other, and the world fighting against us, dropping bombs, napalm, shooting artillery, killing those we love. We are afire everywhere," Tweet said somberly.

"Also, in a different way, religion is a conflict for us. My father and Papasan practiced Catholicism, but my mother was a Buddhist. She married my father against her family's wishes, unheard of in their village. He was Catholic and below her social status. Also, their birth years were not compatible; she born in the year of the Tiger and he the year of the Horse. It was believed misfortune would befall both sides of the family with this marriage. But they loved.

"She was cast out by her parents for marrying my father. These are the old ways of those in my country. People living in the city are more progressive, but many, including those in the city, still hold to the old ways of prearranged marriage. We Vietnamese are very superstitious, and our lives are dictated by old customs even as we live in a modern world," she finished with a sigh.

"We have lost much to this war." Tweet looked at Mike sadly.

A simple but accurate validation.

148

Mike's bravado melted, as did his heart for this young woman who'd endured so much. Her story was one of hardship and loss, much like his own. The will to carry on is sometimes all we have, he thought. As tears rolled down her cheeks, Mike found his arms encircling her, trying to offer comfort.

She did not resist his kindness, his tenderness. He stroked her hair and spoke the words she needed to hear, "I'm sorry."

Tweet's words moved him, and Mike found himself wanting to protect this unusual woman who had experienced so much pain. She felt like someone he'd known all his life. In turn, Mike's warmth and empathy touched Tweet. She had not been held or touched since her parent's death, and she'd felt lost and alone.

His kindness allowed her to trust. She felt safe with him, safe enough to show her true feelings. She sobbed quietly.

"I miss my parents and brother so much. I see what no one should see at the hospital. We have so little to eat. Sometimes I don't even recognize the land beyond my village. It has changed so much from this war. There is no beauty for me anymore," she sobbed harder.

In soothing her, their lips met. Two strangers, a wounded man and an orphaned woman-child clung to each other. They allowed themselves the comfort and warmth of touch, and then, a surprise to both, their kisses turned to passion. They made love.

By trusting each other, they found a home for their needs, knowing well that mortality was fleeting, and the word "tomorrow" was not guaranteed. In the quiet aftermath, they recognized a most beautiful thing, the capacity of another for kindness and compassion could be absolute. They remained in each other's arms, not wishing to separate, not wishing the reality of the outside world to intrude. Miraculously, each found protection and love amid chaos and war.

TWENTY-NINE

HOME AWAY FROM HOME

1967

As Mike's wound's continued to heal, his mobility increased. Not yet well enough to survive travel in a cart, he remained with Tweet and learned about the Vietnamese culture and way of life.

He learned the interiors of Vietnamese homes were much the same. Near the entrance stood a table of worship. Family members, alive or dead, were remembered with incense, candles, and a statue of Buddha or the Saints, depending on their religion. Tweet's table displayed one small Buddha, a golden container burning incense, a white candle, photographs, AND statues of Saints, a true amalgamation of the husband and wife who, until not long ago, were alive in this home.

The right side of the house entertained guests and had rooms where the men slept. The left side was for the women. The kitchen was the center of the home and the heart of the family. The entire house was built of bamboo, wood, and mud. Papasan's roof, corrugated metal, was an improvement from most dwellings which typically used thatch. In this hamlet, all homes were built on stilts to avoid the monsoon floodwaters.

This house faced crop fields rather than the visible mountain peaks of Con Thien. Mike found this odd as a view of the mountains would have been more valued in the States.

"We believe that peaks, shaped like arrows, have the potential to injure or harm residents in their vicinity," Tweet explained. She added, "We associate the trees with beasts, and our culture believes beasts bring bad luck to animals and livestock near our home."

150

She looked around and seeing no one, took his hand and led him out the front door. "We paint the outside of our door red to ward off evil spirits. The mirror hanging from it will safeguard us from marauding dragons with evil intent. If they come to our door, they will see their reflection and believe a dragon already occupies this home. They will leave in search of another home to trouble." She laughed.

"Do you really believe that?" Mike asked.

"Well, of course, I do! We've never had a dragon here! Not once!" She put her hands on her cheeks and laughed a little harder, her eyes daring him to challenge this. When he shook his head and said, "No more," she pointed to the rice paddy nearby.

"What do you see?"

"I see a pole in the paddy."

With lifted eyebrows and a daredevil look, she stated matter-of-factly, "That's my 'spirit pole' stuck in the water, also meant for protection."

Mike chuckled, pulling her close to him, "I get this Tweet, and it's working!"

Looking into each other's eyes, they both laughed.

"And I'm grateful for it," he said huskily.

He looked softly at her upturned face, eyes closed and lips in a pucker, like a little bird waiting for food from its mother. *How lucky am I?* He leaned forward and kissed her waiting mouth.

Mike learned it was taboo to touch anyone on the top of their head, as the Vietnamese believed this to be where the individual's spirit lives.

"Many still believe that to do this is an insult to the person and their ancestors," Tweet explained.

He learned that the genie of marriage, somewhat like "Cupid," had a name. "It's the 'Rose Silk Thread God,' not a 'great God,' a 'smaller God,' whose protection and help must be requested as part of any wedding ceremony."

151

The superstition Mike liked the best, perhaps because it was so visual and sweet-natured, was the practice of dripping dew from a sweet-smelling flower into the mouth of a baby. Doing this would ensure a sweet speaking person.

They were standing together looking out toward Tweet's paddy, Mike's arms encircling her from behind, their hands locked.

As Tweet explained, she leaned into him, and he couldn't stop himself from whispering into her ear.

"In the South, we grow a sweet-smelling flower called Jasmine. I will plant a vine by our window on the first day we get our own home in America. Can we go out in the morning when the dew is still on the Jasmine and drip it in the mouth of our firstborn?"

Tweet turned to face Mike. She looked into his eyes and whispered, "Yes."

He took her inside, and they laid together. The ache from his wounds was nothing compared to the ache he felt now. So, this was love. He kissed Tweet hard, taking in her mouth, cupping her breasts with his hands, then pushing himself deeper inside her body. It was like being a god while inside her. He knew Heaven while holding her after, and they lost themselves in each other.

~~~

They heard the voices of Papasan, Tran, and his young friend, returning from the rice paddies after the day's work. Tweet jumped up, hurriedly dressed, and went to the kitchen. Mike straightened out his freshly washed uniform and tried hard to hide the look of satisfaction and contentment on his face.

THIRTY

RETURN TO MADNESS

1967

Papasan and Tran walked to the hut, while Tran's friend continued to his family. They were one of the few 1,200 Vietnamese who had not evacuated. With Papasan and Tran working in the fields, Mike and Tweet were given a pause in time to share gentle days, to fall deeper in love. A moment granted. The soothing solitude, broken only by the sound of rustling bamboo trees, created a spell of sorts. They pretended to be the only people in the world, and it soothed their souls.

Today, watching Papasan and Tran approach, Mike's instincts went on alert. Something was wrong. Agitation existed between them.

Like most children of addicted parents, Mike was intuitive and hypervigilant. It was a way of coping and necessary for survival when sharing a home with a mother and father involved in drug abuse. He was good at reading others and paid attention to body language, tone, and affect.

Vigilance included familiarity with the rituals involving "the habit." A door locked when it was usually open, a blind drawn, a candle burning. While living in the addict's world of cobwebs and paranoia, reading people and situations was crucial to avoid trouble. When he was young, Mike's eyes watched, and his ears listened. He was on alert when Big Redd came by. He was on alert now. Papasan was scowling, and Tran's head was down. He'd wait and see what the problem was.

The evening meal was a pleasant concoction that looked and tasted like chicken and rice. Mike suspected they were serving him the best they had. He complimented Tweet and thanked Papasan. Tran was unusually quiet.

153

During the meal, Papasan told them Tran had confided to his best friend that a wounded American soldier was staying with them. Although his friend had sworn secrecy and was honorable, he was still a boy. Tran's mistake created a dangerous situation, and Mike's presence endangered them all.

Tran hung his head in shame.

Seeing Tran's reaction, Mike said, "Tran, hold your head up. We all make mistakes. I've made plenty. No hard feelings, buddy."

Tran raised his head and looked at Mike. A tear rolled down Tran's face.

Mike continued, "Hey, I've forgotten to thank you. If it wasn't for you, we might never have gotten to know each other. Meeting you and Papasan and your Aunt Tweet has been about the best thing that's ever happened to me."

Tweet translated Mike's words, and as Tran looked at Mike, a smile took shape. Tweet squeezed Tran's hand, and the young boy visibly relaxed. He returned to eating, the sadness gone, living in the moment as children do.

Tweet thanked Mike for the kind words, then, in a serious tone, continued.

"Expedience is of paramount concern, Mike. Gio Linh is within six miles. You will be too vulnerable traveling alone, so Papasan and I will accompany you. We will use the cart and buffalo on a lightly traveled road. We should leave before midday, avoiding both the VC traveling in the early morning and the farmers walking home for their noon meal. All you must do is what you've done before, stay covered, lie still, and be quiet."

"That won't be hard," Mike said, grinning.

"Mike, your wounds are healing, but a doctor should examine you," reminded Tweet.

Tweet turned to Papasan, "We must get through the night without discovery."

154

"Yes, yes," Papasan agreed.

He called for Tran. "Yes, Papasan?"

"Tran, I want you to walk through the hamlet and look for any signs of the Viet Cong. Listen for them singing their communist songs or stealing supplies. Be careful, the hamlet is almost deserted, and you may come upon them suddenly. Stay hidden as much as you can. If you see any signs of the VC, do not draw attention to yourself, but come back immediately and let us know. Can you do that for me?"

Tran smiled, and eager to make up for his mistake, nodded, "Yes."

Papasan turned to Tweet and said, "We will leave in the morning."

This incident was Mike's wake-up call. The real world was coming back, and fast. Time to get back to his unit. Time to get back to life and death. He took a deep breath and nodded to Tweet.

Mike and Tweet would wait for Tran's return and asked Papasan to rest.

Mike promised they would wake him should there be a need. He also reassured Papasan he'd take watch tonight while remaining hidden, just in case.

The VC could still pass through during the night, you never knew, and it was a risk he couldn't take, not with Tweet and not with her family. She had lost enough, and they were now risking their lives for him. He knew only too well how to stand watch, and he'd move heaven and earth to protect them. He'd fallen in love. Sure enough, he'd fallen in love.

To himself, Mike shook his head in amazement. Life was strange. Who would've thought?

Only need to keep them safe one night. Tomorrow their risk is behind them.

~~~

With no marauding VC, Tweet and Papasan hitched the buffalo to their cart the following morning. Tran understood they expected to return sometime late afternoon, but if not, he was to go to his friend's house. Surprisingly, as Mike went to shake hands with Tran, the shy boy stepped forward and wrapped his arms around Mike's waist in a quick hug. He moved away just as quickly, looking a little embarrassed. Mike got into the cart filled with thatch and was hurriedly covered with mats and light furniture to appear as if they were leaving the area. His head remained free at the front of the cart so he could hear what Papasan and Tweet said and be part of the conversation. Tweet made him as comfortable as she could, but Mike found maximum comfort from the loaded M-16 by his side.

~~~

She clenched tight the reins to her water buffalo, keeping him from wandering where he wanted to go. Tweet knew his soul was capricious, and only vigilance would keep him on course. The bombed-out roads, pockmarked and barren, looked every bit like the dusted craters on the moon. She worked hard to keep Mike from being jostled and reopening his wounds.

Her country not only looked foreign, it felt foreign and repugnant, no longer a paradise of lush blues and greens that lived in the lakes and mountain mists, places of mystery and enchantment. Only a few years earlier, this countryside filled her eyes with exotic splashes of yellows, oranges, and reds in the trees and on the ground.

During the cherry blossom season, blooms were everywhere and looked like pink clouds from heaven.

Her country was now a paradise lost. She was a stranger in a land once her home. Worse, a stranger to the story she had once shared with her family. All was gone. A shroud of weariness, as gray and foreboding as the scenery, descended upon her.

Tweet focused on the road. It would do no good to engage in this sadness. She spoke gentle words to Petrichor, her water buffalo, and clicked her tongue to encourage his now steady, rhythmic ambling.

~~~

She remembered the day she learned the word "Petrichor." Father Joseph offered "petrichor" to the class as a lesson in word roots. He said it was a Greek word. The root "petra" meant "stone" and "ichor" the fluid which flowed through the veins of the gods in Greek mythology. His gift to the class was the meaning of the word, one that did not exist in the Vietnamese language, making it even more precious.

"Petrichor is the earthy scent produced when rain falls on dry rock and soil," Father Joseph said, his own eyes twinkling with anticipation. He watched each student reflect and allowed their minds to linger on a scent known since the beginning of time to reach that "aha" moment. His smile was as broad as their own for this "gift." Petrichor, what a wonderful word!

That afternoon, while walking home from school, Tweet wondered what she had that was deserving of such a word, and there, before her, wallowing in a puddle of mud and dust, filth from nose to tail, with surely a smile on his face, was her family's huge "Cong bo," their water buffalo. *"Petrichor,"* she called out to him. He craned his thick neck in her direction. With a grace that defied logic, he stood and walked toward her. Now and forevermore, he would bear this godly name.

Tweet sighed in remembrance of those days. She had loved learning. And she loved her Petrichor.

Now Petrichor, you are the gatekeeper of our safety. Our lives depend on your sure-footedness.

When passing villages, all three knew that trouble could occur, even in "friendly" villages. Viet Cong or Viet Cong sympathizers were seldom far away.

Mike thought once again that the fight is won by whoever wants it most. He'd fallen in love with Tweet from the moment he saw her at the clearing, and he would fight the fight, to the death if need be, to protect her.

She looked tense. Maybe small talk would relax her vigilance.

"You never told me what your name means," said Mike from behind her.

"It means 'smooth,'" she replied perfunctorily.

His smile grew, and he couldn't resist relying on his southern drawl once more.

"Does that mean smooth like a Georgia peach ma'am or smooth like in 'smooth operator?'"

"Both," she muttered, preoccupied, flicking the reins ever so slightly to get better speed. "It can also mean heavenly."

"Ahh, very nice, I can see that," grinned Mike. "And Thanh's name?"

"Sunny and intelligent." Before he could ask further, she volunteered, "My parents liked the name Anh, but Anh means seventh child. We often name our children according to birth order. They named my brother Bao because he is the third child, but the name also means protector."

Casually, she dropped her hand and wagged a finger near his face, stopping him from further conversation.

"I don't want to alarm you, but someone is coming toward us riding a scooter. This is very unusual, and they're coming quickly. Cover your head."

Mike moved the M-16 fire selector switch from "safe" to "automatic" and put his head under the heavy blanket as he heard Tweet speaking rapidly but quietly to Papasan. Before long, the rider came upon them.

"Thuy, is that you?" asked a Vietnamese man.

"Yes, Nhat," Tweet replied, not slowing the cart.

"Is everything all right?" he asked, nodding toward Papasan's direction.

"Yes, Papasan has been violently sick. We don't know what he has or if it's infectious, and I'm bringing him to Mother to see if she can tell us what it is and offer some herbs. He falls asleep with fever. I would not get close. It could be contagious."

158

"Mother" was a Vietnamese woman who lived in a village nearby. She was part prophet and part healer. People from many miles came to her with their problems.

"Yes, yes, Mother is the person to take him to. I'm in a hurry with pressing business, or I would gladly help. You understand?"

"Yes, Nhat, surely you must hurry then."

"Good luck to you, Thuy." And with a second nod, he was off, traveling fast to make up for the few moments lost.

Both Papasan and Tweet relaxed. Tweet spoke to Mike.

"You can pull the blanket from your head now."

"Who was that?"

"He is the brother to my husband,"

"What?" Mike stammered.

"My dead husband," Tweet added quickly, smiling a little at his reaction. "It was a pre-arranged marriage. We were betrothed when I was thirteen, and he fifteen, a usual age in our culture. We married two years later. A month after the marriage, I heard an owl outside, a grim omen, and went to find Hai in the field. We have a snake here. You call it the "two-step," two steps after it bites, you die. I found Hai in the field dead with bite marks."

Mike was silent for a while.

"Does Papasan understand the risk we are all taking?"

Tweet translated for Papasan and then told Mike his reply.

"Papasan has been in Vietnam his entire life, and he's never known peace. He has decided that he will do what he can to help you because he's seen the brutality of the Viet Cong and the NVA. He's tired and just wants peace in his life. Oh, and he likes you!"

Papasan said more to Tweet. She giggled and replied to Papasan, and he too chuckled. Not wanting to be left out, Mike asked Tweet what was being said.

"Papasan congratulated me for being so quick to answer Nhat. He's nicknamed me 'Lanh Huu.' Lanh means 'smart,' 'street smart' as you Americans say. And Huu means 'very.' Papasan now calls me 'Very Street Smart.'"

Mike, Tweet, and then Papasan all broke out in laughter, feeling relief that Nhat had been in such a hurry.

"From the way you handled this situation, you deserve the name Lanh, excuse me, Lanh Huu! Maybe you'll be my 'Lanh Girl' from now on! What business was Nhat in such a hurry to get to?"

"He is a VC list maker."

"A list maker? I've never heard of that. What's a list maker?"

"He travels through nearby villages pretending to be friends to those who support the American GIs and the families of ARVN soldiers. He watches everything and everyone in the villages, then reports on who is helping the Americans and who is helping the communists. Informants like these are everywhere, some even in ARVN uniforms! There are also VC secretly making lists of names for the day the communists win this war and control us. Then the names will have their day of reckoning with the VC and communist government officials. Supposedly, Nhat is one of their chief informants. If he had seen you, you undoubtedly would be dead by now, and me too for helping you."

Mike sat in quiet reflection. *Saved by a woman. A cool, calculating, smart woman. Saved not once, but twice!* He secretly thanked God for sending her to him, then, just because, he thanked the monk.

~~~

They arrived at a crossroad on Highway 1. As they were getting the cart onto the road, they first heard, then saw a large convoy of U.S. Marine trucks. Mike got out from under the mats and pulled himself out of the cart. He held his hands high with the M-16 in one hand and waved for the convoy to stop. The lead truck began braking, rolling up next to them with five or six trucks behind.

"Tweet, you and Papasan stay here."

He walked toward the vehicles. Two Marines got out of the cab of the truck with their M-16's ready.

"What the hell are you doing, Marine? We're sitting ducks here!" shouted the Staff Sergeant.

"I was wounded around Marketplace, Gunny, and this woman took care of me. She's a nurse in Da Nang. I'm trying to get there and have someone check my wounds and get back to my unit."

The Sergeant took it all in, "Get in the back of the second truck and take her with you. We've got a corpsman in there with some walking wounded that are heading to Da Nang. Let him take a look at you."

"Roger that, Gunny!"

He turned to Tweet, "Your carriage has arrived m'lady!" Mike tried his best to bow without wincing as he swept his M-16 toward the idling truck nearby.

Laughing, Tweet turned to Papasan and told him what was going on. He nodded his head, yes, several times while motioning for them to move along with his finger. Mike and Tweet walked to the back of the truck, where two Marines helped them climb in. Tweet sat beside him as "Doc" looked at Mike's dressings, taking them off and examining the wounds.

"Who's your Doc, jarhead?" he asked Mike, smiling.

"She's right here. Good job, huh?"

"Damn fine work, but there's a minor infection that's deep, and there may be fragments left. Best we get you and Nurse Nightingale here to Da Nang for a good once over and X-Rays. Sit back and relax, Marine, ya hungry? We got a whole case of Ham and Lima Beans."

Laughing, Mike said, "Just when I thought life was getting better."

The Doc got it, "Man, we can't give this shit away!"

Looking through the dust left by the trucks, Tweet saw Papasan heading back to the hut along the small dirt road.

161

At the hospital, Mike's wounds were examined by a corpsman. Then, seeing Tweet happier than she'd been in a long time, Lieutenant Campbell dropped by to see what was going on. He was one of the doctors who worked with Tweet, evidently glad to have her back. He signed Redd's papers indicating the need for a few more days of rest to ensure complete recovery before returning to Hotel Company. He did this with a wink and smile at Mike and passed by Tweet's radiant face saying, "You owe me."

Tweet took Mike to the tiny place she rented, and they made love. All night, until the alarm clock sounded. He walked Tweet to the hospital, where she was back on duty once again. As they walked through Dog Patch, hard stares and derisive gestures came their way from a few locals. He was on their turf, and they were not friends of the American soldier. Mike hoped nothing would go against Tweet for walking with him, and he hurried her along. Someone shouted, "Get out, American!" just as the hospital came into view. What the hell are we doing here, Mike wondered for the hundredth time.

He pulled Tweet close to him for a kiss when they were out of view. As he pulled away and looked into her face, her hair caught a breeze he didn't feel. It blew everywhere. She responded to Mike's quizzical look, "Chi," she said somewhat abashedly as she tried smoothing her hair with her hands. Then added, "Chi is a belief of inward energy that sometimes finds its way out."

They shared three more glorious days before it was time for Mike to return to the gun team. His wounds had healed well enough. Their time together would now be a memory, but one each would carry for life. The gun team was due for R&R at China Beach in a few weeks, and he would be near her soon enough.

As he returned to Hotel, he couldn't have felt better. The platoon cheered, seeing him alive, and the gun team cheered the loudest when they saw their buddy, who'd been classified "MIA," Missing in Action. He grinned wide as he told his story and suffered through their jokes and laughter. In the end, with hugs and backslaps, they welcomed him back. The gun team was whole again.

~~~

Three weeks later, while enjoying R&R, the team met Tweet, and to a man, thought she was really something. Jesse thanked her with gratitude for taking such excellent care of his friend. Beau, whose accent she recognized as similar to Mike's, gave her a bear hug and said, "Hello Lanh Huu! Good work, darlin'! You're a regular Rock of Gibraltar in a soft little body! Welcome to our family, Tweet."

Chingas nodded to Redd, grinning from ear to ear, "She's got her shit in one sock, not like you brother. Your sock has a hole in it."

"Whatcha talkin' about city boy, I'm from the south, remember?"

"Oh yeah, that's right," remarked Chingas sarcastically, "You southern boys probably never even wore socks 'til you got to boot camp! It means you got your shit together, man, and it's tight. It means you know what's going on! She's got her shit together and saved your ass bro, twice, but you've got a hole in yours, my friend, 'cause you continue to need saving! I think you've got more problems than a math book!" This opened the door for the rest of the group to start the joking.

That night, while trying to get some shut-eye, Redd perceived a flash of orange at the edge of his dream.

~~~

Chingas, trying to get his own shut-eye, did not see orange. He was proud of the banter he'd contributed today, unusual for this quiet Marine. A memory of hanging around the school's basketball court with his friends came to him.

One of them talked about the size of his "Mexican mud snake," when Miguel, Chingas' closest friend, had taken over the conversation,

"I have three inches and proud of it!"

163

The group stared at him, not sure how to take that statement, then snickered at its ridiculousness. Miguel had them on the hook, then threw out the punch line, "But most women I know like 'em that wide." That was a funny one! That was Miguel, always the cut-up.

Chingas promised himself to remember this one when Beau and Angel started their bullshit. Chingas was not quick with jokes, but he knew this was a good one! Then he too dozed off, hoping he'd see Miguel again one day, and wondering what he was up to, safe in "The World."

THIRTY-ONE

WHO ARE WE WHEN THE FIGHTING'S DONE?

1967

Incoming!" was the word. It meant dive, then push hard into the mud or dust, flatten yourself into what might become your grave. The artillery shells rained down in random locations, on random days, at random times, for random minutes, or hours.

The Marines at Con Thien lay there amid the thunder of explosions, the ground heaving, while they silently plead for help.

Lord, please let me live through this.

Lord, please don't let me be a cripple.

Some bargained when facing the possibility of death.

Lord, if you let me live, I promise I won't fuck with that son of a bitch Killer Kell again.

Lord, I promise I'll be a better son if you let Joe Clark live. He saved my life.

Bargaining always came down to an "if/then" proposition with God.

By bargaining with God, you acknowledged his power and indebted yourself. Now you had to make good. That was the way of an agreement.

Later, with the crises over, many who bargained with God rationalized they'd done so under duress. God had them over a barrel. It was extortion of the worst kind. And many reneged on their promise.

They would deny the promise until the next "Incoming!"

But it was a debasement to bargain a second or third time if you didn't make good on your promise the first time. To ease their conscience, many Marines rationalized their behavior.

Jesse believed their humanity suffered for it, and ultimately, their integrity.

In war, rationalization had many faces.

Jesse knew most Marines rationalized the obscene into something tolerable. The buddy who was blown apart or burned beyond recognition "died for his country." The Marine who cut the ears off the dead enemy or killed the prisoner of war "put fear in the enemy." Those who killed the innocent, civilian men, women, or children did so "to win the war."

Jesse knew, they all knew, there was a price to pay for these obscenities. Seen by many, known to all, those obscenities became part of who they were. The abominations exacted by Marines in war were heavy burdens for the soul.

~~~

Each Marine attempted to make sense of the words of war, such as killing, survival, loyalty, patriotism, surrender, mortality, justice, and morality. Their meanings had seldom been considered until now. There had been little need in "The World."

Now there was a need. It concerned survival. Immediate physical survival, and future emotional survival. Each Marine got to know these words, then came to terms with them in his own way.

A majority of fighting men in Vietnam were young, green, and wet behind the ears, most just out of high school. What did they know about life and its complexities? What skills did they have to analyze words and actions with far-reaching consequences and rules that seemed to vary according to circumstance?

Marine Officers were forced to answer tactical questions from their men.

"Do I shoot the old man stepping into the free-fire zone? How can I tell if he's the enemy or just an old man walking along?"

The moral dilemmas were even harder.

"Do I give medical aid to this peasant, who might be a genuine peasant, or perhaps a VC trying to kill me tonight?"

Many moving parts with life-or-death considerations every step of the way. Hard to stay focused on the cause with so much ambiguity and incessant stress.

Invariably, for each Marine, there came a time for reflection, a need to make sense of it all, and, hopefully, a way to live with it. It was a steep learning curve for sure, with many considerations and lifelong consequences.

~~~

Why do we fight? Jesse gave a lot of thought to this question. As the intrinsic thinker of the gun team, he collected ideas to mull over. He kept what was useful and discarded that which would hinder his journey. In the end, he concluded the world fought for power and material goods. Simple.

The question that remained was, what became of the warriors?

How did they live with themselves?

Jess never questioned his faith, but neither had he given it much thought.

One quiet evening, he had an epiphany. The two words most important to a Marine were forgiveness and redemption. Acknowledging the power of those two words could lead to emotional and spiritual healing.

Forgiveness, if asked for and granted by God, promised salvation on earth and in heaven. Forgiveness freed the soul and brought peace.

Redemption. Jesse thought about redemption for a long time.

Redemption was thought about by many who were near death but still hanging on. It was a concept and a process that involved a promise to yourself and a Higher Power. Redemption required action. It demanded

167

an effort to restore your soul, reclaim yourself, undo the bad if possible, or at least change for the better.

Redemption required you to honor a promise made, commit to change, and correct trespasses. It was an opportunity for hope. Without hope, there was nothing.

Yes, those who sought the path to redemption, who delivered on their promise, found honor. Even with death, especially in death, those men were the lucky ones.

That thought comforted Jesse. It gave him solace. He knew he could deliver and deliver in the best way.

He would lead, knowing that men would act decently and honorably even in the worst situation if it was expected of them. He would lead by example. He could do that. It was in his soul to do the right thing. It had always been there. The Corps just put a shine on it.

THIRTY-TWO

THE BROTHERHOOD

1967

As Operation Kingfisher neared, Mike Redd finished his letter to Tweet and folded the forms he'd signed into the envelope. He'd designated Tweet as his beneficiary and provided copies of permission forms for them to marry. Redd was walking to the Command Post to drop his letter in the outgoing mailbag when he heard Angel yell, "Beau's back!"

There was just enough time for a picture of the gun team sporting wedding cigars, some rough-housing between Beau and Jess, and for Beau to pack up when the order to "Move out!" was heard.

As Mike predicted, it took the 400 Marines most of the day to arrive at the overnight assembly area, a mere mile west of the Hill of Angels.

Redd wiped away sweat and dead mosquitos. Anyone who wasn't there could never understand the unbearable heat. Men were dying because of it. It was suffocating! When Redd felt Tweet's letter in his fatigue jacket, he realized he'd neglected to mail it.

"Dammit!" He muttered and felt anxiety about the mistake.

Redd knew the dangerous leg of the mission was ahead, but they were safe this evening. Accompanying the Marines were eleven armored vehicles, Amtraks, Ontos', and tanks, and a platoon of combat engineers. A battalion of 400 Marines, LAWS Rockets, and untold numbers of weapons with plenty of ammo surrounded him. Most comforting, with Beau back, the gun team was whole again. Yes, Redd would sleep better tonight.

~~~

"Hey friend," Jesse said to Beau as they were bedding down, "Might you be interested in telling us what's happening in "The World" and about your wedding?"

"Thought you'd never ask," came Beau's immediate reply.

Four young men, warriors with the future of democracy resting on their shoulders, sat like patient children while Beau cast his spell like a wizard. The master storyteller.

"Let's see, California had a thing called a 'Pop Fest,' Mammas and Pappas, Janis Joplin, Otis Redding, and other groups played outside in Monterey for free. Scott Mackenzie, a newcomer, sang, 'If you're going to San Francisco, wear some flowers in your hair.' The Hippies loved that! Heck, I love that song! What else?

"Lots of racial rioting happening, also demonstrations and protests about us fighting here. I had no problems. Still, I heard GIs are getting harassed by the long hairs when they see us returning in uniform. Like I said, I didn't have any problems, but the news covered the incidents."

Jess breathed deeper. He'd been feeling "off" since yesterday. He wished he hadn't heard this, and to the team, he said, "Guys, do me a favor, don't mention this to anyone else until we're finished with this mission. It's a downer."

"Good thinking, bro," responded Redd, appreciating Jesse's concern.

Beau continued with talk of the wedding, the bachelor party his groomsmen gave him, the wedding cake, how Helen looked coming down the aisle.

"What movies are playing, Beau?' Angel asked after listening for a while.

"Okay, now you're talking my language!" Beau responded excitedly. "Since all of you have been singing falsetto to Lulu's song, 'To Sir with Love,' Helen and I went to see the movie she sings it in. Definitely worth the money. The teacher in the show is a black actor named Sidney Poitier. Now dig this, we saw him in a preview for a movie coming out next month. That movie is getting a whole lot of attention because of

Poitier's role. He plays Virgil Tibbs, a black police detective working in Sparta, Mississippi. Called 'In the Heat of the Night.' Virgil Tibbs thinks highly of himself and has a great line in the preview. Man, he looks the white Sheriff in the face and cool as a cucumber says, 'They call me MISTER Tibbs!' Straight in the eyes, with no part of him backing down! Man! I would sure like to buy some popcorn, get a pack of jujubes and a big coke, settle in my seat with my arm around Helen and enjoy THAT show!"

It was a typical 'Nam night, so black a hand in front of a face was impossible to see.

The boys in the group leaned back and thought about what Beau had told them. They were quiet for a while.

Beau, realizing his stories of "The World" had brought on a feeling of nostalgia and quiet reflection for the gun team, broke their reverie.

"Angel, did I see you with an AK-47 today? What's up with that?" Beau asked.

Angel looked at Beau and said straight-faced, "Beau, I just got sick of it, all of it. Shitty food when we DO get it, and a shitty rifle that damned near got me killed while you were gone."

"What the hell happened, Angel?" Beau asked, leaning forward.

"We had a skirmish with a VC patrol right after you left. We finished checking bodies, and Gunny was reporting to the CP while we sat down to grab some chow. Remember Roy Coltrane, the only guy in the squad who liked Ham and Lima Beans? He was always willing to trade my beans and ham for his beef stew. I had just swapped out with him.

"We were all sittin' around, like now, shootin' the shit. Coltrane was telling us about a winning touchdown he made back home, spoon headed to his mouth, mid-sentence, and bang, there's a hole in his forehead. Sniper got him; spoon never made it to his mouth. We scatter and fire in the shot's direction. I'm shootin' at anything that moves when my fuckin' M-16 jams!

"I roll over on my back to clear the jam, and the sniper gets off another round. Missed me by inches. That's when I swore that would never happen to me again.

"We got the son-of-a-bitch, and he had an AK with a scope on it. I took it from him and all the ammo he had. Then I went back to the other bodies and took as much AK ammo as I could carry. Took the scope off later that day. I thought about not keeping it but then figured I haven't come across a dead VC or NVA that had a jammed AK-47. I'll search for ammo after every firefight. Now that Coltrane's gone, who're we gonna trade our Lima Beans with? Roy, you left us in a pickle, brother!"

They sat quietly for a moment, dealing with the absurdity of a man who loved Ham and Lima Beans and how a bullet in his head would affect their daily routine.

Beau broke the strained silence once more and asked, "Guys, when I left, Lieutenant Tom was transferring out? What happened with that?"

Redd answered, "We got lucky, the Lieutenant was supposed to leave, but with this big operation, the brass figured something right for once and kept him here. I bet we're happier about this than he is!"

The team chuckled, but to a man, they felt good having an experienced Lieutenant lead them in an operation of this size.

Hotel Company had experienced the loss of junior officers in Vietnam, much as the rest of the Marine Corps had.

Redd continued, "Yeah, we finally grew us a good leader. When he showed up, Lieutenant Tom knew he didn't have all the answers. He listened and worked with who we were.

"The Lieutenant told us what the Captain wanted done and talked with us about the best way to do it. He figured out which one of us was wound too tight, who can be counted on, and who can't. He knows us and our history.

"We look out for him because if he takes a hit or the brass moves him to some other platoon, there goes our history, and the new guy won't know shit from Shinola. A new Lieutenant can get someone killed quick if he doesn't get killed himself. It's bullshit the way the brass moves these new officers around. Guess they forgot how dangerous it is with a new guy."

The guys were agreeing with Redd when Chingas chimed in, "As the new guy here, I gotta tell ya I learned fast from all of you.

"I look at all the fresh faces in the Company, and I'm grateful for you guys in this cosmic jungle shooting gallery. I can rely on you. One less thing to worry about. I just wish you weren't so damned ugly!"

Even through the pitch-black night, the empty C-Rat cans and a few stones found their mark as Chingas ducked from the counterattack.

Unable to contain himself further, Beau began, "Redd. I have a joke for you."

"I'm all ears, bro."

"Do you know why so many blacks get killed in Vietnam?"

"Tell me, man," Redd was already chuckling, not at the joke, but at Beau's audacity to tell racial jokes to a black man after just discussing race riots back in the States.

"Because every time the Sergeant yells, 'Get down!' they stand up and start dancing!"

It brought a round of laughter.

"Okay, Beau, one back at you," said Redd. "Tell me this, man. Why did God invent golf?"

"Don't know, bro."

"So white people could dress like blacks!"

More laughter. Then, surprisingly, Chingas spoke up. "Angel, I got one for you, man. What's the difference between pick and choose?"

"Don't know, Chingas."

Chingas was smiling, but no one could see that in the dark.

"Pick means to select something, and choose is what we Mexicans wear on our feet."

Laughter from men who were no longer black, white, Mexican, or Cuban, but brothers. And so it went until one by one; they fell asleep.

THIRTY-THREE

MY PRAYER

July 1967

B egrudgingly, Jesse realized dawn was approaching. He didn't want to wake up to this day and felt a dread he'd never felt before. Yeah, he'd been scared before, plenty of times, but this was something different. His insides churned.

Christ, could it get any hotter? Supposed to hit 105 today, already feels like 120, and the day's just startin'.

Feels like breathin' through a straw, hard to take in, burns the nose.

Just breathe easy. Slow and easy.

Soon it would be time to move toward Thon Cam Son.

Jesse ignored the beads of sweat rolling down his face. Weariness held his body to the ground, and he sought refuge from a world that pushed into his dreams.

At the periphery of Jesse's thoughts and senses, he heard, then felt, the large armored equipment start, their diesel engines catching, then settling into a drone that helped him go to a place in his mind used to escape while not able to dream.

It was a refuge of sorts, a dream-like state, where he could be with his family and friends in as normal a life as he could imagine. He went there now, back to Forest Heights, the front porch of his home as the people he knew and loved spoke with him ....

~~~

A breeze blew across the lawn as Jesse played with Duchess, the family's black standard poodle. Crazy how much he loved that dog. His sister Janine claimed her, but she was his dog. Duchess was smart and probably Jesse's best friend.

Duchess jumped high in the cool air for her Frisbee. Yellow Frisbee, black fur, pink tongue. She looked like she was smiling when she had it in her mouth. Her Frisbee. No one else's. Get it if you can. Her eyes dared Jesse to try.

Jesse threw the Frisbee for Duchess again and watched her track it down as he heard his family laughing inside the house, the aroma of Mom's Sunday cooking reaching his nose.

Steaming hot Maryland fried chicken, the smell of the gravy from the chicken drippings meant for mom's fluffy mashed potatoes.

There was Jeff, standing on the sidewalk.

"Hey, Jeff! How ya doing? Man, I hope you're lucky with the draft board. I guess you've met them by now. Be smarter than me, buddy. Avoid this shit at all costs. This place would blow your mind. Get your student deferment, go to college, and make your parents happy. You'll be safe that way. Peace back to you, and thanks for the letters."

Janine popped into his head next.

What's she up to?

Probably in the bathroom preparing for a date.

Strange, she hasn't married and settled down.

Three years older and a school beauty queen, life with Janine had been a series of scents and visuals, best amplified in their "shared" bathroom with stockings, bras, and other unmentionables hanging in that small space to dry

Yes, he missed his sister. She'd been kind to him, probably better than he deserved, sending mail and baked goods regularly. Not the best-baked goods he'd ever tasted, but she was trying! Her last cake was her worst and best, a rum cake, with what must have been an entire bottle of rum.

176

It arrived as a mush, disintegrated en route, but the boys scooped it up with their fingers and told Jess to ask Janine for more!

Jesse spoke to his sister, "Janine, find yourself an honorable man with money, one who can buy you a house with an enormous bathroom. I'll buy you some perfume when I leave this hellhole."

So much taken for granted back home. Cool air. Clean water. A bed. Daily showers. Edible food. Feelin' safe. The simple things in life taken for granted.

~~~

There was Russ, a best friend, and a fellow Marine that understood what was happening "In Country."

"Russ! How are you, bro? I was at Marketplace when I heard the explosions at Dong Ha from a rocket attack a couple of months ago. I hope you weren't hurt. I also heard that the tin roof you guys put on your Better Homes and Garden hut saved your butts.

"Hey Russ, have you noticed that on some nights the sky and the countryside around here sure look beautiful, like a picture, almost, and on some nights, it reminds me of the woods by the pet cemetery. Remember how we climbed those trees, hung out on a branch, and talked and joked instead of going home? Spooky strange that Vietnam could look like Maryland, huh?

"That pet cemetery. Remember the old lady that passed out pennies to the trick-or-treaters instead of candy, her house just across from it? Remember?

"Have you heard the Cong can fight for a week on a handful of rice? Christ, are they indestructible, or what?

"I'm getting' short Russ, thirty-two days left, counting down and getting' squirrely. Just hoping this doesn't turn negative. Gotta tell you, bro, I'm creepin' out. Feels like something terrible is squattin' on my doorstep, and it's comin' to get me.

"I'm sure as shit gettin' the hee bee jee bees. Gonna work on stayin' numb.

"Gotta move on Russ, thanks for being here for me. Thanks for listening while I get all this out. Send a prayer my way, buddy, I could use that. Keep your head down. Stay safe."

Thirty-two days and I'll be back with the things I miss and love.

Annie, walking down the stairs at her "welcome back" party. Beautiful. I miss her. I'll find her when I get home.

~~~

"Hey, Annie! Wow, it's good to see you again. The memory of you has gotten me through more than one night here in Vietnam. It was sure nice seeing you at the Stone's house. Wow, you coming down those stairs looking like you did, you took my breath away.

"From the second I saw you, I realized you'd been gone too long. I don't remember asking you to dance. I think I took your hand and put you in my arms. I remember we'd danced once before, in my basement, when Janine had that screwball boyfriend over. Remember? He had Jerry Lee Lewis hair and thought he was something. How old were we, Annie? So young.

"I'd never taken a girl in my arms like I took you in mine that night at your party. Didn't want us to part. Couldn't get close enough to you. Couldn't get enough of you. I can't remember the song we were dancing to. You remember it, Annie? It was slow, and the words were for us.

"You changed so much the year you were gone. You went from girl to woman, or maybe I just never really saw you before. I saw you that night.

"Sixteen! You were sixteen at that party! Sweet for the lucky guys who got a kiss from you. Glad I was one of them.

"Your kisses tasted so good lying out there in the grass. We sure were quick to get time for ourselves. Guess we both felt selfish. I was sure glad for it.

"Feels like I'm in a trance, Annie.

"Never felt like this before.

"The sky is full of stars tonight, and they're all reflected in your eyes... until my face shadows them.

"It feels so right to lie on you like this, our arms outstretched, my heart racing, yours too, I feel it ....

"You're an angel lying in the grass, your blonde hair everywhere, kissing me for all the years we missed because we were young. Kissing for such a long time, for all the times we wanted to, but couldn't.

"I'm getting so turned on by you. Annie, you taste so good ... can I ...?

~~~

"Jesse, wake up!" Beau gently shook Jesse's shoulder and then said above the din of machinery and 400 Marines packing up to move out, "If I gotta leave my dream, you gotta leave yours, Pard." Then in a serious voice, "Pack it good Jess, get some grub, today is gonna be a motherfucker."

Jess looked up into the eyes of his friend and said, "Yeah, probably hotter too."

He gazed at the stark, harsh world of men and machines that had but one purpose.

His stretched his limbs. It was a new day. While he lit a cigarette and looked for leaches to burn, Jesse pushed back the impending dread and reminded himself that Second Battalion, Ninth Marines grunts were battle-hardened and experienced. They knew how to handle themselves. He knew he and his team would hold up their end.

Stop thinking.

Jesse swung his rucksack across his shoulders and felt its weight as he adjusted the straps. He picked up his M-60, stood tall, and looked toward the sky.

In silent prayer, he said, "Annie, please stay close."

THIRTY-FOUR

THE REAPER

July 1967

*Y*ou couldn't have picked a worse time to return my friend, Jesse thought to himself. He saw by the look on Beau's face that he knew it too. *One more day in hell to get through. Let the day begin.*

What the hell am I doing here?

Beads of sweat clung to every pore.

His remembrance of Annie moments before left a longing for the comfort he felt in her arms. He wished for that now. One moment more....

A breeze would be nice, any breeze.

Jesse washed two salt tablets down with water to stay hydrated, then pushed back his hair and lowered the three-pound metal helmet onto his head. Designed to protect his head in the scorching sun, it baked instead.

The 400 trekked along Provincial Route 606. To call 606 "a route" was a stretch; it was a narrow dirt road, a cart path, but one that would lead to deadly consequences.

Today's destination was Thon Cam Son, close to the DMZ.

~~~

Second Battalion, Ninth Marines, Hotel Company, marched with Echo and Golf Companies, accompanied by 11 armored vehicles. Foxtrot would be flown ahead by helicopter to a hill near the Ben Hai River. They would provide support should the column be attacked.

Their estimated arrival time to Thon Cam Son was late afternoon, where the 400 would bed down for the night before heading into the DMZ the following day.

This spoiler mission was to root out Giap's NVA regulars, who continually shelled Con Thien, Gio Linh, and the Marines clearing vegetation from the Trace near the DMZ. This would disrupt Giap's efforts to drive the Marines from Con Thien.

Lieutenant Tom walked among his men, checking on them.

"Your head here, or back home, Parker?"

"Here, Lieutenant. I'm good."

"Sorry you returned to this, Beau, but I'm glad your back."

"Wouldn't have missed it for the world, Lieutenant!" Beau grinned.

The jungle vegetation along Route 606 was thick and blocked any breeze that could cool a sweat-soaked body. The temperature rose from stifling to oppressive, and men began to drop from heat exhaustion. The armored vehicles remained off the road to avoid presenting an easy target or block movement if one broke down. After only a short distance, the invasive jungle forced the vehicles onto the road with the infantry. The large tires and tracks kicked up Vietnam's red dust, and every grunt breathed it into their lungs. No longer an asset, these vehicles became a liability, obligating Marines to watch out for them, and their buddies.

Out ahead, on point, Scouts searched for an ambush, but they too were forced closer to the road, their task compromised. Route 606 transformed into a closed corridor with minimal protection of the flanks, one way in and one way out.

Every Marine stared into the jungle and searched for signs of an ambush, knowing the first sign would be the ambush itself.

Two hours into the march, eight Huey helicopters passed overhead, each carrying Marines from Foxtrot. Everyone knew the term "military intelligence" was an oxymoron but felt good that Foxtrot was a designated backup. Most of the time, HQ provided additional backup plans "just in case." For this operation, Foxtrot was the only backup.

Tributary rivers hidden by the jungle bordered both sides of Route 606, their existence either not known or discounted by Intelligence. These rivers further limited any chance of dispersion of infantry or vehicles. Ultimately, men and machines moved as one concentrated mass, along the narrow dirt road, penned in, easy targets for enemy fire. There was no escape.

~~~

"You okay?" asked Jess.

"Yeah, guess I'm ten days out of shape. Feels like we're walking backward in this heat. Christ, could it get any worse than this?" Beau grumbled.

After the second mile, the jungle gave way to a clearing. Hard to miss. It had been cleared on purpose and provided a wide field of fire. Hotel Company's Commanding Officer noted this on their map.

Beau pointed it out to Jesse, "See that shit?"

Jesse nodded with a contrived smile, "See? It can always get worse."

Not the answer Beau was looking for, more like a quip he would toss out, not Jesse.

What's up with Jesse? Not like himself. Seems detached. To hell with it, we aren't coming back this way.

Why am I having trouble humping? I got plenty of exercise at home with Helen, the best kind, but something's up. Must be the heat, forgot how it sucks the energy, wears you down, faster than any Florida sun I've known. One step in front of the other, man. Just keep moving. It'll be over soon.

Beau trudged on. But it wasn't just the heat. It was something he'd never felt before. A dread gripped his gut as though everything he had was about to be ripped away.

~~~

The sun was setting as they reached Thon Cam Son four miles later. Beau was puffing harder than usual.

Command issued orders to set up patrols, establish listening posts, and protect themselves from an enemy well versed in nighttime attacks.

Battalion Scouts returned with details on the bunkers and spider holes in the clearing the column passed earlier. Bunkers were sometimes part of an extensive underground tunnel system, and Vietnam was a country full of such labyrinths, dating back hundreds of years to the days when the Vietnamese fought the Chinese. The tunnels allowed for troops' movement to surprise an enemy and for materiel storage, hospitals, command posts, and sometimes housed Vietnamese families.

The Marine Command Staff notified Headquarters of the locations should artillery or airstrikes be required. No doubt, HQ had planned this operation in cool tents with large maps on tables. Although it required coordination, it should have been a simple maneuver. The men who orchestrated this had probably fought in a war, maybe even this war. Headquarters plan was sound when the mission began yesterday morning, but it had fallen apart step by step as the Marines advanced toward the objective. The road was narrow, dense jungle growth confined them, and limited any chance of escape. Marines had passed out from heat exhaustion in the claustrophobic environment and slowed the movement more. The narrow road forced vehicles and Marines to walk closer together, easy targets. Now, a clearing with bunkers and spider holes.

Still, the grunts whose lives hung on decisions made weeks ahead and miles away understood one thing; in war, the battle's first casualty was usually the plan itself. They would be right. No words were spoken; the mood turned grim.

~~~

Jess felt alone, and for the first time, questioned everything about this war. He ached for a world he was no longer part of.

Probably spooked about nothin'.

Seems like something's always going wrong.

Something would happen. It shouldn't, but it did—something unbelievable, followed by head shaking, then a shudder when the details were heard. A dead Marine was usually the result, and almost every time, due to piss-poor planning.

With each story of things gone wrong with this Marine or that Marine, the more it felt like bad juju attached itself to you. More stories meant more juju, and the more likely you would become the next main character. Shabby planning at many levels resulted in too many dead Marines, that's what every grunt thought. The question of the day was, "Who's looking out for the regular grunt takin' the hits?"

As Jesse prepared to bed down, he was acutely aware of his concerns. His stomach knotted. He felt removed, unfocused, and began to shake.

What the hell is wrong with me?

This fucking dread is coming back! Shut it down!

Get yourself in check, McGowan! Don't give it life! It will feed and grow stronger!

Shut it down now!

Keep this shit to yourself, Jess, you're the fucking leader, act like it!

Jesse's world was closing in on him. He imagined a hallway becoming ever narrower, like Route 606, pressing him tighter as he moved down the hallway. No escape possible. He was powerless. There were many doors, but each was locked and denied his escape, herding him to one door, and he knew where that door led. It led to death. His death.

Jesse understood the source of his terror. It was fear of death.

Jesse clenched his fists as the anger welled up. He wanted to scream, to rage at the world, but couldn't, wouldn't. He had a responsibility to his brothers. He buried his rage, pushed it down deep where it would remain, entombed. He shook again, then took slow and deep breaths.

With focus and clarity of mind, Jesse realized he was not powerless and would keep his head in the game until "it" happened.

My last act will not be of capitulation.

185

If I can't live, neither can they.

I'll take out as many of these bastards as I can, take out those who will rob me of the rest of my life.

They must earn the right to take me out, and it will cost them dearly.

I'll fight to the death.

More deep breaths. And then a calm came upon him.

I've lived well so far. If it's my time to die, I'll die without fear!

I'll die with honor and purpose. It's not just how you live, but also how you die.

No matter what, I won't be left behind.

My brothers will take me home.

After several deep breaths, Jess promised himself he would do all he could to keep Beau safe for Helen.

~~~

Beau dropped his gear, spread out his poncho liner, and sat down. He needed to eat. He needed something sweet. Smiling to himself, Beau found a can of peaches and a tin of pound cake in his rucksack. He ate slowly and savored the sweetness. Beau hoped it would ease the discomfort in his gut.

Finished, he laid back to relax and get some sleep. It didn't come. This was not the unease he'd carried with him to `Nam. He'd resolved that when he arrived. He wouldn't play it safe. This feeling was different—rooted deeper, menacing.

What the hell is going on?

I went through this yesterday and made the right decision.

What am I feeling now? Dread? Fear?

Dread.

Beau stretched out, head on his rucksack. He closed his eyes and emptied his mind of everything except Helen. Memories were vivid, but when sleep finally came, it was an uneasy sleep.

THIRTY-FIVE

INSIDE THE WORD "EVERYTHING"

1967

Because they had known and trusted each other for years, Beau and Helen's love, with marriage, enriched their lovemaking. For Beau, his days with Helen had been like a dream, one day better than the next. Unique and more beautiful than he believed possible, Helen fulfilled him in every way.

They'd make love, then lay entwined, skin on skin. When Beau tried to pull away, to reposition, Helen held tight, and the more he tried, the harder she held, like a Chinese finger puzzle. Enmeshed, they were their own paradise. Perhaps so poignant because each knew these shared moments might never again be theirs. "Would these memories be their last?" was the question. Neither gave voice to it, but it loomed, ever-present, at the edge of their inseparability.

Beau took in every detail of Helen so he could remember it all. Helen's full red lips curved upwards into a smile with Shirley Temple dimples on either side of her mouth. She was lovely, intelligent, and his. Luxurious brown hair cascaded across her white pillowcase, whose edges were embroidered with tiny red roses and forest green leaves, smelling of outdoors from drying on the line; sheets infused with lust, a testament to the days and nights of intense lovemaking, sometimes carnal but always joyful.

They hungered. They laughed. Then they cried.

~~~

Laying together their last morning, wind chimes serenaded them. They sounded like cathedral bells, deep, resonating. They evoked a new day and the sweetness of the morning and a remembrance of their wedding. The large chimes hung from a Live Oak tree close to Helen's window. The tree's height and breadth offered shade and coolness to her room. Long strands of silver moss hung from its branches, looking like straggly beards coveted by ancient men. The moss was perfect for nest making and a welcome invitation for songbirds to build their homes. They put forth a melody now. Beau listened gratefully and told himself to remember it all.

Helen's tree. She had always loved it. It was part of her.

Wrapped in each other's arms, oh so quietly, time was only two hands on a clock, its passing measured by the melody of chimes and the song of birds, both surely just for them.

Helen leaned close and whispered, "Do you know this wind has traveled across our planet? Perhaps it comes from Africa, maybe from the Serengeti?

"It knows of things we can only imagine or read about. Wondrous things! Terrible things! Listen to the chimes, they play the stories of the wind!"

She pulled back to look at him, her eyes wide, seductive, teasing, her smile growing on those very red lips. She pressed her finger against his lips and murmured, "Shhh. Listen!" They smiled with their eyes, then with their lips. It was easy being silly with her new husband. She loved that part of him.

A thought came to Beau. If Helen could be a word, she would be the word "very." Exposing his heart, he whispered, "Inside the word, 'everything' is the word 'very.' You, my sweet wife, are 'everything' to me because you are 'very' incredible, 'very' beautiful, 'very' intelligent, 'very' funny, and 'very' much my fantasy woman."

She smiled as he continued, "The word 'everything' also has the word 'every'… Helen, I will love you 'every' day of my life."

Grinning, she asked, "Marine, have you been reading Hallmark cards?" and pulling him closer, she whispered, "I think I'll send that to a card company. We'll be rich by the time you return!"

The smile left her face as she saw Beau look at the clock. It was time for him to leave. The tears began. She wrapped herself around him tightly, "Thank you, my sweet man, thank you for knowing me and loving me."

Beau's heart sank. He wanted to keep the bedroom door shut forever. Stay with her, forever. He sighed, kissed her forehead, then rolled out of bed to shower before his flight back to Vietnam.

~~~

Huffing and trudging, Beau growled, "It can't get worse than this!" Helen had been his only two days ago. He longed for her now. The reality of Vietnam, compared to what he left behind, was glaring.

Jesse replied, "It can always get worse, Beau. Keep moving forward. Let life take care of itself."

Grinning at his friend, he added, "Keep thinking about Helen. But stay focused!"

Beau muttered, "What do I have to complain about?" while he humped 80-pounds of equipment in the heat toward Thon Cam Son.

Yeah, I'll keep thinking about Helen.

Jess, you know me too well, brother!

For Jess, being the gun team leader meant looking out for the guys on his team. He knew they complained little enough, took it, and then some, but sometimes a dose of bitterness got caught in a man's gut. The Marines Jess served with felt comfortable going to him with problems, not because they thought he would agree with them, but because they knew he would acknowledge their complaints, not judge, and, if asked, offer some solid advice. Even if he only told them to keep moving forward or that good enough was good enough, which was often what was said, that was enough in their book. To have their complaints heard and validated, even if only by another grunt, well, that meant something.

Listening was a small thing that produced big results. Jesse understood this and felt good he could be there for these men.

THIRTY-SIX

GENTLE SOLDIERS GOING HOME

July 1967

Throughout the night, sounds of heavy truck traffic to the north, near the Ben Hai River, were reported by Hotels listening posts. Foxtrot reported sounds of digging in the jungle, and in the twilight of the early morning, the Marine command staff met to discuss the plan.

"Are you sure?" was the question asked with disbelief and asked by everyone even remotely involved.

The scouts returned with a simple observation that laid waste months of planning, weeks of preparation, and now placed 400 Marines in grave danger. The situation seemed to be something from a Charlie Chan movie with Charlie buying a beautiful trailer, only to realize travel would be impossible without a car to tow it.

The command staff stared at the scouts, then stared into space, incredulous.

Division Headquarters, with their maps, orders, and battle plans, had not thoroughly analyzed the route the mission would use. Tactical planners, who saw to the broader strategic plan's specifics, either neglected, failed to consider, or outright ignored a narrow, ancient bridge spanning a tributary.

The tanks, Ontos, and Amtracs were too wide and too heavy for this small bridge, and the tributary was too deep to cross. Armored vehicles could not pass over.

With no way to circumvent this obstacle, the simplicity of the solution was unequivocal. They would not abandon the machinery, so the 400

192

could not proceed forward. The Marines and the accompanying vehicles were to return on the same path that brought them here, Route 606.

A cardinal rule repeated once, if not a hundred times during military training, was about to be violated.

Never return the way you came. It was suicide.

Poor, poor planning. Inefficient and reckless incompetence. Lives could, and likely would be needlessly sacrificed if the noises heard last night were from the NVA or Viet Cong. Every man present recoiled from the consequences that might result.

HQ issued the order. "Return the way you arrived."

The command staff disassembled, and the officers returned to their companies to brief the senior enlisted personnel on the situation and the solution. Within minutes, every Marine, whether infantryman, armored vehicle gunner, or driver, knew the plan and collectively knew they were royally screwed. To a man, they knew the danger they were about to walk into.

Jesse got his gun team together and passed the word. Beau piped up first.

"Jesus Fucking Christ, Jesse! Headquarters doesn't know their ass from a hole in the ground these days!" was all he got out before Jesse stopped him short.

"Ya know Beau, it seems lately the more you complain, the worse it gets! No griping will change the fact that we're in a bad spot, so let's get outta here before Charlie figures this mess out and slam dunks our asses! We'll do wide-dispersion formation as much as we can so these bastards can't take out a group of us. That's presuming the NVA or VC is out there right now. The only thing that will happen with bitching and worrying is that we'll be that much longer in gettin' outta here, and then we won't be able to pay attention because we'll be playing catch up. Unless one of you knows how to widen that bridge, I suggest we get our asses moving! C'mon."

Redd spoke up, "Jess, are they gonna call in an airstrike and soften up our path outta here? I'm not feeling too good about walking through a shooting gallery. I wanna get back in one piece, bro."

"I'm telling you guys what I was told. Again, we need to get our asses out of here now!"

No one said a word. Jesse was right. They loaded up, and Angel, Mike, and Chingas moved out.

Beau remained in his spot, looking at the ground, then at Jesse.

"Jess, I'm not pissed at you, I'm just pissed. How in the fuck can someone forget to think about a fucking bridge not being wide enough or strong enough to support these vehicles? Shit, these vehicles are here to help us! Not only are they not helping us, but now we've got to babysit them through an ambush site two fucking miles long! They're a liability! We should drive them to the river, blow them the fuck up, and move toward the DMZ as planned!"

Tactically, Beau was smart. It's what should happen, but the brass wasn't into the business of blowing up weapons to save lives. Beau didn't bitch much, but when military tactics made little sense, he was hard to shut up, and this time Jesse thought Beau was right. They were quite possibly being ordered to die needlessly.

Jess stood there for a moment and let Beau fume. He understood that Beau and Redd had Helen and Tweet, two good reasons to be pissed. Jess also knew that to let Beau stew over Headquarters' fuck up would only produce bad results. He had to move Beau forward.

Jess put his hand on Beau's shoulder, "Get your gear brother, we gotta get movin'. Hotel is on the way out."

Marines would pay the ultimate price for their country, but none wanted their lives taken in senseless sacrifice. Jess was seething inside, not only for himself but for his team.

~~~

The 400 Marines and their equipment walked out of the area, stunned and hypervigilant. Echo Company led with the Command Staff, the tanks, Ontos, and Amtracs. Hotel followed Echo, and Foxtrot left their nearby hill's safety and hurriedly joined them, not wishing to be stranded. Golf Company provided rear guard.

Jess and Beau walked in wide dispersal with weapons at the ready, staring into the jungle, looking for any sign of movement or existence of the enemy. Jesse could see Angel, Mike, and Chingas in front of them about 100-yards. Hotel recalled the noise of trucks the night before and the digging sounds during the night reported by Foxtrot. Jesse motioned for Beau to pick up the pace to catch up to the rest of the gun team. Everything warned ambush.

The warning was answered as a massive explosion erupted in the middle of Echo Company.

The Viet Cong remotely detonated a 250-pound bomb they'd buried in the ground the night before. Marines still alive hit the ground or ran to either side of the road, down into the ditches. Many who sought the ditches landed on booby-traps or sharp punji sticks smeared with human feces, placed there by the enemy the night before.

The Marines of Echo Company who caught the direct impact of the blast were blown into the air. Hotel came upon the horrific sight of body parts and entrails hanging from a tree near where the bomb exploded.

Machine gun and small arms fire opened from both sides of the jungle. Every man knew to stand still was to die, so they kept moving forward as quickly as they could, returning fire and keeping low while searching for cover that didn't exist.

It was the NVA who produced the spoiler attack. They knew the Marine plan and realized the bridge would block their maneuver, require them to reverse course and return the way they came.

Overnight, the NVA established a half-mile gauntlet of death and destruction. Mortars, machine guns, rifles, and booby-traps, all carefully placed for this ambush.

Jesse evaluated his surroundings, then searched for the rest of the gun team. He saw only Beau in a ditch on the opposite side of the road, his head popping up and down as he returned fire into the jungle. Redd, Chingas, and Angel were nowhere. *They must've run forward for cover.*

The small arms fire hadn't come Jess's way yet, but it was only a matter of time. The jungle was alive with specters running between the road and the tributaries. Because they wore helmets, a Marine shouted, "Friendlies!" But that Marine wasn't looking carefully. They were clad in loose-fitting black pants and shirts, carrying the distinctively shaped AK-47 assault rifle. Cong. They were everywhere. It would be a slaughter.

Last night's knot was tight in Jesse's stomach. His heart raced. His pulse pounded. "Get out of here," his brain shouted. He motioned for Beau to keep moving on the right half of the road, and he would take the left. Beau gave a nod, and both moved forward. They fired into the jungle where they saw motion or the muzzle flash from weapons. They made it as far as a tank, gutted by a rocket-propelled grenade, its driver dead and aflame, hanging over the turret. Seeking cover, they huddled together in front and slightly underneath its metal tracks. Bullets from behind bounced off the tracks and hull with hollow "thunks."

"We need to get the hell outta here, Jess! There's enemy fire from the jungle and the bunkers in the clearing. They got us in a crossfire! They're gonna spot us, and we'll die right here."

Jesse grinned at Beau and shouted above the din, "See, I told you it could get worse!"

Beau's fear shattered. They grinned at each other. At that moment, in the face of death, each man shed the dread.

They'd fought before; they were together again, knowing what to do and how to do it. Superman, John Wayne, and the Lone Ranger wrapped up into two Marines! They were invincible and would take on the world!

"Hell In A Helmet!" They yelled Hotel's Company motto as they moved out.

Jesse got up first, headed left over the ditch, and shouted back to Beau, "Watch out for booby-traps!"

Beau came out from under the tank as another RPG round rocked it violently. A large cloud of flame and smoke covered his exit as he ran after Jesse, firing indiscriminately into the jungle.

Jesse heard Beau's M-16 stop, and through the haze, saw him load another magazine. He crouched low and fired into the trees to cover Beau. He hoped Beau would move fast enough to catch up. Jesse felt a pat on his helmet as Beau ran past, dropped to his stomach, and fired to cover Jess. Jess sprinted forward, passed Beau, and tapped his helmet as he ran by.

With a goal in sight, Jesse darted fast but fell short. Confused, he laid there, willing his body to move, but it failed to respond.

Something was wrong.

Beau landed next to him, shouting, "You're gonna be okay! I'm here!"

Jesse looked at Beau, not understanding. "You're supposed to keep going while I cover you!" he yelled but couldn't hear himself. The blast from the RPG must have temporarily deafened him, he told himself.

"You're hit, Jess, you're hit, but you'll be okay!"

The damage was beyond repair, but Beau's psyche disconnected from the obvious. He was there to save the life of his best friend.

Beau's attempts to collect and cover the intestines that moved away from Jesse's body were fruitless. They were bloody, wet, and slippery. He handled what he could, and without thinking, said, "I can't collect them all!"

He instantly regretted those words and hoped Jess hadn't heard. Beau ripped the first aid kit off his back and grabbed the large field dressing. He placed it over Jesse's wound to keep what he could intact.

Beau pushed Jesse's head to the ground and yelled, "Keep your head down, dammit!" as bullets shredded the surrounding earth.

Jesse saw an NVA machine gun firing from the road while the enemy fire from the bunkers caught Marines jumping into the ditches. The NVA moved into the road and fired down its length at any Marine unlucky enough to remain there.

Jesse looked down. They'd hit him above his hips. His intestines were open to the air, and Beau was trying to cover them.

Beau knew the bullet that hit Jess was a 12.7 mm round. It came from the heavy machine gun being wheeled on to the road. Its size and velocity were used against light armored vehicles, but today, it was the weapon that eviscerated his best friend.

"You're gonna be okay, buddy. Hold on! We're getting outta here!" Beau yelled above the sound of the battle.

Beau grabbed the back of Jesse's collar and crawled on his belly, pulling Jess with him.

Beau pushed through the dense foliage toward a patch of trees. The largest looked to him like Helen's tree. He gently placed Jess in the tree's shade.

Jesse looked at Beau and spoke in a soft, calm voice indicative of shock and impending death. "It's cold, Beau. This is nice. It feels like winter in Maryland."

Beau took Jesse's face in his hands, looked into his eyes, and said, "Don't you leave me!"

Jesse heard less and less of the battle raging around him as a quiet peace settled over him.

He didn't care about anything anymore. The cold felt good, and the sounds of battle faded.

Jesse gazed into the blue sky as dusk fell.

He laid under the stars with Annie, and she smiled at him. Annie wrapped her arms around Jesse and comforted him, holding him close.

Then they were dancing, once again, to "One Summer Night," the song he'd tried so hard to remember.

Jesse fought the good fight. He gave his best.

Keep me warm, Annie, dance me through the cold.

All was good in his world.

Jesse closed his eyes and let go.

~~~

Beau cradled Jesse's head in a farewell embrace and watched his friend's face relax as his eyes looked to the sky. Beau knew that Jesse was gone, gone from the hell of Vietnam to a peaceful and pleasant place. He whispered, "Thank you, Jess."

Jesse gave the gift of friendship, but he'd given an even greater gift. Jesse showed Beau that death was not to be feared. It was the gift that released Beau from all doubts and enabled him to move forward.

~~~

Beau laid Jesse's head down and ran back for the M-60. He heard a wounded Marine cry out, "Help me," and when Beau recovered the M-60, he pulled the wounded Marine to safety. Beau placed him near Jesse and suddenly became aware of many wounded near him. Staying low to the ground to avoid being shot, he rescued them, one at a time, placing each near the safety of the tree.

Beau made it to the tree with the fifth Marine when he felt a bolt of fire surge through his back. The pain brought him to his knees.

And there, leaning against the tree, within arm's length, waited the M-60.

God is good.

With all he could muster, Beau grabbed Jesse's machine gun, turned in the direction of the enemy fire, and let the M-60 rip.

He would protect these men. He had lost Jesse. He would not lose these Marines too. His finger pulled the trigger. It fired and fired, then fired some more, as though seeking its own revenge. Like dominoes, the NVA fell, including the gunner of the heavy machine gun who had killed Jesse. One hundred rounds were spent in less than a minute, and the M-60 became silent.

Satisfied, John Beau Parker crawled to where Jesse's body lay and collapsed. No shame or regret. He had not wavered. He had proven worthy.

In Beau's mind, he was a boy again, standing between rain and sunshine with arms outstretched. But this time, he didn't stand still. He stepped to the right, into the sunlight. Beau felt a breeze and remembered Helen's chimes. He wondered if this small wind could carry his words to her. "I love you," he whispered. Not able to do more, Beau slipped into unconsciousness ... among his brothers and best friend ... under what he believed to be Helen's tree, a haven for birds, now a haven for men who had proven their worth.

THIRTY-SEVEN

FATHERHOOD

1967

"Hey Morris, the Lieutenant, okay'd me to catch a ride with you and the convoy to Da Nang and get supplies." Redd lit his cigarette, eyes unwavering as he looked at Morris.

"No need, man, I've got the list," came the reply.

"Morris, for the record, I'm going with you to pick up supplies, but between you and me, I'm catching a ride to check on a friend who got shot up. The Lieutenant knows I'm going to check up on Beau Parker."

"Parker? The grunt who took out the NVA and saved a lot of Marines?"

"Yup," replied Redd.

"C'mon, then, climb aboard."

Redd climbed into the truck and offered Morris a cigarette.

"Thanks, man," replied Morris, accepting the Marlboro, then placed it behind his ear. "Were you in that mess?"

"Yup."

"Then, you probably could use this, friend." Morris offered him a joint.

"Thanks, man, but this cigarette will do."

"To each his own," Morris replied nonchalantly. He lit the joint and took a long, slow hit.

"You know how many body bags went to Da Nang?" Redd asked, wondering if Morris knew any specifics since he'd heard about Beau.

"Yeah, man, 23 tagged and bagged. Two hundred and fifty wounded, with 190 of those medevac'd out."

Redd sat there, stunned. He knew it was bad but didn't realize almost half of the 400 Marines had been wounded badly enough to be medevac'd to the hospital. One was too many, but this was fucking incomprehensible!

Morris kept the conversation going. "That was some kinda fucked up mission. Every grunt in Quang Tri Province heard what happened. It's all anyone's been talking about for the last two days. Man, they fucked you but good. What happened to you guys has soured more attitudes than anything I've heard of!"

Morris spat out the window in evident disgust and took another hit.

"Yeah, it was bad," Redd replied as he tried not to think about it. Still feeling raw, Redd hoped Morris wouldn't ask him for details.

"Morale is pretty stinkin' low in Da Nang. The hospital's been working round the clock, trying to patch up all those guys who got blown apart. Jesus, I just don't dig how upstairs could fuck it up like that. It's all dinky dau shit, and we're getting killed right and left for no reason."

Silence. Each man lost in thought.

The joint took effect, and Morris continued, "I'm not one to wax philosophical, I take it as it comes and make the best of the shit coming down the pike, but in my book, their fucked up plan sure put a low price on everyone's life. We might only be grunts, but even grunts should have value. Like Gunny put it, it's the common man, grunts like you and me that win a war. We outta have value."

Chingas and Angel had spoken those exact words to Redd before he left to catch this ride. They both noticed the same thing, a definite shift in attitude, a souring, and anger they hadn't witnessed before among the grunts at Con Thien.

Listening to Morris, this battle must've had widespread repercussions in terms of morale if grunts in Da Nang were reacting to 2/9's pain and disillusionment. For sure, a vast military grapevine existed, and this was proof.

Later, Redd and others would come to see this battle as a turning point in their motivation to fight. It seemed like they were target practice for Giap at Con Thien or bait in the bush for Westmoreland so he could justify the need for more troops.

Hell, wherever we go, we're just fodder for the fire, boosting the egos of military leaders.

Sacrifice, yes, that's what Marines do, but needless sacrifice, no. Higher-ups didn't have the right to forget that.

There was silence between Morris and Redd for another few minutes, each lost in thought.

"Yeah," Morris continued, "What's your name, bro?"

"Mike Redd. I go by Redd."

"Where you from?"

"Georgia,"

More silence. Then, unable to stop himself, Morris resumed.

"Yesterday I heard we're getting spat on in the U.S. by protestors, more dinky dau shit! We're here to protect America's freedom with our asses. Just that simple. I'm puttin' my life on the line to keep the commie's from spreading their shit, so don't turn on me man, I'm not the enemy, and I sure as hell don't need to be a scapegoat or to carry this country's shame on my shoulders. I know we're not gettin' a ticker-tape welcome for fighting in this hellhole, no 'hoorah's' or 'thank you boys,' but give us something more than a hard time! What the fuck!

"I wonder how these protestors see us. Do they think we're so different from them? Our shit stinks, and theirs doesn't? So, my dad's a firefighter, and their father sits on his ass at a cush office job. We're all still Americans. Don't we have that in common? Isn't what each of us does important to the whole? What if we didn't have trash collectors? Rats and roaches would be everywhere, including in the homes of the rich and famous."

Redd smiled to himself, thinking that was some excellent pot Morris was smoking. It was getting him in the groove!

"When are we gonna get it that all jobs are important in their own way to make the system work and that all of us count and are connected?

"Don't we all believe in democracy? Do any of us want to have that bald, fat fucker Khrushchev speaking to us, or our kids, as the leader of our country? Holding us all hostages to his beliefs? Wash off the dumb, people!

"Hey, the way I see it if I'm willing to do the dirty work over here just like my dad is willing to do the dirty work in 'The World,' that's okay. My choice. Not askin' for permission or even a thank you, although that would be nice, but I think a little respect is in order. I love my country, and I never said who should fight in this war. You don't want to fight this war, you want to stay at home and make money, or you don't believe in killing, alright by me if you can pull it off, but don't judge, or worse, condemn me for my choice to be here and fight communism.

"You know, when I came over here, I felt proud! I was serving my country like my dad did in WWII. I was giving back like Kennedy asked."

Morris took another long hit on his doobie, held it in, then exhaled slowly, with contentment. Redd was going to agree, but was interrupted as Morris began again in earnest.

"Okay, so what's the common ground between us and the protestors?

"I guess the common ground is that we all see this war as a phony-baloney war starting with the Gulf of Tonkin. We've been lied to. This is Johnson's 'conflict,' and I guess plenty of us think he created the whole Gulf of Tonkin fiasco to get us over here to stop the communist spread.

"Congress hasn't declared this a war, so I get that some of the protestors say since it's not a declared war, why should they fight? And technically, I suppose they have a good argument. It's messy. Hell, it's messy over here and vicious. There are atrocities and moral issues. I've never seen brutality like we have here.

"But hey, this is the only fight I've been in. I don't know if it was like this in other wars. I wonder if my parent's generation saw the slaughter of their war on TV every day, would they, or my grandparents, have tried to end it? That box showing faces and wounded is a powerful medium and might well be the most powerful factor shaping this war."

Redd looked over at Morris with newfound respect; this was quite the philosophical truck driver!

"Look how we treat them! Napalm landing on civilians! Look at our disrespect when we gun down civilians or their water buffalo for sport. How about the way we're throwing full C-Rat cans at kids wanting candy? Yeah, I know they want something from us all the time, and if we don't deliver, they scream, 'Cheap Charlie, you number ten, you not number one.' Yeah, it grates on your nerves, but throwing cans at kids? C'mon, we can do better than that!

"And then there's the disrespect they show us, like the South Vietnamese helping set booby traps against us, or planting punji sticks, figuring taking care of a wounded Marine is a bigger liability than a dead Marine. Or even villagers stealing anything left out in the open.

"Hey, I heard some prostitutes put razors in their wahoo's, then take our money and leave us for dead. Atrocities on both sides, but aren't we supposed to be on the same team? In the meantime, our real enemy in the North is slicing off the private parts of our dead and stuffing them in our Marine's mouths while we slice off the enemy's ears and collect them on our belts.

"I don't know, man. I figure every war brings out the rage and the worst in some men, but this guerrilla warfare, it seems to allow for more of that. No one seems to be held accountable in the same way as they were in the big wars. I get that they seem primitive to us, and that can translate, by some, into thinking of them as being less than us, that we're superior. But hell, we don't even know how to communicate with the

South Vietnamese, and we haven't been taught anything about their culture or way of thinking to bridge some of this.

"How do you make a friend like that? How do you get the best out of them or a sense of camaraderie under those circumstances? We're pissed at them because they don't show gratitude. They use us to get money. What we don't take into account is that many of them have family and allegiance in the North, so they sell us out. Seems like the side we fight for is often our enemy! A slippery slope.

"Then there's Westmoreland, counting dead civilians as enemy bodies, civilians we've shot or napalmed in McNamara's body count war. I heard he said, 'If they're dead and Vietnamese, count them as the enemy.' Don't know if that's true, but I sure hate this idea of a 'war of attrition' and what it's causing. Guess he figures if he justifies enough battles and bodies, he'll get more troops because winning is the name of the game in any war.

"You know, sometimes part of me wonders if maybe I shouldn't have signed up. This whole gig is not what I thought it would be. I feel fucked over, no denying that. No front to win like in the old days with a 'normal war.'

"Coming over here, I figured to find the Vietnamese grateful for my help to keep their democracy intact. Not seeing much of that either. Not seein' the so-called democratic leaders that I expected in the Vietnamese government. I do see dirty little government officials that can be bought and bribed, but what country doesn't play the 'you scratch my back and I'll scratch yours' game?"

Redd saw a chance to say something come and go in the time it took Morris to fire up another joint.

"What sticks in my craw, what hurts, are the Vietnamese civilians that would just as soon sell us up the river as keep us here. 'Yankee Go Home' signs are popping up on the streets of Saigon. How often are we betrayed by some teenage Vietnamese kid pretending to be a friend, then stealing our tactical maps? Or some prostitute getting information as she's holding you close, helping you forget the world outside, then passing it to the Cong so they can set up an ambush?

"But hey, we've bombed the hell out of this country, making holes as big as moon craters, destroying the villages and villagers we're here to protect. We've poisoned their land with defoliants, leaving 'em homeless, millions of them. There's good reason to want us gone. There's a good reason why we wonder about the hypocrisy of it all. Maybe they never wanted us here in the first place. I don't know anymore.

"Who knew this was a civil war? I didn't. Guess I didn't know much of anything. Yeah, not a neat or tidy package for sure. It's a dirty war alright, no doubt about it, and I'm part of it, so I guess I'm dirty too."

Morris paused. "Sure, you don't want a joint man?"

Morris started this trip by saying he was no philosopher. Redd realized that wasn't the case! Morris had plenty to say, and he was right on with most of it.

Redd shook his head. "I'm good, bro."

"I'm talking your ear off," admitted Morris. "It's the Mary Juana talking. Want me to shut up?"

"No man, I'm right there with you."

"Am I repeating myself? If I am, just tell me."

Redd chuckled, "So, with all that said, would you sign up again?"

Redd then wondered how he'd answer that question.

Morris didn't take long to respond. No surprise there!

"Yeah, man, I would come here again, 'cause I figure the Domino theory is right. One country falls to communism, then the next and the next. A chain reaction of falling dominoes coming right at you. Then it's only a matter of time before the Russians are in our backyards. I, for one, do not want to add to their power by giving them Vietnam, then all of Indochina.

"Even if the Gulf of Tonkin were a lie generated by Johnson to get us to fight the commies, I'd still come here. Yeah, even with all this shit, I'd do it again.

"We live in a great country, and I want to keep it that way. Johnson apparently decided he'd do whatever it took to make that happen. I'm not sure I'd do any less than that, but it feels like we were lied to in order for him to carry out his plan. Why didn't he just level with us? That's what pisses me off! He sold us a bill of goods.

Redd jumped in quickly, "So, man, we started out talking about protestors and common ground. You said you could find some. What comes to mind?"

Morris chuckled. "I like you, man. You're a good listener."

"I'm a talker too, Morris, normally, just have a lot on my mind right now."

Morris looked hard at Mike.

"You okay, man?" he asked, sounding genuinely concerned.

"Yeah, I'm good. Just a rough couple of days. So, go on about 'common ground.'"

The invitation was all Morris needed.

"So, on the topic of protestors, I asked myself why so many protestors these days? What's that all about? Then one night, I heard the 2-S Student Deferment is no longer a 'get out of the war' card for the college students. Males, whose college ranking is low, with grades shall we say, 'less than,' now run the chance of gettin' drafted.

"Sounds to me like the middle-class boys are now gonna have skin in the game too. They'll be asked what price they're willing to pay for their country, just like us. I get it that they think things are wrong over here. Things ARE wrong over here, but I wonder how the college boy who gets drafted will personally, NOT theoretically, logically, or existentially feel when he's made it home alive, after 'Nam, standing on Terra Firma at the airport, and someone calls him out for being over here.

"Call him 'baby killer' or whatever. Will he be able to separate himself from the uniform and stoically say, 'They're attacking the uniform, not me personally?'"

"I think not," laughed Morris. "After doing time in this hellhole, I think the middle-class boy will be just as pissed as us working-class mutts. And it'll cut deep and hurt him like it would hurt you or me.

"Maybe the long hairs truly don't want to get their hands dirty. Maybe they honestly believe it's an immoral or illegal war. Call me base, but I am of the opinion that most are protesting to protect their asses, covered by brand name boxer shorts. I think most of them are so wrapped up in their private world of drugs, sex, and rock-and-roll AND self-import, that giving to the greater good is difficult, if not foreign, to them. They've been pampered.

"Requiring them to protect the liberties we all enjoy in the U.S. just might have the happy spin-off of them appreciating this country. We value what we have to work for. We value less what's given without sweat equity. Hard work and sacrifice keep us morally straight. But hell, those are just my thoughts, and it wouldn't be fair for me to generalize and lump everyone into one category, the way they're categorizing us with the word 'soldier.'"

"What's our common ground?" Morris asked, then answered, "Actually, I agree with a lot of the causes the protestors are marching for outside this war. I don't have any trouble with equal rights for blacks, including equal rights for jail time if blacks are doing something stupid like looting businesses or homes while rioting, but I'd be having the same trouble with whites if they were acting stupid in the same way.

"Not a matter of race, it's a matter of stupid. I'm walking right next to you, man, in this war, and would fight as hard to keep you alive as I would a white brother, and I'd expect you'd do the same for me."

Redd nodded in agreement at Morris, quite the truck driver extraordinaire, a philosopher in his own right, and a sharp thinker at that.

Feeling utterly relaxed with Redd now, Morris began again.

"I have three sisters, all older than me. I was the kid brother they all loved on. I want to see my sisters make the same pay I make for the same work. No question there. I'm with equality for women and equal pay for equal work—no difference between them and me. Hell, one of my sisters is protesting back in the States. She wants an end to this war and see me home safe. What can I say? That's her right.

"Shit, I go fishing and hunting in Colorado, where I come from, and I care about the rivers stayin' clean. Pollution is a concern, and so is the environment. What the hell? It's not like I'm a Martian or something, just because I'm over here. I care too.

"We DO have a common ground. Sometimes it just takes a little patience and good communication to find it. Don't take us out of the equation or make us the enemy just because some of us believe this fight needs to happen to keep the commies in check or that we're willing to fight the fight for our belief.

"This much I know, these issues would have a slim to no chance of ever being heard under a commie government. Our government might be crooked and imperfect, but I'll take it over what Khrushchev or Chairman Mao offers any day. They'd strangle all our freedoms if their regimes took over. Don't the long hairs get that? Look at how Mao murdered anyone not agreeing with him!

"That's the big picture. Keep the communists out first, then talk about freedoms and discuss the changes we want to see in the States. No need for these knuckleheads to turn on us and make this into an 'us or them' head game. As soon as that happens, both sides have lost."

More silence, followed by one last explosion from Morris as he threw the roach out the window, then slammed his fist against the door of the truck.

"What the fuck is going on anymore? That's what I want to know. What the fuck," and Morris spat out the window again. His anger and frustration intense. He was worked up.

"Life shouldn't be this hard."

Not much conversation after that, each man disgusted by the turn of events in-country and "The World." Heavy shit. Both Marines felt overwhelmed and exploited.

Morris dropped Redd off at the hospital. It was almost noon.

"The convoy will be back around 1500. I'll watch for you," Morris promised.

~~~

Redd had three hours. He hoped that would be enough time to check on Beau and locate Tweet. He entered the hospital, and a nurse directed him to where he could find Beau. Redd found the correct ward, saw a lot of guys on their backs, some with legs in traction, some without any legs. IV tubes hung from hooks extended along the ceiling, attached to many men needing blood, plasma, or drugs. He walked up and down the line of beds looking for Beau, periodically stopping to check names on the bottom of the beds where faces were either covered or unrecognizable.

Redd saw a doctor nearby reviewing a medical chart and walked over to him. He looked incredibly tired, understandably so, as this hospital had received over 190 wounded Marines in the last two days.

"Excuse me, sir. I'm looking for Marine Lance Corporal Beau Parker, came in late two days ago with lots of others from Operation Kingfisher. Can you tell me where he is?

"Sorry, son, I know who Parker was. He didn't make it. He died last night of unsustainable wounds."

Redd felt his legs buckle. First Jesse, now Beau. Three days back from getting married and now dead.

The doctor, seeing the impact on Redd, took him to an empty room to compose himself.

"That was a fierce battle son, take your time; no one will disturb you. What's your name, Marine?"

"Mike Redd, sir."

"Mike, be grateful you made it out alive and in one piece."

His head still spinning from the news, Redd appreciated the kindness of this Navy doctor. There was something familiar about him.

Redd looked at his nametag. "Lt. Campbell."

"Lieutenant Campbell, are you the doctor that helped me when I came here in May with a shoulder wound? Tweet brought me in."

"Ah, yes," he replied with a smile. "Tweet's friend. Not much I wouldn't do for that young lady. She's a sister of mercy around this place. Everyone loves her. Full of energy and kindness, that one."

"She looked after your friend, that's how I know he didn't make it. She hardly left his side and still managed to care for just about every other Marine coming out of that ambush. She said she knew Lance Corporal Parker.

"Tweet hasn't been home in two days, snatching bits of sleep here and there, like all of us. She was scared to death you might come here wounded, or worse. You're in luck. She's here now. Sit tight, and I'll find her for you."

He walked away, then turned, "I'm glad you made it, son. I'm sorry about your friend."

Redd sat down, placed his head between his hands, and sobbed.

~~~

When the bomb detonated, he, Angel, and Chingas were traveling ahead of Jesse and Beau, and once the action started, it took everything they had to fight their way through the VC. They'd tried to get back to them but couldn't make it; the bullets were too thick.

Redd took it incredibly hard because he was the designated third member of the gun team. Now, for the hundredth time, he wondered if Jesse and Beau's lives might have been saved if he'd walked with them instead of with Chingas and Angel.

Redd had already suffered through Jesse's death, but now Beau's too? He should have stayed closer to them. Why, why hadn't he stayed closer? It had been his responsibility to protect them.

212

Dear God, I tried to get back. You know that, Lord. I tried. I tried. Oh God, is it my fault they died?

Mike Redd, in that quiet spot inside the Da Nang Station Hospital, wept openly.

If it was my fault, Jess, if it was my fault, Beau, please forgive me. God, forgive me. Why wasn't I there for them?

~~~

"Mike, Mike, you're safe! I've been so afraid! Oh my God, thank you, thank you for keeping him safe!"

Tweets arms were around him, sheltered him, held him close, and they sobbed in each other's arms.

"Tweet, I should've stayed with them instead of walking ahead. Jess and Beau were talking, so Chingas, Angel, and I left when we were told to pull out. I wasn't that far ahead, but I should've been with them. If I'd been with them, it might be different. This could be my fault, Tweet. They might be alive if I'd stayed closer. Oh, my God. My God," he cried in anguish.

"Mike, listen. Listen. Calm down."

Tweet cupped his face in her hands and waited until his eyes were looking into hers.

"Breathe and listen. I've seen many things in this hospital, and when it comes to someone dying, there is usually another someone thinking, 'If only.' If only this, if only that. We who survive live with the 'if only.' But we cannot blame ourselves. We must not blame ourselves.

"There is a plan, and you have been granted life because He made sure you were walking ahead. We don't know what His plan is, but it was Jesse and Beau's time to meet Him, and your time has not yet come.

"You must believe and accept that; without questioning or living in guilt. Neither Jesse nor Beau would want that for you. Please, please, my love, hear me and accept this. This world needs you. I need you." Then in almost a whisper, "Our baby needs you."

"Our baby?" Mike looked into Tweet's eyes, shocked and confused.

She took his hand and pressed it to her stomach.

"Life is in me. Our love made life," she whispered to him and continued to hold him close.

~~~

Leading the convoy, Morris picked Redd up at exactly 1500. As Redd climbed up into the cab, he saw a sandwich wrapped in white paper on his seat.

"Thought you could use some grub," Morris said with a smile. "How'd your buddy Parker make out?"

"He didn't make it," Redd replied.

He looked at Morris, then said quietly, "I'm going to be a father."

THIRTY-EIGHT

MY NEW ORDINARY WORLD

1967

The scent of Beau was still on her pillow when word of his death arrived at her parent's home.

Beau died in the Da Nang Station Hospital.

Crying hysterically, Helen went crazy in a way. She screamed into her pillow in anger. She tore at her skin, needing the pain to keep her from feeling numb. She sobbed in her father's arms. How could her bed still smell of a man who no longer existed?

Daily, her father, Ben, stayed with her in her room. He sat in a soft, sage green chair by her bed and made sure his little girl had the comfort of his quiet presence. He knew how many tiny burgundy roses made up one sheet of wallpaper. One Hundred and Twenty.

Helen's mother, June, stayed busy in the kitchen, making Helen's favorite foods, trying to tempt her to eat.

Helen refused to come downstairs. She stayed in her upstairs bedroom, where she and Beau had shared their last days. She refused friends and phone calls. Helen closed her bedroom door and made a sanctuary of their memories. Neither parent could coax her from her self-imposed isolation.

Beau's parents received a desperate call from June, asking if they would stop by and spend time with their daughter-in-law, hoping it would do some good. Helen liked Beau's family, and perhaps they could speak with her about funeral arrangements. It needed to be done, and it involved the Parkers.

In speaking with them, June discovered they had already contacted the groomsmen at Beau and Helen's wedding to tell them of Beau's death. Beau's parents then had to broach the subject of possibly being pallbearers, should Helen wish Beau to be buried in Fort Myers.

June didn't know what to do about the many wedding gifts still stacked throughout the house, including Helen's room. Should Helen keep the gifts or return them? More importantly, was this the appropriate time to approach Helen with this?

Everything normal suddenly took on a sense of the surreal.

"Dear God," she prayed aloud, "Give me the strength to get through this, and show me how to provide comfort to my daughter."

~~~

The Parkers arrived and brought Helen's favorite dish, Norwegian waffle cakes, little heart-shaped waffles, crisp and warm. Helen would not see them, but she would see Kristian, Beau's older brother, in her room.

~~~

"Now that Beau is dead, you will have to live life for Beau. Beau lived his life as a Marine for you and himself," Helen said distantly. "You must relax and lighten up, Kristian. It's what Beau would want. I only see you now to tell you this."

Kristian watched Helen as she stood by her window and stared at the tree outside.

Did she really tell me to "lighten up"? Doesn't she realize I've just lost my brother?

Helen walked from the window and leaned on the edge of the bed across from where Kristian sat. He looked into the eyes of a woman who had once been exquisitely beautiful. They were red and swollen, her long brown hair disheveled. She was wearing Beau's football jersey, so large it looked like a dress.

Kristian's eyes drifted from Helen to the large window that overlooked the lawn, then returned to the bed where Beau had slept three days before. He could hear his brother's hearty laugh, almost see him. Eyes beginning to burn, and not wanting Helen to see his tears, he looked down and tried to focus on her words.

The thought, "she isn't all here," crossed his mind. Helen was not the person he'd known. This woman was harder, colder. Kristian was afraid for Helen and, believing this change came from grief, hoped it would be short-lived.

They had played together when they were young. Many times, Kristian came along as the third wheel while Beau and Helen dated. Neither ever minded and were happy for his company. His heart ached for her, remembering all the kindness and joy she had given to him and those around her. That was the Helen he knew.

"So, Kristian, you realize your responsibility to Beau; to relax and enjoy life," she said, wrapping things up perfunctorily, as though he were a tidy package, ready for a Christmas tree.

I'm being dismissed!

"Yes, Helen, I hear what you're saying, and I'll do my best. I'll look out for Ronny like Beau did and keep him on the straight and narrow. No promises there, but I'll try. I'll do what I can to fill Beau's shoes with Mama and Papa as well.

"I promise to God I'll laugh more, for Beau, and enjoy every day granted. Beau's life will not be wasted by me.

"Helen, would you come downstairs and say hello to Mama and Papa? They want to hold you. Dark days at our house too, Helen."

Helen declined. "Please give them my best. I'll come to visit when I can."

"Alright. Know we're here for you, and you'll always be a part of our family. I'll never forget the good times we had. Please stay in touch, Helen. Please?"

217

Helen inclined her head toward the open door, guided Kristian out, then softly closed it behind him.

~~~

It was hard seeing Kristian. He was large and blonde like Beau. Helen turned her back to the door and leaned against it. As glimmers of her reality once again took hold, she sank to the floor. Helen wrapped her arms around her knees and pulled them close to stave off the loneliness, and rocked. Tears slid down her ravaged face, hands too tired to wipe them. Helen's sorrow overwhelmed her. She had made it through seeing Kristian without breaking down.

~~~

Two weeks after Beau's death, she missed her period.

By three weeks, Helen's breasts were more tender than she had ever known them to be. By four weeks, she instinctively knew she was pregnant. At six weeks, she missed her second period, the rabbit died, and her doctor confirmed what she already knew.

Helen was pregnant with Beau's child.

~~~

June brought up meals and chattered about what Helen's friends were doing. Ben sat in the chair in her room for a few hours each day, not saying much but continuing to offer support with his presence. Ben did everything in his power to carry her through the ordeal to bring her peace. Helen wanted Beau buried at Arlington National Cemetery. She believed it's what Beau would have wanted.

At Beau's service, the Chaplin presented Helen with an American flag and Beau's Silver Star for Valor in combat against an enemy of the United States.

~~~

After weeks of isolation, Helen came out of her room and roamed the house. She strayed into the kitchen one morning while her mother was baking, the Settlement Cookbook on the counter open to the cookie section.

"Hello, sweet pea, good to see you up and about," June said as she smiled.

Helen looked at the recipe her mother was following. On the opposite page was the recipe she'd followed while making a care package for Beau. A different time, a different life. A smudge on the page caught her attention, probably her finger covered with butter, making the Snickerdoodle cookies Beau loved. She stared at the smudge, captivated, and mindlessly traced her finger around the butter stain, remembering. It was from a time when she was happy, and Beau was alive, and the world was full of possibilities ….

She felt as though she was in a trance, and that smudge held a secret.

It was then, on this ordinary day, in this ordinary place, that God spoke to her.

Go to Vietnam.

She heard the voice, clear as a bell.

Go to Vietnam.

She looked around. No one there. Just her mom and herself in the kitchen. Everything normal, but for the voice of God!

For the first time since Beau's death, her spirit soared. Was there hope? Was there a way she could quench her scorched soul?

Go to Vietnam, He'd said.

A great need consumed her. And she knew her need for Beau was not exhausted, would never be exhausted. He burned as strong as ever. The emptiness in her heart could be filled. Their love was not finished. It hadn't died. She only needed to breathe air into it; breathe the air Beau breathed, smell the earth Beau smelled, hear the sounds, gentle or not, that Beau heard … step into his world, and he would be there, hers once more.

Because God had told her to go, it would be so.

She would have this baby, and when the baby was old enough, she would put her nursing skills to use and volunteer for duty in Vietnam. She would be close to Beau again.

She confided in her mother about what just happened. June looked at Helen as though she'd gone mad.

"Go to Vietnam? Helen, that's lunacy!" June almost shouted.

"You have a child to consider! How can you even think of something like this? You're young. I know it's been terrible for you, but you'll get through this, and you'll move on with your life. Your baby and time will help you heal!"

"I'm not sure what this is, Mom, or where it will lead me, closure perhaps, maybe to something else, but God told me to go to Vietnam. He spoke to me!"

June stared at her daughter in utter disbelief. Had she lost her mind?

Helen answered her mother's incredulous look, "I need to know the details of his life and death over there, Mom. I need to be near Beau's spirit."

He's waiting for me in Vietnam. I know it.

That, she kept to herself.

THIRTY-NINE

BREATHING LIFE INTO AN ECHO

1969

The Naval Support Activity Station Hospital in Da Nang was situated between a Vietnamese village, an Army Special Forces Base, and the Marine Air Group. Composed of Quonset huts and tents, it was the largest Naval/Marine medical facility in South Vietnam.

The helicopter was critical in the war in Vietnam. It could land in battle zones to insert and extract troops and could rescue the wounded. The wounded could be delivered from the battlefield to the Station Hospital within 30-minutes. Those who arrived alive at the Station Hospital had a 90% chance of survival. The Huey helicopter was a weapon of war and a vehicle of rescue.

In the hospital triage center, rows of sawhorses supported canvas litters for the wounded, often carried in by other wounded Marines, stretcher-bearers, or corpsmen coming from the landing zone.

Expedience was the name of the game if the wounded were to survive, and everyone pitched in. The nurses were all volunteers. They worked twelve-hour shifts, six days a week, and were on call 24-hours-a-day every third day. When the choppers arrived, "incoming" was the word that shot electricity into the room. It was the cry that demanded urgency and pushed adrenaline through the veins of the doctors, nurses, and corpsmen on duty.

No matter how bone-tired, when "incoming" was heard, anyone on duty showed up and prepared for another round of grisly work; mangled bodies, horrendous head, facial, chest, and abdominal wounds, horrible burns from napalm and phosphorous, and thousands of amputations.

221

When they could speak, each Marine poured out the same plea, "Please don't let me die." Or, "Please, don't let them cut off my leg," when unbeknownst to him, the leg was already gone, blown away by some cruel device, a Bouncing Betty, a Claymore mine, exploding artillery, something—just blown away. Never to return.

Corpsmen or nurses triaged and classified the incoming.

"Expectants" were the less fortunate. Alive for the moment, these were the Marines "expected" to die. They were placed against a wall and made as comfortable as possible. Effort and attention were first given to those who had the greatest chance of surviving.

"Treatables" were taken to a cavernous room. Here, the staff went about the task of saving them.

In this room, life and death played out at a frenetic pace. Cries from the wounded were heard until they succumbed to anesthesia, some never to wake up. Commands were shouted. Large pans of bloody bandages found their way to the floor. Staff's shoes were quickly covered with blood from the bodies on stretchers that doubled as operating tables. Throughout it all, blood was tracked everywhere, making floors slick from its profusion while ten, fifteen, or more surgeries happened simultaneously. These were the images of mercy conducted at Da Nang Station Hospital.

The hand that once held a weapon, caressed a face, wore a wedding band; the arm with the tattoo of "Mom," that swung a bat, threw the football; the legs that ran and jumped as a child, skied in snow or water, pedaled a bike, walked; were all summarily dumped into a tub for burning.

Those working here were 5-star caretakers, encouraging, confident, and skillful. They worked as a team with many varied specialists to save who and what they could.

~~~

Dogpatch was an encampment of refugees and disenfranchised adjacent to the hospital, the population growing exponentially. A hodgepodge of humanity; huts, dilapidated shacks, restaurants, barbershops, movie theaters, and bars. It was filled with refugees from North Vietnam, as well as the Vietnamese whose homes or farmlands had been bombed or destroyed by the rainbow of defoliants used by the U.S. Sprayed from the air to destroy vegetation and expose the enemy hiding in the jungle, the colorful sounding agents, white, pink, green, purple, and blue were used with various degrees of success. The most successful, and memorable, was orange. Agent Orange. It poisoned not only the earth, but also the water, livestock, and humans. Americans and Vietnamese alike would live with the insidious effects of Agent Orange for decades.

Tweet's walk to the hospital through Dogpatch took no time at all.

~~~

She had been working alongside a new nurse. Today they carried away a large tub, heavy with recently amputated limbs. The nurse was trying hard not to wretch, gagging despite her efforts.

A fresh recruit.

"You are new here, yes?"

"Yes." Helen gulped the answer and swallowed to keep her lunch from coming up. "My name is Helen Parker."

"Hello, Helen, welcome to Da Nang. Come here, by the doorway. Let's sit down and breathe some fresh air. I know I need some. It was a terrible battle today."

She patted the threshold of the door for Helen to sit on.

"Don't worry, they're not always this devastating. We have time now. The surgeries are done, and this is the end of the clean-up, so it's alright for us to sit and breathe." Tweet reached over and gave Helen's arm a reassuring touch.

Today's ambush was costly to American Marines who had fallen victim to the U.S. made Claymore mines and Bouncing Betty's, stolen by the Cong, and turned against the Marines. What the Claymores didn't maim with their deadly half-circle spray of steel balls, the Betties took out with their explosive charge, leaping out of the ground, ripping through legs and guts of anyone unlucky enough to step on one.

"So many bodies blown apart. I knew it was bad here from the coverage we saw on the news, but I never thought it could be this grotesque," whispered Helen.

Helen wrapped her arms around her knees, keeping her bloody hands from touching the fabric of her uniform. She sobbed, her head resting on her knees.

"It will be alright," Tweet whispered, moving a little closer to Helen. In a motherly way, she put her arm around this young woman.

Beyond the doorway, Helen looked at Dogpatch through tear-filled eyes. Children played with a soccer ball, an old man led a water buffalo, and two women in black pants, colorful silk tops, and coolie hats sat in a cart drawn by a goat. She gazed at the scene of "normalcy" while assailed by the powerful odor of iron-laced blood from the tub next to them. The buzzing sound of flies grew loud as they descended upon the carnage. It was then that Helen realized how insanely irrational her world had become.

~~~

Helen heard her name called, over and over, and as she opened her eyes, she saw Tweet's face above her.

"Helen, are you alright?" Helen realized she had passed out and slumped into Tweet's arms.

Tweet helped her to sit up. Still lightheaded from days of stress and lack of sleep, Helen took a moment to allow her world to settle. Tweet left, returned with a cool, wet rag, and wiped Helen's face and hands. A corpsman removed the tub. After a few moments, Helen looked at Tweet and said, "Thank you."

Tweet replied, "This is my country. I've lived here my entire life. I, too, am sickened by what I've seen today. My name is Tweet. I'd tell you my last name, but you wouldn't be able to pronounce it. I've shortened it to 'Dai,'" and Tweet smiled widely.

224

She and Helen laughed at the blatant truth of this statement, and each felt the beginning of a camaraderie.

"How did you come to be here, Helen?" asked Tweet, trying to make conversation with this fragile woman, talking about anything or nothing, to keep her focused on something other than the limbs and surgeries.

"My husband died in this hospital. I'm trying to come to terms with his death. I needed to come here, see his world, and where he died."

"Your last name is Parker?" Tweet asked, her interest piqued.

"Yes," Helen replied.

"I knew a Parker once. What was your husband's first name?"

"Beau, his name was Beau Parker."

"Mon Dieu," gasped Tweet, as the shock of those words coursed through her. "I not only knew Beau Parker, but I was also with him, by his bed, when he died."

Helen's face was emotionless, unable to react. She leaned against the door frame to steady herself. She would not humiliate herself with a second blackout!

Tweet took Helen's hand in hers and clasped it tightly.

"One and all, life and death, always the same interconnected circle. You were meant to come here and find me." Then squeezing Helen's hand, she added, "We Buddhists don't believe in coincidence."

Tweet's statement, "You were meant to come here and find me," made more sense to Helen than anything she'd heard since Beau's death. Life and death, an interconnected circle, no coincidences.

She'd made the right choice by coming. She was meant to be here. She could let go of the insecurity she'd carried since she'd come to Vietnam. She was justified, no matter what anyone said. She now knew she was on "her" path.

"Please tell me about my husband, every detail. Please Tweet. I need to know," Helen pled.

"Yes, I'll tell you all, but first, let's wash up, then I'll take you to a shaded spot where we can sit."

FORTY

BEAU, I HEARD YOUR CALL

1969

Tweet answered all of Helen's questions, telling her everything she knew and remembered about Beau. Then reassured Helen he was at peace and had died quietly, a hero. Tweet chose not to mention the anger felt by Marines and medical staff over lives lost and terrible injuries sustained from that poorly planned battle. It was not information that would have eased Helen's pain, nor did she mention her relationship with Mike. Beau was the focus today. Tweet's sad story of Mike would be for another time. Small steps, and in due time, the rest would be revealed.

Tweet finished her account, and the two women sat in silence. Both filled with sadness.

After a while, Helen looked at Tweet.

"Tweet, I'm interested in what you believe. What you said earlier resonated with me and validated not only my thinking but also what I've been feeling. Would you tell me a little more about your beliefs, and Buddhism? I feel as though I was led to you for many reasons."

"Yes, I will tell you something about our beliefs," She looked at Helen for a while, wondering what teaching would be relevant to her spirit, then began.

"There is a Vietnamese Buddhist monk, Thich Nhat Hanh, nominated last year for the Nobel Peace Prize by your peace activist, Martin Luther King, Jr. My mother was a Buddhist who read his works and taught them to me. One teaching that I believe will have meaning for you is impermanence. Do you wish me to speak on that?"

"Yes, Tweet. Go ahead. I'm listening."

"Something Thich Nhat Hanh considers important for us is the concept of 'impermanence.' He teaches there is no such thing as 'permanence.' Everything in our life is impermanent.

"Without impermanence, life as we know it could not be; a child could not grow into something wonderful, a tyrannical government would govern until eternity, the sky would look the same every day. Ideas, feelings, governments, trees, flowers, people, all impermanent.

"We want things to be permanent, steady, familiar, remain the same. We believe permanence is that which gives us a sense of security. But it's a false sense. Nothing is permanent, and everything is subject to change.

"You Americans know something of this when you say, 'The only thing permanent is change,' and some of you funnier Americans say the only thing permanent is 'death and taxes.'

"Flowers decompose, but knowing this won't stop us from loving their beauty or their scent. It's because the blossoms are fleeting that we love them more. It is because something is impermanent that we should treasure it more, respect it more, appreciate it more.

"The practice of 'seeing' in this fashion promotes understanding, acceptance, and an opportunity to appreciate and engage in every moment. To live in the 'now' is to live fully in the moment. We come to recognize that every moment is precious but fleeting, and we should rejoice in the gift of life.

"Your memories of Beau and the love you shared is a reality, but it is not the same today as it was then. It has changed. Nonetheless, the reality of your memory and the knowledge of your love should give you confidence and a reason to rejoice every day. It can carry you forward, Helen, and provide you with peace.

"You've had someone precious taken from you. But you still carry Beau's love. Let that love strengthen you, make you more resilient, and understand that more can and will be taken from you. But when living fully in the moment, the loss won't hold the same suffering. You will be at peace knowing you gave and received all you could, appreciating each moment of each day. Your days of appreciation will become years of rejoicing. Peace comes from living in the present and accepting that impermanence changes all things."

Understanding the power of these words and their concept, Helen decided it was a practice she would incorporate into her life. She took a deep breath and squeezed Tweet's hand in thanks. Helen was grateful to have shared love with Beau AND, equally as important, was the knowledge that she could continue to share this love with him. He had changed, but their love was real and would continue. She was grateful to have met this wise woman.

Helen had never thought like this. She realized she and Beau had lived in the moment and all their moments were precious. That was why their love was so deep.

She remembered when she and some high school girlfriends visited a psychic one Saturday for fun. The psychic had said, "Even in death, we continue to grow and learn." Helen now wondered if Beau was continuing his journey of learning. These ways of approaching life and death were new to her. For the first time, Helen recognized that she could let go of Beau's death and her grief, understanding that he and his love would remain.

Helen relaxed as she focused again on Tweet's words. She looked around and saw Vietnam differently from when she'd arrived. She liked this woman.

"I've had to deal with more impermanence than I've wanted to," Helen confided.

"As have I," replied Tweet quietly.

~~~

Helen felt stronger after that conversation. She found immense comfort in caring for the wounded. In nursing Marines back to health or by offering a safe presence in death, she did it all and did it well. They were all "Beaus" to her.

With time, Helen's concept of life and death changed dramatically. She believed that she took care of the wounded here on earth, and Beau's strong and capable hands would accept those who passed. He would know what to do. Earth and Heaven, one circle. He was her angel looking over her and those she cared for. Beau and all these young men were in a different place, call it Heaven, call it a parallel universe, or nirvana, it didn't matter because they were all safe.

Helen was comforted with the idea of one fluid process between Earth and Heaven. She and Beau were still a team. She came to understand that by helping one, she was helping all. "One and All, the same," as Tweet had said at their first meeting. Not precisely the Southern Baptist way of thinking, but it made sense to Helen.

Do unto others, as you would have them do unto you. Wasn't that The Golden Rule? Couldn't "others" mean a collective all?

In time, Tweet told Helen about Mike Redd and their love story, and that Mike, Beau, Jesse, Angel, and Chingas were the gun team for 2/9 Hotel Company. "No coincidences," remarked Tweet shaking her head and smiling gently. "Life is amazing, yes?"

Helen responded with a smile of her own, "Yes, you and I are a 'club' of two. The cheerleaders for Hotel's fighting gun team!"

Tweet laughed at the thought of being a cheerleader. Helen, yes. Tweet, no! "We were meant to be here for these men, Helen, but we were also meant to meet, help each other, and become friends."

~~~

Tweet had given birth to Lucky within months of Helen giving birth to John Jr.

Tweet's little girl's name was Lucky, for the day Tweet met Mike.

Helen learned many Vietnamese considered babies born of American soldiers to be cast-offs. They were called "Dust of Life" children. Communities often shunned Amerasian children, and children born of black soldiers were especially ill-treated. Vietnamese, particularly those from rural villages, with stronger ties to the past, believed "skins should not mix," Women involved with American soldiers, especially black soldiers, were held in contempt.

This didn't worry Tweet. She lived life on her terms. Her daughter Lucky was a beautiful, sunny toddler.

Helen missed John dearly, especially when playing with Lucky. She recognized all too well the sacrifices made at home for her and her son.

She'd wrestled mightily between staying with John Jr. or leaving him to go to Vietnam. Helen knew she had no choice. Her need to understand and make sense of Beau's death would cast a lifelong shadow if left unresolved. She had to go.

Truth be told, she secretly believed that by going to Vietnam, she would be close to Beau once more. Their story remained unfinished. She would return to John when this great yearning no longer consumed her. She felt guilty for leaving him, also for asking her parents to care for him while she searched for her inner peace. She understood John was her responsibility. If she could have taken him, she would have, but that was impossible. She vowed she would make her absence up to John, someday, somehow.

FORTY-ONE

J ohn stay clean, so you look good for your Mother," June said for the third time in the last hour.

She sat on the porch swing, enjoying the smell of sea air mixed with orange blossoms. It was April, and the blossoms were early. "Lots of oranges this season," she mused, watching bees fly from flower to flower, pollinating each. Fresh juice for breakfast and screwdrivers when the girls met for their bridge game. John's fourth birthday was tomorrow.

Helen was returning from three years in Vietnam. She'd seen John each time she took a leave of absence. A week, maybe two. Within days after his first birthday, she'd left John and June reflected on the many changes and experiences Helen had missed with her beautiful son. A shame. Precious years she would never retrieve.

June thought back to the year John Jr. was born, 1968. A year unlike any other she had experienced in the United States. A year of blood and violence. Rioting in Chicago after Martin Luther King Jr.'s assassination. Rioting, burning and looting in Washington, D.C. The assassination of Robert Kennedy, The Battles of Khe Sanh, Hue, and Tet.

All the anger in hell seemed to erupt outward and fill the soul of every man and woman in the United States. Fighting, bloody faces, clubbed bodies, National Guardsmen, and police, summoned to quell disruption on college campuses and America's cities.

Families became divided politically and socially, seemingly at odds at every turn, much as families had been during the Civil War.

June realized her daughter's feelings of anger, frustration, and loss were reflected in London, Paris, Berlin, Prague, and Stockholm, where demonstrations called for an end to the violent war and an end to humanitarian and political inequities.

Nineteen sixty-eight began with North Vietnam attacking Khe Sanh in the most prolonged and deadly battle of the war. U.S. Marines were surrounded and under siege for seventy-seven days. Aircraft delivered vital supplies of food, ammunition, and medicine since all roads in and out of Khe Sanh were in enemy hands. America watched on television every graphic detail while eating their evening dinner.

Khe Sanh pitted thirty-thousand Viet Cong and NVA regulars against six-thousand Marines and other American forces.

One week later, the Tet Offensive began. The Viet Cong conducted simultaneous attacks on thirteen major South Vietnamese cities over 26 days. It took U.S. forces almost nine months to regain lost ground.

The enemy failed to win either Khe Sanh or Tet, but the U.S. paid the price with human life. In April 1968, 520 American soldiers returned home in caskets.

That same month, the Broadway play "Hair" premiered. Helen, June, and Ben went to the movies to see Stanley Kubrick's film, "2001, A Space Odyssey," Otis Redding sang, "Sittin' on the Dock of the Bay," on the radio. After a long and intense labor, Helen delivered John Parker, Jr. to this world of contradictions, and divisiveness ... screaming.

~~~

Now, four years later, June anticipated Helen's return with unease. Who would Helen be, and how long would she stay this time?

The last time Helen returned, it was from New York City. She had addressed the United Nations on the plight of the Amerasian children in Vietnam, fathered by American soldiers. The prohibitive American bureaucracy, combined with restrictive Vietnamese red-tape, deterred U.S. soldiers from marrying Vietnamese mothers or adopting their children.

Lovingly, but sadly, June's eyes rested on her grandson, busy at play, pounding wooden pegs into a bench with a little blue hammer. He was also an orphan of sorts. How different his life would have been had Beau lived. This damned war destroyed everything, and for what? Helen was never here for John, tending to her needs first by nursing America's Marines, now abandoning her son while hypocritically advocating for abandoned Vietnamese children.

Yes, the situation was sad, deplorable, and John was another shameful human casualty of the war. As in all wars, June thought, the women and children were the long-term casualties, hardest hit, and impacted for generations to come.

She breathed a little easier, looking around at the comfortable beauty she'd created. Her "nest" looked perfect today; her home and furnishings could grace the cover of a Better Homes and Gardens magazine.

Be thankful for all you have! There are many with so much less!

June told herself everything would be all right this time. Helen would return to them and become a mother to her son. President Nixon promised an "honorable end to this war," and the Paris Peace Accords, conducted by Henry Kissinger, were underway to meet that goal. Life was getting better, but the uncertainty of Helen's plans festered.

John Jr., what a treasure! Helen's absence left a void greater than June could have imagined, and caring for this sweet boy minimized June's loneliness. Sometimes she wondered if her anger toward Helen resulted from the twinge of guilt she felt for the gift of John. Perhaps her anger was legitimate; a single parent had no right to leave a child, especially to place herself in harm's way when the child's other parent was dead. Period. It was irresponsible. Well, perhaps irresponsible was too harsh a word, but Helen's actions showed a lack of priorities. June softened and tried to justify the choices of her errant daughter, who'd known too much pain early on. Yes, Helen's causes were meaningful, but she was a mother first, not some visitor in her son's life. They'd argued vehemently the last time Helen came home.

When was that, how long ago?

Would she ever get over Beau?

Would she ever become whole and allow herself to love again, love her son or another man?

No matter how the conversations began, it always ended the same, "I may not be doing what you think is right, Mom, but I need to do it!"

Helen was a casualty, like Beau; the only difference was Helen's suffering was never put to rest. June's heart ached for her daughter, and her stomach tightened. She hoped Helen would show some inner peace, but she'd prayed that prayer before.

My sweet, beautiful, cheerleader daughter ... how I miss you.

Will you ever return to us?

June sipped her martini and rocked herself into a state of numbness on her perfect white porch.

~~~

Helen arrived with an excitement June hadn't seen since before Beau's death. That evening, after reading a bedtime story to John and tucking him in bed, Helen joined her parents for drinks on the porch.

Ben made small talk, a true gentleman of the south, catching her up on John's antics. There was laughter when he described John's attempt to sing Little Bunny Foo Foo or dance the Hokey Pokey. June held her breath, hoping this might be the beginning of a reunion. It felt like it. She would not allow her smile to waver. During a pause in the stories and laughter, Helen took a deep breath and began.

"I've met a French doctor working with Médecins Sans Frontières."

June's heart sank as Helen continued.

"He helped create MSF last year. We call them Doctors Without Borders. I'm sure you'll be hearing about them in the news. They're international relief doctors who've recently united to reduce political interference and obstruction of medical aid in war or crises.

235

"Since the Paris Peace Talks have resumed, the scuttlebutt in `Nam is that we'll be pulling most of our troops out soon. Anyway, my tour is up in July. If you'll have me, I plan to come home for a few months, spend time with you and John, then join this group in late October."

Helen saw the disbelieving and disappointed looks on her parents' faces but continued.

"I want to be a part of this effort. I hope you'll support me. There are hundreds of thousands of Burundian refugees who have resettled in Tanzania and need help. I think I've done all I can to help in the efforts of the Vietnamese and Amerasian children. Working with these doctors will allow me to help refugees who have no tools or means in place to deal with their horrific losses."

Ben's eyes teared as his head dropped slowly to his chest.

Helen saw his reaction but pressed on.

"Dad, there's no justice for these children or women. The kids who have lost limbs stay that way. Prosthetics are expensive and require adjustment as they grow. They face trauma and live in fear of bombings or attacks. The girls are often raped, as are their mothers. They live with wounded and disfigured people, loss of parents, schools, medicine, normalcy, or hope. They become the world's throwaways. They need all the help the world can give them. I want to help."

June could contain herself no longer.

"Helen, STOP! What about John? He's a child too and needs his mother!"

"Mom, John has you and Dad. I would hope someone would do this for John if he became one of these children. They have no one and need so much more than you can understand. Please support me and give me your blessing to go."

June leaned forward and took Helen's hand's in hers.

"Helen, you're John's mother. Not me. John doesn't have a father. He has Ben, a grandfather. Neither of us is a replacement for you. You've found a good cause to follow, another good cause. It's always something else to distract you from the reality that Beau is dead. He's DEAD, Helen, and you need to face that! I will support everything you do in your life if it involves becoming a better mother to John, but I will not give you my blessings to continue to run away."

~~~

John's 4th Birthday Party was the following day, and neighbors came to wish him Happy Birthday and Helen a welcome home. The Parkers stopped in as did John's Uncles, Kristian and Ronny. It was a day of forced happiness. Three days later, and with more tears than words from everyone, Helen left John Jr., her parents, and Fort Myers.

FORTY-TWO

DEATH TAKES US ALL

1967

The trip back from Da Nang Station Hospital to Con Thien was a quiet one for Morris and Redd.

"So long, Redd, hope we meet again. Keep the faith, brother. Oh, and congratulations man!"

"Thanks for the lift, Morris, and the sandwich. That was nice. Keep on keepin' on."

"Sure, man. Hey, sorry if I talked your ear off on the way down."

"No worries, Morris."

And with that, Morris put the massive truck in gear and drove off, leaving diesel exhaust and the red dust of Con Thien to settle over Redd.

Redd caught sight of Chingas, holding a mirror and shaving. It had been a surprisingly quiet day on The Hill with no incoming artillery. Everyone was using the opportunity to get caught up on shaving, mending clothes, writing letters, cleaning weapons, all the while listening to the latest songs on the Armed Forces Radio station.

"To Sir With Love" was playing, and several Marines were laughing hard at the Marine who loudly sang falsetto, hands pretending to hold his heart, and eyes looking upward toward the heavens. Lulu, was London's newest pop-singer.

Beau was gone.

Redd walked toward the remnants of the gun team, searching for fresh faces, the replacements for the wounded and dead. Jesse and Beau's replacements.

238

Someone yelled, "Look out!" and he instinctively ducked as a football landed next to him, a poor throw by someone out of practice.

Angel was sitting on a poncho liner, leaning against a sandbag bunker. With pencil in hand, a drawing pad rested against his pulled-up legs. He saw Redd approach, and both Chingas and Angel stopped what they were doing and looked at him with questioning eyes. Mike shook his head and quietly said, "He didn't make it."

Angel looked away, then down at his drawing. Using the new Faber colored pencils Aunt Rosalina sent, he'd sketched a big Marine carrying a wounded Marine to safety. Now, at the bottom, he wrote, "Death Takes Us All."

The new Lieutenant walked over to Redd along with other grunts from the platoon wanting news about Beau. Redd just shook his head, "No."

Without saying a word, they either sat down or slowly walked away.

The big Norwegian was gone. Every Marine felt the pain and loss of both Jesse and Beau, honorable men who would be missed. One brought strength and wisdom, the other strength and humor.

These fighting men were young. Like Jesse, many were teenagers away from their families for the first time. Only wanting to be told what to do, they would then, by God, do their damnedest to get the job done. A true family, they looked out for each other, and did what they could to ease life for their brothers. The boys in Vietnam in 1967 were America's best a General had said of them. When one brother died, it felt like a family member was gone.

It was a somber evening on the Hill of Angels, filled with memories and reflections … and sadness.

Redd decided not to share news of Tweet's pregnancy. It was a time for sorrow. It was a time to honor the two they had lost. He would pass the news to Chingas and Angel another time, a more appropriate time. He did, however, seek out the new Lieutenant the following day.

~~~

"Lieutenant, Sir, do you have a minute?"

"Sure, Redd, whatcha need?"

"I didn't want to say anything in front of the men yesterday, the news being what it was, but I need help. My girl lives in Da Nang, and she gave me fantastic news yesterday – she's pregnant. I want to marry her. What paperwork do I need, and how do I get it started?"

"Redd, do you know what you're doing? Is she a bar girl?" was the immediate response.

"No sir, she saved my life near Marketplace and works at the hospital in Da Nang. She's someone of value, and I love her."

The Lieutenant paused a moment, then replied, "It's a complicated process, Redd, and involves a helluva lot of paperwork on our side and the South Vietnamese side. The South stalls a lot; I hear it's a deterrent to make it more complicated than it should be. They don't want their women 'mixing skin' with American soldiers."

"I'm doing this Lieutenant, and I'll re-up if it takes too long on my present tour. I'm not leaving without her." Redd stubbornly replied.

"Long as you know what you're doing, Redd, I'm on your side. I'll find out specifics and help you any way I can. I'm told you're a good Marine."

"Thanks, Lieutenant, I appreciate it."

It would remain relatively quiet for these Marines for the next few months. Unknown to them, the North's focus had shifted from Leatherneck Square to Khe Sanh, where a buildup of NVA regulars was about to engage in an all-out effort to displace 6,000 Marines from their combat base.

240

FORTY-THREE

THE END OF A DREAM

1967

In the days that followed, Redd thought of the Monk who appeared in his dream while he lay wounded in Tweet's home. He'd gotten into the habit of referring to him as his "hallucination."

"Sow your seed" was the phrase the Monk had used in Mike's dream, and it ping-ponged around in his head as he trudged through heat and rain, ate his C-Rations, smoked his cigarettes, and laughed with the men in his squad when there was something worth laughing about.

Angel and Chingas had laughed hard when Redd told them Tweet was pregnant.

"So, you got it in you, man!" Angel patted his back.

"You're the man, alright! Livin' life in the middle of a war!" Chingas congratulated him.

"We know you love her Redd, so whatcha gonna do?" Angel asked.

"I've already asked the Lieutenant to start the process for us to get married. I'm getting' hitched fellas and damn happy about it!"

It was good news for all three and lightened the grief they'd been dealing with. Both men liked Tweet and were happy for Redd.

~~~

Several weeks later, Morris showed up unexpectedly.

"Hey man, the Lieutenant said to come get you when I told him I could use some help with supplies on this trip."

Morris was smiling big. "C'mon, let's get to Da Nang!"

241

Redd grinned back, losing no time following Morris to the idling truck.

"Hey man, thanks for whatever you had to do with this!"

"It ain't nothing, just lookin' out for a fellow Marine. You needed this. And thank your Lieutenant when you get back, he had a little something to do with it too."

Redd smiled wide and said, "Let's get truckin' man!"

~~~

"'Choi oi'… good heavens!" Tweet exclaimed as she greeted him in her doorway. "What a beautiful surprise!"

She wrapped her arms around Mike and pulled him inside. He stepped into her small space and pulled her close, kissing her hard, his body responding to the nearness of her.

"Ummm, my American soldier want some boom boom?" Tweet laughed, teasing him, and mocking the speech of the Vietnamese prostitutes. "Me love you, long time soldier," she continued.

They both laughed, knowing how special these captured moments were.

She was on call as always but was off-duty today.

"No coincidences, Mike," she whispered. "We have just now. I could be called to the hospital any minute, so we must be 'rikkitik,' very fast. Then we can take our time."

They made love. Not as 'rikkitik' as Tweet suggested but thoroughly as Mike needed, lost in each other, during and after, laughing, kidding, holding, and just being.

How lucky am I to be holding and loving this precious woman, who is mine? I am blessed.

Afterward, Tweet asked, "Are you hungry?"

"Yup, hungry for more," he replied with a grin on his face.

"Ahh, no. Now we eat. Let me make you some food."

"Let's celebrate! Is there a place I can take you?" his eyebrows up, his eyes smiling, love and contentment covered his face.

"Yes, we'll go to the best restaurant in Dogpatch! The Blue Dahlia. Homemade coastal food and cheap!" she replied.

"Speaking of money Tweet, I've made arrangements for money to come to you out of my pay. I think it should start in a few weeks, so be on the lookout."

"No, no, my love," began Tweet. "I'm not that kind of girl. I'm proud. I can take care of myself and make it on my own!"

"You're my girl Tweet, and I WANT to take care of you. I know I don't NEED to. I want you and our baby to have a nest egg just in case. That's MY baby you're carrying so 'sinloi minoi,' 'too bad honey,' the money's coming, and you're taking it with no more discussion."

Tweet laughed harder.

"'Sinloi minoi,' is it? Who's teaching you Vietnamese?"

"You're my love, Tweet, and I want us to communicate in every way we can. I don't know much about marriage or how two people can stay in love with each other. I never had a family to learn from, but I want that for us. I want us to stay together forever.

"I've been thinking a lot about this Tweet, and I figure talking, really talking with each other and listening, really listening to what the other is saying must be the secret of a good relationship. That's why I'm learning Vietnamese."

Mike then got down on one knee and, with tears in his eyes, quietly asked, "Tweet, will you marry me?" Tweet's eyes welled with tears.

"You know my heart has already said 'yes' to yours. I want to be yours forever too. Yes! Yes! Mike, I will marry you! I have loved you since the first day we spoke.

"Tweet Redd! That sounds friendly, yes?"

With a large grin, Mike replied, "Yes! That sounds very friendly, my Cong Khi, my sweet monkey."

243

"Ha, Ha! I like that! I like that you wish to learn my language! I love you, Mike Redd, from Macon, Georgia, but more importantly, my lover, I like you, I like the person you are.

"And as we are to be husband and wife, I will gratefully accept your money and 'put it in my sock' as you Americans say, for our baby. Our sweet baby! Thank you for your kindness and thoughtfulness, Mike. Thank you for loving me. Thank you for wishing to be my husband!"

They stayed in Tweet's room a little longer, making plans for their future. Mike gave Tweet the notarized papers he'd been carrying in his pocket, addressing his intentions to marry her and that she was pregnant with his child.

"Just in case, Tweet, you never know."

They left for food, both feeling ravenous. What a beautiful day it had become. The best day for both.

~~~

As they turned the corner, heading to the Blue Dahlia, Mike's arm around Tweets waist, they collided into a man.

"Nhat," Tweet said, surprised. "What are you doing here?"

"I'm here looking for my sister- in- law. I've heard you keep company with a black soldier. I see the rumors are true."

"It is none of your concern, Nhat," Tweet angrily replied.

"It IS my concern. You still carry my brother's name, and I will not have you disgrace it. My name is being dishonored as well!"

"Your brother is dead, and I can be with whom I please."

"You have no rights! You shame me, Thuy. Tell me you will stop seeing this American or live to regret your choice. I have a name and a position to think of."

His voice was threatening, and his presence sinister. Not understanding Vietnamese, but clearly sensing the threat to Tweet, Mike grabbed Nhat's shirt.

"Get the hell away from Tweet," he said menacingly and pushed Nhat away from where they stood.

Nhat spat on the ground by Mike's boots and, in English, snapped back, "She's my brother's wife."

Mike moved close to Nhat's face, his eyes icy and steady, and growled, "That's in the past brother, she's about to be my wife. Now get the hell away from us."

Mike took a step closer to Nhat, his fingers clenching into a fist, and Nhat stepped back, not wanting to feel what he knew would be a hard blow from this large Marine.

Mike took Tweet's arm and walked away. Nhat shouted, "You will regret this, American nigger."

"I'm afraid, Mike," Tweet said solemnly when there was distance between Nhat and them. "He's a reckless man and full of, how do you say it 'aggrandizement'? We must be careful."

"Yeah, he's full of shit alright, and a loose cannon to boot. No need to worry, Cong Khi. Are you not with Lanh Huu, your street-smart man?" And as they walked on, Redd smiled to himself as he thought of Jesse saying, 'Just keep moving forward.'

~~~

They ate quietly. Mike told Tweet he would finish his degree with the G.I. Bill and become a journalist, then told her about life in the United States. Tweet asked Mike if they could bring Papasan, her sister Thanh, and nephew Tran to the U.S. after the baby was born and after Mike finished his last semester.

"Tweet, your family is my family. They've been good to me. I want them to join us in a new and better life."

Mike tried to keep Tweet's spirits up, but Nhat had tarnished the sparkle that was theirs only moments before.

Mike paid the bill and escorted Tweet out of the Blue Dahlia.

Stepping into the sunshine, Mike felt a cool breeze across his face. He was about to say it was the first cool breeze he'd felt in months when a shot rang out.

Mike was dead before he hit the ground. Tweet, on her knees, held Mike's head in her lap and looked up at a rooftop from where the shot had come. There stood Nhat with a rifle. "Nhat! Xuống địa ngục đi! Nhat! Go to the Devil!" she screamed.

A crowd gathered as she openly wept and cradled Mike close to her. She heard someone say, "Black American soldier" with disgust.

"His blood is red like yours," Tweet screamed at those around her. Covering Mike's face from their view with her now blood-covered body, she would not let Mike hear their words. She would protect him from their unkindness.

"Mike, Mike," Tweet sobbed, well aware that some of the bystanders had disdain for her as well.

I will never feel shame for loving you, Mike! Never! Never! Stay with me!

Tweet felt a presence, then a soft touch on her shoulder. She looked up into the face of a monk in orange robes.

"You gave him peace and all he ever needed. He is well with himself, child," the Monk whispered to Tweet, and then like an illusion, vanished.

~~~

Morris arrived at the hospital to pick up Redd and heard the news. The Military Police were working with the South Vietnamese to locate Nhat, but everyone knew he would never be caught. He disappeared as quickly as he'd shown up.

With a heavy heart, Morris drove back to Con Thien, knowing how bad this would be for the men on The Hill. He looked down at his shirt and realized it was wet from tears.

246

FORTY-FOUR

WE ARE ONLY CARGO

1968-1975

A ngel flew back to the states on his Freebird in '68, his tour of duty in Vietnam complete.

Before leaving Da Nang, he stopped by the hospital to say goodbye to Tweet, giving her a small-framed picture of the five Marines, cigars in hand. Angel told her about the picture and how happy everyone was for Beau's marriage. He provided his Aunt Rosalina's Chicago address and phone number on the back of the photo and something else for her to read after he left.

"Tweet," he said, smiling, "I'll always be a Marine, and Marines don't cry, but I'll miss you. I wish things could've been different for you and Mike."

That night, Tweet slid the cardboard from behind the frame and read Angel's words.

"If you ever need anything, I'm here to help you. It's what Mike would have done for my girl if I had one! Your good friend, Angel Santiago, once upon a time known as 'Sweetness.'"

Chingas also stopped by to say goodbye to Tweet before returning to the States.

He'd re-enlisted, completed his second tour, and now it was his time to go home. He had a few days in Da Nang before shipping out and stopped by the Station Hospital to look in on Tweet and say goodbye. To his surprise, Tweet introduced him to Helen, who'd arrived a few months before. She had baby pictures of John Jr. to show Chingas. It felt like a most wonderful small reunion!

"Why did you re-up, Chingas?" Helen asked.

"Well, I'll tell you. I had a friend named Jesse McGowan, who took me under his wing when I arrived in Vietnam. He looked out for me and cared about me. He showed me the ropes. Might well have saved my life because of that. Jess took care of me like Beau took care of Jess when he arrived. Time for me to do my part. What goes around, comes around, and I decided to pass this forward."

Then he laughed and said, "Hell, I'm a Mexican boy living in New York City. I had nothin' better to do!"

He wrote his name, address, and parent's phone number on a piece of paper and said, "If there's ever a need, please call."

As he turned to go, he said, "Say a little prayer for me, ladies, I should be fine flying home, but I've learned anything can happen in Vietnam. If I don't make it, I'll send your love to Mike and Beau!"

He bowed once again as he did the day they took the picture and walked away.

~~~

Helen said goodbye to Tweet in '72. She would sorely miss everything and everyone. The people who served had done so with their hearts and their skill. They were top-notch, to a person, and both women could hold their heads high for what they'd contributed.

Tweet and Helen met as widows, Tweet had not had the chance to get married, but she was a widow nonetheless. Both pregnant when they'd lost the men they loved, they were survivors. They had shared the deaths of Marines and civilians, friend and foe, and the visions of gruesome carnage that would live in their souls forever. Together they'd endured hospital bombings and knew palpable fear. They'd shared questions of "why" and then made resolutions not to ask "why," but to do what was necessary to save lives.

Helen departed, grateful. By helping in the healing of others, she had moved forward in healing herself.

It had been a long, arduous journey for Helen, an intimate process shared with no one. So often, she felt Beau's presence, especially during the most heart-rendering moments of a soldier's death. Passersby sometimes noticed this beautiful woman speaking softly to someone not there.

Helen left her contact information with Tweet, and both women, teary-eyed, promised to keep in touch. As a goodbye gift, Helen gave Lucky a small white teddy bear with a bright pink ribbon. Tweet received a bottle of Arpege, a fragrance Tweet commented on each time Helen wore it.

"Remember me when you wear this," Helen whispered as she hugged Tweet. They had shared so much. They had been good friends to each other.

~~~

President Nixon began withdrawing troops, and it was apparent to everyone that soon, only the ARVN would remain in the fight against North Vietnam. By November 1972, a mere 27,000 Americans remained, down from over 536,000 four years prior.

In mid-March 1975, the North Vietnamese Army overtook Quang Tri, causing panic and an exodus of 50,000 South Vietnamese civilians, who fled south to Da Nang.

Because Lucky was the child of an American Marine, and Tweet worked at Da Nang Station Hospital, saving American lives, she knew Nhat, her brother-in-law, would report her as a traitor. The North persecuted traitors and the families of traitors. Her actions would implicate her grandfather. She, Papasan, and perhaps even Lucky could be executed or taken to a communist re-education camp to "clear their thinking" if they stayed. Tweet knew Papasan would not survive those camps.

She returned to her village and convinced Papasan to return with her to Da Nang. Tweet's sister pleaded with her to take Tran to ensure his safety. Thanh would remain in Da Nang.

Dr. Campbell told Tweet that ships, and planes would rescue refugees, mainly the civilians who helped Americans. Five hundred thousand Vietnamese waited in Da Nang for that rescue mission.

On March 28th, the freighter SS Pioneer Contender picked up approximately 6,000 refugees from Da Nang; the USNS Andrew Miller took away another 7,500 refugees.

Tweet, Lucky, Papasan, and Tran walked up the gangway of the Andrew Miller. They became part of a sea evacuation involving 90,000 refugees. The destination of their ship was the island of Phu Quoc, a Vietnamese island off the coast of Cambodia in the Gulf of Thailand, but, for reasons unclear to the passengers, they landed in Vung Tau, a port city on a peninsula in southern Vietnam, and near South Vietnam's capital, Saigon. They remained in danger.

By the end of March, Da Nang fell to the North Vietnamese, and without protection from the Marines and the airborne divisions, Hue surrendered. Tweet and her family had left just in time!

Tweet knew they could not wait long for a ship to take them away from her country, and soon, tens of thousands of people would try to escape South Vietnam. She remembered an American phrase she liked, and it became implanted in her mind, "The early bird gets the worm." Tweet searched for anyone who could take her family to safety.

After days of inquiries, she secured passage to the Philippines on a large fishing boat that appeared seaworthy. The "Captain" seemed trustworthy, and travel to the Philippines would increase her family's chances for relocation to the U.S.

~~~

The Captain would leave when he secured enough passengers to make his trip worthwhile. Days passed into weeks, and Tweet heard no word from the Captain. She and Lucky walked to the waterfront, where she believed his vessel was moored.

It was April 28th, and mayhem ruled the dock. Lucky, now almost seven, took tight hold of her mother's hand, eyes wide. She heard children cry out for lost mothers, and people screaming. Gunshots echoed in the distance.

One man jumped toward the deck of a small boat, missed, and fell into the water. People stared as he flailed wildly, unable to swim. Exhausted, he stopped moving and sank. No one moved to help him.

Passengers in an already overcrowded fishing boat pushed a man overboard, but he was lucky enough to grab a rope that hung from the pier and pulled himself up.

Tweet located the Captain, frantically getting equipment ready for their journey.

He shouted over the din, "I just sent someone to fetch you! We leave tonight! Get your family here and hurry, the North Vietnamese are not far away!"

Tweet was already packed, and as she turned to go, the Captain yelled, "No, suitcases, just satchels! Hurry!"

~~~

Tweet, Lucky, Papasan, and Tran huddled together on the fishing boat, with roughly sixty others leaving their homeland as the North invaded Saigon. The weather was warm and the night balmy as the ship departed under a star-filled sky, the Philippine Islands a week away.

Tweet opened her bag to search for her important papers, ensuring once again that she had them. Tweet touched the half sheet of onionskin paper Mike gave her the last time they were together. Notarized, it stated the child she carried was his, and the birth would be around March or April 1968; that he was a Lance Corporal in the United States Marines and an American citizen.

A second sheet was the preliminary filing of intent to marry Tweet and the amount of the allotment he had designated for her. "Just in case," she remembered him saying. How prophetic he had been.

These papers were invaluable.

God bless you, Mike, Tweet said to herself, ever grateful for this responsible, loving man who had looked out for her and their child, even in death. She missed him so!

Lt. Campbell also wrote a letter for her addressing her employment at the hospital, the "innumerable lives she helped save," and ended it with a personal plea to help her in any manner possible.

On a scrap of paper, she'd written Helen, Angel, and Chingas' contact information.

Two days later, on April 30th, the North rolled their tanks into Saigon as the last Marines helicoptered out of the U.S. Embassy.

The war ended with honor, so said the American politicians.

Most American's sighed with relief.

Finally, the killing of America's sons would stop. Some believed it was the most shameful day in American history as they watched thousands of South Vietnamese abandoned at the American Embassy.

Nowhere to run, nowhere to hide. They were left behind to face the wrath of the proud and victorious North Vietnamese Army; communists who came with revenge in their hearts for those who fought them for so many years.

Approximately 65,000 South Vietnamese were executed, and one million men and women would be sent to re-education camps, some for many, many years. Nearly 165,000 are believed to have died in those camps.

South Vietnam ceased to be a country, and Uncle Ho's dream was realized, posthumously.

~~~

During the second night of travel on the China Sea, a storm bore down on the unsheltered vessel.

Powerful and violent waves rocked and pitched the boat while torrential sheets of rain pelted them. The unrelenting storm lasted for hours and brought on severe seasickness. Lightning cracked around them as they huddled together and prayed for survival.

The storm blew over before dawn, and they greeted the sunrise with prayers of thanks, and hopes for a better journey.

Their prayers were not heard.

As Tweet shared water and bread with her family, Lucky and Tran pointed to a large vessel approaching.

The Captain had seen it as well and increased speed. He altered course away from the menacing craft.

Tweet's stomach knotted. She knew this was trouble.

The Captain's face, taut and determined, knew his boat was no match, and they were soon overtaken.

The women knew they would likely bear the brunt of the trouble coming their way.

The documents from Mike were Tweet's most valuable possessions. They guaranteed safety and relocation.

Tweet took the documents from her bag and folded them into the smallest square she could. With a finger to her lips, she pressed it into Papasan's hand, letting him know to remain quiet and keep it safe. He nodded slightly. He understood.

Mon Dieu, Tweet thought, it is a Thai ship, and there are many men aboard. Her eyes now scanned the faces of the women here, all looking as afraid as she.

The pirates boarded and searched satchels and bodies. They made the passengers show their hands, palms down, to expose rings and bracelets. Tweet saw Papasan deftly hide the paper square with his thumb pushed against his palm, and the Thai adversary failed to notice. Now, no matter what, her family would be safe with the documents secured.

One pirate stepped before Lucky, touching her face, fascinated with her amber eyes tinged with chocolate blue around the edges. His fingers brushed her lips as his other hand traveled down past her belly. Afraid, she turned away from him and clung to her mother's waist.

"She is too young," admonished Tweet. "Wouldn't you rather have someone experienced?" she'd asked boldly, face close to his. He smiled, and Tweet saw brown crooked teeth, then smelled his rancid breath.

Her heart pounded so hard she was afraid he would hear it, know her fear, and turn back to Lucky.

"Me. Take me instead," Tweet's words poured out before she knew she'd said them. Her hand went to his crotch. He took the bait, threw her on the deck, and began to rape her.

Tweet watched as Lucky sobbed in Papasan's lap. His hand covered her eyes while he placed his other hand around Tran, who looked away.

I'm sorry you see this, Papasan. Forgive me, Tran. Please, Papasan, do NOT lose the papers.

She endured the best she could and bit her lip not to scream aloud. His thrusts hurt beyond belief, and when he'd finished, he left her silently crying on the deck of the ship.

~~~

Tweet pulled herself up from where she had been lying. All eyes averted hers. The men who had been too afraid to help looked down in shame.

The Thai pirate, like a magnet drawn to steel, touched Lucky's face again. Tweet screamed and clawed at him, biting when she could, shoving her knee hard and quick into his groin, using every ounce of strength left in her.

She pushed him away from her child. He drew his dagger, and with wild eyes, grabbed her by her hair, pulled her head back, and drew the blade across her throat.

Her shocked eyes stared into his … too long, almost mocking him in death.

He pushed her backward into the water.

254

Mercilessly he'd killed something of beauty, and for a fleeting moment, his skin crawled with revulsion at his act as he continued to stare at the floating body.

Why didn't she let me do as I wished and save herself? Why did she make me kill her?

Her ripped throat gushed red. It framed her body as she floated through it. Her burgundy top billowed in the water, then something, a smear of orange, appeared beside her. The pirate couldn't make out what it was, a large fish perhaps, but never had he seen a fish of that size and color.

Then both burgundy and orange sank slowly and disappeared into the blue-green waters of the South China Sea.

The Thai Captain called them to return to their ship. The pirate wiped Tweet's blood from his face and wanted no more to do with this boat or the people in it. Cursing them all, he turned and left.

Papasan remained frozen.

He watched his lovely granddaughter float from him and then disappear. He would never hear her laughter again. She was gone from him forever, just as his wife and son were gone.

He covered his face with his hands to hide the tears, not wanting others to see his pain, thinking it would bring him shame. He looked at a motherless and fatherless Lucky. Now she had no one and nothing but himself and her cousin Tran.

Resolve replaced the pain. He would never feel humiliated or helpless again. No more would be taken from him or his family because of this cursed war. He would get Lucky and Tran to safety, fight for them by God, kill for them if necessary. He gripped the papers in his hand.

Later that night, when most were asleep, Papasan unfolded the pieces of paper to see what Tweet had given him.

As they were unfolded, the small note with Helen, Chingas, and Angel's address fell out and blew into the water before Papasan could catch it.

He wondered what was on that note.

FORTY-FIVE

DRAWING LINES

1968

1968 was a significant year for Annie, Helen, and Tweet. Annie was married in the summer and became pregnant with her son, Thomas. It was the year Tweet and Helen gazed into the eyes of their newborns, Lucky and John Jr., and wondered what their futures held. Three women, three mothers, who would impact the world with their quest for justice and mercy.

And Angel returned to "The World."

~~~

"Angel! Angel! Here! Over Here!"

He heard Aunt Rosalina long before spotting her in the crowd. She was waving a "Welcome home, Angel" banner. He chuckled as he walked toward his Aunt and Uncle Maximo. Leave it to her to do something so provincial, so Cuban. But he couldn't keep from smiling, and it felt good they were happy to see him.

Before he could say "Hello," Rosalina was hugging him. She held his face in her hands and repeatedly kissed his cheeks. In the car going home, Uncle Maximo kept his eyes on the road and drove like the perfect chauffeur while Rosalina told Angel everything about everyone since he'd left for boot camp. It seemed like a lifetime ago to Angel. Maximo gave Rosalina full berth to enjoy her nephew's return and unleash thirteen months of pent-up anxiety... thirteen months of hell for her, which meant thirteen months of hell for him.

Maximo had recently read a sign, "When Momma ain't happy, ain't nobody happy," and that, in a nutshell, told the whole story since Angel had left for `Nam. Church had become their second home and Father Roberto, their new best friend.

Maximo had spent a small fortune contributing to the candle business, with one always burning in the church for Angel's safety. He wondered if Angel had any idea how many had been praying for him during his tour. Probably not. Angel was young, perhaps too young to be aware of anyone outside himself.

It had been hard, but now it was over. Rosalina baked and prayed Angel home. She no longer had to worry about her sister's son, a sister who still lived in Cuba under Castro's communist regime. Now, this family could breathe again.

~~~

Angel arrived at O'Hare International Airport on Easter weekend.

He hoped to avoid some dumbass challenging him on his service. Too many brothers had sacrificed their lives for this uniform, and he would not allow it to be dishonored. Angel strutted through O'Hare like a Kuban Kurvar, a Cuban stud, and turned many female heads. He wore his uniform with pride for his brothers and his own service. Sorry would be the person who did or said anything disparaging.

~~~

They drove directly to Easter Sunday Mass, and the circle of his experience was completed as Father Roberto again focused on Angel Santiago. He thanked Angel for serving the country and thanked God for returning him safely. The congregation clapped, people behind Angel patted his back, and others shook his hand in gratitude. Aunt Rosalina looked so proud that an unknowing person might have thought she was the one who'd returned from fighting the communists.

With Mass complete, Angel turned to his Aunt and Uncle. "Would you two mind if I remained for a few minutes? I can walk home."

Alone, Angel thought about the last time he was inside this church. He'd enlisted for adventure and freedom, not to be trapped in a mundane life.

258

What an ignorant fool I was.

I didn't have a clue what I was getting into. I was so green.

Thirteen-months in a combat zone! That'll be easy I thought.

Stupid. Stupid. Stupid.

Angel looked at the high ceilings and the graceful wooden beams that arched over him. His gaze moved down to the stained-glass windows to take in the serenity of the scenes. He felt comforted by the messages they conveyed. This was the world Angel wanted to live in, one of love and peace.

War ... the opposite of love and peace.

Angel recalled the desolate stare of a small Vietnamese girl curled against the body of her dead mother, killed in a firefight. What love or peace will that child have? Who would she become? Who might she have become had her mother lived?

And Beau's son, who would never know the largeness of his father, a father who would have shaped him into an honorable man. The country lost not one but probably two incredible people with Beau's death.

Then there was Lucky, another little one with no father. Angel knew Mike Redd grew up poor in the States, often felt invisible and voiceless, but made something of himself by establishing goals, then put his back into achieving them. He was a man of integrity and would have been the best of fathers to Lucky. How often had Redd spoken of his wish for a family and becoming a journalist to effect positive change? He'd wanted to be a role model for his three younger brothers; prove injustice and prejudice could be overcome. He would have been a loving husband to Tweet, and Tweet would have had a wonderful life in the States.

When Angel said goodbye to Tweet, she told him about the papers Redd had given her to safeguard their baby and herself. Yeah, that was Redd. A solid brother-in-arms and a credit to his country. A success by anyone's standards. He'd made a difference already. No telling what he could have accomplished had he lived, his golden eyes an outward reflection of his golden heart.

War ripped away what the world might have gained.

It ravaged possibilities. It stole.

Angel wondered how Tweet and Lucky would fare, a Vietnamese woman with a mixed-race child? *Prejudice, just another word for fear and hatred, one group believing they have more value than another. When will we learn every individual has value? Every group, every person, brings something of value to us all. Jesse knew and respected that.*

What hardships would they endure because of the love Redd and Tweet shared? So many lives wasted, so much potential lost.

Had the war killed the next astrophysicist who could have taken us to safety to a new home in the stars? Or the research scientist who could have discovered the cure for cancer? Perhaps.

Didn't we ALL deserve nurturance to grow and flourish in a safe and just world?

What remains for the children of Vietnam with their country and homes destroyed?

How will they grow and flourish with no homes, perhaps no family?

Tweet would have said, "War anywhere is war everywhere." And she would have been right. War was a waste that left only death, destruction, rage and sadness in its wake.

Between war and hell, Angel decided he might choose hell. No, he would never again take part in that evil. The price of war was too high, and generation after generation paid.

Angel would live with the memories of those he'd killed or maimed, the men he'd served with, and the families they'd left behind. He realized that the seeds of those thirteen months would germinate and shape who he'd become now, be part of him for the rest of his life.

Yes, `Nam had changed him.

He was grateful to be inside this peaceful sanctuary, a place of reverence and solitude … a place for reflection.

It was a privilege to breathe in and "be" in this beautiful church. Just breathe, he told himself, but his brain refused to listen. It was not yet time for Angel to relax. He still had much processing to do.

Chingas, where are you? In a firefight? Dodging incoming artillery?

Who's got your back now that the gun team is gone?

I'm here, my brother, and I'm with you, take care of yourself!

His thoughts returned to Jesse, Beau, and Redd.

May each of you be in a peaceful place.

I miss your banter, Beau; you were so good at it. You brought laughter when it was needed the most. We knew we could count on you. You could make the impossible possible.

Jess, you were the leader we needed, our moral compass. In a way, you were the dad I didn't know. I grew up under your support. You listened and taught me to value myself and others, and you supported us all. Thank you, my friend.

Redd, well buddy, you were the rock. Responsible as the day is long. I always knew you would be there for me if I needed help, needed anything, no doubt about who you were.

I will never forget you, my brothers, Semper Fi.

Angel bowed his head and unashamedly let the tears fall freely, lost in memories of the pain, horror, and terror he'd just left behind. Let the thoughts come out as they need to, he told himself.

It seemed they had a will of their own and apparently would be remembered no matter how much he wanted to forget.

The children's choir came to practice for the 11:00 Mass. As they rehearsed songs of salvation, appalling images and noises of war surfaced from his soul, faceless screams, bombings, fire, the smell of death, and the look in the orphaned child's eyes ....

Angel never realized killing others resulted in killing part of himself. He understood it now. How innocent he had been.

He felt small in this place of worship and life weary. He felt shame for what he'd done. This was God's house. Perhaps he had no right to be here.

Studying his surroundings, he slowly shook his head, amazed.

It was just the day before yesterday that I was wearing a frayed and tattered uniform, pulling off leeches, praying I would stay alive long enough to get back home.

The sudden shift from the horror of war to sitting inside a church was incomprehensible; no time to process, no time to transition.

I need time to myself, to think through what's happened, make sense of it all.

Father Roberto ambled toward Angel. He saw something familiar in Angel's face, pain, self-doubt, defensiveness, guilt. He'd seen it before in other returning Vietnam Veterans.

He hoped Angel's transition back to "The World" would go well but wondered if this would be the case.

"Hello, Father, I'm not sure I should be here inside God's house," Angel said quietly.

A sad look crossed Father Roberto's face. He'd guessed correctly.

"God's house is for everyone Angel, especially those feeling alone and suffering. God's love is shockingly personal. The door is always open to you, and my company always available.

"Remember this, my son, Jesus walked on water, as did Peter

… as long as Peter kept his eyes on Jesus.

"The moment he took his eyes off Christ and lost focus, he began to drown. When he asked Jesus to save him, Jesus extended his hand and saved Peter.

"Keep your focus on what's essential, Angel. Your salvation. Jesus only wants to extend his hand to you.

"This church is your home, and we, too, are your family. Find peace, do things for yourself that will put you on the path to peace."

~~~

Watching the news that week, Angel realized not only had he transformed in such a brief time, but the United States, in fact, the world, had also transformed. Everything and every place seemed on fire, with revolution, protest, and violence.

London, Paris, Berlin, Stockholm, Rome, and Canada protested in opposition to the war in Vietnam.

Social movements raged across France, almost toppling its current government.

Northern Ireland began its revolution against British rule, and guerrilla warfare erupted in Brazil against the military dictatorship.

Czechoslovakia, Poland, and Yugoslavia protested for freedom of speech and civil liberties denied under communist rule.

The repressive governments of Mexico, Spain, and China fought back protestors using police and military to crackdown and even execute demonstrators.

Denmark and the Netherlands protested environmental violations.

And Japanese students protested to reduce the U.S. Military presence in Japan, stationed there because of the war in Vietnam.

People questioned the establishment and distrusted its authority. Students became the anti-establishment. Baby boomers had taken part in bomb drills related to the Cuban Missile Crisis and the Cold War. Now, young people worldwide were aware of the ever-present potential of nuclear warfare, a threat a thousand times more menacing than the atomic bomb.

Television made possible the viewing of worldwide demonstrations and fanned the peace movement's flame, the revolution.

In the United States, the women's liberation movement disrupted the Miss America Beauty Pageant for five days. No longer comfortable being defined by "looks," the Feminist movement believed it was time for the woman, like her male counterpart, to be defined by her ability to contribute to society. A woman was an individual also designated with rights regarding reproduction, jobs, and pay equality.

Civil liberties, racism, feminism, ecology, biological and nuclear weaponry reached a crescendo in 1968. Freedom was the word of the day, and "second-class citizens" would fight repression. The world was at war with itself, and revolution was everywhere.

Martin Luther King Jr. was assassinated on April 4th, and his death was fresh when Angel returned to the States. In response to Martin's assassination, riots took place in Chicago and Washington, D.C.

~~~

Alone for the first time since his return, and grateful for the solitude, Angel sat down to watch the evening news, a documentary on Martin Luther King Jr. Attentively, he listened to excerpts of King's speeches.

The doorbell rang. And Angel opened the door to his cousin Phoebe.

Her father was black, and her mother was one of Rosalina's Cuban sisters. Phoebe had one of the largest afros Angel had ever seen and wore enormous silver hoop earrings. Around her neck hung multiple colored love beads, each strand displaying a different Ankh, the Egyptian symbol of life. She wore a honey yellow suede vest with fringe that reached the knees of her faded bell-bottom jeans.

"Hey, great, you're home and watching the special on Martin! I was hoping you'd be watching this! So many great quotes." She wrapped her arms around Angel and kissed him on the cheek.

"Glad you're back, cuz," and without an invitation, she walked in, sat down on the couch, and patted the seat next to her for Angel to sit.

"To ignore evil is to become an accomplice to it," King was saying. These words resonated with Angel. Jesse, Tweet, and Mike immediately came to mind, and they would have liked those words. Then came the quote, "Our lives begin to end the day we become silent about things that matter."

Wow! Those words are a call to action! This guy got it!

"God, he was wise," Phoebe chirped in. "The only problem is that the peaceful approach he promoted doesn't work here. Seems like you gotta get violent to be heard by the government."

She looked at Angel and asked, "Have you heard of the Black Panthers, Angel?"

"No, who are they?"

"Their motto is 'Freedom by any means necessary,' and I believe that's true. There's someone I want you to meet, a friend of mine; his name is Bobby Seale. Bobby's the organizer and leader of the Black Panther Party. He'll be visiting the Chicago Chapter of the Black Panthers for a few days. They'll be part of the demonstration against the Democratic National Convention in August.

"Huey Newton and Bobby Seale organized the Black Panthers. They have chapters in almost every major city in the U.S. They're the aggressive end of the black movement. The Panthers believe in armed self-defense and combat police brutality against Blacks.

"They're also part of the Black Consciousness Movement and helped get the Fair Housing Act passed, which prohibits discrimination in real estate purchases or rentals. No more keeping people out because of race, religion, nationality, or sex."

"Not sure I want to get involved in more violence, Phebes," Angel said, hoping she wasn't in over her head with this group.

"Oh, they're not just militants, Angel. They do community work too. They organize free breakfasts for school kids, free medical facilities, an emergency-response ambulance program, drug and alcohol programs, even sickle cell testing. Believe me, they look out for the poor and working-class, and they believe in equality for women. It's an empowerment Party, to mostly address racial inequality, but gender and economics are part of the equation too."

"I'll think about it." But Angel's heart said no more violence.

In May, Angel watched Robert Kennedy's assassination on TV.

~~~

August brought five days of brutality at the Democratic National Convention; its events witnessed on television by most Americans. The brutality of the police and National Guard in "containing" the protestors appalled Angel.

The irreverence of the Chicago 8 on trial for conspiracy to incite a riot shocked him.

Angel was outraged that Bobby Seale, Phoebe's friend, could not defend himself because his attorney, undergoing surgery, was unavailable for Bobby's defense. When Seale was bound, gagged, and chained to a chair for contempt during the trial, Angel turned the TV off in disgust.

What's happening to this country? It's become unrecognizable.

~~~

Angel sought support from the local VFW, Veterans of Foreign Wars, and was told by a WWII Vet, "Vietnam isn't a declared war. You're not eligible to join."

Burning draft cards became as commonplace as burning bras.

The news covered the inadequate medical help in VA hospitals. Returning Vietnam Vets were coming home with a 300% higher amputation and crippling wound rate than World War II Vets.

It sure seemed to Angel that the pain and suffering of Vietnam Vets wasn't being addressed.

John Kennedy, Martin Luther King Jr., and Bobby Kennedy ... all assassinated. Turbulent times. Sad times. Lonely times.

Angel often found himself at Lincoln Park, sometimes thinking, sometimes just watching children play. He drew, and that helped his soul. He thought of the words of Martin Luther King Jr., "Our lives begin to end the day we become silent about things that matter."

266

In those quiet moments, Angel Santiago came to realize that before Vietnam, he'd spent most of his waking hours preoccupied with himself, women, and plans for pleasures of the night. But in thirteen short months, in an environment of chaos and immediacy, where death could snatch you away in a heartbeat, his priorities had radically and permanently shifted.

No longer were carnal pleasures at the top of his list. Because of this war, he'd moved from selfish toward selfless. He learned to love life, the lives of others, help where he could, and listen with a compassionate heart. Angel knew what mattered. Soldiers in pain mattered. He would not remain silent to their pain.

~~~

Angel met with Father Roberto, who knew other `Nam Vets going through hard times. He and the Father met with them, and asked if they'd like to get together, talk, maybe journal their thoughts, perhaps draw or paint their experiences, get their feelings out, ease their pain.

Those were the ways Angel helped himself, and he knew these men could and would help each other here, as they'd helped each other "in-country." The military was a fraternity, and they understood each other.

It filled a need in Angel to start this group. As Jess had often suggested, he was moving forward, and he would take these fragile men with him. By refocusing his anger into helping his brothers, he began to feel a sense of release, and slowly, very slowly, they all began to return to "The World," to the elusive normalcy each needed and wanted to embrace.

~~~

With the help of "Father R," they began to heal.

"Vets 2 Vets," they called themselves. The name, as with most good names, came by accident because of two dog tags.

One Vet, a quiet man, still wore dog tags around his neck. Issued in boot camp, dog tags came as a set of two. One tag was worn on a long chain, the second tag on a shorter chain connected to the longer chain. If you were killed, the dog tag from the short-chain was taken for reporting; the longer-chained tag stayed with your body. This Vet had a habit of fondling both tags and would often say, "Still got two. Thank you, God, I still got two."

After a while, whether to kid him, loosen him up, or just enjoy some well-deserved camaraderie, the other guys started wearing their dog tags. They'd pull them from under their shirts, shake them playfully, and say, "Two right here, buddy, right back at ya."

"Vets 2 Vets" was born in the basement of an old church, a collection of soldiers in fellowship. By focusing his anger and feelings of isolation into active help for his brothers, Angel felt a sense of release and began his journey back to "The World."

He entered college in September, using the GI bill to study Graphic Arts.

FORTY-SIX

NO COINCIDENCES

1969

Chingas returned from Vietnam also seeking normalcy.

He discovered normalcy was subjective, complicated, and elusive. It often depended on who you were, what you were going through, and where you were in the pecking order.

He could categorize as absolute that normal in Vietnam certainly wasn't normal anywhere in the U.S.A., so, for him, it was all up from there.

Sitting in a bar in Dog Patch the night before his flight home, Chingas thought about the reports he'd heard of protestors in the States screaming obscenities at service members. He considered options should this happen to him.

~~~

The flight from Vietnam was surreal. Chingas didn't know what the word "surreal" meant until he heard a young Captain use it to describe his emergency leave home, but he would think of that word repeatedly during his flight.

A clean utility uniform, showered and shaved, he'd departed on a Military Airlift Command flight for Okinawa, then flew almost thirteen-hours to McChord Air Force Base, south of Tacoma, Washington.

The flight to the States had been strangely quiet. It was as if everyone was holding their breath, praying that no monster would slither from the luggage compartment, no shadow would creep up from hell to get you... the twelfth hour.

They'd been living in the twelfth-hour for what seemed an eternity, waiting to be eviscerated by demons, a sinister presence hidden in plain sight, only revealed by its stench of death. Staying safe in Vietnam was like trying to snatch the wind. It just couldn't be done.

All who fought in 'Nam lived with fear so long that expecting their world to be blown apart had become the "normal." Would they ever feel safe again? Now was not the time to feel confident or secure. Fear demanded respect. They would claim relief when boots touched American soil. Not before. No one would tempt the monster with talk of the future. One should not tempt fate.

Thirty minutes from McChord, Chingas could visibly see the tension melt from the faces of Marines who shared his flight. Talk began.

Seated between two white boys, he looked at their nametags. One read "Bailey," the other "Gant."

"Where you headed, Ramirez?" asked Bailey.

"New York City. You?"

"Bozeman, Montana."

"How about you, Gant, where you headed?"

Gant stared out the window and listlessly answered, "Charleston. Been a long time since I've seen home."

Bailey asked, "What are you guys gonna do when you get back?"

"First thing I'll do is visit my draft board and burn the place to the ground!" Gant volunteered with a grin and steel in his eyes.

He was smiling when he said it, but there was something ominous in his voice.

Bailey chimed in, "Not what I had planned, but it sure seems like an excellent idea now you mention it!"

"How about you, Ramirez, you in for some of that?"

Chingas smiled slightly and admitted, "I did this shit on my own, guys. I enlisted, then re-upped. Put it down to a case of terminal dumbass and let it go, okay?"

Gant replied first, "Well, wash off the dumbass. You made it."

The remaining time in flight was conversation about divisions and companies they'd been in, locations, battles fought, and friends made and lost.

~~~

As the wheels touched down, a collective cheer erupted. The good old "U.S. of A." was underfoot, and the level of anxiety to get off the plane was palpable.

The door opened to misty Tacoma air, feeling colder than any of these men had experienced in a long time. They walked down the steps to the tarmac, where a few men dropped and kissed the ground, some in jest, others with tears in their eyes. Cargo lifts began removing caskets from the hold of the plane. It was a sobering sight, and there was less laughter as they walked toward the terminal to be processed.

Steak dinners and new dress uniforms greeted them. It shocked many to discover that, on average, they'd lost almost six inches from their waists, an equivalent to roughly fifty pounds. After eating, a bus drove them to SeaTac, the Seattle-Tacoma International Airport, to catch connecting flights to their hometowns.

They walked in ever-thinning groups toward their gates, happy and excited, each step taking them closer to home. Thoughts of trouble from protestors lingered, but now on terra firma, they didn't seem as important.

These Marines had dealt with "official," yet incorrect messages, plans, and information throughout their tour. Maybe this was simply another incorrect piece of information. Gant, Bailey, and Chingas walked on.

They passed a small group in robes with shaved heads, chanting, "Hare Krishna, Hare Krishna, Krishna Krishna, Rama Rama." The Krishna's meant no harm. It was their meditational mantra of peace.

Then the shit hit the fan, and it all unraveled.

~~~

"Hey, soldier boys, kill any babies today?" The three turned and saw a long-haired young girl in bell-bottom pants and a loud flowered shirt.

"Yeah, you, baby killers, I'm talking to you!" she yelled, and soon several other similarly dressed people joined her. They came closer.

Chingas spoke to Bailey and Gant, "Don't pay 'em no mind. They don't have a clue what happened or what they're talkin' about. Just be cool. It's like walkin' point, you hear shit, but you can't shoot right away. Just stay cool."

The three made their way to the men's room with seabags in hand, planning to change into civilian clothes as recommended back in 'Nam. By then, the crowd of harassers grew to nine or ten, and the insults came rapid-fire. Chingas knew most of what they said meant nothing because it was lies and bullshit.

We'd make fun of each other in-country worse than what we're gettin' here.

But that was different. We could talk that way to each other, in-country we were family.

These assholes haven't earned that right.

Bystanders watched the show and said nothing.

When the three Marines neared the restroom, two young women put themselves at the entrance, stood their ground, and spat as they passed. Chingas did everything he could to prevent Gant from striking out. Hell, he felt like smashing heads himself! Yeah, this was bad. His anger was rising. So, the military reports were right on this one.

Airport Security handled the protestors and regained control.

Everyone heard one protestor shout, "Hey pig, in case you haven't heard, we have freedom of speech and expression in this country, so fuck you!"

~~~

As they dug through their bags for civilian clothes, it was Bailey who spoke first.

"I know about twenty guys who died to protect their rights to protest. I wonder if they'd think it was worth it."

No one answered.

Rage boiled in each of them.

Shortly after, two male protestors walked into the restroom, stood there, and silently stared as the three Marines changed clothes. Headbands, shades, bell-bottom pants, vests, and long hair. Bailey looked at them and said, "What're you looking at, assholes?"

Neither of the two said a word, but one gave the finger. It was a quick gesture, but he'd made his point. Either from cowardice or a wise second thought, he'd tried to invalidate his gesture by quickly saying, "Nothin' man, absolutely nothin'."

That was all it took.

Before he could get the second "nothin'" out, Gant, the southern boy from Charleston, drove his fist hard into the side of the protestor's face, and his sunglasses flew across the room.

"Hey, man! Peace!" exclaimed the other as he held his hands up, offering two peace signs to the oncoming barrage.

For him and his friend, there would be no "peace."

Bailey struck him on the jaw, and as he spun, Chingas hit him hard and fast in the gut. The three beat the two well past submission, then stuffed them unceremoniously into a toilet stall.

Ramirez, Gant, and Bailey turned to leave and came face to face with two airport security guards.

273

The older of the two spoke first, "Korea, '54 to '55. Get the hell out of here."

They grabbed their gear and left.

The three Marines walked down the main concourse and winced as they shook goodbye.

They laughed off the pain in their hands. It was worth it.

It was a good landing, after all.

Chingas remembered a saying by John Kennedy that he'd liked enough to memorize.

"Those who make peaceful revolution impossible will make violent revolution inevitable."

~~~

Boarding a Pan Am jet, a beautiful stewardess greeted him wearing a tailored blue uniform, white gloves, black heels, with a set of wings above her left jacket pocket. A blue hat was perched atop perfectly coiffed hair. He stared at her for what must have seemed an uncomfortable amount of time. She was clean and tidy in her uniform, the polar opposite from the uniform he had worn for years, serving his country.

Chingas had no word for what he saw. Years later, the word "antithesis" found its way into his vocabulary. It was the right word for that moment.

Chingas found his seat and was soon in a dreamless sleep as he flew toward home.

Surreal indeed. Unbeknownst to Chingas, "surreal" would typify his life from that point forward.

~~~

Finally, at his parent's home, Chingas slept for the next two days, uninterrupted, in his own bed.

Like so many Mexican parents, Chingas' parents were proud he'd served in the military. They believed it was a duty to serve your country, and they were incredibly proud when Chingas joined the most machismo branch of the military, the Marines. A large framed picture of Chingas in uniform hung in their living room for all to see.

Chingas worked in his Papa's small grocery store for several weeks before realizing he didn't want to work in a small grocery store, nor did he want the hustle of New York City for the rest of his life.

He stayed with his parents long enough to see his father once again extend IOU's to those unable to pay for groceries.

His heart was filled with love for this man as he witnessed these gifts of trust, faith, and kindness. Chingas' father was a living example of a good man. Papa was a simple man, but one who personified dignity and compassion and carried love in his heart for others.

His Papa understood man's imperfections and would say, "You're okay. Nobody's perfect. I'm your friend."

Chingas knew that at the end of his father's life, when God measured a man's worth, his father would not be found wanting. Papa had given more than he'd taken.

In that small food store in New York City, Chingas came to understand and believe in the tenets of trusting in something bigger than himself. Those few weeks were what he'd needed to remember who he was, what he'd come from... and it refreshed his soul.

His parents reaffirmed that he could still believe in the goodness of humanity.

~~~

He decided a vacation was needed and mapped out a visit to Angel in Chicago.

It had been over a year since he'd seen Angel, and Chingas hoped a get together would be the ticket for them both. Then he'd swing through Atlanta and visit his best friend Miguel, who'd moved there a year ago.

Chingas would've liked to look up Mike Redd's brothers in nearby Macon, but since they had different last names, and he didn't know Redd's grandmother's last name, he decided to let that go for now.

~~~

Chicago was cold, bone-cold even in early April.

Chingas thought his blood would freeze, and the name "Windy City" didn't tell half the story. Walking against the wind was almost as hard as walking in the heat of Vietnam, each step measured and difficult. Good to see Angel, though ... and meet Corinna.

Chingas chuckled. *Fate caught up with you, "Sweetness."*

And Angel was going to college!

It was a short but pleasant visit. They were brothers, relaxed in each other's company, with lots of catching up to do. The two shared a long embrace before parting company, and each promised to write and stay in touch.

He left for Atlanta to visit his friend, Miguel.

~~~

Chingas had never been in the south but found its slower pace and charm soothing.

Atlanta's streets were lined with blooming dogwood trees, their branches hiding beautiful architecture waiting to be discovered. Each corner revealed more beauty than its predecessor ....

The food was new to his pallet and delicious. People were friendly.

Piedmont Park, in the middle of the city, was a lush, green area with plenty of benches to sit and watch. Chingas often walked there and sat while Miguel was at work.

After weeks of sleeping on Miguel's worn leather couch, Chingas decided Atlanta felt right and looked for a place to rent. He didn't stand out as "different" here, but blended, and blending was fine.

Miguel had no trouble finding Mexican friends, and neither would he, although, since Vietnam, people were people to Chingas, their race far less significant than when he'd enlisted.

"Everyone has value," Jess had said, and he was right. Jess led by example and had only been kind to Chingas when others would've stayed away. Fresh recruits got you killed, and a new Mexican recruit, well, that was a double whammy for some. Not for Jess. He took Chingas under his wing and taught him.

No doubt saved me from harming myself!

Chingas smiled sadly at that thought. He'd served with the best, even when each man was so different from every other team member, from race to attitude, to the way they faced life.

Yes, he felt at home in Atlanta. It was peaceful, forgiving, and what he needed.

~~~

While at the park, Chingas noticed a newspaper on a bench and sat down next to it. Folded open to the Want Ads, he saw three insurance agent jobs circled in red. Tweet had always said, "No coincidences." He heard her voice say it now.

So, Tweet, if there are no coincidences, why don't I check out these advertised insurance positions? They're even circled in red for me! Ha Ha!

His thoughts traveled to Tweet and Helen. He wished them well. Service in Vietnam had gotten pretty dark by the time he'd left.

The government was drafting young men who knew they'd caught the tail end of an unpopular war, perhaps a losing war, so why get killed? Draft card burners were being drafted; some were slackers who moved under the radar with attitudes Chingas hadn't dealt with earlier. He heard of soldiers killing officers they didn't feel safe with. It had a name, "fragging." Pull the pin on a fragmentation hand grenade and roll it into the tent of the officer you wanted dead. No one would know who did it.

Some of these Marines were from a much different club than the one he'd entered in 1967.

~~~

"Well, yes, Mr. Ramirez, we think you'd be an asset to our firm. We would be pleased to hire a Vet and send you through school for a series of insurance-related classes you'll need for your Georgia State Licenses. You can work for us while taking those courses paid for by the GI Bill."

Why didn't I know about this "no coincidence" thing earlier? This is golden! Thank you, Tweet!

~~~

His new apartment was not much, but he could afford it with the money he'd saved while in the Marines. Part of a little strip mall, he lived on the second floor over an empty office space. It was private, and Chingas didn't have to worry about making noise, plus he could have music as loud as he wanted. He seldom played music in his parent's home, but it felt good to know that should he want to, he could! AND it could be loud!

~~~

Miguel helped Chingas study by asking questions for the tests. Chingas discovered he liked this line of work because he could protect people from the unseen and the unknown. Those were circumstances he knew only too well!

He passed the State Insurance examinations and obtained his licenses.

Chingas was honest, thorough, and understood the importance of these contracts for their owners. His clients sometimes had little money, much like his own family, but wanted to ensure the future of their aging spouse, children, or grandchildren. They were people who cared about the ones they loved.

They entrusted Chingas not only with their money but with their hopes. Because he understood, he paid close attention to details and considerations.

278

He educated his clients and gave them the time and information necessary to make knowledgeable decisions. Chingas took his responsibility to heart. His clients trusted him and referred many of their friends to him. His clientele list multiplied.

FORTY-SEVEN

HELPING HANDS

1973

G oddamn it!" Chingas exploded as he left the VA Hospital in Atlanta.
"That Gringo wasn't going to help the likes of me, come back next week, he says. I thought he'd give me something for this swelling, but he just talked! Talked the world flat! He's a fraud, and these hospitals are another crooked business, like the war, like our government! No one cares about us Vietnam Vets!"

Miguel stayed quiet. It took a lot to get Chingas mad, but when he was, nothing anyone could say or do would make a difference. He remained silent until they got into the car.

Miguel held the keys in his hand and didn't start the car, allowing a few moments of tense silence.

"Chingas, he doesn't know what's wrong; he just does intake.

"That swelling in your armpit could be anything. He doesn't know what it is. It could be nothing. If it's nothing, what's your worry, it doesn't hurt. If it's something, let a doctor take care of it and get real help.

"A week is only seven days. You now have a doctor's name and a time to see him on that slip of paper in your hand. Relax. I understand you wanted something done today, but you saw a lot of people in that room. I'm guessing a week is probably a pretty fast turnaround."

"Yeah, you're right, amigo. I guess his attitude got under my skin. Maybe I should bring him a taco next week and thank him for his excellent treatment. That will make him wonder!"

"Now you're talking," replied Miguel. "Let's go get a beer," he added with laughter.

"You know, it's a funny thing. The swelling doesn't hurt, but when I drink beer, it gets really tender. I'll get a sweet tea. You get a beer …."

~~~

"Are you a Vietnam Vet? Are you fatigued? Do you get night sweats? Any fever or itching? Any sensitivity in this area when you drink alcohol?" the doctor asked the following week.

"Yes, yes, yes, no, yes," replied Chingas.

"I'll order a biopsy, and I want you to return in a week. We'll have the lab results back by then."

"What do you think it is, Doc?"

"Not sure. It doesn't look to be an infection. I'll know more when I see the lab results."

~~~

Chingas left and decided not to worry until he knew what he was dealing with. He had a meeting scheduled with his landlord, who owned the still-vacant space below his apartment.

Chingas had worked hard in the insurance field during these past two years and had done well. He'd been considering starting his own insurance agency and needed an office. It was risky, and he knew he'd be taking a big chance, but what did he have to lose? He'd developed a faithful following of clients who would hopefully come with him to a new location. He'd taken greater risks in 'Nam. Hell, anything after 'Nam was a cinch. He'd see what his landlord would ask to rent the space below his apartment.

~~~

Charles Walker extended his hand to Chingas.

"Hello son, what can I do for you today? Everything okay with your rental, I hope?"

"Everything is fine, Mr. Walker, the apartment is great. It's not the apartment I've come to see you about."

"Well go on, son, tell me what I can help you with."

"Well, Mr. Walker, after I returned from 'Nam, I began working for Jefferson Life Insurance. I've done well by them, and they've only been good to me, but I'm ready to branch out as a Jefferson Agent. I'd like to try my hand at running my own agency and need an office. The space below me has been empty for two years. I'm wondering if you're interested in renting it out, and what you'd charge."

A pained look crossed Charles Walker's face while Chingas was speaking.

"So, you served in Vietnam, Mr. Ramirez?"

"Yes, sir, I did."

"What branch and where were you stationed, may I ask?"

"I was a Marine. I served in Con Thien by the DMZ and then fought in Khe Sanh, sir."

"Two very rough places to have been. May I call you Chingas?"

"Yes, sir, I'd like that."

"What's Chingas mean, by the way? I saw it on your rental application and haven't heard it before. I assumed it was Hispanic."

Chingas smiled at Mr. Walker before replying, "I'm Mexican, Mr. Walker. I was the youngest of a good-sized family, and you know how it goes with the youngest. I had my mama's heart and could get away with pretty much anything.

"I was a little badass, a redheaded stepchild crossed with a hellion. Everyone began calling me 'Chingas' because that's what it loosely translates to. When I started school, my Papa gave me 'The Word.' Only Jesus has a 'Word' stronger than my Papa's. 'You better be respectful of your teacher, or you'll have me to deal with, not your mama, Chingas Ramirez.'"

"I never acted out after that. I kept the name but stopped misbehaving. When I joined the Marines, I put 'Chingas' down as my first name by habit, and I never corrected it."

They both laughed about that for a minute before Chingas asked Mr. Walker how he knew about Con Thien and Khe Sanh.

"Well, Chingas, my boy Charlie fought over there too. He was a Huey pilot and a special one. He volunteered to fly the Huey's that had been shot down, then repaired. His job was to make sure they got repaired well enough to fly again. His last one wasn't, and it blew up on him. He was killed just a little while before you moved into your apartment.

"Your apartment used to be his. He and I had plans to open the space below and turn it into a record store. Charlie had already thought of a name for it, 'Sounds Impossible,'" he chuckled.

"Charlie loved music, me too, and that had always been a dream of ours. After he passed, well, my wife Bunnie and I haven't had the motivation to do anything with that space. We should have, I know, but my heart's just not in it, and she needs me around more than in the past. It's been mighty lonely without him."

It saddened Chingas to hear of another family with a lost son.

"I'm sorry to hear that, Mr. Walker. He must have been one brave man to have taken on that kind of job."

"He was. He was one of the bravest. We miss him terribly. But let's not speak about Charlie just now. Let's talk about you. I like that you want to take a chance on something like this; take a chance on yourself. It would be an honor to support you, yes sir, an honor. We can work out something here, and I can come up with a good price, especially as you're already a renter and proven you're dependable. That space has been just sittin' there, doing nothing. Your venture will be good for both of us, Chingas!"

Charles Walker looked at Chingas, a soft look in his eyes.

"What do you think you can afford for that space, son?"

They struck a deal, then shook hands.

"Thank you for working with me to pay what I can afford, Mr. Walker. Please understand we will have continued conversations about this. As I become more successful, I'll be able to pay more."

"Understood and appreciated," Mr. Walker replied with a twinkle in his eye. He liked this young man.

Chingas added, "Oh, I forgot to ask, I haven't researched the local ordinances on the POW-MIA flag since it's new, but I'd like to hang one outside my business if that would that be okay with you?"

"I do know the ordinances regarding the POW-MIA flag, and you're well within your right to hang that flag, son. It would be more than all right with me."

It was a very, very good deal for Chingas. He walked away with his head spinning. This man had been very kind to him. Yes, he was right in moving to Atlanta. It had been a great new beginning. He would call home and let his parents know how good everything was going. He could not have asked for a better outcome.

As he entered the apartment that afternoon, Chingas turned on his transistor radio and found a station he liked. Tomorrow he would buy a stereo for this apartment, and music would be part of its world again.

~~~

The news for Chingas at the VA Hospital didn't turn out as well, and for a second time that week, he left a situation with his head reeling.

"Mr. Ramirez, the lab report shows you have Non-Hodgkin's Lymphoma; cancer that starts in the lymph nodes, and if not treated aggressively, can spread to the rest of your body. We'll do other work-ups to make sure it hasn't spread, but I think the prognosis will turn out well from the preliminary biopsy results.

"I think we've caught this one in the early stages. It would be best if you considered chemo for cancer, though, and that will be a rough road for a while. Do you have a friend that can drive you home when it gets tough?" asked Dr. Bourne.

"Yes, my friend Miguel will help me," replied Chingas, sitting there, stunned.

"What causes this, doctor?"

"We're just starting to see cases of this type of cancer, but my guess is, since you were in 'Nam, it results from the herbicide we used as a defoliant to kill jungle growth and clear out areas where the Viet Cong like to hide. It's a spray called Agent Orange; you're probably familiar with it. It's everywhere over there.

"The Vietnamese farmers are mad as hell at the U.S. for ruining their crops with it. They're going hungry and looking at Uncle Ho as a potential friend because we're destroying their food source. You probably had the mist come down on you a hundred times from overhead.

"Agent Orange contains a highly toxic chemical called dioxin, and the government is looking into the linkage between dioxin and human disease. Hell, it turned my stomach when I heard you boys use the barrels for sitting and for barbequing, essentially cooking with poison. I've even heard you split the barrels to make shower stalls, showering in contaminants.

"They've recently sent groups over to 'Nam to see what its effects have been on the Vietnamese. They're finding a lot of preemies, stillborns, and babies with birth defects. I've seen an increase in what you've got.

"My guess is you might be in the first wave of soldiers to show its effect as cancer in the lymph nodes, but I'm speculating—nothing definitive about any of this.

"I'm sorry the news is bad, but on the bright side, I think we've caught yours early and that you will come out of this all right. If you agree, let's get started on a complete evaluation, so we know exactly where we stand and then start the chemo process."

~~~

A few months later, Chingas stepped outside his new insurance office after he completed the upgrades.

On either side of two white framed windows were Wedgewood Blue shutters, looking good against the red brick. The white framing around the black door provided an excellent contrast.

He'd found a Vietnam Veteran nearby who was a professional sign-maker and who created a beautiful white sign. CHINGAS RAMIREZ, INSURANCE AGENT, in black calligraphy letters. Chingas hung it above the doorway with quiet pride. An American flag hung on the left side of the door, and a POW-MIA flag hung on the right. He stood back to take it all in.

Yes, it looks inviting yet professional. It rivals any other business for many blocks in any direction.

Bunnie Walker drove up with two large terracotta pots in her trunk, one for each side of the doorway, past his flags. She'd filled them with an array of seasonal flowers. Smiling, Bunnie claimed them as hers to tend, adding that this would give her a reason to stop by for a visit from time to time. He offered to pay her for the pots, but she refused.

"Are you trying to insult this Georgia peach?" she kidded him. Then her eyes rested on the flags, and Chingas saw they misted a little.

"I surely do like seeing those flags here, Chingas," Bunnie confessed. His heart went out to her, knowing she was thinking of her son Charlie and the music store he planned to have one day. Bunnie cleared her throat, and in the style of a born and bred, true southern gentlewoman raised her head proudly and went on to say, "I brought my Polaroid camera, Chingas. Shall I take your picture standing in your beautiful doorway to send home to your family? I know they'll be proud."

And there he stood, grinning from ear to ear, when the photo arrived at his parent's home, in New York City.

~~~

The chemo was exhausting.

After treatment, Chingas usually scheduled time for paperwork, not clients. When even that became too hard, or he became nauseous, he put the "Closed" sign on the front door and walked upstairs to his apartment.

Charles Walker stopped by to tell Chingas how elegant he thought the outside of the agency looked and learned of Chingas' chemotherapy, most likely from Agent Orange. He volunteered to take Chingas for treatments on the days Miguel couldn't, and Chingas, liking this man's company, gratefully accepted. Soon, Charles was bringing Rubbermaid containers of chicken soup from Bunnie, and, in time, Chingas was eating Sunday suppers with them.

~~~

Not long after opening the agency, the owner of the dry cleaners, a few shops down, walked in.

He was Vietnamese and had seen the POW-MIA flag. Mr. Nguyen was interested in meeting the person who rented this office and flew those flags. North Vietnam had been his home, but he left to escape communism. Thanking Chingas more than once for his service in trying to save his country from communism, he left with a handshake saying, "It is an honor to meet you."

~~~

A few days later, Mr. Nguyen returned with insurance papers. "Would you look at my policy, please? My wife believes we are paying too much."

Chingas looked it over while Mr. Nguyen sat quietly in the chair across from his desk. Chingas couldn't understand why he was being charged so much for his coverage. He showed Mr. Nguyen how he could get more coverage for the same amount of money or the same coverage for much less than he was currently paying. It became apparent to both men that Mr. Nguyen was being taken advantage of.

Chingas explained concepts and answered questions for over two hours. Mr. Nguyen left, armed with knowledge. He planned to sit down with his agent and see why his fees were high, and if not satisfied with the answers, would cancel his policy and go forward with the insurance Chingas recommended.

Because of Mr. Nguyen's enthusiastic recommendations, more Vietnamese began coming through the Jefferson Insurance Agency doors. With the language barrier, Chingas was spending hours on meetings that should have taken half the time. He drew on paper, he repeated, he had them bring relatives who spoke broken English.

~~~

After a few months, Chingas walked to Mr. Nguyen's dry-cleaning business and asked if he knew someone who would like to work as a translator for his increasing number of Vietnamese clients. Mr. Nguyen said his friend's wife spoke English very well. He would talk to him. Within a few days, a middle-aged lady came to Chingas' office. Her name was Kim, and her English was excellent. Chingas explained what his agency did regarding insurance and that he desperately needed a translator for his Vietnamese clients. He would pay her top dollar for her service. He added that if she was interested, he would teach her about the policies he sold, and she could study and get her licenses while working for him as a translator.

Kim went home to discuss his offer with her husband. She'd returned the next day, saying yes.

~~~

As time went by, Chingas' business thrived because the tightly-knit Vietnamese community from the Atlanta metropolitan area came through his door. He was trusted and accepted.

Kim became a full-time agent, as did four other Vietnamese women. His business boomed. Chingas opened other agencies in the Atlanta suburbs and then in nearby cities. All agencies had one or two Vietnamese-speaking agents on the payroll. As fortune would have it, Chingas became the top salesman on the East Coast for the Jefferson Life Insurance Company.

~~~

Many years later, Charles Walker dropped by the office. "Chingas, I'm considering selling this strip mall. Time for Bunnie and me to move on and start something new, maybe even look into one of those retirement communities popping up all over Florida. Who knows? Property values in Atlanta have increased substantially over the past few years, and it's probably a good time to think about selling. You're the first to know."

"How much is your realtor suggesting you ask?" inquired Chingas.

"A million four," Charles responded.

Chingas went to his desk, pulled out a checkbook, and handed Charles a check for $1,400,000.00.

Chingas had done very well for himself.

FORTY-EIGHT

SWEET SURRENDER

1968 – 1980

"Angel, you have a visitor," Aunt Rosalina called. Glad for a break, Angel closed the book he was reading for a class.

"Hello, Angel," Corinna said shyly. She stood in a practical beige coat with a light blue turtleneck peeking out from the coat's upturned collar. Modest. Her cheeks pink as though it embarrassed her to be there. In her hands was a covered dish. She held it out for him.

"Raspberry flan," she said. "I remember you once said it was your favorite. I've just come by to see how you're doing." Touched that she'd remembered, Angel invited her in.

"I'm glad you made it home safely, Angel. It must have been hard for you over there."

"Hard? Yes, it was hard," replied Angel, with an edge of bitterness.

"I prayed you would be safe and that you would find friends there who looked out for you. I know Marines do that." And with that statement, Angel told her stories about basic training and the men he had served with in Hotel Company.

He opened up, telling her more about his experiences in 'Nam than he'd told anyone since coming home. She asked unassuming questions, listened well, and he found it easy to confide in her. Angel, to his surprise, was sorry to see her leave.

The cooking classes Corinna loved taking made her an exceptional and creative cook. Sometimes she shared new recipes with Rosalina, and when they baked together for a church bazaar, there was laughter and singing. The house felt full of Corinna's presence when she visited.

He watched as she pumped air into the flat tires of her younger brother's bike, moving efficiently and filling both tires in the time it took him to make her a cup of coffee. In thanks, her brother had reached up and placed a brief kiss on her cheek. Angel realized he was wondering if it was soft skin that had met her brother's lips. He wondered if she was a competent or impassioned kisser. Perhaps she had never kissed, and those were virgin lips. Lately, he wondered a lot of things about Corinna Delgado, and it made him nervous. Very nervous. He quickly thought instead of the party his cousin Phoebe was taking him to. Passionate or not, he realized he couldn't deny that he appreciated Corinna.

She was not flashy, certainly not that, not the kind of girl who had typically caught his eye, but for the first time, Angel noticed qualities in Corinna he hadn't seen before; she was attractive. In fact, she was beautiful in a quiet way, and carried herself with pride, gentleness, and was genuine.

Corinna came by more frequently, making few demands of him. She anticipated his needs and was like a sweet balm to his spirit. He began to notice of the shine in her black hair, now worn long and loose, the sweet way her mouth curved as she listened to him, and Angel, being Angel, took notice of her round, very large breasts.

But best, she was an artist like himself, enjoying the meditational quality of drawing or embroidery while listening to music or just being at peace with silence as they sat together on the family's porch."

The beautiful, healing heart of this woman brought comfort. She appealed... more and more. He discovered she saw with her heart as well as her eyes

Everything she does, she does well, and with tenderness, he observed one day. He looked forward to her company. She was a presence who, in some inextricable way, offered solace and comfort. He missed her when she was gone. Over time, Angel discovered somewhere in the "betweens" of "each day," he'd fallen in love with Corinna Delgado. He knew he would love this woman always. He knew he wanted her for his own.

Because he loved her, he saw a therapist to work through the feelings trapped inside. Corinna deserved a "whole man," and he would not give her less.

"I want to be something close to the man I was before the war... but the mature version of that man," Angel volunteered, smiling at the therapist.

After some initial conversation, the therapist said, "You've frozen yourself, Angel. You keep the emotions you fear in a safe, contained place. Before we begin, I will warn you, thawing out hurts physically, emotionally, and psychologically. It won't be a cakewalk, but I think you'll find self-discovery to be rewarding.

"If you can trust me and lower your defenses, we can address your fears and come to terms with the horrors of war.

"Will you ever go back to becoming the person you were? No. You've experienced too much and insulated yourself to survive the trauma. Think about this, can a pickle ever return to being a cucumber? No, the cucumber was immersed in brine and changed into something else. The war, the brine, in this case, has changed you.

"However, don't dismiss that parts of you have evolved into a better version of yourself. Perhaps there's more compassion, tolerance, or the ability to see gray. I can't tell you the answer, but those are possibilities we can explore. You see yourself as damaged goods. I see you as a survivor. You changed because it was necessary. I'm a big believer in the heart's ability to travel from darkness to light if it has the 'want' to do so.

"So, the question is, will you let this war define you, or are you more than the war? Again, something only you can figure out. You came here wondering if you are worthy of love, Angel. I'd like to help you discover the answer if you're comfortable with me and willing to trust."

Angel let out a sigh of relief. *This man is not here to judge me.*

He visibly relaxed. The therapist knew what the issues would be.

I've hit the jackpot and made the right decision to come.

"Yes. I'm ready to start. The sooner, the better."

~~~

In 1972, upon graduating from college, Angel and Corinna Delgado married. As he watched his bride-to-be walk down the aisle, Angel remembered Jesse, Beau, and Mike. *I'm sure you guys are laughing down at me.*

Corrina's beauty shone through a most beautiful wedding gown, cut low, and showing a remarkable cleavage. Corinna had chosen a low-cut gown to please Angel. She took his breath away as she floated toward him.

He could hear the boys in Hotel now, "Hey Sweetness, you never stood a chance!" He looked at Aunt Rosalina's face.

Yes, Auntie, you won. You knew what I needed all along. I only knew what I wanted.

He nodded toward Rosalina and smiled. He knew that she knew what that nod meant. It was a joyous day!

~~~

Years later, Angel read there were as many suicides among Vietnam Vets as there were combat casualties during the war itself, and worse, the numbers were increasing each year. Angel hid this article from Corinna, not wishing to worry her.

His depression had come and gone for years, even with ongoing help. He'd fought it and tried his best to keep it from Corinna, out of protection for her and perhaps, if brutally honest, out of fear of losing the anchor she'd become.

Angel loved the family they'd created and worked hard at staying positive, using strategies learned from therapy. The statistics gripped his heart with cold fear, for he, too, had thoughts of ending it all, even in his happiness. They had all seen too much, done too much. Thank God for Corinna! He knew full well that without Corinna, Father Roberto, his buds at Vets 2 Vets, and his creative outlets, he might have been one of those statistics. Vietnam was a far-reaching horror that Angel fought and would continue to fight every day of his life.

~~~

Angel's sculptures and paintings were representations of his Vietnam experience and received wide acclaim. They became part of a traveling exhibit of works of art by Veterans of the Vietnam War. Art that captured the personal expressions of the fear, pain, horror, and sometimes joy of war.

A few pieces were works by Angel's Vets 2 Vets group. He was especially proud of those because he understood what they represented and knew he'd played a part in the catharsis this art encouraged.

Public interest supported these traveling pieces. Thereafter, Angel became one of several Vets instrumental in establishing a permanent Vietnam Veterans Art Museum in Chicago. The museum featured multi-media works relevant to the Vet experience, the only museum of its kind in the United States.

Angel came to realize he'd written many rewarding chapters in his life.

~~~

Suicide found the Vets-2-Vets group. They didn't realize it until one of their brothers missed one, two, then three meetings. Father R brought the bad news. "Two Tags" was gone. Another statistic. Another human being whose existence was not missed by anyone.

Along with Father Roberto, the "Vets-2-Vets" group attended the funeral, as did "Two Tags'" probation officer. The Rabbi spoke slowly and solemnly about John Abraham Lincoln. He had returned to "The World" and found friendship within the Veterans group. The Rabbi thanked everyone from the group and said, "It kept him alive longer than anyone imagined." After the service, they attended the burial at the Abraham Lincoln National Veterans Cemetery. The irony was lost on no one.

A pall permeated the room as the group gathered for their following weekly meeting. Father Roberto sensed it immediately and challenged them to create something positive from this soldier's death.

"I watched him flip his tags every week, and I returned the gesture because I made it back to 'The World.' I didn't think about what he might have gone through to get here," one said.

Another said sadly, "I didn't know his real name. He had those tags out every week, and I never asked." He looked up, glanced at each man present, and said, "You all know me as 'Short Stuff.' I have a name. My name is Michael Murphy."

With that, each man, in turn, spoke their name. One by one, they became new men in the other's eyes and took another step forward from where they'd been.

That evening, another weight from the war was lifted.

~~~

During one of the group meetings, an idea formed in Angel's mind, and he talked about every man he'd known killed in Vietnam. They had names too. He understood everyone who served "in-country" knew someone who'd been lost. They ALL had names, over 58,000 names that needed to be spoken and remembered.

Years later, other vets had those same thoughts, and their creativity led to the creation of "Above and Beyond," an exhibit at the Vietnam Veterans Art Museum in Chicago. Over 58,000 dog tags were suspended from the ceiling, each with a name, branch, and date of death.

The somber display included one black dog tag that hung to remember every Vietnam Veteran who died from service-related conditions during the war. That black dog tag hung for "Two Tags."

~~~

"Daddy, Daddy," cried out Angelina, climbing into Angel's lap.

"Maria won't let me color with her. She says I'm too messy."

295

Angel looked upon the face of his beautiful young daughter, wiped away her tears, and gently kissed her forehead. He reached over for something.

"I have magic pencils your great Aunt Rosalina sent to Daddy many, many years ago." Angelina spelled out each letter on the blue metal pencil box.

"F. A. B. E. R. See Daddy, I'm smart."

"Yes, you are my sweet girl. These are my special pencils, and when you use them, you can go outside the lines or mix the colors, or press and make them dark, or look, you can color lightly like this. No rules, my sweet, just color, and draw the way you like. Magic will happen."

"Will you color with me, Daddy?"

"Of course, I will. We'll color together until Mamma calls us for dinner. After dinner, if you'd like, you and I can walk outside, under the moon and stars, and discover what our enchanted world looks like at night. Do you know Angelina that trees are the oldest living things on our planet? We can stand in the middle of our lawn and let the crisscross shadows of the tree branches move around us. Maybe we can find some night flowers to smell and see if the silver moonlight has dripped on their petals. Or hear old father owl hoot hello. And perhaps, if we're very lucky, we might even spot a fairie or two playing near the gnarled tree roots! Would you like that, Angelina?"

"Oh, yes, Daddy!"

FORTY-NINE

A NEW BEGINNING

2006

John sat in Lucky's car and put the key in the ignition. He realized the key wouldn't move because of pressure on the steering column. *Simple fix.* He moved the wheel back and forth, taking the pressure off the column, turned the key, and the car started.

"Wow, so simple!" exclaimed Lucky. "You are a bricoleur!" she added when the car started.

"Bricoleur? I'm not familiar with that word …."

"It's a French word stemming from bricolage. A bricoleur is someone who can succeed using only what's at hand. Like the TV show, 'MacGyver.' He could get a machine going with a bobby pin or a rubber band," Lucky laughed.

"I call my Papasan the MacGyver of the senior set; he can fix anything just like MacGyver! He likes when I call him that and says it makes him feel young and competent."

"How old is he?"

"He turned ninety this year. He is my great-grandfather and has seen a lot in his life. He lives with me."

"So, I guess being a 'bricoleur' is a compliment!" John laughed. "I wasn't sure for a moment. I thought you might be saying I needed a breath mint!"

"Choi oi, good heavens, no!" laughed Lucky. They laughed together.

Laughter, the shortest distance between two people, and John and Lucky were already feeling a connection.

"I listened to your speech. You did an outstanding job. It was a very moving speech, and truthfully, I felt honored to hear it."

"Thank you! Yes, I saw you standing in the back of the crowd."

"I'll be honest with you, Lucky. May I call you Lucky?"

"Yes, of course."

"Your speech stirred up many memories of a time that was painful for me. My father was a Marine. He served in Vietnam between '66 and '67."

"Mon Dieu, no!" replied Lucky, her beautiful eyes filled with surprise and expression.

"My father was a Marine who served at that same time!" she replied.

"I was just having a drink and a bite," John said, motioning to where he'd been sitting.

"Perhaps you'd care to join me? My name is John Parker."

Lucky gasped and stumbled slightly.

"Are you alright?" John asked, concerned. "Come with me, and let's sit down."

With his hand on the small of her back, he guided her toward the restaurant.

Lucky stopped to look at John. "John, I believe your father and my father served together and were very good friends, as were our mothers!"

Now it was John's turn to look amazed. "What? How could they all have been friends? I don't understand! Can we sit down and talk?"

"Yes, I think we need to!" Lucky replied, still unsettled by her discovery.

Sitting at the table, John asked, "What will you have Lucky? Lunch, a drink, or both? I'll definitely be ordering another drink!"

"Yes, both, please. I was too anxious to eat before my speech this morning, and now I think I could use a drink as well."

John held Lucky's chair for her as she sat down, and he sat across from her.

"Okay, let's start from the beginning. Why do you think our parents knew each other?"

Lucky smiled. "I have stories for you, John. But some of these stories have amazingly only come to me in the last few weeks. First, let me say to you that your father was a very funny man, a cut-up. You obviously get your humor from him! I enjoyed our laugh a moment ago."

"Me too," grinned John, and continued, "I've always wanted to find someone who served with my father, to hear stories about what he faced during his tour. I wondered if that would ever happen. Please go on with your story."

Lucky settled herself with a long breath, "Let me start by telling you that two days ago, I received your grandparent's address in the mail."

"My grandparent's address?" John asked, his head now swimming. He stared at her incredulously.

"Yes, that's how strange this river flows, your grandparent's address in Florida. I see now that both our worlds will change because of Hurricane Katrina. In her fury, she has stirred up and released energy from earth and water so our stories can be known."

"You're not making sense, Lucky. What do you mean?"

"John, are you the son of Beau and Helen Parker?"

"Yes!" he replied with a disbelieving look.

"Then let me begin," Lucky replied as she took another deep breath.

"My mother and your mother worked together at the Station Hospital in Da Nang. They were great friends. My mother was a self-proclaimed 'spiritual mutt,' having learned Buddhism from her mother and Catholicism from her father and Papasan. She collected spiritual ideas like a florist collects flowers, and she studied religion, quoting monks and Bible verses in the same sentence.

"The first day they met, your mother confided in mine that your father died in Da Nang, and that she came to Vietnam as a nurse to see where he died, to know what his world was like, and to stay close to his spirit. Helen was beautiful and caring. Every Marine, doctor, and official that passed through the doors of the hospital fell in love with her. Many wanted to marry her. She could have had anyone she wanted.

"She was called 'The Angel' because she would sit at night with Marines in critical care whose injuries were severe and who would probably die. Your mother would hold their hand and whisper to them about their home, their mothers, or their sweethearts. My mother once told me that your mother was the most compassionate woman she'd ever met.

"Here is the strange part, and you'll probably have trouble accepting this... your mother believed your father was always near her and kept her safe so she could care for these men. She swore she saw him, and when she could do no more to sustain life, she relinquished the dying Marine over to your father's capable hands.

"She never wavered in her love for your father; she stayed true. Has she remarried?"

John looked down and shook his head. He put his hand on his forehead to shield his eyes.

"No," he said quietly. Lucky saw a tear fall.

"I'm sorry," he said, his voice husky with emotion. "My mother came and went, mostly went, and we've become estranged. I just found out she lives in Washington. It's where I'll be living, and I didn't know it was her home too. I resented her; I should have been the most important person to her, a fatherless son. I've heard nothing about my mother's life at the hospital, and I've heard nothing like what you're telling me now! My father, a spirit? It's more than a little hard to believe."

"John, I was a young girl when my mother told me these stories. I was only seven when my mother died, but I remember these stories very well, and I remember your mother. She played with me sometimes and would tell me about her handsome son back in the States. She helped in an orphanage to be around children because she missed you so much.

"My mother told me that your mother once took in a young Marine who had what we call today, PTSD, Post-Traumatic Stress Disorder. Back then, they didn't have a name for it, and certainly no treatment. A booby trap had severely injured him. He had what they called a dirty wound, gaping flesh with mud, metal, and clothing fragments embedded inside, a common injury among soldiers in Vietnam. Anyway, he developed a dependency on the drugs they had given him for pain, so they needed to put him through detox.

"Your mother discovered he had nowhere to go, no one to go home to in the States, so she convinced the doctors to give this Marine a few weeks to get himself together before shipping him out. She promised to oversee his care and brought him to her place. Things were fine for the first two days, but her home had been wrecked on the third day when she returned from work.

"She looked for him, found him, and brought him not to the hospital, but back to her home. She understood the rage and confusion associated with this brutal fighting and how difficult it was for him to let go of his anger and reconnect with his humanness. She also knew he had the right to feel rage, the same rage she must have felt with your father's death. Your mother brought him to her home to get through another day. And that's what it took for that Marine to get it 'right.' That's how intensely she cared."

John mused, "I believe what you're telling me and what your mother told you. You have no reason to tell me anything but the truth. And I know my mother went to 'Nam to see where my father died and that she wouldn't give up on their love. Actually, as a man in a man's military, what's always amazed me is that she did this as a woman alone, on her terms.

"But to stay there to be close to my father, believing he was with her to help the wounded, well, that's more than bizarre, Lucky.

301

"I know why none of us heard these details from my mother. It's something a person wishing to be considered sane wouldn't disclose.

"So, I either accept she's slightly insane or that there's more between heaven and earth than I'm aware of." He looked at Lucky in disbelief.

"No, John," Lucky said, "She didn't do it alone. She did it with your father.

"He's been with her every step of the way. Your mother believes she takes care of those in need on earth, and he takes care of them in death. It might not be what you believe, John, but it's what your mother believes.

"Perhaps your mother believes that as long as she helps those in need, your father will remain with her."

John remained still for a few moments in reflection. Then, with an amazed look on his face, as if a great mystery had been solved, said, "This makes complete sense to me. It's why my mother has pursued one catastrophic situation after another.

"Lucky. I'm grateful. I was hoping to hear about my dad, but here I am, learning about my mother instead. Maybe she's not the remote statue I've always imagined her to be, and I'm wondering if there's a chance for my mother and me to have a relationship and find peace between us. Something I never expected, but something I'm willing to explore."

John was silent a few moments longer. "My father and mother were best friends for years before they were married. I know from my uncles how deeply they were in love. I suppose if there were a way to be together, those two would find it. We don't see the wind, but it exists. Who knows?

"What an opportunity you've given me, Lucky." He smiled at her and covered her hands with his own and said, "Thank you."

"Now, can you tell me anything about my father?" John asked, hopefully.

Happy and relieved, Lucky smiled and continued with her story.

"My mother was introduced to the gun team by my father, Mike Redd. After the DMZ battle, she was at the hospital, frantically looking at every arriving Marine, fearing she would find my father. She never found him, but she found yours. My mother took care of your father and was at his side when he died."

She held John's hands tighter and looked directly into his eyes. "He didn't die alone, John."

John released Lucky's hands, excused himself, and left the table for the restroom. He returned a few minutes later, and with a shaky voice and moist eyes, said, "Thank you again, Lucky. This is a lot for me to take in all at once. How about if we move to the story of you? How did you come to be in New Orleans?"

"It's hard to speak about some of this, John, but I'll try my best for you. I can see we share the same pain, but already I trust you, so I will tell you."

She took a deep sip of her rum and coconut milk and told John many things about her life in Vietnam, her father's murder by the list maker Nhat, and their escape from Vietnam ending in her mother's murder.

"Here is the vital part for us, John, and why I say Katrina has ripped apart earth and water for us to understand our complete story. As we left Vietnam in the Captain's fishing boat, my mommy carried with her a small satchel. In it were documents that would help get us to America, money, a bottle of perfume your mother gave her, and a small picture of the gun team that Angel Santiago gave her as he was leaving for the States. Angel was one of the five Marines in the picture, and he particularly loved your father. They would spar with words.

"That picture is the only picture I have of my father. He stands between your father and another Marine, Jesse McGowan, your father's best friend. It is the picture taken on the day of your father's return to Vietnam commemorating his marriage to your mother, and just three days before he was shot in battle."

John's eye's widened as he interrupted her, "I have that picture on my dresser. I was told a friend of my mother's gave her the picture."

They sat and stared at each other, then smiled. It was true. The universe was revealing its secrets. They both took another sip of their drinks, and Lucky continued.

"Like you, I've also wished to find people who knew my father, but for me, that too never happened, until Katrina. As the hurricane approached, I remained undecided if Papasan and I could stay in my apartment and wait things out or go up the street to our church for sanctuary. The force of Katrina's wind was just to the point of requiring a decision when, suddenly, the wind's intensity increased. I hurriedly gathered essential items, knowing we needed to get out.

"As I held that small picture in my hand, Katrina slammed into our apartment window. I never saw exactly what flew past. It looked like an orange sheet with a large stone inside. The thunderous noise caused me to drop the picture. Our window never broke, but the glass in the picture frame did.

"Last month, I finally had time to look for a new frame. As I disassembled it, I saw a note written on the back of the photo in green pencil. Angel Santiago's name, address, phone number, and message were written for my mother.

I called the number and asked if Angel still lived there, and the person answering said she was Angel's aunt and gave me his new number. I spoke with him, John! He's so friendly and forthcoming.

"He told me how he was young and stupid then and liked nothing better than to throw banter at your father, watch his reaction, then wait for him to dish something back. Angel suffered from depression when he returned from the war. He is an artist, and he's sending a picture of his wife, two daughters, and four granddaughters, all gathered around him.

"Angel said a bevy of beautiful women finally surrounds him, and that this has always been his dream. He's a funny man. I'm excited to see it when it arrives! He also helped establish the Vietnam Veteran's Art Museum in Chicago, John! He told me many stories. How he'd enlisted to avoid marriage with the woman he, in fact, married when he returned; that the squad was blackmailing your father over another picture taken while they were on R&R, a picture of your father in a pink coolie hat with someone called Mai Mai. Angel didn't give me details, but I bet he would give you the entire story from the way he was chuckling. I think it will be a good story but one you might not want to mention to your mother.

"Angel, and Chingas Ramirez, the other Marine who is also still alive, have continued to stay in touch. I wrote to Chingas and received a reply a few days ago. He wrote that my father would have been a great journalist, someone like Ed Bradley, a black journalist wounded while reporting in Vietnam, and who, like my father, believed 'the harder he worked, the luckier he got.'

"In his letter, Chingas suggested a reunion of sorts. I know you and your mother would be welcome! He has a large home with plenty of space for us when we visit. He also said he had Helen's address once, and they stayed in contact at the beginning, but with subsequent moves for each of them, they lost touch. He sent me your grandparent's address but didn't know if they were still living.

"Just so you understand how strange this is, my mother's two favorite sayings, her two beliefs were, 'no coincidences,' and 'we don't have endless grains in the hourglass.' She was so right, so wise on both accounts. We are not immortal, and every day counts. Here I sit with Beau and Helen's son while my poor mommy lies at the bottom of the ocean!"

For a long time, John looked at Lucky, aware that her pain and loss were even greater than his own.

He wasn't sure what to say to her but let his heart speak. "And here I sit with someone who's known so much more pain than a person should ever know, certainly more than I've encountered in my life. I'm so sorry this has happened to you and your mother and father, Lucky.

"War is a thief. Yet, here we sit together and share the pain of the loss of our parents. But also, to know how much our parents loved each other. Well, it's incredible, all of it, to say the least, and I think I must agree with your mother, 'no coincidence' rings clear.

"So Lucky, if there are no coincidences, then we've been brought together by a force greater than ourselves. If not that, then our meeting is stranger than science fiction. I want you to know, for me, I'm very grateful to be here with you! You feel like someone I've known all my life. I don't want to let go of this. I want more time with you. As much as you're willing to give me, I promise whatever that amount is, I will only be appreciative!

"Do you have time to walk by the river with me, talk more, have dinner, see me tomorrow? There are but so many grains of sand in the hourglass, Lucky. Please say yes!"

"Yes, I say yes, John Parker!" And as John Parker looked into Lucky's eyes, he noticed a tear rolled down her face, but she smiled a happy smile. She cried for the beauty of life as he leaned over and gently brushed the tear away. They'd both waited so long …. And so it began … again.

FIFTY

THE CIRCLE CLOSES

2006

A nnie traveled to the places Terrance, the waiter at Café du Monde, recommended she see. The lower 9th Ward, hardest hit, showed little activity of rebuilding. It was all but deserted. One lone house on Florida Avenue had a hole in its roof, and Annie guessed that this had been Terrance's sister's home. Other areas showed various stages of renovation.

A few days after she'd heard Lucky Dai's speech, Annie drove to see the progress made in the Vietnamese community. She parked her car at a small strip mall near Versailles Arms Apartments, hoping to speak to store owners or customers about their experiences with Katrina and to see if she could be of any help.

Her offers were politely refused. A store owner showed her pictures of boats navigating this very parking lot, the water so high it looked like a river, but no, help was not needed. They were a community unto themselves, and she could tell immediately there was organization in the way they carried out their tasks.

She leaned against her car and noticed people went to one of two men for instructions. She learned from a different owner that most residents of this community attended the Vietnamese Catholic Church, whose leadership had structured its parishioners into groups responsible for church and community events. These responsibilities had translated efficiently into tasks involving the reconstruction of their community. Significant rebuilding was occurring here, and everywhere she looked, people were working with purpose.

Annie noticed a pharmaceutical sign in the window of a store and wondered if this was where Lucky Dai was a pharmacist. She walked toward it, and as she was debating whether to go in, she heard someone shout, "Watch out!"

Katrina had damaged an orange marquee displaying the names of the Vietnamese stores. The damaged section had not yet required replacement but broke free when a sudden gust of wind came from nowhere. The fragment flew against Annie's back and knocked her to the ground.

People ran to help. The door of the pharmacy opened, and Lucky came out to see what had happened.

"Are you hurt?" she asked, taking charge. Annie, more embarrassed than anything else, stood up.

"No, no, I don't think so." The two women recognized each other. "I stopped by to see what was going on regarding rebuilding. I was told this was a community to visit if I wanted to see coordinated community effort." Annie said, smiling.

She looked down to see her knee was bleeding under a tear in her jeans.

"Come inside my shop, please. Let me take care of that. Are you sure you're okay?"

"Yes, just feeling a little silly," Annie replied, wishing to get away from the on-lookers who had crowded around her.

"Come inside," Lucky repeated, taking Annie's arm. Lucky said something in Vietnamese, and the crowd disbanded.

Annie's pride was injured more than her knee, and a flash of Thomas crossed her mind. She was glad her son had not been here to see her get hurt! Some alcohol, a few dabs of peroxide, and a Band-Aid took care of the mishap.

"That sign knows how to get a customer's attention!" Annie laughed and then confided, "I'm glad my son didn't see this strange event. He thinks I'm too old to be 'gallivanting around dangerous places' and takes every opportunity to tell me!"

Lucky laughed at Annie's revelation. "I have a cousin, Tran, who hovers over me like that. Cuts into our feeling of independence, doesn't it? I don't know about you, but I love it and hate it at the same time!"

"Exactly!" exclaimed Annie, feeling a bond with this woman.

"I live around the corner," Lucky volunteered. "I'm finished for the day and ready to go home. Come with me, and I'll tell you a little of the story you asked for. We can share a cup of tea or something stronger; you've earned it! It's not every day someone gets attacked by a sign!"

Annie let Lucky drive the rental car to her home.

"Papasan, my great-grandfather, always likes company," Lucky told Annie as they entered.

In the foyer, a small plaque caught Annie's attention. She had the same one in her home. It was a quotation from Eleanor Roosevelt, a woman she admired, "Justice cannot be for one side alone, but must be for both."

"I have the same quote in my home. Justice and fairness are concepts a boy in my neighborhood and I talked about when we were young. He had a big heart and strongly believed in fairness for all. I bought my sign with him in mind. He was special to me."

"Yes, this is a saying close to my heart as well. I liked Eleanor's stance on Black rights, something Franklin was ambivalent about, and using the word ambivalent is probably giving him every benefit of the doubt," laughed Lucky.

"So, you're a history buff, Lucky! I am too," said Annie as she stepped farther into Lucky's home, surprised by its modern décor.

White walls, stark furnishings, with a focus on line and color. Bright pictures and splashes of color in the upholstery defined the living area.

"Is that a Peter Max?" Annie asked, amazed, and moving closer to the large picture.

"Yes, I attended an exhibit a few years ago and fell in love with this piece. I like his freedom and vibrant color. It's exciting artwork and reminds me of the times in which my parents lived. The freedom in this giclee is reminiscent of the sixties and is why I purchased it.

"I buy with my heart," she said, smiling. "And I'll never get rich collecting," she confessed sheepishly.

"I also liked that Max's parents were refugees of sorts, like me, leaving Berlin to escape the Nazis. He painted many pictures of his Nanny, a young Shanghai girl, who is the woman in this picture. He was purportedly in love with her," said Lucky with a broad smile that held a hint of mischief, "Or maybe he just loved her for taking good care of him, we will surely never know!"

Laughing, she handed Annie a drink, a sweet mix of coconut milk and rum. "With that fall you took, I took a liberty and thought you could use a proper drink," Lucky said in a conspiratorial manner, handing Annie the drink in a simple black raku cup that fit comfortably in the palm of Annie's hand. "No need to tell your son about your fall! Just enjoy this moment. It is the unexpected outcome which your fall has given you! I hope you like it. It's my specialty."

Papasan walked slowly into the room and sat in what must be his chair, Annie thought, a weave of leather strips that had over time shaped to the contours of his body. They nodded to each other, each giving a smile. Without asking, Lucky poured Papasan some tea as if this were a ritual, and he sipped while Lucky introduced the two.

Papasan said something to Lucky in Vietnamese, patiently pointing a long, crooked forefinger her way, then waving it towards Annie, apparently saying, "Tell her, go on, tell her."

Lucky turned to Annie, "Papasan wishes me to tell you he doesn't speak English, but he'll enjoy sitting and drinking tea with us." Papasan smiled, looked at Lucky, and shook his head, no. He admonished Lucky again with that long finger, bringing a laugh from her as he spoke a friendly reprimand.

"Those were my words Annie, not Papasan's. I apologize, Papasan. Papasan wants me to repeat his exact words to you, so please take note, as he wishes me to be very clear on this. He said he enjoys drinking tea with us and being part of our company, but he wants you to know it's not that he doesn't speak English. He does. He just does not wish to speak English. He would rather speak Vietnamese and let me translate. It is easier for his ninety-year-old brain to do it this way."

Lucky looked affectionately into the eyes of her very old Papasan, and they shared a smile, a private joke between them. He nodded, yes.

"He thinks at his age he has earned the right to do exactly as he pleases, and he is likely correct. He has been through much in his lifetime."

Smiling at this animated, devilish old man, Annie said, "Then please tell Papasan that I understand and agree completely. Life should be easy. It should be as simple and wonderful as a child's kiss, or a breeze on the face!"

Papasan beamed. He beckoned her toward him. Endearingly he reached for her hand with his own gnarled, almost translucent fingers and kissed it softly. "He agrees with that beautiful sentiment," Lucky translated once more.

Annie turned back to Lucky and sat where Lucky indicated, on a carved mahogany chair with a saffron silk seat.

"I'm interested in hearing about your life and challenges, Lucky. If you feel comfortable, I'd be grateful to hear a little of your story as a child and your experience as a boat person. I ask because, as I mentioned before, so many women and children in the Middle East today find themselves refugees, as you were upon leaving Vietnam. Their struggle is hard, and help needs to come their way. I'm hoping to help with my position on the Post. Justice is not on their side, and they might never retrieve what's being taken from them. You've done so well, Lucky. I wonder what kept you going and how you made a success of your misfortune."

"Yes. I will tell you some of my story, how we went from Vietnam to the Philippines to Fort Smith, Arkansas, a relocation center for refugees. Then, with the help of Catholic Charities, how we came to our final destination here in New Orleans. As I mentioned in my speech, my mother was Vietnamese, and my father, an American Marine in Vietnam. Here are their pictures."

Lucky took two pictures from an end table near Papasan. One was of a beautiful young Vietnamese woman looking very much like Lucky herself; the other was a black-and-white photo of five Marines with cigars.

Annie gasped and almost dropped the picture.

At the end of a long, tearful but joyous visit, Lucky and Annie promised to meet again. Lucky wanted Annie to meet John before leaving New Orleans. She told her all she knew about each Marine in the photo, and about John and Helen, also mentioning Helen's present work.

It seemed the two women lived within miles of each other in the Washington/Virginia area and had worked toward similar goals, protecting women and children who were refugees and victims of large-scale violence and war. "No coincidences, Annie," Lucky said.

As Annie stood to leave, Papasan slowly pushed himself out of his chair. He walked towards Annie and gave her a long and warm hug, something very uncustomary for Papasan.

He pulled away, saying in his best English, "Take care of yourself. You are a child of the universe. It would please me, and my granddaughter Thuy, if you stayed friends with my great-granddaughter, Lucky."

"I am so happy for today, for our meeting," a teary-eyed Lucky said. "Forces greater than us are here today, working their magic. It is as though my mother and father are here with us and have brought us together to close their circle of love. We were meant to meet each other and help each other in our loss and grief. And then there is John."

Lucky and Annie hugged goodbye. Lucky whispered to Annie, shyly confiding, "I think I'm falling in love with John."

What a strange and wonderful world we live in, thought Annie as she drove over the bridge back to the Hilton, and much that exists between heaven and earth.

~~~

Sitting at the writing-table of her room that evening, Annie jotted down notes relevant to Lucky's conversation. She had been a descriptive storyteller, vivid in her recollections. For a young child, she had many detailed memories. Perhaps trauma implants recall in some while others are blessed with forgetfulness, all according to need, Annie reflected.

Lucky, well, she had remembered. The pain was hardest when she spoke of her mother's rape and brutal death. It was then that tears rolled unabashedly down Lucky's face, and she was forced to pause, overwhelmed, pulling in air. She regained her composure after a few moments and willed the horror of her memory away.

Annie had been quick to say, "Stop, this is too painful for you," but Lucky shook her head and continued her story. The story was for Annie to know. Annie had a significant connection with the picture and had become part of the circle, part of the family. She had a right to know.

Lucky spoke of what gave her the strength to carry on, of her dual religious upbringing and the blend of Buddhism and Christianity that formed her personal faith. Since a child, she had learned all life was temporary; therefore, each precious day spent in pursuit of honor, love, purpose, and beauty was a day well spent.

Lucky became a pharmacist to honor her mother and continued to help others as her mother had done with nursing. To honor her father, she became someone of substance and helped her community whenever and however she could. Per her father's faith, she treated others the way she wished to be treated. Her parent's death would not be in vain. Their lives would count for something.

Lucky spoke of hope, peace, and balance and the desire to live up to what she believed her parents wanted for her; would have expected of her, had they lived. She carried them in her heart, and in so doing, knew she kept them alive.

FIFTY-ONE

GHOST OF A HERO

2006

It had been an incredible day, and Annie was emotionally exhausted. With notes of Lucky's journey complete, Annie looked out the hotel window and watched the sun cast its last rays on nearby buildings. It was the golden hour when the sun gave its last burst of radiance, illuminating all before darkness consumed its light.

Tomorrow she would call Mary, her closest friend, and tell her what happened. Annie would also call Russ and tell him what she'd discovered about Jess, who he was in 'Nam, how he lived, and how he died.

Annie tried to imagine what fighting in Vietnam was like, the jungle, the heat, the filth, the terror. The unknown moment of meeting death, the shadow around a corner. Would death come suddenly with no time to suffer, or would it punish you slowly and with searing pain? A meeting undoubtedly considered by every soldier in combat.

What did Jess think about death? So close to coming home when it took him. He'd survived twelve of the thirteen-month tour of duty.

She knew now that Jesse had a best friend there, and they were mortally wounded on the same day. Had they talked of death or dying? Was that subject taboo? Did these two men individually prepare themselves, and if so, how? How did Jess process the fear of death? Did he reconcile himself to it? Did Beau?

If so, were they more than "casualties of war?" Were they survivors?

Annie's father habitually taped parables, statements, or poems to the refrigerator door, meant to touch the soul if one took the time to understand it. Annie particularly liked one tattered poem by Kipling that had spent an inordinate amount of time on that door, and she'd memorized it.

"If you can force your heart and nerve and sinew

To serve your turn long after they are gone,

And so hold on when there is nothing in you

Except the will which says to them: 'Hold on!'

If you can fill the unforgiving minute

With sixty-second's worth of distance run,

Yours is the Earth, and everything that's in it,

And... which is more... you'll be a Man, my son!"

Annie imagined this writing described Jesse and Beau. They had become men in this war.

She now understood she'd loved a boy who, in that struggle, became a man ... then a hero in his own right.

Jess. How she missed him.

Annie relaxed and allowed her thoughts to drift. She became aware of the melody playing on the radio. It was a Thomas Newman piece and one she particularly liked, every piano note deliberate, rich in its simplicity and purpose. Lost in its slow, haunting sound, her mind wandered to Forrest Heights. There, for her to remember, was the heavy sweet smell of honeysuckle on a summer's night. She was on her family's back porch again, watching the tiny spider doing what its DNA demanded, stringing together a web in the moonlight, strand by strand, creating a pattern unique to its species. A turn here, a thread there, details, serving a purpose, much the way each piano note served a purpose tonight, taking her heart slowly and methodically to a memory of long ago, playing a melody to a place in her heart, meant to recapture an ache long since left behind.

What becomes of a heartache? Does it sit on some obscure shelf with other tarnished memories? Does its pain lessen with each passing day, only to die into a tired sigh, or worse, something indistinguishable fading into inaudibility? Do heartaches become ghosts, occasionally resurrected on nights like these, by a familiar song, a remembered smell, or a special gesture?

Would she find the courage to accept death with dignity and grace when her moment came? She let go of the pen, her eyes heavy, her body tired. Annie stepped toward her bed and slid into the silky comfort of the sheets. *Did you ever feel anything so smooth, Jess?* She pulled the covers over her.

So much between heaven and earth, Lucky had said.

Annie's eyes closed. *I've missed you Jesse. You've been gone too long, and it's been cold without you.*

And then ... somehow, perhaps in her dream, somehow ... perhaps through this thing called a parallel universe, somehow ... because she'd willed it, Jess traveled eternity to be with her.

Hello Annie, time is different for me. I miss you always. His voice familiar, his touch warm.

In a swirling mist, they were together again, on the hill behind the Stone's house. A galaxy floated above them and found its way into Annie's eyes. Not a word spoken between them. His gaze was long and traveled through her, his kiss tender.

"Annie, can I?" he asked without speaking.

Her arms wrapped around him; tears streamed down her face. He was with her once again. She kissed him deeply and surrendered.

"Oh yes, Jess, I've waited so long."

FIFTY-TWO

UNTIL WE MEET AGAIN

"We're here to awaken from our illusion of separateness"

Thich Nhat Hanh

2006

It was a gray November day when Russ Stone Jr., now an old man, stood on one leg and crutches on the Chesapeake Bay pier. A punji stick and the subsequent infection took his leg at the end of his second tour in 'Nam.

The sun would soon set. His eyes found the point where the water met the sky. It was his meditational spot that allowed him to "be," a place of solace. It was the water on the Bay he often sought and needed, an old friend he could rest with before making the lonely trip home.

Annie had called him to talk about Jesse, Vietnam, and the events of New Orleans. How could she know Vietnam still had the power to wrap itself around his gut and wake him soaked in the sweat of relentless and inescapable fear all these years later?

"The best way to destroy your enemies is to make them your friends," a friend once told him. It struck a chord, and he'd lived by that motto most of his adult life. Since 'Nam, he sought only to coexist with others, to be at peace with himself and nature.

Russ became a recluse of sorts after Sally died. They had a wonderful life together and were married before he left for 'Nam. Now he lived alone in his small house in Rosehaven, near the bay.

He knew he should head home soon as driving in the dark was difficult for him, but he couldn't resist lingering a little longer. The water sparkled like diamonds this evening. It is beautiful, he thought in appreciation as geese flew overhead in a chevron heading to their home on the Patuxent River.

Russ thought of the many birds that sat on the telephone wires. He'd see them soon enough on his way home, as they were there every evening. Small, white-winged birds that either sat together like clothespins on a line or flew together like a school of swimming fish, swooping and soaring in complete accord, not a bird out of sync; a flight of unison, a flight of one body, a part of something bigger than themselves. A unit. Then they'd stop as quickly as they started, as though heralded by a silent trumpet, and land on that telephone line. Always the same line.

He watched night after night, transfixed at this feat of nature, and wondered what it would feel like to be in total synchronization with others of your kind. He would like to be one of those birds, to be one with others, sharing a perfect moment. The closest he'd come to that experience was serving in the Marines. There, he was part of a unit, and it felt good.

He thought of all the fallen heroes he'd known.

After talking with Annie, he thought about Hotel Company and the gun team. He knew each of their stories from letters written to him by Jesse. He wondered what the men of Hotel Company would say if they had voices?

Standing on this dock in the dusk of life, Russ carried on a conversation with the silent Marines of Hotel's gun team who could no longer be heard. Whatever they said to this old warrior made him laugh, tear up, and slowly shake his head. Those who had not fought the good fight, taken lives, or saved lives could never understand the words that described their feelings, their experiences of fear, pain, relief, and joy in the camaraderie. Russ knew. The old warrior dried his tears and returned to the world of the present. He knew if they could speak, they would say, "Remember me."

He watched the fishing boats return with their catch of the day and turned to go. A cold wind blew on his face. He was getting old and was tiring of this world.

Years ago, he'd driven through the old neighborhood of Forest Heights and recognized Jesse's dad, Mr. McGowan, sitting on the top step of their front porch. His gaze was vacant. He hadn't remembered Russ standing in front of him. "Did you know my son served in Vietnam?" Mr. McGowan asked, not listening for an answer, seemingly just wanting to make sure that Jesse's young life had been worth something. Russ smiled and said, "Yes, sir, I did. Thank you for your sacrifice." Mr. McGowan didn't respond but continued to stare off somewhere that only he could see.

Russ walked away and thought once again, dead is dead. War, 58,220 dead from a "conflict." These men were once human beings who cried, loved, and wanted. With death, their dreams, as with their breath, moved away from those who loved them, never to return.

Will we ever learn to fly in unison like the birds, swim in unison like the fish? Dear God, let this world find a way to live in harmony. Let there be peace for all.

Talking with Annie brought back memories of long ago when life was so different.

I'll keep believing parallel universes exist. In one of those universes, a group of innocent kids are playing hide and seek under the streetlights of Forest Heights. All of them safe, without the threat of war, a universe at peace.

"Ollie Ollie Oxen Free," he heard Bobby Dougherty call out, and he saw the kids from his neighborhood emerging like shadows from the dark, Jeff, Julie, Mary, Annie, and Jess.

"Every gun that is made, every warship launched, every rocket fired signifies, in the final sense, a theft from those who hunger and are not fed, those who are cold and not clothed. This world in arms is not spending money alone. It is spending the sweat of its labors, the genius of its scientists, the hopes of its children."

General Dwight D. Eisenhower, Head of Supreme Headquarters Allied Expeditionary Force, during his "Chance for Peace" speech.

AFTERWORD

Here are statistics relevant to my story. Research led me to "aha" moments and conclusions that enabled me to interpret and understand the soldier's story. By sharing, I hope you will feel compelled to learn more about this war and what a tumultuous time it was in our history! I also hope the reader will realize the parallels of the 1960s with the ongoing conflicts our nation is engaged in today.

More than 2,700,000 American soldiers served in uniform in Vietnam from March 1965 through May 1975.

Vietnam Vets were the best-educated forces our nation sent into combat, with 79% having a high school education or better.

The Department of Defense cites 6,250 Army nurses served.

The average infantryman in the South Pacific during WWII saw about 40 days of combat.

The average infantryman in Vietnam saw about 240 days of combat in one year.

Two thirds of the men who served in Vietnam were volunteers, 2/3 of the men who served in WWII were drafted.

Roughly 80% of those who served in Vietnam came from working class, or low-income families.

Of those Vietnam Veterans killed, 61% were younger than 21 years old. This is why the "Class of '65" is called "the lost class."

58,220 American soldiers died in Vietnam. That number also represents the number of families and future generations impacted.

Missing In Action (MIA's), to include Veterans and civilians, was estimated at 1,592 as of 2018.

Amputations and crippling wounds were 300% higher in the Vietnam War than in World War II. A large number were dirty wounds from booby traps or Claymores, Bouncing Betties, and punji sticks.

75,000 Vietnam Veterans were severely disabled.

Let us not forget the Vietnamese families who lost loved ones in Vietnam's fight for freedom from communism.

The Army of the Republic of Vietnam (ARVN) combat death statistics vary widely, perhaps between 220,000-250,000.

Statistics of South and North Vietnamese civilian and soldier deaths in the Vietnam War also vary widely. An approximate estimate is 1,700,000 Vietnamese killed.

Approximately 1 million South Vietnamese, men and women were sent to re-education camps after the communists took South Vietnam. Approximately 165,000 died in those camps. It is believed the communists executed 65,000 men and women.

Approximately 400,000 boat people from both North and South Vietnam died trying to escape communism.

In recent years, the Vietnamese government released information that approximately 1.1 million North Vietnamese military died in the Vietnam War. As ferocious and relentless as the Viet Cong were portrayed, when we combine the Viet Cong (VC) and North Vietnamese Army (NVA) deaths and compare them to the U.S. and ARVN deaths, an obvious conclusion can be drawn. We were every bit as good and, in fact, three times better than the North. The war was our win if body count was the determinator. But body count was not what determined win or lose in this long-standing conflict.

Because President Johnson failed to get authorization from Congress to declare this a war, America's soldiers entered a fight that was defined as a "conflict." Had Congress voted on behalf of their constituents, this "conflict" would have become the people's war. Johnson could easily have won the vote of Congress, but this was not to be. Johnson failed the soldiers in this decision. A declared war would have required decorum from its citizens, a correct way of behaving, as past wars had required. Demonstrating or fighting against war was considered an act of treason in the past. As an undeclared war, the door was opened for discourse, demonstrations, and dissent. Some protested because they honestly believed we had no reason to be fighting in Vietnam. Others demonstrated to avoid the draft, especially worried were those college students with lower academic standing who were more likely to be drafted.

We, the spectators, year after year, watched America's longest war in our living rooms on our televisions, first in black and white, and later in the colors of war; napalm orange, Huey green, smoke on the water brown, body bag black, all the while protected from its stench of death.

Before television, Americans obtained news through the commentators "take" on the radio, or they read the newspaper. Past generations were protected from the rawness of military events. Innocence was spared. With television, we saw our boys "upfront and personal" taking on multiple layers of the jungle, wearing heavy flak jackets, carrying 60-80-pound packs, in heat and humidity regularly over 100 degrees and fighting for their lives in unimaginable conditions.

We saw our boys during the monsoon season, and bullets rained on them faster than the cold pelting rain, while they fought and died in knee-deep mud. We saw them struggle to conquer a hill, Hill 593 or Hill 861, the numbers designating the hill's elevation. The Marines who conquered those hills, however, would recall tales of death and heroism at the mere recollection of that number. The Marines would capture a hill, force the enemy to retreat, only to return soon thereafter, and begin the cycle of fighting and dying again.

The war effort was failed by a media that reported live daily. Sometimes the reports were biased and indicated a U.S. loss; the Tet Offensive is one famous example. In the end, Americans at home saw too much of a war that was personal and controversial to the point of polarizing. We were a country divided, with intense feelings about whether we should be fighting in Vietnam or not. Our nation was divided and out of control. We took our anger out on the returning Vet, but when the news showed the exhausted, sweat-soaked, scared, and lonely faces of the soldiers that fought that war, we realized they were, after all, OUR faces, and OUR boys. Many of us felt guilty from our lack of support for the soldier.

Perhaps with the daily confrontation of this guerrilla war, we became as crippled in our souls as those soldiers, fighting the fight. When our Vietnam veterans turned to us for help in ministering to their wounds or accepting their visions of hell, many Americans couldn't muster the courage, or nurturance needed.

With wars end, we hoped for a fresh beginning, but our soldiers were daily reminders of what we fought to forget, and their nightmares enshrouded us as they enshrouded them.

We failed to care for them in our VA Hospitals. For years Vietnam Vets sought help for effects caused by exposure to Agent Orange and are, even today, still being denied.

Many Chapters of the Veterans of Foreign Wars (VFW) turned their backs on the Vietnam Vet, citing Vietnam was not a declared war.

The combined effects of these actions left the soldier exposed and unprotected, emotionally, psychologically, and physically.

We abandoned our Vietnam Vets as we abandoned those South Vietnamese who had fought beside us and sought refuge at the American Embassy before the last U.S. Marine helicoptered from the roof of the U.S. Embassy in Saigon.

Most conclude the Vietnam War's end was determined by the American public, who grew weary of seeing American boys killed in a war with no exit plan. Those who fought did so to win the war, but in the end, the war was lost due to the tide of dissent of the American citizen.

Nationally, it is said we lost the graduating class of 1965 to this war … thousands of nineteen-year-olds. It is also said the class of 1965 was the last class of an era, just kids, who, to their credit, believed in what our country's core represented and who were willing to uphold those values and rights. They were the last of what was once called Camelot.

They came from all walks of life and were true blue patriots. Weekly followers of Prince Valiant, these Marines were the bubblegum chewing boys who shared company with Bazooka Joe and his comic strip buddies.

After this graduating class and this war, our country profoundly changed its perspective and trust of the government.

For all the negativity the Vietnam Vets encountered, these are their final statistics and my "aha" moments.

Vietnam Veteran's personal income exceeds that of our non-veteran age group by 18%.

85% of Vietnam Veterans made successful transitions to civilian life.

97% of Vietnam Veterans were honorably discharged.

91% of Vietnam Veterans say they are glad they served.

74% say they would serve again, even knowing the outcome.

These men and women offered their lives to preserve America's freedom and to fight the most gruesome war the U.S. had encountered to date. They received the least recognition, appreciation, or respect. The Vietnam War was and continues to be a stain on America's conscience.

How does one repay a debt or an injury? The answer is to first acknowledge the wrong, apologize with sincerity, seek justice, and finally, request forgiveness. Only then can we heal.

There is a fable of two wolves in conflict. The question is, which wolf will win? The answer is … the one we feed. When will we choose to feed with "communication" as a way to peace? We live on a small planet. It is one world. As one world, I ask, when will we stop living in a state of separateness? The laughter of a child is a universal sound. When will the world realize that what we do to one we do to ourselves?

I remember and honor those who fought in Vietnam.

I especially remember and honor the gun-team of Hotel Company.

I have tried my best.

Acknowledgments

First and foremost, my heartfelt thanks to my partner Geoff Warnock. Twelve years ago, I asked him to explain what "ROE" meant on an online dating service. A retired Navy submariner, he forwarded a one-page single-spaced answer detailing "Rules of Engagement." I believed he copied them from a military manual. He hadn't. They were his words and the beginning of our long-time love. His countless hours of support, encouragement, and patience, especially with my many technical issues, have immeasurably helped bring this novel to fruition. Deepest thanks, Geoff!

Thank you, Clare and Roy for standing with me before Jesse's headstone where this journey began. Thank you, Janet Brown, my school's reading coach, who, after reading my prologue, said, "You have to keep writing and tell this story." Thank you, Elle Stocum, for your endless encouragement after reading my first draft. Thank you, Debbie Doblar and Julie Cordray, for reading, re-reading, then re-re-reading again with solid feedback. Thank you, Lisa Kirby, and Lt. Col. Wayne Dreyer, for feedback. Thank you, Bruce Gant, HM2, USN, Fleet Marine Force "Devil Doc," a military reader who served "In Country" 1968-1969. He has never forgotten those fallen heroes who served in Vietnam and consistently posts information about them. I dearly appreciate his fidelity and remembrance. Thanks to these Marines for their time discussing their tours and proofing my story: Ray Barry, Sgt. USMC, "In Country," 1967-1968; Leo Harris, Cpl. USMC, "In Country," 1968-1969; Howard Boyte, Cpl. USMC, "In Country," 1968-1969. A heartfelt and big thanks to Barney Barnes, Cpl. "In Country," 1967-1968 for his continuing support and contributions. Also, thank you to John Ligato, USMC for the use of his wonderful quote describing "the most ferocious fighting machine in the world!" Thanks, and good wishes to Mike "Chingas" Medina, who graciously allowed me to use his nickname when I discovered its delicious meaning. Thank you, Tim O'Brien, *The*

Things They Carried, who, although we never met, significantly motivated me after attending his speaking event.

Thanks to my daughter Alexandra for her support and help with ideas and edits, her journalism degree paid back to me in spades. Thank you to my daughter Elizabeth for constant support and bringing me coffee after my all-nighter's of writing! Thanks to my son Timothy, and his family, who smiled as I came to visit, computer in hand, on the off chance I would have time to write (of course, that never happened).

Good wishes all.

RESOURCES

Thanks to the following individuals for the information I obtained from their writings for this story. These are all great references for further information on Vietnam and the War.

Clark, Johnnie M. (2004). *Gunner's Glory, Untold Stories of Marine Machine Gunners.* New York, Ballantine Books.

Cohan, James P. (2004). *Con Thien, The Hill of Angels.* Tuscaloosa, University of Alabama Press.

Hayslip, Le Ly with Wurts, Jay. (1990). *When Heaven and Earth Changed Places, A Vietnamese Woman's Journey from War to Peace.* New York, Plume.

Logevall, Fredrik. (2012). *Embers of War, The Fall of an Empire and the Making of America's Vietnam.* New York, Random House.

Minh, Ho Chi. (1973). *Ho Chi Minh, Selected Writings 1920-1969.* Hanoi, Foreign Languages

Publishing House.

Parrish, John A. MD. (2012). *Autopsy of War, A Personal History.* New York, Thomas Dunne Books, St. Martin's Press.

Raskin, Marcus G. and Fall, Bernard B. editors. (1965). *The Viet-Nam reader, Articles and Documents on American Foreign Policy and the Viet-Nam Crisis.* New York, Vintage Books/A Division of Random House.

Steinman, Ron. (1999). *The Soldiers' Story, Vietnam in Their Own Word.* New York, The Fall River Press.

U.S. Army. (1962). *Department of the Army Vietnamese Phrase Book*. Headquarters, Department of the Army.

BIOGRAPHY

I came to America in 1954 at the age of six. My mother and I left a small town near Heidelberg, Germany, and traveled to Little Rock, Arkansas; she a war bride with her handsome Lieutenant, and I, a little girl with my new father. In Germany, I played in castle ruins with my cousins and swam with tiny fish and lily pads in the Neckar River, which flowed past my grandparents' home. In Arkansas, those memories were replaced with playing in dusty ditches, visiting snake farms, catching fireflies in the moonlight amidst the smell of jasmine, and watching my new father grow watermelons so big they required shelves for support.

My biological father flew with the Luftwaffe in WWII, and later, as I grew up in this great country, I came to understand that he had been the enemy America fought against. Until I reached my late twenty's, I seldom spoke about my German heritage.

War affects us throughout generations, I realized. It's the closest thing to hell on earth that I can imagine. Living through the Vietnam War gave personal attestation to that.

There must be better ways to process when conflict arises. Destruction can never be the answer; the toll is too great. Let us find a path toward the light, toward peaceful coexistence.

My work with substance abuse/addiction affirmed every life has value; my work with the incarcerated and the judicial system verified that injustice for one is injustice for all; and my work with children confirmed resilience, trust, love, and hope are the cornerstones of every human relationship.

I live in Florida with a wonderful man, have three children I am proud to call my own, and four happy grandchildren.

University of Maryland, B.A.

Bowie State College, M.Ed.

Made in United States
North Haven, CT
30 May 2022

19680244R00211